FREEFALL

EARTH'S LAST GAMBIT

VOLUME 1

FELIX R. SAVAGE

FREEFALL
EARTH'S LAST GAMBIT, VOLUME 1

First published in the United States of America in 2016 by Knights Hill Publishing.

Cover art by Christian Bentulan
Interior design and layout by Felix R. Savage

ISBN-10: 1-937396-24-X
ISBN-13: 978-1-937396-24-4

FREEFALL

EARTH'S LAST GAMBIT

VOLUME 1

FELIX R. SAVAGE

CHAPTER 1

The final space shuttle flight in history lifted off from Cape Canaveral on a sunny afternoon in 2011. "*Atlantis,* Houston, you are go at throttle up." *Atlantis* was flying like an angel. "Feel that mother go," Jack said jubilantly. "I mean, roger, we are go at throttle up." The gee-forces were *insane!* The vibration rattled the teeth in his head. Waiting for the SRBs to burn out and detach, he grinned. Nothing could prepare you for this. But he was prepared. He'd been preparing all his life.

The roaring stopped on cue. The vibration lessened as *Atlantis* climbed out of the atmosphere. Gravity released its hold on the astronauts, and Jack engaged the orbital maneuvering system (OMS) thrusters with a noise like an artillery barrage. Time to go to work.

Atlantis hadn't been wheeled out one last time so that four astronauts could enjoy the view.

Oh, no.

STS-136—a classified mission for the National Reconnaissance Office, one of the 'big five' US intelligence agencies—had a specific, secret goal. The *Atlantis* was a delivery truck, and their package was going to Keyhole-12a, aka *Frostbite,* a digital imaging satellite whose very existence was kept a secret from the public.

A year ago, *Frostbite's* main mirror had cracked catastrophically. A huge flake of glass had spalled off, degrading its capacity to take high-resolution pictures of Chinese, Russian, North Korean, and other foreign military installations.

The DoD contractors couldn't craft a replacement mirror

in under a year, so they'd missed the cut-off for STS-135.

And so NASA's partners, the United Space Alliance, had processed *Atlantis* for her *absolutely definitely* last flight.

When Jack heard he'd been selected as pilot, his shout of elation had brought people out of nearby offices in JSC's Building 4 South, asking if he'd won the lottery. "Yes," Jack had said. "I did!"

Now here he was, driving the world's fastest delivery truck.

Thundering around Earth at orbital velocity of 17,500 miles an hour, the *Atlantis* first had to be inspected for any damage the heat shields might've sustained during launch. Everything checked out. "This bird could keep flying for decades if they'd let her," said Mission Specialist Linda Moskowitz. Mission Commander Greg Howard shook his head at that. No political talk. Not when everything was being recorded. Jack kept his mouth shut. He wasn't even American. British, dual nationality. He knew better than to say what he thought of Congress.

Anyway, they had this: Earth in the windows, streaky blue and white, the most stunning sight an astronaut would ever see. Jack admired the view in the sliver of time before the start of their sleep period. It fascinated him. He found Europe, shy of the terminator. A blanket of cloud hid Britain—of course—but he imagined he could see Nuneaton, where he'd grown up, and the Mach Loop in Wales, where he'd learned low level flying as a Tornado pilot. He imagined his parents standing in the garden, looking at the sky, knowing he was up there somewhere.

Something weird happened then. His headset made a pipping noise. The faint tones reminded him of the BBC radio pips—*beep, beep, beep, beep, beep, beeeep*—and then they blended into a whine that flowed up and down the scale. Jack was in the pilot's seat, just keeping an eye on things; he leant forward and checked his comms panel. Receiving on the S band. Automatic antenna selecton enabled. *Wheeeoooo-eeee.*

He turned the antenna selection dial, cycling through all eight positions, forward and aft.

The tone went away when he limited reception to the aft antenna positions.

Came back when he selected the forward positions.

UL FWD—upper left forward—strongest of all.

Line of sight away from Earth.

Receiving from the outer solar system.

Jack drew breath to call to the others, who were on the mid-deck, put on your headsets, do you *hear* that, and then he grew abashed. His cheeks heated.

It's just cosmic noise.

Some clever-clogs hacker pranking the space shuttle.

Yet he kept listening, hunched tensely in his seat.

Wheeeooooeeewww …

The whine grew fainter, and then suddenly scaled up into a tone that stabbed his ears, loud, startling, and repugnant—nails on a blackboard, the electronic version, at 150 decibels.

Jack snatched his headset off. The sound continued to shriek from the earphones for a second, and then stopped.

"What was that?" Howard called up through the hatch—the shriek had been so loud, it must have been audible even on the mid-deck, even over the shuttle's background noises.

"Nothing," Jack called, making the decision to pretend it away on pure instinct, before he consciously weighed it. "Just pushed the wrong button."

His headset swayed in the air on the end of its cord. Ears ringing, he eyed it like a poisonous snake.

Eventually he held it to one ear.

Nothing. Not a whine, beep, or pip.

The mysterious signal was gone.

He sat dissatisfiedly fiddling with the antennas for a few minutes, checking the other comms systems. Nothing.

It was just a glitch.

Seen too many science fiction films, Kildare.

Yeah.

No astronaut should watch *Contact* five times. Let alone *Alien.* (Jack's favorite film in that franchise was actually *Alien vs. Predator.)*

Resolving to forget all about it, he tethered his sleeping-bag to the wall and closed his eyes.

I mean, who knows what's out there? Who knows, eh? No one knows. And we'll never find out, at this rate …

They woke to The Drifters crooning *Up On the Roof*, piped up from Mission Control.

"STS-135 got a special message and a song from Paul McCartney," Mission Commander Howard said. "What are we, afterthoughts?"

"Is that your official statement, Greg?" said Mission Control.

"Aw, stick it up your ass. We are honored and proud to be the last astronauts who'll ever have to endure Mission Control's taste in music. And now, we're switching to encrypted comms as we wipe the sleep out of our eyes and start prepping for EVA."

Dipping lower towards Earth, *Atlantis* was overhauling *Frostbite* in its lower reconnaissance orbit. They caught up with it on Day Three. By that time they'd run successful tests of the Canadarm, using the OBSS camera system to check the heat shields, and the two mission specialists were enduring their 'camp-out' in the airlock in preparation for their EVA. Jack maneuvered the shuttle neatly into synchronization with the bus-sized, gossamer-winged satellite.

"You could drive for UPS," Howard congratulated him.

"The second career I've always aspired to."

Howard smiled. He was fifty-nine. His second career would be a victory lap through the executive boardrooms of the private aerospace industry. He would speak at elementary schools, urging children to take an interest in space, when their government was sending the opposite message.

Jack had no second career planned. He'd stay with NASA until they carried him out feet first. Even if he never got to fly again, there'd be interesting work to do in flight dynamics. The thought made him die a bit inside. He decorated it with the images of a wife and kids, the family life that no astronaut had time for … Still not feeling it.

Funnily enough, his imaginary wife had the elfin face of Mission Specialist Moskowitz. Linda was known as NASA's secret public relations weapon. There hadn't been a female astronaut as hot as her since Anna Lee Fisher. Not that she knew it, or anything.

Jack leaned forward, spoke into the radio. "Looking good out there, Linda." Howard smirked sideways at him. All they could see of Moskowitz from the flight deck was the rectangular top of her life support backpack.

"So how're you liking that digital camera, Jack?" Howard said, gesturing to the Canon Jack wore on a band around his wrist.

They didn't know each other that well, but Howard knew Jack was a keen amateur photographer. It was pretty much all he did outside work.

"It's flipping great!" Jack said. "Trust me, in five years, no one will be using cameras that take *film.* This is the future. 15 megapixels of digital beauty."

Howard scoffed amiably.

"I'm removing the mirror tray now," Moskowitz said.

Jack was controlling the Canadarm, the space shuttle's robotic arm. It looked like a fifty-meter white crab claw. Moskowitz balanced on the tip of the arm, facing the aft avionics bay of the satellite.

"Go for it, Linda," Howard said.

She fell gently backwards, holding the 1.2-tonne mirror.

"Whoops," she said. "Dropped it."

Mission Specialist Rivera, waiting in the shuttle's payload bay, let loose a stream of curses.

"Just kidding," Moskowitz said sweetly. "Jack, can you take me back to the bay now?"

Jack maneuvered the Canadarm, rolling the joystick gently between the balls of his fingers. "Sure you can manage that, Linda? It's not too heavy for you?"

Just kidding! The mirror had mass, and could get away from them if they weren't careful. But it weighed precisely nothing up here. Like each of them did. This was Jack's second shuttle flight, although it was his first time as pilot. He loved freefall—the sensation of having grown longer, the freedom to decide that 'up' was the way his head was pointing. He'd never gotten spacesick. Headache, yeah, but you pissed that out by Day Two.

Rivera did get spacesick. He was on his fourth mission, so obviously he could handle it. But Jack could tell how crap he must be feeling from his grumpy tone. "Careful, Linda … Just put it over there in the return bay."

Jack and Howard, in the two-man station at the back of the shuttle, could not see either of the mission specialists now. They were out of sight in the payload bay. In a moment, Rivera would request Jack to maneuver him out on the Canadarm, with the billion-dollar replacement mirror.

Then it happened.

A clangorous boom reverberated through the space shuttle, as if someone had hit it with a giant hammer.

Moskowitz: "Holy shit what was—"

Rivera: "It hit us! Jesus H. Christ guys, I saw it! It *collided* with the fucking *fuselage*!"

Howard sprang forward in his foot tethers. "Jack, get that spin under control or we're going to torque out the arm!" He keyed up the comms. "Houston, *Atlantis,* be aware we've just suffered a suspected debris impact."""

Jack nulled the slow rotation the impact had imparted.

Rivera: "I'm going out—"

Howard: "No, Jesse, you are not going out. Have we got any visuals? Jack, gimme what we've got."

"Here it is," Jack said. He played back the view from the camera on the Canadarm.

In a series of still frames, a bright point of debris shot out of the blackness. It tore through the *Atlantis's* port OMS housing and exited stage left through the side of the cargo bay.

The *Atlantis* continued to fall serenely around Earth. But liquid hydrazine spurted out in a straight line before forming globules, like water from a high-pressure hose, from a hole in the port OMS thruster's spherical fuel tank.

Jack fought the shuttle's sudden loss of attitude control, struggling to counter the additional thrust caused by the venting fuel.

"At your discretion, Greg, slap a patch on that hole," said Mission Control. "We're looking at options for you. Now, run the flight check-lists for OMS fuel venting."

Jack could imagine the pandemonium down there right now. Fifty mission controllers had just been plunged into a scenario no one could prepare for, even though it could be, and had been, anticipated. It was like *Armageddon.* They were playing the odds. And this time they'd gotten unlucky.

He collected the repair kit and flew through the shuttle to the airlock, faster than he'd ever moved in his life.

CHAPTER 2

Jack wrenched open the inner hatch of the airlock. He placed the tools, insulation, and glue in the airlock for Rivera and Moskowitz to pick up.

Then he looked around for a piece of paper. Nothing. OK. In his pocket—a letter from his mother. He tore little pieces off the fragile sheet of airmail paper. Moving around the inside of the crew module, he let the scraps go one by gone, and held his breath to see which way they'd fall. If the scraps were pulled towards the wall, it would indicate a hairline crack in the pressure vessel. That could kill them all faster than any fuel leak.

No damage.

Their unexpected visitor had confined its destruction to the OMS pod, the side of the shuttle, and the starboard wing.

Rivera, spacewalking aft, struggled to patch the hole in the OMS pod. Jack watched him from the window into the payload bay, and took photographs for Mission Control's viewing pleasure. The struts connecting the fuel tank to the fuselage were crumpled like bendy drinking straws. The thermal blankets had caved in like the bonnet of a car that had been in an accident. There wasn't even any point patching it, but they did anyway, before starting on the rest of the damage.

While that was going on, Moskowitz completed the installation of *Frostbite's* replacement mirror.

NASA gets the job done.

It wasn't like there was anything else she could be doing

right now, anyway.

Back inside, Mission Control confirmed what they already knew: OMS B was a dead loss. Worse still, the impact had mauled the sensors and wiring in the side of the payload bay and wing.

Jack floated, upside-down to the layout of the upper deck, one finger on the hole leading to the mid-deck. He was wrung-out and stinking like a pig. He'd been working flat out for five hours. Howard looked like he hadn't left the commander's station all that time. You can't slump in zero-gee, but the mission commander's face sagged, his age showing. "Listen," Howard said to Mission Control, "we saw the debris. You've seen the pictures. There's no question in anyone's mind, or there shouldn't be: it was a piece of the Great Chinese Science Experiment."

That made sense to Jack. The lump of debris that disabled the *Atlantis* had most likely come from the Great Chinese Science Experiment—as it was known in the Astronaut Corps—of 2007. In that year, the Chinese had blown up one of their own old weather satellites with a kinetic kill vehicle, strewing 750 kilograms of debris throughout low earth orbit. They pretty much admitted they'd done it just because they could. The potential consequences for future spacecraft were foreseeable, and had been disregarded. Now, the inevitable had happened.

"Either that," Howard said, "or the Chinese just conducted another satellite kill test. Missed *Frostbite,* hit us."

Jack grimaced to himself. Even given the aggressive stance that the Chinese military had recently been taking, that seemed unlikely. "Maybe aliens did it," he murmured, remembering the odd electronic screech he had heard over the radio before the disaster. *Wheeeooooeeee … EEEEEE!*

Nah. It was the Great Chinese Science Experiment, no question about it.

"It could have been debris from Iridium-Cosmos," Mission Control said, referring to the 2009 collision between a Russian communications satellite and an Iridium GPS sat.

"You know it wasn't," Howard grunted.

"Greg, we're not going to go public with any kind of speculations until we do some analysis of the damage."

"Fine," Howard said. "Let's get back to that. The insulation is too seriously damaged for us to fix."

What he meant was: the *Atlantis* now had no re-entry system. Without extensive repairs, she was never going to return to Earth.

"If we're going with the ISS lifeboat option, I want to change orbit to catch up with it."

Jack pulled himself 'down' so his head poked into the mid-deck. He flashed a thumbs-up to Moskowitz and Rivera.

"Jack, get up here," Howard said. "Need you to do an orbit change. We're going to be cutting our margins thin on this, and you've got to do the burns with only one OMS online."

On the mid-deck, Moskowitz and Rivera, in their underwear, holding hands, spun around in a clumsy zero-gee victory dance.

Jack bounced back up into the cockpit, buoyant with relief. The *Atlantis* had suffered a fatal blow, but unlike in decades past, that wasn't an automatic death sentence for the crew. The International Space Station—humanity's home away from home in low Earth orbit—was ready and waiting to take them in.

CHAPTER 3

Almost two days later, four weary astronauts rose out of the *Atlantis's* crew hatch. Jack was the third to exit. Someone seized his wrist and hauled him into the airlock of the ISS's Harmony module. "Now the ISS has problems," growled cosmonaut Alexei Ivankov.

Jack grabbed Alexei's shaved head in both hands and pretended to twist it off. "The only problem with the ISS is it's infested with bloody Russians."

The two knew each other well. They'd overlapped in Star City, the Russian counterpart of NASA's Johnson Space Center, when Jack was undergoing his Soyuz training. On icy nights—not that there was any other kind of night in Russia, as far as Jack could tell—they used to drive out into the forest and blast away at tree-trunks with Alexei's service weapon. Other times, they'd venture into Moscow and try to pick up astronaut groupies. There were astronaut groupies in Russia. Not in the US.

Mission Commander Howard floated out of the shuttle's crew hatch. He looked tired and older than ever. Their ordeal nursing the nearly-fatally wounded *Atlantis* to the ISS had taken a lot out of him. Jack saw a glint of wetness on Howard's eyelashes, and looked away in a hurry as the mission commander futilely blinked. Tears didn't flow in microgravity, but that didn't stop them coming. Howard had been saying goodbye to the *Atlantis*.

America's longest-running spaceflight program hadn't been meant to end like this. They should've touched down at Kennedy Space Center to quiet congratulations, the satisfaction of a job well done, the bittersweet pride of having been the last astronauts to fly on a space shuttle.

Instead, they'd be flying home by Soyuz, one by one, over the span of the next year.

Alexei explained the tentative schedule for their return. It was going to take that long because custom seats had to be made for each of them, molded to their bodies, as well as specially designed Russian re-entry suits.

The nature of the Atlantis's original mission was a delicate subject, and neither Alexei nor Jack alluded to it. But Jack knew Roscosmos had to be pissed as hell at having to bail out an NRO mission, and would charge a hefty price for the rescue. At least NASA had taken seat molds for the crew themselves. Some difficulties you *could* anticipate.

Rivera would go first, on account of his spacesickness, although no one mentioned this. Then Howard. Moskowitz third. Jack last.

"I was due a holiday," Jack said, eyeing the science experiments lining the walls of the US lab module.

"We will keep you busy," Alexei threatened. "You can start by looking after my lettuces. They don't grow properly."

"I don't have a green thumb. More like a brown one," Jack said uneasily.

"There are toilets to clean, too," Alexei offered, grinning.

The two mission specialists from the *Atlantis* had gone ahead into the Tranquility module, eager to visit the famous Cupola. Jack was saving that for later. No matter how much busywork they gave him, he'd surely have plenty of time to revel in the views. He showed his Canon to Alexei, who asked if he had any dirty pictures on the memory card.

The two men floated through the Russian storage module,

and down a tunnel lined with white plastic pillows, barely wide enough for two people to pass each other. It felt like taking a trip down a robot's esophagus. At the far end of the tunnel, Alexei braked with one hand. He put a finger to his lips. Jack, coming up alongside him, heard voices in the Russian module ahead, the heart of the ISS, known as Central Port.

Howard had gone past them while they were shooting the breeze in the US lab module. One of the voices was his. The other had to be Katharine Menelaou, the current station chief.

"—needless," Howard was saying. "It could be parked in a graveyard orbit, where its orbit wouldn't decay due to atmospheric drag. Power it down, fix it up, bring it home later."

He was talking about the *Atlantis.*

"It could be, Greg," said Menelaou. The station chief had a folksy Midwestern lilt to her voice. But you could hear the hard edges under the Ohio niceness. "I'm just telling you since you asked, it probably won't be. They are leaning towards deorbiting the shuttle in a reasonably short timeframe."

"Well, I guess we might be able to scoop some of her out of the Pacific, after she burns up in the atmosphere."

Howard didn't sound happy about that. But personally, Jack thought a fiery deorbit would be a more honorable fate for the old space shuttle than NASA's original plan to decommission her and display her alongside her sisters. The *Atlantis* deserved better than to be flayed and wired up in a museum for an indifferent public to glance at.

"It's a shame," Howard said. "That's all. It's a damn

shame."

"I know," Menelaou said. "But it'll be decided way higher up the food chain."

Alexei raised his eyebrows at Jack. He whispered: "Ball-breaker." Jack suppressed a laugh.

They pushed off and floated out of the tunnel, into Central Port. There was no 'up' and 'down' on the ISS, but the little portholes set into one wall, framing views of Earth, made that wall feel like the floor, and that's the way Menelaou and Howard were oriented.

"Hi, Kath," Alexei said. "I'm just showing Jack around. It's his first time on-station."

"Yeah?" Katharine Menelaou looked Jack up and down. "Jack Kildare, OK. The Brit. First mission?"

"No," Jack said. *No, ma'am* was on the tip of his tongue. Something about the rail-thin, hard-faced Menelaou triggered old military habits he'd largely shaken off. He rudely scratched one armpit to undo any impression of subservience. "My first mission was STS-125, the last Hubble servicing mission, in 2009."

"Ah. Well, welcome aboard," Menelaou said. "It's gonna be a bit crowded, obviously …"

The ISS had already been fully staffed, with a total of six people on-station: three Russian cosmonauts, two Americans, and a Japanese robotics researcher. The crew of the *Atlantis* brought their numbers to ten—the most in ISS history. However, with so many modules separated by tunnels and 90-degree angles, it didn't feel crowded. In fact, compared to the crew module of the space shuttle, this was a McMansion. Jack smiled blandly at the station chief.

"We've got plenty of food, so don't worry about that,"

Menelaou went on. "As far as sleeping areas go, you can take your pick of walls."

"He can sleep in Zvezda, with us," Alexei said.

After a moment, Menelaou said, "OK, yeah, that'll work." Jack smiled in thanks, while privately wishing Alexei hadn't made the offer. He did appreciate it, as he knew he wouldn't be getting one of the deluxe sleeping booths in the US lab module, anyway. But it underlined his separateness from the American contingent, something he was never eager to draw attention to.

"Jack," Howard said, "we're going to organize a series of EVAs to inspect the damage to the *Atlantis*. While that's being prepped, I want you to take as many high resolution photographs as you can to cover the impact points, and make sure you have enough angles for 3D reconstruction. The post mortem on this is going to be huge. There might even be a Congressional investigation, depending on what the cause of the impact ultimately turns out to be."

You mean, if they can prove it came from the Great Chinese Science Experiment, Jack thought. Which will be a lot harder if the *Atlantis* is de-orbited and burnt up on re-entry. He suddenly realized that Howard might have other motivations besides sentimentality for opposing that plan. On the other hand, he could understand that the bureaucrats at the top of the NASA food chain might *not* want China openly blamed for the catastrophe.

"I'll have to testify in committee, anyway," Howard said gloomily. "Related to that, we'll need to pull all the logs and transcripts, and everyone will need to prepare a statement and personal report."

"You got it," Jack said.

Alexei hadn't been kidding. They were going to be kept busy.

Yet even with a full daily schedule of duties, including two hours a day of exercise, the astronauts on the ISS had free time from about eight o'clock until lights-out at midnight. Some wrestled with the appallingly slow broadband connection to exchange emails with their families. Some squeezed in more exercise. Alexei was carrying on a long-distance relationship with a Russian female military pilot stationed in Syria. He agonized over love-emails to her, while fending off uproariously bad advice from the other cosmonauts—well, Jack gathered it was uproarious, the way they all laughed.

Despite only speaking a few words of Russian, Jack found himself getting along better on this side of the 'Iron Curtain' … yes, it existed. There was a barrier between the Russians and the rest, no matter how much everyone insisted they were all colleagues working towards shared goals. It was the language barrier, but not just that. A hint of coolness in the air. A slight reserve on both sides.

Jack came to believe it started with the other Westerners taking their cues from Menelaou. The station chief never behaved less than professionally, but now and then she made a throwaway comment that revealed her political views. She was such a hardcore neocon, she could've understudied for Dick Cheney.

But Jack himself was a brick in the wall, too. Hell, he couldn't even tell Alexei and the other guys what the *Atlantis's* last mission had been about. Because bloody *Frostbite* spied on the Russians as well.

Thank God there weren't any Chinese on the ISS, anyway!

The atmosphere would have been so frigid, they'd have frost on the inside of the portholes.

Staying aloof from the tensions as best he could, Jack loitered in the Cupola whenever he could get it to himself. The seven-sided bay window lived up to its reputation. When the ISS was orbiting over Earth's dayside, you got spectacular views of home. When night hid Earth, the stars blazed out, undimmed by light pollution, and auroras danced over the poles.

Jack hadn't seen such amazing skies since he was a child in Warwickshire. Actually, *ever.* He took picture after picture.

Most amateur shutterbugs in space photographed Earth exclusively. Jack had been the same, until he heard those weird sounds on the *Atlantis.* He'd tried to bury the memory *(Wheeeeooooooeee ... EEEEE!)* but it kept repeating on him, like a dodgy kebab. He'd considered telling Alexei about it, asking him if he'd ever heard anything like that out here, but he knew that would destroy his reputation with the whole cosmonaut corps. It wasn't worth it.

Instead, reasoning that the best way to satisfy his curiosity was to give in to it, he spent time in the cupola gazing away from Earth, taking pictures of the fathomless darkness beyond humanity's home planet.

The pictures were usually a waste of pixels. You couldn't even see the outer planets in any detail, although the views out here were much better, naturally, than from Earth.

But shortly after he arrived on the ISS, he had a rare opportunity to photograph Jupiter in full color. He claimed his spot in the Cupola in plenty of time, feeling excited. Google told him Jupiter was 400 million miles and change beyond Earth. It would probably only be a few dozen pixels total, but that wasn't the point. Jack cranked the external shields of the Cupola's windows open, and drank in the black eternal night.

They'd had a treat for dinner: fresh apples, sent up on the Soyuz that had come to take Mission Commander Howard home. Howard's custom Soyuz seat had been made and delivered, so he'd be heading home to face the Congressional music. The rumored investigation into the causes of the *Atlantis* disaster had materialized, and Jack was certain that Howard would milk the chance to air his firm belief—neither conclusively proved, nor disproved, by their impact analysis—that the accident should be laid at the feet of the Chinese. Jack was just glad he wouldn't have to poke his own head above the parapet. Much better to be up here, far away from petty political games—even if politics *did* infect the atmosphere on ISS itself.

Never mind.

There's Jupiter.

Oh, you beauty.

Click. Click.

He imagined he could even see Europa, Jupiter's second moon, a pinprick on the bright blob of the gas giant.

Click click click.

All quiet on the ISS. Not a sound except for the constant, comforting white noise of the fans. No eerie pips from outer space. No ear-stabbing electronic shrieks. It was just Jack and the 2-inch screen of his Canon.

Click. Click. These pictures are going to be bloody fantastic. Who needs aliens?

"Oh my God!" Mission Specialist Moskowitz's voice, high and raw. "Oh my God! I need help in here, get the first aid kit!"

Jack dropped his camera. It bobbled on his wristband as he flew towards Moskowitz's scream.

"It's Greg! He's not moving—he's not *breathing!*"

CHAPTER 4

Earlier that same night, a young man named Skyler Taft drove at the stipulated 5 miles per hour up the side of Mauna Kea. He swung his rented 4WD Subaru into the parking lot of NASA's Infrared Telescope Facility and got out. It was dusk.

Way up here, 13,700 feet above sea level, the only sound was the wind. The dry, thin air tickled Skyler's throat. He shivered and zipped his parka all the way up against the cold. Patches of snow dappled the slopes around the parking lot, although spring had already come to Hilo, down on the coast, where he was staying. He walked around the Subaru to get his guitar out of the trunk. His hiking boots crunched on cinders from the dormant volcano.

Golden and orange clouds swathed the western horizon like an exploding quilt. It was a spectacular sunset but it made Skyler's shitty mood even worse.

He needed clear weather. Yes, everyone had to cope with bad weather while observing, but come on! The last two nights, the clouds had been so thick, even the IRTF's three-meter telescope couldn't see anything. They only had two more nights on the telescope after this.

Ye gods, am I ever gonna catch a break?

He trudged up the slope to the IRTF's snowglobe dome. The already-opened letter crackled in the inside pocket of his parka.

Letting himself into the windowless control room, he faked a bright tone. "Yo Pete! How's it going?"

At the C-shaped arrangement of desks on the far side of

the room, a balding white head turned. Glasses caught the light from the anglepoise lamp above the computers.

"Says it's gonna clear up tonight," said Peter Tamura, the telescope operator. He was a full-time employee of the University of Hawaii.

"It better," Skyler said. He dumped his guitar case on the floor. With a ta-*daaah!* gesture, he placed a grease-spotted paper bag on the desk. "Donuts from Lanky's."

It had been Odo's idea to pick up the treats, not Skyler's. But Skyler saw it had been a good one. The plump telescope operator's eyes lit up. "That stuff'll kill ya," Tamura grunted, reaching for the bag.

"Brain food," Skyler said, biting into a glazed donut roughly the size of a dinner plate. "How do you think I got my Ph.D?"

Not that getting his Ph.D had made one damn bit of difference to Skyler's life. Before, he'd been a graduate student at Caltech. Now, he was a post-doctoral fellow at Harvard. Harvard! Sure, it sounded nice until you realized that the Ivy League—hell, the *world*—was oversupplied with elite Ph.Ds. Astronomy might not be as popular as some fields, but that's because the number of good jobs available was pitifully tiny.

So Skyler had cast his net beyond the Ivy League, and damned if he didn't get the door slammed in his face, *again.*

"Didja hear back from NASA?" Tamura asked. They'd been chatting about Skyler's job hunt last night. You had to talk about *something,* sitting here from dusk to daybreak, waiting for the clouds to go away. Skyler had confided that he'd applied for an astronomy job at NASA's Jet Propulsion Laboratory. Yesterday a letter from NASA had arrived for him at home in Arlington, MA. Too impatient to wait, he'd asked his housemate to Fed-Ex it to the motel where he was staying in Hilo.

$25 for a buttload of nothing, as it transpired.

"Yeah. I struck out," Skyler said. He pulled the letter out of his parka, which he was still wearing—you didn't use heaters in the IRTF control room, as heat would distort the telescope's images. He held up the offending envelope and dramatically tore it in half, then stuffed it into the trashcan. Tamura laughed.

Later, while Tamura was in the bathroom, Skyler got the letter out of the trashcan and cut it into small pieces with the desk scissors. It was just common sense not to leave personal information lying around.

But that was later.

Now: "Big Dog is ready," Skyler announced, through the donut clamped in his teeth, as he checked the Big Dog array in the XUI.

"Roger," Tamura said. "Big Dog is on."

Big Dog was the software that controlled the spectrograph—the key piece of the IRTF, which measured infrared wavelengths to provide information about planets and stars that conventional telescopes could not. Guide Dog was imaging / guiding software. It documented where the telescope was pointing.

"Guide Dog is ready," Skyler said, swallowing his mouthful of donut.

"Roger. Guide Dog is on," Tamura said.

The veteran operator focused the telescope on Skyler's objective: Jupiter.

With the professor he worked for, Dr. Odo Meiritz of

Harvard's Department of Astronomy, Skyler was looking to obtain more information about the atmosphere of the solar system's largest gas giant. Dr. Meiritz had a theory that there were sharply defined differences in cloud composition at different depths that might give rise to simple life. The IRTF could 'see' the separate cloud layers of Jupiter: colder at the top, hotter the further down you went, and each point could give you a separate spectrograph. If the weather over Mauna Kea ever cleared up, they might be able to prove that compounds were present that could support life.

Skyler didn't really give a crap about Jupiter. This project was Odo's baby. Skyler himself was more interested in Herbig Ae/Be, and to a lesser extent T Tauri, gravitational collapse, and development of main sequence stars near reflection nebulae.

But any crumb of success might count towards the next phase of his so-called career. So he silently begged the weather to improve as the night wore on. Cracking his knuckles, munching donuts, drinking Diet Coke to stay alert, he entertained Tamura with horror stories from previous observations in Atacama and other facilities on Mauna Kea, and tried not to look at the shreds of the NASA rejection letter in the trashcan.

Around eleven o'clock, when it seemed like they were never going to get a break in the clouds, he got bored enough to take his guitar out. Tamura complained, but hell, *he* listened to NPR, so he had no business objecting to noise. Anyway, the operator grudgingly admitted that "Lucy In The Sky With Diamonds" was a good song. Skyler played the Beatles; he played Dylan and Guthrie. He didn't have any great talent, but he could pluck the chords and carry a tune.

Just before midnight, the clouds disappeared.

"Hey hey," Tamura said placidly. "Got Jupiter for you."

Skyler dumped his guitar in its case and sprang to the console.

"Got Europa, too," Tamura said. "Just came around the limb there."

"Screw Europa," Skyler said inattentively. If there was anything less interesting than a gas giant, it was a gas giant's frozen, radiation-drenched moon. He selected the points for spectrograph capture. "Sweet," he said, watching the grainy black-and-white guide image with his points overlaid. He could see the great eye of Jupiter's famous storm, and on a whim flagged it for a spectrograph capture. "Odo's gonna love this."

"Hope he feels better soon," Tamura said. Dr. Meinritz had come out to Hawaii with Skyler, because who wouldn't jump at the chance of a holiday in Hawaii, even if it was March? The buff, outdoorsy professor had planned to drive around seeing the sights while Skyler put in the long hours at the IRTF. On their first day Odo had promptly come down with a bug. Who was it said schadenfreude is the spice of life?

"Yeah, he was feeling a bit better today," Skyler said. He stared at the data on his screen. "Are you sure this thing is working?"

"Ya know how many years I've been operating this 'thing'? It is working. Something wrong?"

"Yeah … not sure."

What he was seeing *couldn't* be right.

Save data.

"Nuh uh," Skyler muttered, glued to the graphs appearing on the screen. "Nothing out there is that hot.""

Save data, he commanded again.

1.7x106 Kelvin? *Seriously?*

Then temperature readings returned to normal, and the graphs resumed a more reasonable shape.

Skyler checked the data dumps from 23:45 and 23:47 to make sure they were really there. They were.

The weird temperature readings were there, too, in black and white.

Tense as a cat on a windowsill, he pulled out his cell phone.

"Odo?"

"Yeah, hey, what is it?" The professor sounded suspiciously perky for a man who was supposed to be in bed.

"Are you at the motel?"

"I am very sick," Odo replied. He was German. "Do you need something?"

"OK, this is what happened," Skyler said. And then the voice of caution tickled at the back of his mind. *Not on the cell phone. You never know who might be listening.* "Odo, can you just get up here?"

Maybe Skyler's excitement carried over the phone. Odo arrived barely an hour later in his own rented car, probably having broken the 5mph speed limit by a factor of ten. He blew his nose loudly into a wad of Kleenex. "So this better be good," he said.

Skyler glanced at Tamura. The veteran operator folded his arms. He didn't know exactly what Skyler was so worked up about. But he wasn't going anywhere.

Fine. If this was anything, NASA would have to know

soon, anyway.

"I observed absorption lines at 1950 nanometers, 1450 nanometers, and 1200 nanometers," Skyler said. He opened the first file. He'd already copied both files to his keychain USB, for safekeeping. "See? And look at these overall temperature readings. They're coming from behind Europa and across the disk of Jupiter."

In the space of three minutes, between 23:45 and 23:47, Skyler had developed an intense interest in Europa, which he had formerly dismissed as a boring, radioactive iceball.

"It looks like a plume of ..." he started, but Odo cut him off.

"Water! Those absorption lines, it can only be water!"

"It's *hot,"* Skyler continued. "See? Nothing is that hot out there! It's so hot it's not even vapor. It must be a plasma!"

Heart racing, he snuck a glance at Odo's profile.

The professor stared transfixed at the screen. His face looked pallid in the bluish glow from the screen. His lips trembled. *"Die Außerirdischen,"* he whispered in German.

"What?" Skyler said. He knew that word. *Aliens.* He wanted to hear Odo repeat it in English, to confirm that they weren't both going crazy. "What do you think it is?" he pushed.

The next instant felt very long.

At last Odo straightened up and faced Skyler. He wore a fixed grin. "It could be a sign of new processes going on in Europa. A massive volcanic eruption of water vapor. This could completely alter our understanding of cryovolcanism on Jupiter's icy moons!"

"Hmm," Skyler said. He felt more disappointed than he would have expected. Then again, Odo was a smart guy. He knew that talking about *Die Außerirdischen* got you nowhere fast in their field.

"Come on, Skyler! This is fucking huge! We might even get a Nobel Prize out of it."

CHAPTER 5

This is fucking huge, Dr. Meinritz had said that night in the control room of the IRTF.

But it didn't change anything for Skyler Taft.

They returned to Cambridge, where Dr. Meinritz immediately threw himself into analyzing the spectrographs. Meanwhile, the professor pushed off the Jupiter project onto Skyler. So for the next five months, Skyler was left to write up the composition of Jupiter's cloud layers—for observing conditions had continued perfect on the fourth and fifth nights of their IRTF slot, allowing them to gather massive amounts of incredibly boring data—while Odo jetted off here and there to discuss the anomaly.

The anomaly. That's what they called it at the lab now.

Skyler still thought of it as *his discovery.*

But his connection to it grew more tenuous every day. After all, what had he actually discovered? He'd been physically present in the IRTF control room when the telescope picked up the water plume from Europa. That's all. Just a stroke of luck. It could have happened to anybody.

Still, it had been *his* stroke of luck, the only one to come his way in ages, and it just didn't feel fair that he was getting left out.

Dr. Meinritz was spreading the word about the anomaly to other institutions, and running into predictable skepticism. As the saying went, the only difference between science and screwing around was writing it down. But what really made science was being able to repeat it. If they had seen a genuine volcanic eruption on Europa, you would expect to see another one at some point. So there would have to be a near-constant watch kept on Europa and Jupiter to catch the next eruption. The problem was that no one wanted to commit scarce telescope time to such an unlikely project.

Odo had already contacted NASA's Jet Propulsion Laboratory (JPL) about making an emergency request for observations from their Juno probe, which was scheduled to arrive in the Jovian system shortly. But so far, he wasn't having much luck. One person at NASA had taken a look at the temperature readings and asked if they'd forgotten to top off the cryostat that night.

On the first warm evening in May, Skyler sat on the porch of his house in Arlington, noodling on his guitar. It wasn't actually *his* house, of course. He shared the top floor with a Google employee, a junior researcher from Genzyme, an MIT lab tech, and the MIT guy's druggie girlfriend. That's why Skyler spent so much time, weather permitting, on the porch. The neighbors might not like him playing his guitar out here. They could kiss his ass.

He played Dylan—*Blowin' In The Wind*—and Baez—*Sacco & Vanzetti.* It was a funny relationship they had, Skyler and folk music. He loved the tunes while understanding that the lyrics were, in general, pretty stupid. Sacco and Vanzetti? Guilty as hell. And yet that melody. Oh, boy.

A sleek black Lexus drove around the corner and cruised along the street, as if looking for parking. Both sides of the street were parked up solid, since there was no room for driveways or garages between the hundred-year-old triple-deckers. The Lexus slowed outside Skyler's house, then rolled on. Skyler grinned and started a new song. "Imagine there's no parking," he crooned.

The Lexus came back around the block. It stopped in front of Skyler's house, blocking the street.

Skyler put his guitar aside and lit a cigarette. He smoked rarely, and then only to piss people off.

Two men got out of the Lexus. One was younger, wearing a suit. The other, older, wore jeans and a plain navy blue t-shirt with a logo-less baseball cap.

They squeezed between the parked cars onto the sidewalk. They were probably friends of the Google chick, Skyler thought, while a deeper instinct said, *No, they're not.* It was the plain blue t-shirt. He didn't know why that set off an alarm. It just did.

The men came up the steps. "Hey," the younger one said, smiling. "Looking for a guy who lives here? Skyler, uh, Taft?"

Skyler was sitting on the old porch swing, on a blanket that generations of stray cats had peed on. He didn't get up. "Can I help you?"

"Are you Skyler Taft?"

"Yeah." Skyler took a drag on his cigarette. It was coming in handy now, giving him an excuse to fidget. He was nervous, and he still didn't know why.

"That's bad for you," said the older man.

"Kiss my ass," said Skyler.

Both men laughed. The younger one said. "Kind of chilly for sitting out, isn't it?"

"My housemates are home," Skyler said.

"Wanna go grab a coffee?"

"I saw a Starbucks as we were coming along," the older man said.

"That's the one on Mass Ave," Skyler said. "It's always full of students. You can't get a seat."

The older man chuckled and said, "OK. We can talk right here."

"Just a couple of minutes of your time, if you're agreeable," the younger one added. He had Deep South vowels, and a peckerwood jut to his pale brows. Skyler reminded himself that just because you talked slowly didn't mean you thought slowly. "I'm Josh, and this's Travis."

The two men handed over business cards. There was nothing on the cards except their names—Joshua Beauchamp, Travis Moore—their cellphone numbers, and an address in Augusta, Georgia. Skyler tried to think what was down there. He didn't know, but he was 99% sure it would turn out to be something to do with the federal government.

The older man, Travis, took over the … conversation? Interrogation? He was black, with silver speckles in his hair. He carried some extra weight over his belt buckle. "You probably figured this out already," he said with his chuckle that wasn't a chuckle, just punctuation. "We're extremely interested in the work you're doing with Professor Meinritz."

"I'm not doing any work with him," Skyler said, employing a Clintonian definition of *with.* He was doing grunt work *for* Odo. Not *with* him. Not since his discovery.

"Oh yeah?" Josh said. "Don't you work at the Observatory?"

"At Harvard, yeah."

"That's all the way over in Cambridge. How do you get there?"

"Bike path. It's a nice ride."

"I guess that would be good exercise," Travis said, and

they chatted for a couple of minutes about bike commuting. Josh said that he commuted by bike sometimes, too, but everyone thought he was crazy on account of the heat down south. "Someone should invent an air-conditioned bike!" Travis said. He chuckled again.

"Must be nice in Hawaii this time of year," Josh said. "You were out there recently, huh?"

"In March," Skyler said. His anxiety spiked again. Suddenly, he was back in the IRTF control room, watching impossible graphs take shape on the screen. He leaned down, stubbed his cigarette out on the porch, and tossed it into the street.

"You were working at the …" Travis paused, as if trying to remember its name. "The Infrared Telescope Facility?"

An SUV rolled down the street and stopped behind Travis and Josh's Lexus, patiently waiting for it to move. Boston area drivers didn't honk in this kind of situation. They were too used to it.

Travis jumped off the porch and went to move the car. Skyler was surprised at first, and then not. He'd assumed Travis was the senior man, just because he was older. But it was Josh who'd taken the lead to begin with. Him with his pale peckerwood eyes.

"Dr. Meinritz has been telling the whole world about some observations you made? A water plume, if I've got that right? At a temperature of almost three million Fahrenheit?"

"That's right," Skyler said, while his faint hope that Josh and Travis might turn out to be from NASA, come to offer him a position at JPL working on the James Webb space telescope, dwindled to nothing. Degrees Fahrenheit, for chrissakes! Astronomers used the Kelvin scale. Nor would anyone from NASA struggle to recall the name of the IRTF. And they'd call it the IRTF, not the 'Infrared Telescope Facility.' NASA didn't have any facilities in Georgia, anyway.

"The professor's saying it could be a new type of volcano? Volcanoes in outer space!" Josh marvelled. "How is that even possible?"

""""The same way it happens on Earth. Something gets squirted out of something else by increasing pressure," Skyler said, going into TA mode. It made him feel better to see Josh as an undergrad dozing through Astrophysics 101. Now the man was even taking his smartphone out. *Just* like an undergrad. "On icy moons like Europa, cryovolcanoes can produce eruptions of water vapor. Now we've previously seen cryovolcanoes on Europa, but the hint is in the name: *cryo,* meaning cold. But now Dr. Meinritz thinks there has to be something different out there. Of course, at a few million *degrees,* it's definitely not a cryovolcano! Hell, that's hotter than the magma that comes out of volcanoes on Earth."

Josh slid his phone back inside his suit jacket. When he did that, Skyler saw something that made him go absolutely cold. *The man was carrying a gun.* Was concealed carry even legal in Massachusetts?

"Travis says he's gonna circle around and look for a parking place," Josh explained. "Man, I wouldn't want to have a car if I lived up here."

"That's why I don't. As well as, you know …" Skyler, flustered, rubbed his index finger and thumb together in the universal gesture for money.

Josh smiled slightly. No fake chuckles from him. "If you

lived down south, you'd have to have a car. Not necessarily a truck with a Dixie flag on the bumper. It's a pretty diverse area where we are."

Skyler nodded. He was hyper-aware of his physical vulnerability, his guitar lying stupidly behind him on the porch swing. No one else was out on the street. Curtains glowed warmly. He could smell supper cooking in the second-floor apartment.

Josh made a sudden movement. Skyler flattened himself against the porch swing, like a child shrinking into a corner. Then he saw what Josh had reacted to. Just a rat running across the porch steps.

"Shee-yit!" Josh said.

"We get a lot of them around here," Skyler said. "Because of the recycling laws. The bins are supposed to be animal-proof, but people don't put the lids on properly."

Josh grinned ruefully— "I just about jumped out of my skin!" and suddenly Skyler was no longer afraid of him. He understood that Josh was as nervous as he was, and it had nothing to do with rats.

"So you wanted to know about the Europa observations?" he said.

"Yeah. Yeah. Let me ask you a question, in your personal opinion. What do you think caused that water plume?"

Skyler gazed up at him for a long moment without answering. At last he said, "Aliens. Nothing makes things that hot, in a mature solar system, apart from nuclear fusion … or intelligent life."

Josh grimaced, looking troubled. "That's what we think, too."

Travis came jogging back, having found a parking place

way over on Mass Ave. By that time, Josh had pretty much offered Skyler a job. He had a funny way of working around to it. He said nothing about the benefits and opportunities that his organization could offer Skyler. Instead, he harped on how they needed Skyler's expertise to adequately analyze the 'risk profile' of the anomaly. He said that there were dozens of people with the same qualifications, of course, but Skyler had been involved with this thing from the beginning, so they'd prefer to have him.

Just a stroke of luck. Could have happened to anyone.

Skyler turned to the out-of-breath, grumpy Travis. "So what *is* this organization?" he said. "I mean, maybe I'm supposed to know, but I don't."

"The CIA," Travis said, shrugging.

Which was actually going to have been Skyler's second guess, behind the FBI.

"At the moment, we're with the CIA," Josh clarified. "But there could be changes. It depends how this thing goes. I mean, maybe it just goes away. But there's a possibility that a separate organization could be set up to deal with it. That's kind of up in the air right now, but we'd like to have you on board, anyway."

"Uh huh," Skyler said. He looked up at the darkening sky above the roofs on the other side of the street. Only a few stars were visible. Goodbye, proto-stars, he thought.

"Well, you don't have to make up your mind right now," Josh said. "You've got our cards, you can give us a call. We would just request that you don't talk to anyone about this. It's not like you'd be prosecuted for it. Just, you know, use common sense."

"Hang on," Skyler said. He stood up. He was still holding

their business cards. He took his cigarette lighter out of his pocket and set fire to the corners.

All three of them watched the little rectangles flare up like candles in the dark. When the flames got near his fingers, Skyler dropped them and stamped them out.

"Well, I've been told to fuck off before," Josh said. His face was tight with anger. "But that was a first. Do you burn American flags, too?"

Skyler scuffed his shoe over the soot smears, knocking the unburnt scraps off the porch into the drift of old dead leaves below. His pulse hammered in his throat.

"No, wait up," Travis said. "Maybe he was just destroying the evidence. Like a kind of a James Bond thing."

"Yeah," Skyler said. "That's right."

Josh folded his arms. Skyler smiled fiercely. He'd got them on the back foot.

"So what's up, man?" Travis said. He said to Josh, "If we got this one *that* wrong, I want to hear it from his own mouth."

Josh said grudgingly to Skyler, "You know you're this close to being on a watchlist?"

That shook Skyler. "Why?"

"You don't have Facebook, you aren't on Twitter, you only use your Harvard email account. You're still using a dumb phone. In the year 2012."

"I guess that pisses you guys off?"

"I'm just wondering why you're so …" Josh waved one hand, inviting Skyler to fill in the blank.

"Cautious," Skyler said. "I'm cautious. It's common sense, like you said. I don't understand people who do Facebook and stuff like that."

"So you don't hate America?" Travis said, eyebrows raised.

Skyler decided to be honest. That meant taking a moment to think it over. He had never really considered the question of whether he hated America or not. The closest he'd come was a vague sense that maybe America wasn't all bad, but that was no more than instinctive contrarianism, because everyone he knew in academia did hate America.

"OK," he said. "It's like this. Some songs, the lyrics are stupid, but the melody's beautiful. For example, *Imagine.* The lyrics are a bunch of half-assed utopian bullshit. But the tune is a classic. I guess that's how I feel about America. I love the melody, even if I don't like a lot of the lyrics we're singing right now."

Travis looked at Josh, pooching out his lips. "That's pretty good," he said. "I might steal that."

"So why'd you burn our business cards?" Josh said.

"Because I don't need to call you."

"OK."

"I'm in. You didn't mention the compensation, but I'm in." *It's got to be better than an assistant professorship at Ohio State.* He decided it would be undiplomatic to say that out loud.

Both of the CIA guys laughed. Then Travis shook Skyler's trembling hand. "It's OK. Those weren't our real names, anyway. I'm Tom Flaherty."

"You don't look Irish," Skyler said.

"I'm what they call black Irish." Chuckle, chuckle. "That was a joke, son."

Skyler laughed.

"That's OK, not many people appreciate my sense of humor. I run this here government-funded tinfoil-hat operation, and this's my right-hand man."

"Lance," said the pale-eyed one. His handshake was cold.

CHAPTER 6

Hannah Ginsburg had a hangover, and it wasn't even Monday.

She drove into work with the California sun beating in her eyes, sunglasses not helping. At least the car was OK. Be thankful, as her Jewish grandmother would have said. It could have been worse. She'd rear-ended someone's Tesla last night as she pulled out of her parking place near La Cuevita, the best tequila bar in Greater Los Angeles.

She drove into the western parking lot at NASA's Jet Propulsion Laboratory and parked. She got out, walked around her second-hand Camry, and stopped at the rear fender.

There was a noticeable dent. She'd seen that already. Now she noticed specks of blue paint glinting in the dent. She pulled a Kleenex out of her bag, squatted down, and scrubbed at the flecks for a good two minutes before realizing how stupid she was being.

No one had seen the fender-bender. The owner of the other car might not even have noticed the damage. *(Of course they had.)* She should have left a note with her contact details on the windscreen, but she hadn't, so they'd never know who scraped their fancy-schmancy Model S. It could have been worse, Bubbie. So much worse. Hannah could have wound up with a DUI. She could have woken up somewhere else, instead of at home in her cozy little studio apartment in Highland Park. That happened, sometimes.

She walked towards Building 36. On the way, she grabbed a large coffee from the cart on the mall. She gulped it as she hurried through the woodsy JPL campus.

There were two Hannahs.

One Hannah got drunk, and sometimes woke up in the wrong bed, and now, apparently, also backed into other people's cars.

The other Hannah was the flight dynamics team lead for the Juno Project. She painstakingly calculated orbits and burn timings, nursing the pioneering Juno probe through space. Destination: Jupiter.

These two were not the same person, and never the twain should meet, she was firmly resolved. As long as she kept her work life and her personal life separate, she'd be OK.

By the time she reached her desk, she felt more like her work self. She still had a headache. It would take another hour or so until she was hitting on all cylinders, so she used that time to clear out her email inbox.

"Hey, Richard? Did you get this?"

Hannah leaned around her computer. She pitched her voice to reach across the open-plan office to Richard Burke. The lanky, balding systems engineer was the Juno Project's lead scientist, making him the senior person on the Juno team here at JPL. He was kind of sexy, Hannah thought, with his 70s-style moustache and tanned forearms, although she'd never flirt with him, because he was not only married but her boss as well.

"The thing from Suzanne?" Burke said. Hannah nodded.

From: Suzanne Stone

Suzanne Stone was the Juno program executive. She hid out on the other side of the country, at NASA headquarters, and rarely poked her nose into the JPL team's business.

Subject: Request for emergency observations of Europa

"What's she smoking?" Hannah said. "She wants us to do a fly-by of Europa? That's not in the mission. It's not even *possible.* The probe's aimed for a polar orbital insertion."

"They want to look for traces of that cryovolcanic eruption that was observed a couple of months back," Burke said.

This, too, was in the email. Hannah clicked on Suzanne's link and skimmed the attached academic paper. She'd first read it when it was published last month. The lead author was a Professor Odo Meinritz from Harvard. His conclusion that Europa *might* be tectonically active would be fascinating, if true. To Hannah, it smelt more like an equipment malfunction. Either way, it had nothing to do with Juno's mission to study the composition, gravity field, and magnetosphere of Jupiter.

Ralf Lyons, the mission navigator, looked around the ficus plant between his desk and Hannah's. "No way was that a cryovolcanic eruption," he said. "Too hot."

"What was it, then?" Hannah said. "Aliens?" She laughed.

Lyons laughed, too. "Yeah, the advanced civilization buried under the ice of Europa just blew themselves up."

"Do-doo-do-dumm-dummm," Hannah hummed the famous bit from *Close Encounters of the Third Kind.*

"Well, we *could* alter the orbit to do a longer fly-by of Europa," Lyons said.

"That's what Suzanne wants," Burke said.

"It would depend if the propulsion system could hack it. Is your baby up to the job, Hannah?"

They called the probe Hannah's baby, because she'd worked with the Lockheed Martin team that built it from day one. Juno used a LEROS 1b engine that had been around since the 1990s, but Hannah had personally designed modifications to the engine bell that increased its specific impulse. She scratched her nose. "Of course the system is up to it," she said. "But there are risks involved in increasing the dwell time in Jupiter's radiation belts, and we'll have to calculate the propellant usage really carefully, or we risk not being able to deorbit the craft when we're done. On top of that, anyone who already has their observations planned is going to be, hmm, let's say mildly unhappy, because Juno won't be where they expected it to be, when they expected it to be there. Is this worth it?"

Hannah had achieved success in her profession because she thought deeply about risk, both on the scale of individual component failure and on the complex system level. She never let anything take care of itself. Whatever befell Juno on its way to Jupiter, chances were Hannah would already have planned for that eventuality.

The one thing she *hadn't* planned for was the bureaucratic foot of Washington stomping all over their mission.

When she finished enumerating the risks of altering Juno's orbit insertion, and sketching out how they could be managed, everyone in the office was grinning broadly.

Lyons did a golf clap. "Hannah's so got this."

She gave him the finger. "I just don't get why this is even happening."

"Because Suzanne says it's happening," Burke said in a world-weary singsong.

"Who is this Meinritz guy? How come he gets to go around our investigation team and come in through the Washington door?"

"He's screwing Suzanne," Lyons suggested.

"Suzanne is married," Burke said peaceably. Lyons opened his mouth, probably to say that that never stopped anyone. Hannah saw him think better of it. There was an least one extramarital affair going on in this very office that she knew of. *Some* people weren't as careful to keep their work lives and their personal lives strictly separated as she was. Burke went on: "Anyway, Suzanne wouldn't request this if Bill hadn't okayed it."

Bill Walker was the Administrator of NASA. The big boss.

"I guess the Meinritz dude must be politically connected," Hannah said, shaking her head. This reminded her that she still had a headache. She did a Gollum voice. "Oh, the corruption, it burnsss, my precious, it burnsss."

She reached into her desk drawer for ibuprofen. Time to start replanning the orbits to see how long she could get the craft near Europa, without cooking the avionics in their titanium box.

Over lunch, Burke said to Hannah, "It's nothing to do with Professor Meinritz. He approached our investigation team last month to ask for these observations, but he didn't even get his foot in the door. This is coming from somewhere else within the federal government."

Hannah sipped her Snapple. Hannah's Rule #1, the cardinal rule: No drinking at work. They were sitting out on one of the square concrete benches under the trees. In Pasadena, you could sit out all year round. She thought about what Burke had just told her. "You're being kind of sinister-ly vague," she said.

"That's because I don't know anything for sure. But a lot of this is going to be on you. Sure, you'll have Ralf to help, but …" Burke rolled his eyes and bit into his chicken sandwich. "So I figured you should know as much as I know. Which you now do."

Hannah smiled at the lead scientist. Burke was such a nice guy. When political shit rolled downhill, it landed on him, but he never let it get to him. Never even raised his voice, just did his best to shield his team from interference. He and his wife had three lovely kids at a private high school.

"Don't worry," she said. "I was thinking about it this morning, and it's gonna be a fun challenge. I'm trying to increase the fly-by time near Europa without frying the control systems."

"It's going to increase your workload," Burke sighed.

"I live for my work," Hannah said gamely. The thing was, it was true.

Some other people from the team came to sit with them, carrying food from the franchises and street carts on the mall. They finished lunch while speculating about the *Atlantis* investigation. The Subcommittee on Space, Science, and Competitiveness was hearing testimony in Washington today.

Hannah's cellphone rang. She plucked it out of her bag and stared in horror at an unknown number. This had to be about the car she'd rear-ended.

It was happening. Her work life and personal life were about to collide with disastrous consequences. The insurance wouldn't pay out … she'd lose the car … everyone would find out about her problems … Cold with terror, she answered the phone. "Hello?"

CHAPTER 7

The chairwoman of the Senate Commerce, Science, and Transportation Committee said, "We'll proceed to Mr. John Kildare, mission pilot for STS-136, who was on board the *Atlantis* at the time of the incident."

No one called Jack 'John' except his Irish grandmother. He smiled at the chairwoman, who sat in the middle of the raised dais on the far side of the room, wearing a loud pink jacket. Other representatives and senators dotted the rows of chairs below the dais, facing the trio from NASA who'd been called to testify at the joint hearing on the *Atlantis* disaster: NASA Administrator Bill Walker, his deputy, and Jack. It should have been Greg Howard, but Howard was dead. So here was Jack, in his only good suit. The retired general who'd headed up the accident investigation board was also present.

The big boss and his deputy were relaxed to the point of semi-consciousness. They had ramparts of Poland Springs bottles and Starbucks cups around their memo pads. Jack hadn't asked for anything. He hadn't realized the hearing was going to last all day.

Now, finally, it was his turn. He cleared his throat. "Right. Thank you. It's an honor to be here."

The C-Span television crew off to the side of the room faffed around, turning one of their cameras on Jack.

"Can you pull the mic a little closer, Mr. Kildare?" the chairwoman said.

"Sorry. Right." This time, the mic let out a squeal of feedback. Off to a great start.

The white-haired chairman of the Science Committee, a Republican from Missouri, spoke. "As I said in my opening statement …" He proceeded to recapitulate his entire opening statement. Jack sat patiently, trying not to sink back into the trance of boredom and unhappiness that had swallowed him as the hearing dragged on.

It was just a bureaucratic formality. He mustn't let it get to him. But he kept thinking about Greg Howard, who should have been here in his place. The mission commander had died on the ISS, of cardiac arrest. His death was now fodder for scientific enquiries into causes of death in space, and officially had nothing to do with the *Atlantis* disaster. But it was all connected in Jack's mind. The ordeal of losing the space shuttle couldn't *not* have contributed to Howard's death. Meanwhile, the politicians' longwinded speeches about safety and transparency struck Jack as missing the point completely.

Even worse, they kept implying it had been NASA's fault for putting the *Atlantis* in harm's way. As if the mission planners could somehow have known the space shuttle would cross paths with a piece of deadly debris. As if space wasn't irredeemably dangerous to begin with. They were already in the situation where even the contingency plans had contingency plans. No amount of redundant systems would ever make this job safe, and some of the pieces of debris orbiting the Earth were just too damn small to be seen by radar.

The senator finally got around to his question for Jack, which was simple: "Did you see the piece of debris that struck the *Atlantis?"*

Jack said that he had not, but he'd heard it all right. The

politicians made skeptical faces. He got the feeling that at least some of them had just taken against him in reaction to his accent. Immigration was a big thing in Congress this year. Maybe for politicians, there was little difference between an illegal immigrant from Central America and a British astronaut with dual citizenship.

Prompted by the white-haired Republican senator, Jack walked them through the *Atlantis* crew's reaction to the impact and the actions they'd taken to stabilize the shuttle. About the only thing he didn't mention was how he'd torn up a letter from his mother to check for leaks in the pressure vessel. That was none of their business.

At last the senator circled back around to the lethal piece of debris. "In your opinion, Mr. Kildare, and note I'm saying *in your opinion,* where did it originate from?"

Jack sat without moving a muscle. He felt Greg Howard's ghost jogging his elbow, urging him to lay the blame on the Chinese. He committed himself to telling the truth. "It could have been a piece of the Chinese satellite that was destroyed in 2007. Or it could have been shrapnel from the Iridium-Cosmos collision. Or something else. We just don't know."

The senator sat back, grumpily. Howard's ghost drifted away. Jack felt like he'd let him down. But Walker was smiling, and so was the chairwoman. They approved of the way Jack had managed not to actually give his opinion when it was asked for. The moment of danger was past, Jack had scraped through without damaging the NASA family or himself, and he was going to need a hot shower to wash off the taint of this place.

"I'm done," the senator grunted.

One of the congressmen in the cheap seats below the dais stirred. Jack was mentally halfway out the door already. He sighed and settled back into his chair. This *couldn't* last much longer …

"The chair recognizes the senator from North Carolina. Mr. Colbert, go on."

"Thank you, Ms. Chairwoman. And I would also like to thank Mr. Walker and his staff for their diligence today. Now, I may have missed this, and I apologize, but I would just like to return to the mission, um, STS-136, the reason you were up there in the first place. I didn't catch that, Mr. Kildare?"

"Well, it was an NRO mission," Jack said, assuming the senator knew what that meant. The National Reconnaissance Office provided satellite intelligence and imaging for all the other US intelligence agencies.

"OK," Senator Colbert said. "But I'm not really understanding why it was so urgent, the repairs to this satellite, why it was so important that we had to send a space shuttle up there and put American lives at risk. That part's not making sense to me as we speak at this moment."

Young for a politician, maybe forty, Senator Colbert had a rumpled appearance and a way of talking with his hands that made him seem non-threatening. His question didn't feel hostile at all, unlike the previous questions that Jack had had to field.

"Well, obviously it is vitally important that we can continue spying on our allies," Jack said, allowing himself a tiny detour into sarcasm. He smiled at the senator. "Russia, the North Koreans, China, and of course our friends in NATO—if Frostbite wasn't watching them like a hawk, who knows what mischief they might get up to? If we were willing to risk American lives servicing the Hubble Space—"

Something thumped Jack's leg under the table. Startled, he stopped speaking. Bill Walker, the administrator of NASA, straightened up, his face blank. He'd kicked Jack under the table. *Shut up.*

Flustered, Jack tried to change the subject in mid-sentence. "I mean, there could be anything out there, but if we don't look, we'll never know, will we? So it's better to have these resources in space, than to just sit around waiting to get hit by an asteroid, or invaded by aliens. Ha, ha."

Jack laughed, but no one laughed with him. What happened next was Bill Walker knocked over his Starbucks cup.

Cold coffee flooded across the table and dripped onto Jack's legs.

Walker wasn't a clumsy man. He'd been reaching for Jack's mic, intending to turn it off or pull it away. Or maybe he'd spilt his coffee on purpose because he couldn't reach Jack's mic.

Jack, silenced, cold coffee soaking into his trousers, stared at the frozen faces lining the room, and thought: Oh, *shit.*

CHAPTER 8

On the pavement outside, Walker said, "It's a gotcha game. They got you. Don't worry about it."

Jack wasn't sure exactly what he'd said that he shouldn't have. After the coffee spill, the hearing had wound up quickly. The dishevelled senator who asked Jack about Frostbite had left the room even before the aides were done mopping up.

"Was it what I said about aliens?" Jack ventured. "I didn't mean it, obviously. Or asteroids?"

"It wasn't *that,*" Walker said briefly, leaving Jack with the distinct impression that it might have been.

"That's a relief," Jack said with an uneasy smile.

"We thought it was going to be Howard up there. He was senior to you, obviously. More experience." The subtext was obviously, *HE wouldn't have got got.*

Jack's wet trousers stuck to his thighs. This was his only good suit—or *had* been. It was a wool blend, completely unsuitable for June in the nation's capital. In contrast to the brutal air-conditioning inside the building, the afternoon sun hammered down on the sidewalk. Jack felt sweat coating his body, and not only because of the sticky heat.

"I shouldn't have tried to be funny," he apologized again.

Walker's jaw bunched. "No, you shouldn't have. Senators and humor don't mix. Especially not British humor, if that's what that was." They stood on the U of sidewalk outside the Rayburn House Office building, waiting for their car. Crash barriers cluttered the monumental '60s façade. Jack thought the official areas of Washington were like something designed for Hitler. No one needed this much concrete. "There's going to be a shitstorm," Walker said to his deputy. The deputy nodded and started texting.

"Sir," Jack tried again. "I'm awfully sorry. I'm not sure exactly what it was I said ..."

Walker sighed. "Those idiots in there? Those democratically elected, insecure, narcissistic, monstrously ambitious *idiots?* Before today, three of them knew about Frostbite. The chairwoman, the senator from Missouri, and the ranking member for Science. Now they all do."

For the second time that day Jack was silenced. The possibility that democratically elected representatives of the American people might *not* know about their own nation's satellite intelligence programs hadn't even crossed his mind. After all, this was America, the land of the free and the home of the transparent.

"If you'd been awake during my testimony," Walker said, "you might have noticed that I did not refer to Frostbite in any but the vaguest terms. Even the satellite's code name is classified. It's a kind of a don't ask, don't tell thing. Senator Colbert violated that mutual understanding." Their car came.

"Looks like C-Span's going to play ball," Walker's deputy said, as they climbed into the chauffeured Town Car.

"That's a relief," Walker said.

Despite the welcome air-conditioning, Jack felt more uncomfortable than ever. He had a suspicion that Walker was fobbing him off with a partial truth. Obviously he shouldn't have mentioned Frostbite. But if that were the worst of it, why hadn't Walker tried to grab his mic at that moment? Why wait until Jack made a stupid joke about aliens?

He asked nervously, "How much of a shitstorm are we expecting?"

Walker gave a rictus smile that made him look like a politician. "It won't be that bad. Even democratically elected idiots can be discreet when it serves their own interests." The car turned on Constitution Avenue. "Most of the damage," Walker added, "will be in-house."

"Uh oh," Jack said, trying for a light tone.

Walker touched the intercom button to communicate with the driver. "We'll be dropping Mr. Kildare off at his hotel."

*

"Hello?" Hannah said, trying desperately to sound normal. If this was the police calling about the car she'd rear-ended, she had to come across as the kind of person who had her shit together and never but *never* drove over the limit.

"Is this Aunt Hannah?" squeaked a child's voice.

The tension drained out of Hannah's body. "Isabel?"

"I bet you didn't know it was me, did you?" Isabel giggled. Hannah reflexively grinned in response. Isabel, six, was her favorite niece, not to mention her only niece.

"I did not know it was you, monkey. Where are you calling from?" Horrible possibilities cascaded through her mind. "Oh my God, Izzy, are you OK?"

"I'm fine! This is my new cell phone! Mommy bought it for me today! You're the first person I've called!"

Hannah wondered if Mommy—Hannah's younger sister Bethany—knew that Isabel was busy running up Mommy's phone bill. She decided not to say anything. If Bethany was stupid enough to buy a six-year-old a cell phone, she deserved it. Anyway, it wasn't Hannah's role to play the hardass.

She enjoyed the role of indulgent aunt, taking Isabel for ice cream, or to the funfair on the Santa Monica Pier, whenever she could get into L.A. on the weekend ... which wasn't often enough.

Isabel chattered about her swimming lessons—"I put my face in the water yesterday!" Hannah duly praised her, and promised to come for a visit this Saturday, no matter what.

Ending the phone call, she returned to Burke and the others. They were all clustered around Lyons, some of the team members kneeling behind him on the big square bench. They were all looking at Lyons's cell phone. "That's just weird," Lyons said.

"What are you looking at?" Hannah said.

"I can get C-Span streaming on this. We were looking at the *Atlantis* hearing. It just glitched."

"Alt-F4. That kind of a glitch," said someone else.

"It"s supposed to be live," Lyons complained, shaking his cell phone as if the gadget were the problem.

"They always have a delay so they can bleep out f-bombs," Hannah said. "Maybe that's what happened."

"Well, it was Kildare talking." Several people laughed. None of them had ever met Jack Kildare, as astronauts didn't have any reason to visit JPL as a rule, but astronauts and foul language went together like apple pie and ice cream. Not surprising, as most of them started off in the military.

Burke was silent.

Aha, Hannah thought. It wasn't just an f-bomb. It was a *political* glitch, wasn't it?

She walked back to the office with the others, feeling pensive. Buried in engineering problems on a daily basis, she tended to forget that the charter of NASA was "to advance

US scientific, security, and economic interests." The agency's mission was a political one. If only it could just be about the engineering …

Her mind drifted back to Juno's orbital insertion burns. Although the probe would not reach Jupiter for another four years, the burns could be calculated now.

On Earth, a *lot* could happen in four years. But not in space. That was one of the reasons Hannah loved space, actually. You could plan things years in advance, knowing that nothing would happen in the meantime to throw off your calculations. The planets and their moons were permanent, unchanging. These *alleged* hot cryovolcanic plumes on Europa, for example … if they really existed, that would upend astronomy. But in Hannah's opinion, there was a 99% chance Dr. Meinritz had screwed up his observations.

Never mind. Washington had asked for this fly-by, so Washington would get it.

Mentally immersed in the numbers, she forgot all about going into L.A. on Saturday.

CHAPTER 9

Jack emptied his apartment in Clear Lake. He'd lived there for over five years without accumulating any more stuff than could fit in two suitcases. He drove to Johnson Space Center along Gemini Avenue and Saturn Lane. This dingy Houston suburb was one big memorial to the history he had been so proud to be a part of. Up in the Astronaut Office, he emptied his desk drawers—a small bin liner held everything. A couple of other people from his class, the Peacocks of 2004, came over to offer awkward good wishes. Jack was only the third astronaut ever to be dismissed from NASA. The cause of his dismissal hadn't been made public, although rumors of a Washington shitstorm had done the rounds. His former colleagues seemed unsure whether to sympathise with him or shun him.

Linda Moskowitz evidently had no doubts. Jack met her on the way to the elevator. She was wearing a blue NASA polo-neck, and carrying her laptop, sporting a huge NASA insignia on the cover. Jack was wearing holey Levis and carrying a bin liner. Moskowitz looked straight past him as if he didn't exist.

Flying out of the country, he got that feeling that he didn't exist again and again. Who's watching the day darken above the clouds? Who's pouring overpriced airline wine into a plastic glass? Who's standing at a baggage carousel, waiting for his suitcases to appear between gigantic twine-wrapped cardboard boxes from the Third World? Not an astronaut. Not anymore.

Dear filthy old Heathrow. They lost one of his suitcases.

He abandoned it, caught a shuttle bus to the Park Inn on the Bath Road, simply because it was the first hotel it stopped at, and didn't move from his room for the next two days, except to make foraging trips to the off-license up the road.

On the third day, he showered, shaved, rented a car from Avis, and drove to Warwickshire, chewing spearmint gum the whole way.

"Hi, Mum."

His mother screamed and dropped her pruning shears, which was not flattering, but understandable. She had thought he was on the other side of the Atlantic.

"The garden's looking lovely," Jack added. It was. Now that she and his father were retired, his mother had gone from a keen gardener to an obsessive one. She had strange ideas about planting flowers whose colors clashed with each other, bursting out of crannies in the pocket-sized garden, but somehow it all worked.

She pulled herself together, hugged him, and asked what they owed the visit to.

"I've lost my job," Jack said. "But not to worry. I've got loads of prospects lined up."

He hadn't. His mother, realizing this, made it clear without a word that he was welcome to stay as long as he liked. His father, on the other hand, had a lot invested in Jack's success. A retired science teacher, he used to bask in the reflected glory of his NASA astronaut son. He kept on at Jack for details of his supposed job leads with obtuse persistence. On the fourth night of his stay, Jack blew up at him and stalked off to the pub.

At the end of that too-long night, he brooded over a last

can of lager in his childhood bedroom. He might have a go at processing his photos from the ISS. He hadn't looked at them since he took them. But all he had here was a laptop, and neither its screen quality nor processing software were really up to the job …

He was about to boot up the laptop, anyway, when he got a call from Oliver Meeks.

"How's everything?" Meeks said, sounding as sprightly as if he'd just woken up. It was three in the morning. He probably had.

Meeks had been a friend of Jack's at Bristol University, where Jack studied physics as an undergraduate. They shared a common interest—all right, obsession—with rockets, spacecraft, and all things that went boom. Meeks was hands-on. He built things. A little while after they graduated, he'd built a rocket-propelled car that corkscrewed across the bottom of a quarry in Wales and smashed into a slate cliff-face at a hundred miles an hour. Meeks had lost the use of his legs. A while after he got out of hospital, he'd gone to work for BAE Systems. That was the last Jack had heard of him, until now:

"So you got canned by NASA? Bad luck."

Evidently Meeks had stayed better informed about Jack's movements than vice versa.

"Yeah, how'd you hear?" Jack said.

"Your father," Meeks said, with the whinnying laugh that wrongly put a lot of people off him. "He rang me up earlier. I think he's worried that you're sinking into a spiral of pathetic, loser-ish depression and will finish up an unemployable alcoholic."

"The sly old git," Jack said, with a certain amount of admiration. "He's overreacting, need I say. *One* late night at the pub and he thinks I've got a problem." In fact, Jack's grandfather—his father's father—had drunk himself into an early grave, causing much needless grief and suffering for the family. So Jack's father, himself a teetotaler, tended to be twitchy about booze. Jack opened his window and propped his elbows on the sill to talk with his head outside, keeping his voice lowered. The scent of his mother's phlox drifted up through the warm night. "What are you up to these days, Ollie? And how the hell did my father get your phone number?"

"Off the internet, I expect," Meeks said. "I'm not hard to find if you bothered to look. Firebird Systems."

"I thought you worked at BAE?"

"Not anymore," Meeks said. "I started Firebird a few years back."

Jack suddenly had a vivid flashback of Meeks's rocket-propelled car hurtling across the quarry. It had been a spectacular smash-up. Meeks had cartwheeled out of the fireball in his flame-retardant Formula One style nomex getup, still strapped into his seat, never to walk again. The name of that car had been *Firebird.* It took a certain type of man to adopt a life-altering failure as his personal totem. "Congratulations," Jack said. "How's that going?"

Meeks snorted. "If you want to get old before your time, try starting a company in this bloody country. They might as well just go the whole hog and ban ideas."

In Meeks's case that would probably be a good thing, Jack thought. "What are you making now, then? Rocket-propelled wheelchairs?"

Meeks whinnied. "I considered it, but I decided to stick

to spaceships."

"Ah."

"Yes, a single stage to orbit spaceplane. The thing is in about a year we'll be ready to fly our first test launches. So I'll need a pilot. Of course, you've probably got something else lined up …"

*

Shortly before Christmas 2012, Jack was in Firebird Systems' corporate headquarters, otherwise known as Meeks's house in the Rhondda Cynon Valley. Optimized throughout for wheelchair access, the spread had ramps instead of stairs, and huge picture windows overlooking the forested opposite side of the valley. Meeks came from an extremely well-off family. That was just as well, since Firebird was burning through money like there was no tomorrow. They'd reached the stage where they could get the thing sub-orbital, but couldn't load it with enough fuel to make a decently round orbit, and still carry a payload somewhere useful. But with Christmas coming up, Meeks had issued an edict against doom and gloom "at least until Boxing Day." The small, fanatically committed team of design engineers had been dragged away from their computers to decorate a 12-foot Christmas tree.

Under these circumstances, Jack felt bad about accepting even a token salary, especially since he couldn't contribute to making their existing engines more efficient.

He could hang tinsel, anyway. He balanced on a stepladder, driving thumbtacks into the wall above the picture window in the living-room. He looped fluffy silver tinsel over each tack. The smell of mulled wine filled the house, and on the stereo Psy sang "Gangnam Style." Jack knew he ought to be spending Christmas at home, since he was actually in the same country as his parents for a change, but they were used to being alone. They'd told him not to go to the bother of coming down for the day. And honestly, it was going to be more fun here. Although most of the team would disperse on Christmas Eve, their German metallurgist, Inga, would be staying here over the holidays. Inga had the body of a Valkyrie and a nerdish lack of social confidence. Jack reckoned she just needed to be brought out of her shell. He was still weighing it, but they were all adults, and it shouldn't disrupt the team if they got cozy under the mistletoe after a few glasses of wine.

He climbed down from the stepladder and moved it around Meeks's wheelchair. Meeks was spraying the window with one of those fake snow aerosols. No clichéd season's greetings for him—he was literally writing rocket equations, backwards, so they could be read from outside if anyone ever came up here, which they didn't.

Physically, Meeks and Jack were a study in contrasts. Jack, ruddy, fair-haired, just under the astronaut height cut-off at six foot two and a half, was in the best shape of his life. His revenge on NASA was to stay at peak fitness with daily runs and weightlifting. Meeks was beaky-faced, dark-haired, with an overdeveloped upper body that looked out of proportion to his withered legs. And then, of course, there was the fact that Meeks was in a wheelchair. But their minds worked the same way.

"Why don't you put the Tsiolkovsky rocket equation?" Jack said.

"No, I prefer the vis-viva equation," Meeks said. "No one ever comes out here except for us, anyway."

He strained up in his wheelchair, stretching to write the last figure—and the wheelchair rolled into the bottom of the stepladder.

Jack reached instinctively for the curtain rail, then realized he was going over no matter what he did. He jumped clear, landing on his feet. He was too late to catch the stepladder. It crashed down across the wheelchair. Meeks was no longer in the chair. He'd thrown himself out. He lay at the base of the window, the spray can still clutched in one hand, his useless legs crumpled like sticks. "Sorry," he said. "God. Sorry about that."

Jack picked up the stepladder, as everyone rushed over. "Ach! Are you hurt, Ollie?" Inga exclaimed.

"He's fine. What fun would Christmas be without a prang or two?" Jack said with a laugh. He did not offer to help Meeks get up. He moved the stepladder along and went back to stringing up tinsel, while everyone else fussed over Meeks. Jack knew how much his friend detested being treated like a cripple. He might be a paraplegic, but in Jack's mind, he was exactly the same person as ever. He was brilliant, hyperactive, and right now incredibly frustrated about engine efficiency. Jack watched as Meeks snarled and swore at Inga and the others, who were trying to help, but seemed only to make things worse.

After they finished the decorations, Jack found himself at loose ends. He sat at the three-monitor CAD setup on the far side of the ground floor, sorting through the photographs he'd taken on the ISS. It was about time he got around to them. He planned to enhance and print out his best ones. Inspiration for the team.

Gosh, here's Jupiter!

It was strange to look back and rememb how excited he'd been about capturing Jupiter on film. Greg Howard had died that same night. Jack had forgotten about this photo set amidst the chaotic aftermath of the tragedy.

To his disappointment, the pictures weren't that great. As advanced as it was, his Canon's resolution was not on the level of a telescope. Jupiter dissolved into a clump of pale pixels.

Hang on.

The time-stamp of the photo was roughly midday.

What's this?

Jack enhanced the contrast.

That makes no sense.

Absorbed in enhancing and retouching the picture, trying to make the apparent smear go away, Jack didn't hear Meeks wheeling up behind him. "Are those your space photographs?"

Jack jumped. 'The Fairytale of New York' on the stereo had drowned out the squeak of the wheelchair's tyres. "Yes."

Meeks rolled up to the desk. It was exactly the right height so the arms of the wheelchair could fit underneath. "Was there something wrong with your camera?"

"No," Jack said.

Meeks tugged the mouse out from under Jack's hand. He checked the exposure and processing settings. "That looks like a plume of water vapor. Except it wouldn't have shown up unless it were dense enough to be illuminated by the sun, or very, very hot."

"And that would be impossible."

"Let's say for the sake of argument that it really is a hot plume of water vapor. Plasma, actually. Hang on." Meeks whizzed over to a different computer and began to Google. "Here's something," he said about thirty seconds later. "It's behind a paywall ..." He subscribed to the journal on the spot.

Superheated volcanic water eruption observations on Jovian moons. Jack read the abstract over Meeks's shoulder.

"Well, they've got *that* all wrong," he said when he finished.

"Yup," Meeks said. "They would only have been looking at a very tight view of Jupiter and its moons. I bet they didn't realise how far the plume extended."

Jack nodded. He walked back to the other computer and stared at his photograph.

All his training and experience with NASA had taught him that 'impossible' was a moving target. The things he'd done as an astronaut would have been considered science fiction by their grandfathers' generation. In the space industry, 'impossible' barriers got shattered all the time. It was just a question of overcoming human and technological limitations. *Anything* was theoretically possible with the right people and materials.

Out of nowhere, Jack suddenly remembered the weird noises he'd heard through his headset on the *Atlantis*.

Beep, beep, beeeeep.

Wheeeeooow ...

EEEEEEE!

He shuddered, hard. His entire skin seemed to shrink up tight on his body. For Jack Kildare, that was the moment when two plus two made four and the world changed.

He glanced at Meeks. "Ollie, do you believe in aliens?"

Meeks continued to stare at the photograph without answering. Jack began to feel annoyed and ashamed of his own overreaction.

He went on, a bit defensively, "I'm not sure if you know this, but all astronauts believe in aliens. It's simply impossible not to, when you've been out there and seen for yourself how… big it is; how much there is of it. *Space.* So many stars, and now we know there are billions of potentially habitable planets. There's no way they're not out there. But for the same reason, no one believes they'll ever come here. It's too far from A to B."

"Shut up," Meeks said. "I'm thinking."

"But they have come here, haven't they?" Jack rubbed his face with his hands. If he was right, this was probably the worst news the human race had ever received. A smear on a photograph. "That's a drive plume."

"Of course it is," Meeks said impatiently.

A huge wave of relief washed over Jack. He wasn't going bonkers. Meeks saw it, too.

He said in a false light tone, "Bang goes the Fermi Paradox, eh? 'Where is everybody?' Well, Enrico, they were actually on their way. And now they're here."

On the other side of the room, Inga dropped a Christmas tree bauble. Jack whipped around at the sound of shattering glass. So much for taking it lightly. His body was in fight-or-flight mode.

Meeks turned to watch Inga picking up the pieces of the bauble. Then he said, "Speaking of the Fermi paradox. Where is everybody? I've always thought the most logical explanation is that they're out there, but we're unable to detect their signals. There may be modes of long-distance communication we're completely unaware of, which are standard for a highly advanced species. But that's the trouble. It implies that any other species out there is highly advanced." Meeks brought his thumb and forefinger together. "If they've got the ability to travel between the stars, they also have the ability to squash us like a bug."

"Agreed, but I wonder why they haven't got around to it yet. I took these pictures in April." Jack laughed. "Listen to us! Discussing a bloody alien invasion."

"It was bound to happen someday," Meeks said. "God knows why they're delaying. Gathering data on us, perhaps. The good news is, every day they haven't invaded us is another day we've got to prepare."

Jack touched the smear on the screen. "It'd take us decades to build anything capable of taking on *that.*"

"Not necessarily," Meeks said. He tapped the screen with a pen. A smile slowly spread across his face. "Do you realize what this is?"

"Water plasma. The article said it was heated to 1.6 million degrees Kelvin."

"Exactly." Meeks's smile broadened. "It's the answer!"

"To what?"

"Getting enough fuel on board whilst still being light enough to take off! Water! The answer is water!"

Meeks spun on his wheels. Then he halted.

"Don't say anything, Jack."

"About aliens? Well, of course not. We'd need more proof." In Jack's own mind, no further proof was needed. But the worst of all possible worlds would be for the public to panic—and then move on to the next news cycle, while the threat remained real and unaddressed.

"Say nothing about absolutely any of it," Meeks said. "We

don't want the competition getting hold of this." He rolled down the ramp to where the others were putting the finishing touches on the Christmas tree. "All right, everyone! Change of plans! We're going to be working over Christmas …"

CHAPTER 10

Hannah snacked mindlessly on a bag of spinach-flavored rice crackers as she watched Juno's heartbeat pulse on her screen. It was July 4th, 2016.

Five years since her baby launched from Cape Canaveral.

Four years since the team received the ridiculous, still-unexplained request from Washington to alter Juno's orbital insertion burn for a close fly-by of Europa.

Fifteen minutes until the probe would complete its main burn and settle into orbit around Jupiter.

The mission control room at JPL buzzed with tension. Hannah and the other key team members sat at a long desk with their backs to a wall, facing the cameras. NASA had come a long way in presenting a slick, media-friendly face to the world of the internet age. Everything in the room was branded, from the team's matching t-shirts, to their water bottles—even the snacks Hannah was eating had the Juno logo on the bag, a stylized representation of the tri-winged probe.

If Hannah lifted her gaze from her computer, she would see giant screens on the far wall displaying mission graphics with the same logo. But she didn't look up. She was only vaguely conscious of the video and still photographers circling the team. Nothing mattered except the carrier wave hitting the receiving stations in Madrid, Goldstone, and Canberra, proving that Juno had been alive and well 48 minutes ago.

That was how long it took to send a signal back from Jupiter to Earth.

48 minutes.

Whatever would happen, had already happened. Juno was on autopilot. They could no longer affect the outcome of the orbital insertion burn. But that knowledge didn't ease the tension one jot.

Ralf Lyons, the mission navigator, kept up a stream of nervous chatter on her left. On her right, Richard Burke, the team leader, was calmly working through his emails. His two-fingered typing—which he insisted was highly efficient—grated on Hannah's nerves, making her unconsciously grit her teeth with irritation. She ate another rice cracker.

The snacks were subbing in for what she really wanted, which was a drink.

It had been a tough four years for Hannah. All the issues that inevitably cropped up with a probe operating at the very edge of humanity's technological capability, combined with the demands of redesigning the mission on the fly to achieve the Europa fly-by, had resulted in a lot of late nights at work … and a lot of after-work drinks. It was like a Newtonian equal and opposite reaction. The harder she worked, the harder she had to play, as if to burn off the constantly accumulating stress.

Could you really call it play, what she did? She had eleven bars within her Highland Park territory that she visited on a strict rotation. Hannah's Rule #2: *No drinking at home.* The advent of Uber had made it a lot easier for her to keep this rule. Now, she could head out for the night secure in the knowledge that a few taps on her iPhone could get her home without risking a DUI. She had it all down to a system. *N* units of alcohol allowed per week. *N* Vicodin allowed per hangover. *No* to sexy strangers.

She knew, of course, there was something amiss in viewing her own body as a mechanical system to be recalibrated on a daily basis, but it worked for her. And it would continue to work, as long as she followed the rules.

She had a bottle of champagne in her bag at her feet. Hannah's Rule #1, of course, was *No drinking at work*. But tonight was surely an exception. She planned to bring out the champagne and share it with the team—she'd also brought a sleeve of plastic cups—when Juno had achieved orbital insertion, and they could escape the cameras filming their every move.

She pushed away a fantasy of escaping to the ladies' room, uncorking the champagne, and downing a quick slug.

Right now, Juno's engine was burning, slowing the probe's velocity by 540 meters per second.

This was a big, fast burn designed to slew the probe around and get it facing away from the sun. If something went wrong at this stage, it would all be on Hannah.

The doppler residuals showed that Juno had reached periapsis—its point of closest approach to Jupiter. Bonus points, this was the closest any human craft had *ever* approached the massive gas giant. Juno was skimming just 4,500 kilometers above Jupiter's cloud tops, rotating at 5 rpm, the engine burning sweetly. Not bad for a craft that Hannah had helped to build in a glorified shed at Lockheed Martin.

Suddenly the carrier wave stuttered. Hannah stiffened. Thoughts of champagne vanished. The volume of chatter in the room swelled, gaining an alarmed edge.

"It's just a communications hiccup," Burke said evenly.

Hannah's fingers flew, checking the tracking and receiver.

Communications wasn't her specialty, but there shouldn't be any reason for a hiccup.

Yet the probe's heartbeat had stopped. The icons for all three receiving stations sat mute.

"Have we lost tracking?" Hannah asked. Her voice didn't sound like her own.

"It's got to be a receiver issue," Burke said. "Stay cool, Hannah-banana, we'll check it."

Hannah had mixed feelings about this nickname. It had started when the powers that be ordained that they all needed to tweet. She'd picked @hannah_a_banana as her Twitter handle one evening while drunk, and only found out about it when people at work started calling her 'Hannah-banana.' She couldn't reject it now without explaining how she'd ended up with that Twitter handle. Besides, all her tweets were linked to the @NASAJuno account.

She couldn't even begin to imagine the tweet she'd have to send after this. "#Juno so sorry." Her baby was all by itself, 600 million kilometers from Earth, dying.

Pulse.

The receiving stations picked up a single tone.

Everyone in the control room held their breath.

Pulse. Pulse.

"It's alive!" Lyons shouted.

Hannah whooped in jubilation.

Juno's heart was still beating.

The reporters and bloggers covering the event posted happy tweets. Burke pumped his fists in relief. Lyons hugged Hannah. Other people jumped to their feet and did victory dances.

But their elation died down within seconds, because all

was very far from well.

"Juno has rebooted," Burke said. "It's gone into safe mode. "

As quickly as Hannah's spirits had recovered, she now experienced a roller-coaster plunge into horror.

Right in the middle of the main burn, Juno had undergone a complete systems shutdown. The engine had cut off. The probe was now in safe mode, awaiting instructions.

And all this had happened 48 minutes ago.

For the last 48 minutes, her baby had been spinning like an unpowered frisbee, hurtling through a zone full of rocks and dust—and insanely high radiation—away from Jupiter.

The horrifying reality of the situation sank in. They risked losing Juno altogether. If the probe couldn't insert into orbit around Jupiter, it would plummet irretrievably into the abyss of trans-Jovian space.

"I've got this," Hannah muttered. "I've got this." She called up the probe's orbital parameters. A brief wince of agony pulled at her mouth.

Lyons said, "It's not the end of the world. The probe's been burning for a while. We can still get into orbit, it's just going to be a very elongated orbit. We have to plan a new burn at periapsis on the next orbit to complete the insertion."

Hannah—who was already doing that—spared Lyons a glance. "I would call you brilliant, but I'm in the room."

In the sleepless hours and days that followed, Hannah designed a burn that would fire Juno's thrusters just before the little craft reached its periapsis around Jupiter, dragging the orbit back towards the gas giant … and Europa. This sub-optimal, elongated orbit would still give the probe substantial dwell time near Europa, though not as much as Washington had asked for.

Even when her work was done, and the probe had received its instructions via the uplink, she couldn't rest. She mentally ran over the burn parameters again and again, attacking her own calculations from every side to see if there was any risk she might have underestimated.

Something had caused Juno to unexpectedly shut down and reboot.

And they'd made zero headway in figuring out what it was.

A few hours before the emergency burn was scheduled to start, she sat wearily at her desk in the mission control room. She could have gone home, but she knew she would end up at La Cuevita.

Burke had not gone home in a couple of days, either, although unlike Hannah, he had a family waiting at home for him. He slumped beside her, talking on the phone. The tone of his voice told her he was talking to Suzanne Stone, the Juno program executive in Washington, or someone else at the top of the food chain.

"We're still analyzing the reboot event. At this time, unfortunately, we do not know what caused it."

Hannah tensed, knowing what was coming next.

"Yes, it's possible that this was a recurrence of the same error that caused the probe to enter safe mode just over 90 hours ago."

The words felt like salt in the wound of Hannah's diminished confidence. The terrible fact was they had had warning of the reboot error. Because it had happened before. Almost four days before Juno reached Jupiter, the probe had unexpectedly rebooted itself. That time, it hadn't been critical. The team had ended up writing it off as the result of a shower of charged solar particles overwhelming the probe's radiation hardening. After all, there'd been a coronal mass ejection that might have clipped it.

But now it looked like they had been wrong.

"Nope," Burke said. "Sorry, ma'am. We do not know what caused that event, either …"

His face was a bad shade of ruddy, his eyes bloodshot for lack of sleep. Hannah knew how heavy the burden of responsibility was. She stirred herself from her near-cataleptic slouch, scribbled on the back of a print-out, and held it up for Burke to see:

It's actually quite funny once you get past the tragic elements and the sense of encroaching doom.

Burke laughed out loud. "Sorry, ma'am. Just want to mention, as you know, we have got a great team working on the problem here …"

Hannah smiled. She really, *really* wanted a drink now.

CHAPTER 11

Summer in Las Vegas. Heat shimmered above the tarmac of McCarran International Airport, making the runways look like they were covered with water. Jack settled his Ray-Bans on his nose and walked through the blazing sunlight to Ziggy One. It was July 7th, 2016, and Firebird Systems had been based in Nevada for almost three years.

They'd moved the company to the States in 2013 to access America's startup-friendly regulatory regime, as well as its wide-open stretches of desert where nobody cared if you lit off rocket engines to see what they did.

For Jack, coming back to the USA had been like coming home, unexpectedly so. Though he hadn't realized it at the time, his years at NASA had stamped him with a preference for America's free-and-easy social mores, as well as humongous steaks and bottomless Coca-Cola refills. Iced tea with sugar and lemon, on the other hand, he still considered revolting.

But Las Vegas was very different from Houston. Far from commemorating the history of America's golden age, Vegas celebrated an eternal present of conspicuous consumption. The whole city could feel like an illusion sometimes. And in contrast to the humid Texas summers, Vegas baked in dry heat. This had its points. Jack felt the air get twenty degrees cooler when he walked into the shadow of Ziggy One. He finished checking the aircraft.

The plane did not belong to Firebird Systems. Fat chance when they were operating on a shoestring, with Meeks fighting their investors over every quarterly budget. Ziggy One was a converted 727 owned by The Freefall Experience, a company which offered freefall experiences—just like it said on the tin!—to tourists, for the modest price of $150,000 each. Only in Las Vegas.

Firebird had chartered the plane for the day.

"Have you finished loading fuel?" Jack said to the technician, an overweight man in the bright yellow Freefall Experience uniform. It made him look like a Pokemon. He fit right in with the weird and wild color schemes of the other private planes standing around.

"Y'all are good to go, sir," said the technician.

"Great." Jack turned to climb the air stairs to the cockpit.

"Your co-pilot best get a move on, if he don't want to miss the take-off slot," the man called after him.

Jack paused halfway up the steps, grinning. "That's my co-pilot." He pointed towards the tail of the plane.

A truck-mounted hoist was lifting Meeks—wheelchair and all—into the passenger cabin.

His face shaded by a baseball cap, Meeks gave them a thumbs-up.

"Oh-kayyyy," the technician said. "Guess y'all know what you're doing."

"He didn't have to be such a prick about it," Jack said, when they were inside the airplane. In a land where cheerful smiles and 'you have a nice day now' formed the accompaniment to every interaction, the technician's grumpiness was unusual. "On the other hand, I suppose we're a bit different from the average charter customers."

"Did you tip him?" Meeks said.

Jack slapped his forehead. "Christ. *That* was it." The technician hadn't been dubious about a disabled co-pilot. He'd been annoyed by Jack's failure to tip. Clearly Jack hadn't quite assimilated to American culture yet.

He helped Meeks out of his wheelchair and folded and stowed it. Meeks lay prone on the padded floor of the airplane, near the web of straps and ties that held their cargo. "I'll have a martini," he teased Jack.

"Less aggro from the peanut gallery," Jack said, heading for the cockpit.

He hadn't told the truth to the Freefall Experience man—not exactly. Meeks was listed as co-pilot, and he did have his license. There was nothing wrong with his eyes or ears, after all. But he wasn't going to help Jack fly the 727. He didn't have to.

Pilot's joke: In the airplane of the future, there will be a man and a dog in the cockpit. The dog is there to prevent the man from touching anything, and the man is there to feed the dog.

Ziggy One looked plenty futuristic on the inside. It had just a few rows of seats—currently unused—at the front of the cabin. The whole rear of the cabin was covered with off-white padding. It reminded Jack a bit of the ISS, actually. Ziggy One's airframe had also been reinforced and the hydraulics modified to support its unique flight patterns. But the cockpit was just the same old 727 layout, with the addition of an accelerometer readout.

Jack set the flight engineer's panel up for starting, then crouched between the flight engineer panel and the center console to execute the start sequences. Once he had the engines running, he slid into the left seat and taxied out to the runway. The control tower affirmed that he was cleared to take off.

Up we go!

The thrill never got old.

Reaching across the cockpit to perform the odd flight engineer duty, monitoring all the instruments with an eagle eye, Jack didn't have time to appreciate the Nevada desert spread out below. "OK back there?" he shouted to Meeks.

"Fine," Meeks shouted back. "Great view."

Jack risked a glance back through the open cockpit door. That crazy bugger had hauled himself on top of the aluminum frame that held the boilerplate unit. He was sitting up there like a cross-legged Buddha with atrophied legs. Well, he had to get up there at some point to throw the switches on the pumps.

The boilerplate unit was the whole reason for this flight. From the outside it looked a little like an explosion in a pipe factory, rendered in clear acrylic, allowing easy viewing and filming of the fluids moving inside it.

Firebird Systems had been working on this concept since 2012. The project dated to the day before Christmas Eve, 2012—the day they examined Jack's photos from the ISS. That day still haunted Jack's memory. In the rare moments when he wasn't doing anything else, he would see that smear of hot water plasma in his mind's eye. The doom of the human race, spelled out in pixels.

Well, three and a half years on, doom hadn't struck yet. Jack felt gladder than ever that they hadn't gone public with the photos. They would have been mocked by cretins who thought that if something didn't happen immediately, it was never going to happen at all.

He and Meeks had discussed this reprieve over and over. They had no way of knowing what might have become of the alien ship. They *did* know that at some point, the other shoe would drop.

But maybe, just maybe, if nothing went on happening for long enough, they'd have time to get ready to face it when it did.

Today, Jack felt optimistic about their chances.

The sky was clear, cloudless blue. The altimeter read 33,100 feet.

"Ten minutes until we get out over the Pacific," he called back to Meeks.

"Fingers crossed for @NASAJuno!" Meeks said. "She's about to check up on her husband's first mistress!"

"What?"

Another glance back. Meeks had his phone out. Obviously, he didn't have a signal up here.

"Is that Twitter?"

"Yeah, that was posted earlier today. It's from @hannah_a_banana."

"Who's that?"

"One of the Juno team scientists. That's all there is. There've been no official updates from the @NASAJuno account since they successfully made the burn at periapse."

Needless to say, Jack and Meeks had been glued to the adventures of the Juno probe. The mission seemed to have been designed to take a close look at Europa. Maybe that was just a coincidence … and maybe it was *also* a coincidence that the probe had nearly been lost a few days ago due to "system errors."

And pigs might fly. That Harvard professor's research paper had gone nowhere, but it proved that Jack wasn't the only person to have noticed the anomalous plume. Someone, somewhere, had seen fit to investigate it further. And whoever that someone was, they had enough power to make NASA dance to their tune.

"The silence from @NASAJuno is actually quite deafening," Meeks mused. "So much for NASA's commitment to transparency."

"Don't forget their commitment to the economic and defense interests of America," Jack said. He might have become Americanized in his tastes, but after his career-ending clash with Congress, his trust in America's institutions—including NASA—had hit rock bottom, and there it had stayed.

"Yeah." Meeks chuckled. "Thank goodness for @hannah_a_banana, anyway. She's got a sense of humor, even if she's only allowed to post Greek mythology jokes and pictures of mai tais."

Far below, America ended. The sequined blue sheet of the Pacific spread to the misty horizon. Jack adjusted the throttles and disconnected the autopilot. "Get into position," he said.

Ziggy One had been modified for a specific purpose: to fly parabolic arcs. Jack took the jet up at a steep angle. 1.8 gees pressed him into his seat. In the back, Meeks lay prone on the padded floor again. He had switched the boilerplate unit on before dragging himself down, adding its whirring and gurgling to the cacophony of noise inside the plane.

After 20 seconds, Jack pushed the 727 over. The plane plummetted towards the Pacific.

Everything which was not strapped down rose into the air, nudged by a thousand small vibrations, and began falling at the same speed as the plane—exactly like falling through space in orbit. Jack's body floated against his harness, pressed there as the foam padding of the seat relaxed. His sunglasses, forgotten on the right-hand seat, bounced off the ceiling of the cockpit and spun lazily away.

In the back, Meeks let out a whoop of sheer joy. He kept whooping, and yelling, and laughing like a child as he rebounded off the padded walls.

"This is fucking amazing!" Fifteen seconds into their freefall dive, Meeks finally found words for the experience. "This is absolutely fucking terrific!"

Jack smiled. The sensation of freefall brought back bittersweet memories for him. But this was the first time Meeks had ever experienced it. "Now you know what it feels like," he shouted back.

He heard Meeks laugh the laugh of the freefall virgin discovering what it was like to slip the bonds of gravity.

It happened to almost everyone.

Of course, in freefall, it no longer mattered that Meeks' legs didn't work. He could float free, just like anyone else. No need to worry about steps and staircases. He was free.

Twenty seconds had passed. Jack levelled the plane out. Truth be told, he hadn't flown parabolic maneuvers since he was in the RAF, and he breathed a private sigh of relief when the 727 flattened out into their previous flight pattern.

"Ready to go up again?" he called back.

"Hell yeah!" Meeks lay on his back on the floor, grinning like a loon at the ceiling.

"Don't forget this time, you're actually supposed to be doing science up there …"

*

The boilerplate unit was a one-quarter scale reproduction of the nuclear reactor and Brayton cycle turbines—minus the parts that dealt with superheated steam, of course—that would be used to provide electrical power for the thrusters and engines on their spaceplane. The engines would allow the spaceplane to cast off the bonds of gravity and easily maneuver to drop off a satellite in geostationary orbit … and eventually, perhaps, go further.

They flew 15 parabolic arcs. Bobbling in the air above the unit, Meeks confirmed that the fluids and gasses circulated properly, and that the turbines could stand up to freefall.

The experiment was a complete success.

So Jack flew one more arc, just for fun.

Then he turned the 727 east, and flew sedately back towards Las Vegas.

Meeks propped his back against the unit and drank from a plastic bottle of water. The combination of freefall and experimental success had left him cheerful to the point of bubbliness, a rare mood for him lately. "We can start building the prototype next month," he said. "Then we'll do vacuum tests on the magnetoplasmadynamic engine. We might manage a test launch within the year!"

I hope we have that long, Jack thought. Gazing down at the urban sprawl of Reno, all he could think was how vulnerable it looked.

"I could *live* in space. One doesn't need legs if one can fly," Meeks said a few minutes later. "I'd like to build an orbital habitat. Why not?"

"First things first," Jack said.

"Space should belong to us. Not to *them.*"

Jack shared Meeks's instinctual outrage at the idea that the alien ship, wherever it was now, might threaten humanity's future in space. On the other hand though, the ship *had* given Meeks the idea for the water plasma drive, and they'd just taken a giant step towards making the drive a reality. They touched down at McCarran International in high spirits, planning a celebratory dinner with the rest of the Firebird team.

Jack parked the 727 in their designated spot, a hundred yards from the terminal. The air stairs glided towards the plane. Several men stood on the platform. "Uh, Ollie?"

Meeks was on the phone, making dinner reservations at a well-known steakhouse. Jack made a throat-slicing gesture. He grabbed Meeks's wheelchair, flipped the backrest upright and sent it rolling down the plane to Meeks, and then opened the forward cabin door.

An oven blast of hot air rolled in. The air stairs approached the plane and stopped a foot away. One of the men on the platform held up a badge. "FAA," he said. "You the pilot? Mr. John Kildare?"

"Is there a problem?" Jack said.

The FAA man wore a crumpled business suit. He was the archetypal Federal Asswipes Anonymous bureaucrat. The other two men on the platform wore jeans, navy blue t-shirts, and sunglasses. Jack couldn't figure out their role.

"You bet your ass there's a problem," the FAA man said. "Unless you got a different name for a violation of the Atomic Energy Act."

Jack said the first thing that came into his head. "I'm an American citizen."

All three men smiled. Someone down below laughed. Glancing down, Jack saw the Freefall Experience technician in his Pokemon-esque uniform driving the air stairs. The man looked back at him with cold dislike.

"Step aside, sir," the FAA official said.

Jack stepped aside. "This is a misunderstanding," he said. "We haven't violated any laws or regulations."

The air stairs closed the gap with the 727. The FAA official and his two escorts entered the plane. The smell of sweat hit Jack's nostrils as they passed him. Meeks rolled to meet them, working hard to drive his wheelchair across the padded floor. "I apologize for any miscommunication," he said with a smile. "How can we help you today?"

Meeks was good at dealing with visitors from red-tape land. Courteous and cooperative, that was the ticket. But Jack's hopes that this could be swiftly sorted out faded as the three men simply ignored Meeks. They walked straight past him and began taking pictures of the boilerplate unit.

"Is that a steam generator?" one of the navy t-shirts said to Jack. The other one was unhooking the webbing straps that held the unit in place.

"Yes, it is," Jack said shortly.

"So you admit to flying a nuclear reactor over the continental United States," the FAA official said triumphantly.

"For fuck's sake!" Jack exploded. "It's not a bloody nuclear reactor! It's an acrylic box with a steam generator and some cameras in it!"

"Calm down, sir," said the younger navy t-shirt. He had curly hair in a short white-boy afro and wore a silver peace symbol necklace. His dark eyes stared at Jack down the length of the aircraft. Jack became aware that he was clenching his fists. He relaxed his stance minutely. Then he noticed the lump at the young man's waistband, concealed by his loose t-shirt. Jesus, the guy was carrying a gun!

"That's illegal within the secure areas of an airport," Jack said, letting the little bastard know he was onto him. His heart thumped.

The curly-haired man shrugged. His colleague was slapping nuclear hazard stickers on the housing of the boilerplate unit. "You were offered an opportunity to sell your company in 2015," the curly-haired one said. "You didn't take it. You should have."

"That was *you?"* Meeks said. Jack was tongue-tied, remembering that he'd advised Meeks to take the offer. Meeks stared levelly at the fake FAA agents. "And just who are you, again?"

"Jeez, it's hot in here," said the curly-haired guy, lifting his t-shirt to fan air underneath it. The gun was a Glock.

"Right," Meeks said. "I'm calling our lawyers." He started to dial.

The curly-haired man walked up to Meeks and plucked his phone out of his hand. "We'll have to impound that for inspection." All the blood drained out of Meeks's face. "Your phone, too," the man said, holding out his hand to Jack. "You'll get it back when we're done with it."

"And if I'd rather not give you my phone?" Jack bluffed.

"Then we'll suspend your pilot's license." The man grinned mockingly. "Actually, we're going to do that anyway."

CHAPTER 12

Hannah's ten-year-old niece, Isabel, had made a clay model of Jupiter in science class. She—or more likely, her mother, Hannah's sister Bethany—had sent it to Hannah in a reused Amazon box. Hannah winced in guilt, as Bethany had probably intended, when she found it on the doormat outside her apartment. Bethany and David had been expecting her to visit over the Fourth of July weekend. She'd broken her promise. Again.

At least this time, she'd had a good excuse.

She showered and changed into less-stinky clothes. Then she headed back to JPL, taking the clay model with her.

The mission control room looked like a bomb had hit it. A few people were still wearing their Juno logo t-shirts. That was because they had been wearing them continuously since the near-catastrophe on the 4th. Trash overflowed from the wastepaper baskets. One of the mission control staff snored with her head on her desk.

It was just as well the media had been banned from the mission control room tonight.

Hannah arranged Isabel's clay model next to her computer. Four pea-sized clay balls on the ends of pins represented the Galilean moons. The one made of white and yellow clay smooshed together was probably meant to be Europa.

Sucking down coffee, Hannah took a picture of the model with her phone, and tweeted it.

@hannah_a_banana: "This is what @NASAJuno will be seeing with its science eyes tonight! Kinda ☺ "

"Seriously?" Lyons said. "That is what they're teaching in fourth-grade science these days?"

"Her teacher's got the whole class following the probe," Hannah said. "I think it's great. You're the one who's always complaining about the lack of early STEM education."

"No. No, you're not following me. *This* is what they're doing in *science class?* Playing with modelling clay?"

"Oh, because you were solving rocket equations at that age," Hannah said. "Got it, Einstein."

Lyons's face reddened in humiliation. Hannah churlishly moved the model to the other side of her computer, away from him. She was better at the job than he was—better at the math, better at everything—and both of them knew it. Her *Einstein* crack had been petty. But God, his arrogance was getting on her nerves today. It didn't help to recall that he was sleep-deprived and under a huge amount of stress. Which of them wasn't?

@firebirdmeeks: "No more Greek mythology jokes, @hannah_a_banana?"

Hannah blinked at the Twitter window in the corner of her screen. Someone had actually replied to one of her tweets. That never happened.

@hannah_a_banana: "Trying not to provoke the wrath of the gods again!"

Pretty pathetic, but whatever.

Ostentatiously ignoring Lyons, Hannah settled down to watch the probe's downlink.

On the 5th of July, the probe had switched on its instruments and begun to send back observational data. The spectrographic and visual image data would need to be processed before they would be viewable, but it comforted Hannah just to watch those lovely fat packets of bytes coming home.

Tonight, Juno would swing past Europa at a distance of barely 200,000 kilometers. That was the unspoken reason why the mission control room was packed tonight. Everyone wanted to witness the fly-by that Washington had pushed for at such a high cost to the mission. Because of this requirement, countless other observations had had to be rescheduled, or in some cases cancelled altogether, and Juno would have its orbit altered by the moon. A mood of skepticism clashed with apprehension. Were they about to finally find out what the higher-ups wanted so badly to see? Hot cryovolcanoes, my ass.

As for Hannah, she seemed to have lost her capacity to get excited about the actual content of Juno's observations. The reboot and emergency second burn had drained her to the core. Now she was just hanging in there because everyone else was.

@firebirdmeeks: "A mai tai would be pretty good right now."

Hannah smiled. She liked this guy, whoever he was. Even if he *had* reminded her of her indiscreet first tweet ever, a photo of a flaming mai tai with the caption, "Nom nom!"

@hannah_a_banana: "Champagne if @NASAJuno pulls this off!"

She still had that bottle of Moet & Chandon in her bag. Amid the brutal pressure of the last few days, she'd drunk way too much coffee and taken too many Provigils. But the one thing she hadn't done was have a drink. It felt like part of her was missing.

CHAPTER 13

Passing Meeks's bedroom on his way out, Jack paused.

Meeks lay on his bed with his laptop balanced on his stomach. At least the bastards hadn't confiscated that. They had to have a warrant to search Meeks's home. On that point, Meeks and Jack's knowledge of American law had prevailed.

To Jack's surprise, Meeks was smiling at the screen. Jack wouldn't have expected to see that after the disastrous day they'd had.

"I'm chatting with @hannah_a_banana," Meeks explained.

"You texted her? Tweeted her?" Jack wasn't much of a one for social media. He barely knew how Twitter worked. "And she replied?"

"Yeah. She's nice." The smile faded from Meeks's face. "She says they're doing a close fly-by of Europa tonight."

"Oh Christ," Jack said. "Watch them muck everything up."

He wasn't actually sure how a probe could muck things up, but after today he was taking it as read that the US government would embugger everything within its reach. And it now had a 400-million-kilometer reach. So much the worse for humanity.

"Are you off, then?" Meeks said.

"Yeah."

"Dig the ninja look."

Jack plucked self-consciously at his black t-shirt. "Right, I ought to have a mask."

"I think I've got a balaclava somewhere."

Jack flipped him the bird. "That wouldn't be at all conspicuous in Nevada in the middle of July."

Meeks laughed and went back to his screen. Without looking up again, he said, "Be careful."

"Don't worry. If it looks remotely dodgy, I'll come straight back," Jack lied.

He whistled *Radioactive,* to prove just how confident he was, as he went down the hall to the kitchen. His North Face daypack sat open on the kitchen table. He started to zip it up. Then he grabbed the long butcher knife from the block on the counter, wrapped it in a tea towel, and stuck it in beside his hammer, screwdriver, and boltcutters.

A connecting door from the kitchen led into the garage. Jack started his Toyota truck and drove down the tree-lined driveway.

At least they hadn't suspended his driver's license.

The little town of Bunkerville, NV lay silent and lightless beneath a crescent moon. Jack waited obediently at the stop sign before turning onto NV-170. Not one other vehicle in sight.

He'd been living in North Vegas with Inga until she unexpectedly quit Firebird Systems earlier this year. It was hard to say which had failed first—their relationship, or her commitment to the company. One thing had led to another in a cascade of failures. Inga had gone home to Germany, and Jack had moved into Meeks's spare bedroom.

He didn't plan on staying here forever. The silence and the isolation drove him nuts. But now he had to question whether the company would have a future at all.

Those jerks weren't FAA. The guy with the badge, maybe. Not the other two.

Arseholes! Jack's blood boiled when he remembered how the guy with the peace sign necklace had very nearly threatened him at gunpoint.

A fucking *peace sign!*

Without realizing it, Jack had sped up to 75 mph. He slowed down. There were no cops out here tonight, for sure, and the road ran straight as a ruler through the low hills. But he was very wary of breaking the law at this point.

Which was ironic, considering what he intended to do.

He turned onto an unnamed road and drove out into the Mojave Desert. The Toyota's headlights lit a seemingly endless strip of asphalt laid across barren terrain dotted with creosote bushes. Once, a coyote ran across the road, forcing Jack to jam on the brakes.

Thirty miles out of Bunkerville, he reached the Firebird Systems Launch & Test Facility. The grandiosely named facility was actually just a warehouse at the back edge of an asphalted parking lot. They had been planning to build small-scale test vehicles for when they started test launches.

A chest-height fence, topped with curlicues of barbed wire, surrounded the lot.

Outside the front gate sat a parked car, its headlights off. Jack cursed to himself as he flashed past, hopefully too fast for the occupants of the car to read his license plate.

They'd put a 24-hour watch on the facility. This was definitely not a routine response to an FAA violation.

If he were to keep his promise to Meeks, he would now turn around and head for home. But Jack wasn't giving up that easily. He drove on until the facility was out of sight, then slowed, swung off the road, and bumped at 10 miles per hour over the uneven desert terrain.

If he ever saw Inga again, he'd take her out to dinner to thank her for leaving him the 4WD truck she used to drive out into the desert to go bouldering.

He parked the truck behind a low rise and hiked the rest of the way back to the facility. The night air felt cool on his skin. A breeze carried the faint sweet smell of sagebrush from the hills. Overhead, the moon glowed like a celestial neon sign. Even a new moon could light up the whole sky when you were far from urban light pollution. He couldn't do anything to prevent the pale skin of his face and arms from showing up, but as he approached the facility, he pulled on the beanie he'd had since his RAF days. He should have taken Meeks up on that jesting offer of a balaclava. Somehow, he hadn't expected that he would actually end up doing this.

The moonlight gleamed on the barbed wire. The warehouse hid the front gate and the car guarding it.

Breathing evenly, Jack snipped the barbed wire with his boltcutters. Just as well they hadn't had the money to install the motion sensors Meeks had wanted.

He climbed over the fence, pushing the loose curls of barbed wire out of the way, and walked swiftly towards the back entrance of the warehouse. Strips of yellow police tape crisscrossed the door. DO NOT ENTER. The goddamn nerve of them.

The alarm box shone red, indicating the system was armed. Jack punched his security code in.

The light turned green.

The plods hadn't reset the entry codes!

Grinning, Jack pushed the door open, stepped between the strips of tape, and closed the door after him. He stood immobile for a moment. It was hot and stuffy. He smelled solder and machine oil. The building was divided into two. There was an office space and there was the workshop he stood in now, where they'd built the boilerplate unit. As his eyes adjusted, he made out the hulking silhouettes of the milling machine and lathe. Everything looked untouched.

But his goal was in the other room. He crossed the workshop and entered the open-plan office. This was where the 12-person engineering team had been gathered this afternoon, eagerly awaiting the results of the freefall test flight, when state troopers had burst into the building and escorted them all off the premises.

They hadn't even been given time to collect their personal belongings.

State troopers, in SWAT gear, driving an APV, as if they were clearing a building full of jihadists, not meek rocket scientists.

Meeks had spent the evening comforting the traumatized engineers and promising them that the lawyers would sort it out. Privately, he and Jack were not optimistic. That was why they'd decided that Jack should break into their own facility tonight. It was a crazy thing to do, but it was their only hope of protecting their IP.

The engineers said they'd seen the state troopers unplugging their laptops and taking them away.

But maybe the state troopers hadn't known that those laptops held nothing of value. Firebird's IP existed on Meeks's home computer … and in one other place. Jack was about to find out if the state troopers had gotten to it, or not.

In the moonlight that came through the blinds, the empty

desks looked naked without any computers on them. A potted tiger-tail plant had been overturned, someone's bottle of soda spilled. Desk calendars and kitschy ornaments littered the floor.

Jack crossed the office to a door in the corner and used Meeks's key to open it.

There stood their server, untouched.

"Yes!" Jack whispered.

The state troopers hadn't known the difference between clients and stand-alone PCs. The laptops and desktops they had confiscated hadn't had any data on them. They were mere terminals with no information on their drives, but a lot of processing power for the CAD packages. The data was all on the server.

Jack logged into the server and started to overwrite the drives in the storage array with zeroes. It took an agonizing amount of time, watching the numbers on the terminal climb towards the end of the drives. Finally he was done. All the data was gone forever, beyond the reach of any but the most well-funded labs that claimed they could look for the magnetic ghosts left behind. He had one final trick left for them, though.

He took his hammer out of his daypack, to turn the glass platters of the drives into a million-piece jigsaw, and started to release the handles that held the drives into their bays.

He froze.

The front door had just opened.

Footsteps entered the office.

Jack slid the drives free and backed out of the server closet holding them in a bunch in his hand. With his back to the door, he closed it as quietly as possible. The steel-core, fireproof door nevertheless made an audible *thunk*.

"Shit," said a voice. "Is there someone in here?"

That voice! It was the guy from the airport.

A torch beam flashed across the office, catching Jack's chest.

"Hey! Who's that?"

No point in stealth now. Jack grabbed a coffee mug off the nearest desk and flung it in the direction of the torch. A yell told him he'd made contact. He hurled the drives at the floor, hearing a *snap* as each drive shattered. It sounded as loud as a car crash in the silent office, followed by the tinkling of broken glass. Cringing, Jack dived to the floor after them and crawled under the desks, towards the door. The torch beam flashed all over the office and the guy swore into a two-way radio, demanding backup. Sounded panicky. Sounded like he expected everything to fall into place for him and didn't know how to react when it did not. Jack couldn't wait until he found the trashed server.

They collided at the door into the workshop. The fact was Jack was close to panic himself. If he got ID'd, everything was over. He shoved the guy into the wall. The guy bounced off the wall, swinging his fists wildly. Jack had the butcher knife in his hand. He couldn't remember how it had got there. He slashed at the guy's arms, felt the point catch on flesh. Horror pulsed through him—what the hell was he doing?

The guy screamed and fell back. Jack plunged past him into the workshop and crashed out the back door, tearing down the crime scene tape. He fled towards the back fence.

"Hold it!"

Light flashed around the side of the warehouse. Jack,

halfway over the fence, squinted, blinded. He swung his other leg over and dropped to the desert.

"Stop right there or I will shoot!"

That had to be the state trooper from the front gate. Jack believed him. He sprinted into the desert.

A deafening *crack!* split the night. Jack threw himself to the ground, and pain bit into his shoulder.

CHAPTER 14

"Welcome to Europa, Juno!" Richard Burke said exultantly.

The emotion in his voice pierced through Hannah's apathetic doze. She leaned forward to inspect the latest images from JunoCam, the visible-light camera mounted on the probe. These pictures were scientifically useless—JunoCam was a public relations instrument, not a scientific instrument—but they didn't require any processing, so the team could view them as soon as they were received.

A black sky with a white dot on it.

That was Europa.

The probe was still 250,000 kilometers away from the icebound moon. Over the next few hours, it would swing a bit closer, but for all intents and purposes, this was as good as it would get.

"Maybe JADE or JEDI will pick up particles from the super heated jets," Burke speculated.

Lyons nudged Hannah's elbow. She turned, ready to be pissed at him all over again for belittling her niece's science project.

He angled his screen slightly towards her. It displayed a meme of that wild-haired guy from the History Channel, with the caption: "I'm not saying it was aliens ... BUT IT WAS ALIENS!"

Hannah rolled her eyes and giggled, accepting the olive branch. Lyons was a good guy at heart. More importantly, he was one of the team. Working together, against the odds, they'd achieved the ridiculously difficult goal of placing Juno near Europa. What Washington wanted, Washington had got. NASA gets the job done.

"Mission freaking well accomplished," she said, stretching her arms over her head. "Can we go home now?"

"Hey, what's that?" said an imaging specialist at the end of the long desk where they were sitting.

Hannah's attention snapped back to her screen.

"Zoom in."

"It's like a dot."

"The resolution is so shitty on this thing."

Hannah pulled up the newest still shot and zoomed in.

A dot. A black pinprick on the surface of Europa … or maybe in orbit around it.

Long-range telescopy had established beyond a doubt that Europa did *not* have a moon of its own.

"A rock," Hannah suggested. "A recent capture."

Lyons danced in his chair. "Aliens," he chanted. "Aliens, aliens."

"We have to wait for the spectroscopic data from the UVS or JIRAM," Burke warned.

His caution went unheeded. The room was in an uproar.

As if guided by a sixth sense, Hannah's gaze suddenly snapped back to the small window on her screen that displayed Juno's heartbeat.

The Madrid receiving station had gone mute.

Goldstone.

Canberra.

She couldn't remember which one was facing Jupiter at that moment, but it didn't matter; all three receiving stations had stopped picking up Juno's signal.

"We're not receiving telemetry anymore," she shouted.

She clutched her mouse in a paralytic grip, fruitlessly clicking on signal routing and antenna targeting.

The invisible cord that bound her to Juno, across 945 million empty kilometers, seemed to stretch, twisting around her heart. Then it snapped. She felt the loss of the probe as a physical shock.

"It's shut down," she said between her teeth. *"Again."*

They spent the rest of the night trying to bring the probe back online. Time after time, they uploaded reboot sequences and waited an hour and three-quarters, and another hour and three-quarters.

Nothing.

This time, Juno hadn't gone into safe mode. It had just … *gone.* Its electronics—in their titanium box, hardened to withstand the radiation of Jupiter—had suffered *some* event that fried them completely. Or maybe the probe had been struck by a meteorite. Or something. They had no idea.

At 10 a.m. the next morning, Hannah staggered out into cruelly bright sunlight. She made her way to her car. When she got there, she put down Isabel's model of Jupiter and took the bottle of Moet out of her bag.

In the middle of Friday morning, the JPL parking lot should have been a sea of cars without a living soul in sight. Instead, clusters of scruffy people swirled around news vans with satellite dishes mounted on the roof. Every TV network in the country, not to mention bloggers ranging from serious science reporters to alt-right conspiracy theorists, had descended on the campus. Caught flat-footed, security was still devising a strategy to handle the mob.

This wasn't how NASA would have chosen to announce Juno's final observations, Hannah was sure. But what did they expect, when they made every scientist get a Twitter account?

She hadn't leaked the pictures, but someone had. She suspected Ralf Lyons.

It didn't really matter. Sooner or later, the world would have to know that Juno had photographed a dot that might or might not be an alien spaceship orbiting Europa.

Was it an alien ship? Hannah wondered, wrestling with the cork of the champagne bottle.

A handsome black man in his twenties approached her. "Can I help you with that?"

"Sure," Hannah said, handing him the bottle with a sigh.

"Celebrating?" He didn't ask who she was. He probably assumed a plump Jewish woman struggling to open a champagne bottle in a parking lot could not be a rocket scientist. *Pop,* the cork shot out. He handed the bottle back to her. "It's pretty exciting, I agree. By the way, I'm Todd from *The Atlantic.* You should check out the site if you have a minute. We're live-blogging the first contact event."

"First contact, huh?" Hannah said.

"Did you see what the Dalai Lama said? 'This will mean an end to war and conflict.'"

Until that moment, Hannah had been going to drink some of the champagne and throw the rest away, at least that's what she told herself. She changed her mind when she detected the new narrative impinging on her reality. Standing there with foam spilling over her hand, she said, "Fuck the aliens. They killed my baby."

She upended the bottle of champagne. It splashed onto the ground.

"Um, it's great to get your perspective," said Todd from *The Atlantic,* watching the champagne glug out of the bottle onto the ground. "Could I have your name again?"

"You want a quote for your website?" Hannah said. "If these are aliens, the first thing they did was to shoot down our most advanced space probe. This is not going to end well."

She jumped into her car and backed out, narrowly missing him.

Isabel's model of Jupiter, forgotten on the ground, got squashed flat under the Camry's wheels. Nothing remained but a smear of modelling clay in a puddle of champagne.

CHAPTER 15

The morning sun flooded the kitchen of Meeks's house in Bunkerville. A monitor on the table and a laptop on the counter jabbered. Jack sat shirtless at the kitchen table, bent over. Meeks sponged the gouge in his shoulder. It stung like hell.

"I drove back to the road and took the long way around," Jack said. "I took that road that runs along the Arizona border, then got back on 170 at Mesquite."

"With a bullet in your shoulder."

"Don't be so fucking dramatic," Jack said. He was ashamed of the risks he'd taken. Also, his shoulder hurt, even if it was actually just a graze. "The point is they didn't get a good look at me. They didn't see the truck. DNA? My DNA is all over the office, anyway."

"Yeah, well done," Meeks said. He taped a bandage to Jack's shoulder. "You really need stitches."

Jack shook his head—which sent a twinge of pain through his shoulder. He wasn't going near the ER.

"All right, have it your way." Meeks gathered up bloody gauze and wheeled, one-handed, to the rubbish bin. Jack looked at the monitor on the table. It was streaming CNN.

"… a day of enormous significance for humanity," said Neil deGrasse Tyson. "The big question is, do we greet these cosmic visitors in a spirit of love, or will we cower in fear of the unknown?"

Meeks reached across Jack to the keyboard, minimized CNN, and pulled up the BBC.

Stephen Hawking said, "… ought to continue to project a non-confrontational stance. The fact that they have not yet annihilated us gives reason for guarded optimism."

Click. Al-Jazeera: "… not take for granted that the first contact event will be managed and orchestrated by the West ..."

Click. RT: "… in response to the apparent presence of aliens, Roscosmos has announced a large-scale development program aimed at building a manned spacecraft capable of travelling to Europa ..."

"That's more like it," Jack said. "The Russkis don't mess about."

"They're just posturing. They don't have the money for that," Meeks said. "They *may* have the technology. The TEM project is promising. They were planning their first test launches in 2018. I suppose it could be accelerated if they throw money at it … which they haven't got."

The TEM project, supervised by Russian nuclear group Rosatom, had been initiated in 2010 with the goal of building a nuclear-powered spacecraft for Mars exploration. The focus of everyone's interest had suddenly changed to distant, icy Europa.

"They may get the money now," Jack said. He thought of how excited his old friend Alexei must be. He'd have to ring him.

"It depends whether Putin thinks it's got propaganda value," Meeks said. "At any rate, nuclear propulsion is the only way we're getting there. Which makes all this a rather amazing coincidence, doesn't it?"

Jack nodded bleakly. Firebird Systems, which was developing a ground-breaking nuclear spacecraft engine, had just been shut down by regulatory fiat. If not for Jack's exploits last night, their IP would now be in the possession of the US government.

"They knew what Juno was going to find," he said.

"So did we," Meeks said. He muttered under his breath, "Maybe we should have gone public to begin with."

It was a rare admission of self-doubt from Meeks, who never second-guessed his own decisions, or at any rate never confessed to it. Jack immediately said, "No. We'd have been idiots to pop our heads over the parapet. Let the government take the heat."

On CNN, assorted activists were demonstrating outside the White House, while on MSNBC, the director of the FBI reassured Americans that their country remained safe from attack. It was a completely meaningless statement, given that no one had any idea what the alien spaceship could do, much less why it was here. But the director's calm, authoritative demeanor would count for more than his words.

"Who the hell are they, anyway?" Jack wondered aloud. "FBI? NSA? Or maybe even the Office of Naval Intelligence?" There were so many clandestine agencies operating under the federal umbrella at this point, he could only guess which one had targeted Firebird Systems.

"I got a weird vibe from that guy," Meeks said thoughtfully.

"The bloke with the peace symbol necklace?"

"Yeah. Hard to describe, but I got the impression he was switched on."

Jack raised his eyebrows. Yes, the guy had seemed confident to the point of arrogance yesterday. But at midnight in the ransacked office, he'd gone to pieces. In all fairness, so had Jack. He vividly recalled slashing the guy with a butcher knife. He hadn't told Meeks about that, reasoning that he was fairly sure the guy had not been seriously hurt, so there was no need to mention it. But the memory still horrified him.

He got up and went to make coffee. Meeks had a Nuova Simonella espresso machine, set on a special low countertop. He'd had the whole kitchen remodelled for wheelchair accessibility. Yesterday, the high-end coffeemaker had seemed like a minor indulgence, given there wasn't a barista in sight. Yesterday, they'd had a company with hundreds of millions of dollars in venture capital funding. Today, what did they have? Maybe nothing.

When Jack got back this morning, Meeks had been on the phone with their lawyers. He'd been up all night, too—talking with their investors on both sides of the Atlantic, trying to convince them that this was just a bump in the road.

"We will get through this," he said as Jack sat down again with his coffee. Meeks patted his laptop. "Everything's on here, and I've deleted our cloud storage account as a precaution. If they want our IP, they will have to work with us."

Jack nodded tiredly, drank his coffee. He wanted to be optimistic, but last night's violence had left him in a dark place. He felt as lost and melancholy as he had in 2003, when he realized that a few of the bombs he dropped over Iraq from his Tornado GR-4 had missed their targets, and blown civilian houses—and their occupants' lives—apart. Maybe he'd be able to believe what Meeks was saying when he'd had some sleep.

"That said, I don't think there's necessarily any reason we

have to work with the government," Meeks went on. "I've already reached out to Elon and Jeff. Robert and Fatih emailed me last night. They agree that this is too important to be left up to the ineptocracy."

Now *that* was good to hear. Jack wasn't sure anything would come of it—after all, Firebird was a minnow next to the likes of SpaceX and Blue Origin—but at least it was a step in the right direction. "Sounds like they get it," he said.

"Yes. If this could happen to us, it could happen to any private space company. We've got to stick together, and I think they understand that."

On the monitor, the already-famous JunoCam pictures flashed up yet again. Jack took his coffee mug and went outside. The lawn, recently mown by Jack himself, smelled pleasantly of cut grass. He squinted up at the sky. A hawk soared across the blue emptiness. Another peaceful morning in Nowhere, USA—but Jack couldn't wind down. Part of his brain kept expecting the blue sky to rain destruction. He knew the fear wouldn't leave him until they got to Europa, one way or another, and learned what was out there.

CHAPTER 16

Skyler spent the first day of the crisis in transit. His colleague Lance, he of the peckerwood drawl, who actually held a master's in international relations from Duke, had had some business to take care of at JPL in California. That left Skyler to fly the boilerplate unit they'd confiscated from Firebird Systems back to headquarters at Langley, Maryland.

He felt a bit guilty about checking the unit in as oversized luggage, a few hours after they'd slapped its inventor with an Atomic Energy Act violation for doing the same thing. But by now, they knew for sure the unit wasn't a nuclear reactor. It was just a riddle. A handmade Rube Goldberg contraption that *allegedly* represented America's best hope of catching up with the Russians.

Skyler wasn't a nuclear scientist. He turned the unit over to the DEFSEC experts at headquarters, hoping they could make head or tail of it. He prayed it wouldn't turn out to be a dud. He was in enough trouble as it was. His supervisor, Bob Flaherty, a merciless Marines vet, had a lot of questions about the break-in at Firebird's R&D facility in the Nevada desert. By the time the debrief session was over, Skyler almost felt thankful for his bandaged forearms. At least that proved he wasn't making it all up.

The debrief concluded on a brighter note, however, with a promise that several Nevada state troopers would be transferred to desk jobs. And rightly so. How dumb did you have to be to confiscate the wrong fucking hardware?

In his four years of working for the federal government, Skyler had learned that there existed dimensions of dumb in this country beyond anything he ever imagined. Columbia,

Caltech, Harvard—he'd lived in a bubble. Now he lived in the real world. It was exhilarating.

Understanding, *really* understanding, just how dumb and helpless most people were gave him compassion for them. He and Lance left Langley early the next morning to drive to Dulles. Their route took them through some of the capital's most impoverished suburbs. They passed rusted cars, trash-strewn yards, grown men on kids' bikes. Payday lenders, used appliance shops. Churches, churches, churches. Lance drove with slitted eyes—he came from a working poor background, and would sometimes go off on vitriolic rants about how the collapse of the working class was their own fault. Skyler, a third-generation Ph.D, knew he didn't have the right to opine on that, although he agreed broadly with Lance. He just knew that love 'em or hate 'em, these were his people.

And now their future rested in his hands.

He'd downloaded high-rez copies of the JunoCam pictures, as well as some partial observations recorded by the other instruments on board Juno, during his turnaround at Langley. He pored over his laptop all the way to the airport.

They flew economy most of the time—contrary to rumor, the federal government did *not* enjoy wasting money—but today, because they were flying at such short notice, they got to enjoy Virgin Atlantic's first-class "suites." The sidewalls of the seats meant Skyler could work without the risk of anyone snooping over his shoulder. He completed his review of the data, ate a Thai beef salad with roasted pine nuts and chili dressing, and started typing notes. By the time the plane touched down at Brussels Airport, he'd produced a page of concise, punchy talking points for the president.

US president Barack Obama and his entourage had already been whisked away by the time Skyler and Lance arrived, but they overlapped with the arrival of Japanese prime minister Shinzo Abe. They dodged the voracious Japanese media swarm and cabbed it into a city paralyzed by gridlock.

"Jeepers," Lance said. "And I thought D.C. traffic was bad."

Motorcycle cops on white bikes, in traffic-cone orange helmets, forced their way past the taxi. Grudging drivers made way for a motorcade of black Town Cars and airport shuttle buses.

"Hollande," Skyler said.

"Naw, Merkel," Lance said.

"I saw him texting in the back seat."

"They're hard to tell apart."

This G8 summit had been announced in reaction to the exploding media frenzy. In Skyler's opinion, they should have held off a few days. The alien ships had already been orbiting Europa for five years. Another day or so wouldn't have made any difference. This way, the world leaders risked feeding the hype, instead of balancing it out with gravitas and leadership.

"But hey, I'm not the president," he said to Lance, after explaining his views. They had now been sitting in traffic for 45 minutes. "Maybe this was the right call."

"Holy cow, check that out," Lance said, pointing out the window.

Aging art nouveau buildings lined the street. Skyler sighed at the sight of graffiti defiling every wall and door. *TTIP non merci, donnez-nous des OVNI! Le OVNI est Le DIEU du Paix etes-vous PRET?*

"No thanks TTIP, give us UFOs," Skyler translated with his high-school French. "The UFO is the GOD of peace, are you READY?" He shook his head. "Jesus. People are nuts."

"Yeah, that's fucked-up, but look at *them.*"

A pair of soldiers in green-and-brown camo prowled along the sidewalk, carrying large automatic rifles. Passersby stepped out of their way without a glance, proving that this was normal.

"We need to get us some of that," Lance said.

The taxi crawled into a mob of protesters. A placard written in English—*Tell Us The Truth Mr. President!*—knocked against Skyler's window.

"Everything's up for grabs now," Lance said.

Lance was clearly enjoying the hell out of this. For an undercover operative, chaos spelt opportunity. Skyler was enjoying it, too, for different reasons. He didn't aspire to remake the government of the United States, although it wouldn't hurt. Quite simply, this was the moment he'd been waiting for all his life, without even knowing it. The moment when he could make a difference. Give me partial spectrographic images and I will shift the world on its axis.

Night had fallen by the time they reached the Justus Lipsius building on the Rue de la Loi. Police cordons sealed off the whole block. Hundreds of people queued at the checkpoints. Skyler and Lance's credentials did not possess the magical power here that they did in the US. They achieved entry to the building just in time to see the world leaders rising from a small table littered with plates. Dozens of photographers seethed like piranhas outside a velvet rope.

The politicos had concluded their working dinner in full sight of the world's press.

It was a fairly good bet, Skyler thought, that he and Lance hadn't missed anything.

Dodging the functionaries who were removing the velvet rope, he hurried up to a presidential aide and pressed his talking points into her hand. "Give this to the chief."

The Virgin Atlantic first-class cabin, thank God, had a printer. Paper was considered more secure than digital data these days.

The aide said, "What the heck is this?" She pushed the sheet of paper back at him.

"It's our policy positions," Skyler said.

"Ben didn't mention you," the aide said. She hurried after the president. Skyler was left fuming with his carefully prepared talking points in his hand.

"Depechez-vous," snapped a security guard, physically pushing Lance back as he attempted to follow. Good thing they weren't armed on this trip. Lance would probably have drawn down on the security guard then and there.

"We're from the NXC," Skyler said. The situation was desperate enough to break the protocol against mentioning the NXC in public. "Le Council … Nationale … des Xenoaffairs?"

It was futile. You couldn't translate *Xenoaffairs* into French. The word didn't even exist in English. And neither, officially, did their agency.

The word *xenoaffairs* had been coined in 2013, when the NXC was spun off from the CIA to prepare for the possibility of diplomatic contact with the alien visitors to Europa.

Now their moment had come, and Skyler and Lance were stuck on the outside of the action, leaving President Obama at a severe disadvantage.

CHAPTER 17

Skyler and Lance tried everything to penetrate the onion-like layers of aides and hangers-on around the president. They even got Bob Flaherty to phone Valerie Jarrett. She promised them a meeting with a presidential speechwriter ahead of the first working session tomorrow morning.

They ended up in a grotty nightclub a couple of blocks from the Justus Lipsius building, sucking down Belgian beer. Lance pronounced it "cruddy." Skyler was too upset to care what he was drinking.

Lance leaned closer to him and shouted over the thumping hardstyle music, "I don't understand one bit of that data you were looking at on the plane. So lay it out for me."

Lance wasn't a science guy. Skyler disliked having to explain things in words of one syllable, but over the years, he'd gotten better at it. "The pictures that have been published were snapped with a phone camera off a monitor. But I've managed to grab a whole series of high-rez originals from JPL. I've overlaid several images of the same place, taken from different orbital positions, and managed to interpolate from them, but the resolution is still fairly crappy. However, the ship in orbit is, to be blunt, fucking huge. The best resolution I could get is about 30 pixels long, but even so there are signs of blackened sections on the hull. And you can see on the infrared filter that it's bleeding heat like anything from a section near the middle. So, and this was also the conclusion of the analysts at NASA, there's basically zero chance there is anything alive on that ship."

"And NASA has *not* released this data."

"Jeez, Lance, you're the one who visited JPL with a bunch of Feebs in tow, waving the Espionage Act at them."

Lance frowned. "The Feebs went in way too hard," he said. "It's all they know how to do." He gulped his beer and wiped his lips.

"I know you're worried about unauthorized leaks," Skyler said. "I am, too. The analysts are human. But we've done what we can. Right?"

Lance nodded grudgingly. Skyler knew what he was thinking: the JPL analysts who'd seen the images would not leak it if they were dead. FBI-style intimidation could be counter-productive without a credible threat of follow-through. However, Skyler believed—he devoutly hoped—secrecy could be maintained without killing anyone.

The NXC required all its agents to have basic self-defense skills. Skyler had had to get a gun license, and a concealed-carry permit no less. But he remained morally and physically uncomfortable with violence. The humiliating episode at the Firebird facility in Nevada had underlined that Skyler was never gonna be a man of action. He'd leave that up to guys like Lance.

"Those NASA analysts are patriots at heart," he said uneasily. "They signed up to serve their country."

"You should've been there," Lance said. "Transparency, disclosure, baa baa baa. I looked up their policy. It says *appropriate* disclosure of information. What part of *appropriate* do they not understand?" He leaned forward, grinning. "I had to sit down at a computer at two in the freaking morning and write their press release for them."

"It was a thing of beauty," Skyler said.

The official NASA press release on the Juno observations—penned by Lance, and signed under protest by NASA director Bill Walker—stated that the JunoCam pictures already disseminated were all they had. In reality, the probe had sent back another 300 seconds' worth of data before it crashed. Skyler was one of only a few people in the world to have seen that data. That's what he'd based his talking points on.

He hugged his laptop bag to his side. Even though it had full disk encryption, he was still paranoid about losing it.

"There are no aliens," he said. "There's only a beaten-up old interstellar jalopy. It may have been travelling STL for millions of years, before winding up here."

"STL?"

"Slower than light."

"If the ship was just drifting, why'd it brake at Jupiter and go into orbit around Europa?"

"AI," Skyler said succintly.

"Uh huh," Lance said.

"Now you're getting it," Skyler said, enjoying the sight of Lance's face as the implications sank in. "That ship could contain the holy grail of artificial intelligence. Not to mention an interstellar drive. There must be the mother of all energy sources in that thing too, to survive an interstellar trip of who knows how many years, and still bring it into an orbit. It could be the first workable fusion reactor we've ever seen!"

"Sounds like we should blow it the hell up," Lance said.

Skyler was surprised to hear Lance take that line, even flippantly. "Well, I disagree. And so does Bob."

Director Flaherty had made the NXC's policy very clear to them. They were to push for the retrieval of the alien ship, at all costs.

Skyler had designed his talking points to help the president argue for precisely this objective.

He rubbed his forehead. They just *had* to get a few minutes with Obama before the first working session ...

Lance snatched his phone out of his pocket. Skyler hadn't heard it ringing. The music was too loud.

Clamping his hand to his free ear, Lance stood up and shoved towards the exit. Skyler settled their tab and hurried out into the warm July night. The roar of a demonstration carried from elsewhere in the city.

Lance was already walking back towards the Justus Lipsius building. "Hurry up!"

"Who was that?"

"What's her name, that aide. Prez wants to meet with us *now!*"

*

The media still besieged the Justus Lipsius building, although it was after midnight. This time, Skyler and Lance didn't have to wait in line. They got special passes to hang around their necks. It reminded Skyler of the time a high school friend had gotten backstage passes for an Iron Maiden concert. Skyler hadn't really been into Iron Maiden, even at that age, but he still remembered the overwhelming thrill of being among the elite, walking the same grungy floors as Bruce Dickinson. He'd known—not just felt, but *known*—he was more special than all the wailing fans out front.

Now, his illusions of his own specialness dissipated quickly. Security personnel escorted them to a conference suite on the fifth floor. Every corner of the ante-room was packed with power brokers holding hushed conversations. Half the people in the room held exalted government positions and the other half were there to wipe their asses for them. A seasoned political celeb-spotter, Lance mouthed famous names under his breath. Skyler felt like a pimply teenager in Bruce Dickinson's dressing-room.

"I thought we were going to meet with the president?" he muttered.

"Looks like we're going to meet with *all* of them."

Lance was right. Except for one thing. *He* was not going to meet with the G8 leaders. Someone had told Obama's people that Skyler was the data guy, so it was him they wanted.

"You can't take that in," a Secret Service agent said, pointing to his computer. "Cell phone, too. Gotta leave it here."

So Skyler stumbled into the presence of the eight most powerful men and women in the world, emptyhanded except for the single A4 sheet of talking points clutched in his hand.

The conference room was smaller than he'd expected, a low-ceilinged box with insipid pale blue walls. The fixtures looked as dated as everything else in Brussels. The presidents and prime ministers sat around a large, round table.

Their interpreters sat just behind them. Each politician spoke in his or her own language, pausing now and then to let seven different interpreters catch up.

The outermost circle consisted of aides standing against the walls. Skyler squeezed in between the two advisors who stood behind Obama. "I've got talking points from the NXC," he whispered to the friendlier-looking advisor. That sounded better than 'talking points from Skyler Taft,' which was what they actually were.

The advisor knelt obsequiously, reached around one of Obama's interpreters (he had two), and slid the sheet of paper onto the table near Obama's left elbow. The president glanced down once and then went back to his trademark chin-in-hand listening pose.

Mission accomplished, Skyler told himself. It's out of your hands now.

As his heart rate slowed down to normal, he listened intently. If he wasn't going to be tossed out, this was a golden opportunity to find out what the truly powerful were thinking about the alien spaceship.

The agenda of the summit had called for the 'first contact event' to be discussed at two working sessions tomorrow. Instead, the leaders had decided to hold an unannounced meeting in the dead of night. Skyler figured they wanted to get the drop on the media who would be hounding them for decisions tomorrow. The pressure on each of them must be intense.

Only the flower arrangements didn't look tired.

With mauve bags under her eyes, Chancellor Angela Merkel of Germany presented a nuanced argument for watching and waiting. Oh, that sounds great, Skyler thought. Let's do nothing and hope it goes away.

He scrutinized the Russian president, who sat directly across the room from where Skyler was standing. Like all the other politicians, Vladimir Putin looked smaller and older in the flesh. *Unlike* the others, he appeared relaxed and confident.

The G8 had been the G7 since 2014, when the rest suspended Russia for its actions in the Crimea. As of yesterday, it was the G8 again. No wonder Putin looked like the cat that got the cream. He had to know exactly what had prompted this sudden, embarrassing climbdown.

Russia was the only country in the world with an operational manned spaceflight program …

… except for its Eastern rival, which was conspicuously *not* present at this summit.

No one had so much as suggested inviting China, to Skyler's knowledge.The existing G8 format didn't allow for it, and the G7 powers distrusted China even more than they distrusted Russia, which was saying something.

Even Vladimir Putin looked like a good partner in comparison to the unpredictable, rabidly nationalistic Chinese president.

But of course, Putin was not here to kiss and make up with the Western powers. He was here to extract maximum advantage for Russia.

When Merkel finished speaking, Putin raised one hand slightly off the table. "I can't agree," he said—or rather, his interpreter said. "The people of Russia won't agree to sit and wait for something to happen. Will your people? I don't know." Putin offered a raised eyebrow and a disarming hint of a smile. "But as you must know, we have already announced a manned expedition to Europa. This is independent of whatever is decided here. Would it be better to cooperate? Yes, yes, of course. But that is up to you."

Skyler suppressed a smile. His colleague Lance, for one, had a total man-crush on the Russian president. Skyler was less enamored of Putin's ruthless style, but even he had to admire the way Putin had checkmated the Europeans.

They could watch and wait—and let Putin walk away from this summit clad in the mantle of a global leader. Or they could join the Russian bandwagon. Win-win for Putin.

Unless the USA stepped up to the plate.

Skyler fixed his gaze on the back of Obama's head, willing the president to glance down at those damn talking points.

Obama sipped from his glass of water. The glasses were the finest crystal, relics of a bygone age of elegance. "Well, I get the feeling that we're failing to adequately consider this problem in all its dimensions. Fine, great, Vladimir, so you're going to send a ship out there without any information about this alien craft. That is your prerogative. However, the United States has done years of work assessing potential first contact scenarios. Our allies in Great Britain have joined in that effort." Obama nodded to Theresa May, the recently appointed British prime minister. "Based on these scenarios, and the thinking of the world's best astrophysicists, we believe this is an existential threat to humanity."

Skyler's mouth fell open.

"Therefore," Obama said, "the United States intends to destroy it."

Shocked murmurs filled the room. The president drank from his crystal glass again.

The blood roared in Skyler's ears. This could not be happening. The president hadn't even looked at the damn talking points.

"We'll find out if a Soyuz can outrun a nuke," Obama added. Some people laughed.

Skyler wanted to scream. Where had this idea come from? Maybe from NASA. No, those wimps would never recommend destroying anything. Maybe from the Pentagon. Or no, more likely, it had come from the Brits. He scowled at May, cool and composed as a fashion model. She looked like she'd personally give the order to shoot alien visitors without turning a hair, assuming there were any alien visitors, which there weren't. But none of the politicos knew that.

Obama would know it *if he bothered to look down.*

The Italian prime minister carried Putin's water, denouncing the reckless urge to shoot first and ask questions later.

Obama just listened, his profile impassive. And Skyler realized: this was the president's *own* idea.

The man sitting an arm's length from him wasn't the vacillating, feckless president of Lance's imagination. This was the president who'd watched Osama bin Laden die in real time. The commander in chief who dispatched lethal drones. The cold-blooded realist who'd watched the Middle East go up in flames rather than risk a single American life.

And now he was about to unwittingly throw away the biggest potential advantage America ever had, for the same reasons ...

But wait! Skyler's mind raced. Like a rube, he was taking the president's tough declaration at face value. There had to be more to it than that ...

Of course there was! Obama could not allow the alien craft to fall into Russia's hands. So he had to promise its destruction, on the pretext of eliminating a threat. Because the USA didn't even have a manned spacecraft capable of reaching orbit.

Whose fault was that? Who could say? Successive presidents had slashed NASA's budget to the bone. The US nuclear thermal research program had been put on ice in the 1970s, due to public anti-nuclear hysteria. America's propulsion technology deficit went back to the Carter administration, at least.

But that could change.

Skyler acted without thinking. He pushed past the interpreter in front of him and knelt beside Obama. "Mr. President, sir," he hissed. "I'm from the NXC. Please listen. We have the capability to build a manned spacecraft that can reach Europa."

"I haven't heard about that," the president said quietly.

Hands grabbed the back of Skyler's shirt, trying to pull him away from the conference table. The pulling stopped as the president engaged with the impudent 'data guy.'

"This is the result of very recent breakthroughs," Skyler whispered.

Specifically, the confiscation of Firebird Systems's revolutionary *nuclear* spaceship drive.

"We can do it, Mr. President. I've been on the road for two days straight to tell you that we can do it. We *can.*"

God, if You exist, please let it not be a dud.

"Can we do it without them?" Obama murmured, twitching an eyebrow in the direction of Putin.

Skyler had had an email from the DEFSEC guys, summing up their preliminary analysis of the unit and the intel that went with it. He conquered the urge to over-promise. "No. Realistically, we would need their launch capacity and manufacturing, at least."

He allowed himself to be pulled back from the table, knowing that whether or not the US nuked the alien spaceship, Skyler Taft had probably nuked his own career.

From the New York Times, Monday, July 11th, 2016:

MULTINATIONAL MISSION "SPIRIT OF HUMANITY" ANNOUNCED

President Barack Obama on Sunday, standing shoulder to shoulder with other G8 leaders in Brussels, announced a multilateral project to build a spaceship capable of carrying a multinational crew to Europa. The recent discovery of an assumed alien spacecraft in orbit around the remote moon has roiled international tensions, which the announcement was expected to calm. "We view this as an opportunity for the nations of Earth to come together," said Mr. Obama, citing technology-sharing commitments from the United States, Russia, Japan, and Europe. The ship, dubbed "Spirit of Humanity," will be jointly built by NASA, Roscosmos, JAXA, and the European Space Agency. Its crew, yet to be chosen, will represent all the nations involved. President Vladimir Putin of Russia commented, "We do not know if the aliens are friendly. But we will approach them in a spirit of diplomacy, and this means that first we must strengthen the bonds of friendship among ourselves." Estimates of the project's likely pricetag range from $10 billion up to $1 trillion. While the figures involved dwarf the existing budgets of national space programs, economist Paul Krugman observed, "This is frankly a bargain price for peace on earth. It may be that the little green men have done us a tremendous favor."

CHINA RECALLS AMBASSADOR TO E.U.

BEIJING— Retaliating against its perceived exclusion from the "Spirit of Humanity" project, China on Monday recalled its ambassador to the European Union, dealing a fresh blow to international relations. Chinese Foreign Ministry spokesman Li Diao said, "We strongly protest the decision of the US, EU, and Russia to proceed with this mission without reference to China's global leadership in aerospace technology." However, a source within the CIA commented, "Anything the Chinese could contribute, they stole from us to begin with."

CHAPTER 18

United States Senator Russ Colbert edged into the bathroom alongside his wife. It was a tight squeeze. The realtor had euphemistically described their Georgetown apartment as "cozy" and "characterful." The bathroom smelled of mildew. Colbert wasn't doing this for the money.

He combed his hair and then ran his hands through it, mussing it again.

Xue Hua, stroking a mascara brush over her eyelashes, said, "Why do you even bother with the comb?"

"Likably rumpled: good. Dreadlocks: bad."

She turned and pursed her lips. Colbert pecked her, careful not to spoil her make-up. She was getting ready to go out to some charitable event. One of her Christian things.

She had no idea what *he* would be doing tonight.

She'd never been part of his secret life, although it was all for her. Everything he did was wrapped up with his love for her. With that came an iron resolve to protect her.

"What're you going to be doing in California?" she asked innocently.

"It's just a think tank thing." Colbert rolled his eyes. "The little green men are here. Discuss."

"Sounds fascinating."

He kissed her again, collected his overnight bag, and went downstairs to hail a taxi. Xue Hua's face lingered in his mind's eye. She was as beautiful as the day he'd married her. To this day, he couldn't believe he'd landed such a lovely—and intelligent—woman. The stereotype of the submissive Chinese woman was bullshit, as all stereotypes were.

His flight landed at LAX at half past midnight. No one

met him at the airport. The organizers of the think tank thing—yes, there really was a think tank thing, a panel discussion hosted by the Nuclear Age Peace Foundation—thought he was arriving tomorrow morning.

He'd booked a hotel room in Santa Barbara, near the Foundation. But he wasn't going there yet.

He rented a car. The sullen African-American clerk showed no sign of recognizing the junior senator from Connecticut, even when Colbert showed her his driver's license. Her ignorance didn't surprise him. 77% of Americans couldn't name even one of their *own* senators, according to Pew. Trust in government bumped along at an all-time low. The latest Gallup poll had found that just 15% of Americans said they could trust the government 'always or most of the time,' and that figure must surely have fallen further in the wake of the first contact event.

"The *Spirit of Humanity* project is a cover-up," frothed a pundit on the car radio. "What's happening here is the elites see their chance to create a one-world government. This is the endgame, folks …" Typical far-right nuttiness. But in this case, the asshole was right. The government *was* holding back crucial information about the *Spirit of Humanity* mission.

And Colbert planned to obtain that information, whatever it might be, tonight.

He drove north. Traffic downtown and in Hollywood crawled; horns blew, music thumped, revellers jaywalked. It was 2 a.m. on a freaking Wednesday. Why were all these people awake? Colbert associated LA's restlessness with the first contact event. A new anxiety possessed the earth. Humanity had been given world-shattering news, but no way to react—no answers, no orders, no advice except "Stay calm and carry on shopping," to paraphrase George W. Bush's famous injunction in the wake of 9/11. Colbert had served as a loyal warrior for Obama in the Senate, and he would not hear a word against the first black president. But a new Obama had emerged in the wake of the Juno observations … chilly, close-lipped. It felt like a betrayal.

The media had gone into raptures about the *Spirit of Humanity* project. But for Colbert, the exclusion of China raised troubling questions about the president's commitment to world peace.

Colbert finally reached Griffith Park, the 4,000-acre stretch of wilderness north of Hollywood. The Griffith Observatory was closed, of course. A chain stretched across the entrance to the parking lot. Colbert parked on the shoulder outside the parking lot.

There was one car already there, a beat-up Subaru sedan.

Colbert got out and stretched his back, inhaling the murky scent of the trees. Frogs chirped over the background hum of city traffic. He didn't have a flashlight, but he didn't need one—L.A. lit up the darkness.

He stepped over the chain and climbed up to the observatory. The castle-like building had wide terraces overlooking the city. Colbert admired the view of the city basin full of lights.

A few people loitered on the terrace.

As instructed by his contact, Colbert went over to one of the coin telescopes. He pretended to insert a quarter—no sense actually wasting the money—and waited.

Sure enough, one of the loiterers approached him.

"Senator?" the man rasped in a low voice.

"Russ will do," Colbert said, switching on a smile. Inwardly, he was appalled. The man looked like a bum—scruffy, slouching, jittery. He wore a hoodie with the hood up. He probably thought it was a good disguise. Instead, it drew attention. No one wore a hoodie in July except gang-bangers. "Are you Ralf Lyons?" Colbert asked, making sure.

"Yup," Lyons said. "Here. This is it. It's all here." He thrust a USB drive at Colbert.

Colbert trapped Lyons's hand in a version of the senatorial two-handed handshake. He held on, squeezing slightly, and focused on transmitting his *qi* to the other man. Xue Hua had proved to him that this ancient Chinese healing technique worked. When he came home with a stress headache after an acrimonious debate, she would sit beside him and lay her hand on his forehead. Usually, the pain would go away within moments. Colbert focused on transmitting soothing, reassuring energy. He could not be sure he was doing it right, but after a few seconds, Lyons stopped trying to pull his hand away. When Colbert released him, Lyons pushed his hood down. He seemed to be standing straighter now, as if a burden had slid from his shoulders.

"It's great to meet someone who understands," he said.

"I understand completely," Colbert said. "It's unacceptable that NASA is hiding this information, that they're forcing you to go to these lengths, just to make sure the truth is heard."

"Yes. *Yes!* The FBI, the spooks, my fucking God, they were all over us. They said if we talked, we would be committing treason."

"I am a United States senator," Colbert said. "You are not

committing treason. You are doing the right thing." He pocketed the USB drive. Out of curiosity, he asked, "Can you give me your own take on this data? In your own expert opinion."

"First off, I'm not an expert on aliens," Lyons said. "No one is. This is completely new for everyone. You see these people on TV calling themselves experts on extraterrestrial whatever, they don't know shit. This is an outside context problem. That means we have no context in which to think about the race of alien beings that built that spaceship. The only certain fact is that their technology is far superior to ours. We are the Incas in this scenario, OK? We are the Arawak."

Colbert grimaced. That did *not* sound good. He said, "Is it not reasonable to hope that the aliens have come in peace?"

"Yes! In fact, it's our *only* hope. We have to seek engagement, not confrontation."

"We are told that the *Spirit of Humanity* will be a diplomatic mission," Colbert said, clinging to his dwindling faith in President Obama.

Lyons rasped, "You have *not* been told that the *Spirit of Humanity* will carry weapons. That's what's on there." He gestured at the USB, now in Colbert's breast pocket.

Cobert shook his head. The information confirmed his worst fears. "Does the president know about this?"

"Read the email chains. The president refused to approve the project unless the ship could be weaponized."

"What kind of weapons?"

"Might as well be bows and arrows."

"What … what else is on the drive?"

"Sketches. Preliminary specs. Everything I could access."

"Wow." Colbert inclined his head. "Ralf, thank you for your courage in coming to me."

The JPL scientist shrugged. He turned away and dropped a quarter into the coin telescope. Leaning into the viewfinder, he tilted the telescope upwards, towards the stars—there, of course, but invisible beyond the dull orange glow of the city lights.

"I've spent all my life thinking about outer space," he said. "Wondering what was out there beyond our solar system. There was always this idea that first contact would bring out the best in us. Who'd a thunk it, it's bringing out the worst."

Colbert touched his shoulder, sending more calming vibes. "Don't worry, Ralf. It's going to be all right."

Lyons turned to face him. "Are you going to leak this to the media?" he said.

"No," Colbert said, trying to keep the urgency out of his voice. *Absolutely under no circumstances.* The information would lose its value if everyone had it. "I'm pretty sure that would not be wise. And I strongly advise you not to do it, either. Even if we splashed this all over TV, the only result would be to further diminish confidence in our leaders. I know what you're thinking: they deserve it. Yes, maybe. But it would not serve the purpose of peace."

Lyons nodded. "What are you going to do with it, then? If I can ask."

"It's probably best that I don't share that with you at this time," Colbert said. "But please be assured, I will get this information in front of the people who need to see it."

Lyons reached out and gripped his hand. "Thank you, Senator. This is a massive load off my mind. Thank you for coming all the way out here ... Thank you."

The irony of Lyons's gratitude stayed with Colbert as he drove away. It should have been him thanking Lyons.

Half an hour later, he pulled onto a side street somewhere in Koreatown. He cut the engine. Sitting in the dark, he telephoned Edgar Ho.

"Russell," Edgar said. "Good to hear from you."

"I've got the information," Colbert said.

"Good," Edgar said. "Where are you?"

Colbert gave him the name of the street he was parked on.

"I'll be right there."

Colbert then waited for half an hour. This was the worst part. A tree branch, broken in a recent rainstorm, scraped the windshield. He nearly screamed. As he steadied his pulse, using the breathing techniques Xue Hua had taught him, he reminded himself that he was safe. Perfectly safe.

Edgar Ho was a professor of physics at UCLA, who also happened to work for the Chinese government. In the interests of gathering information—Colbert preferred not to think of it as spying—Edgar had reached out to numerous NASA scientists thought to be involved with the *Spirit of Humanity* mission.

A fishing expedition.

Ralf Lyons had taken the bait.

Edgar had given Lyons's details to Colbert, in person, during one of Xue Hua's events in Washington last week. Edgar and Xue Hua did not know each other beyond the merest nodding acquaintance. They both happened to be Chinese, and both were Democratic activists. That was all.

Xue Hua would never find out.

Nor, needless to say, would anyone else.

Edgar had assured Colbert in the past that Beijing deeply appreciated the work he did for international peace, and of course they understood his need for absolute discretion.

He was safe.

All the same, demons of anxiety wriggled through his body, like the restless traffic snaking through the streets of L.A. On some level deeper than the merely rational, he knew that something very bad was going to happen.

The handover came as an anticlimax. A car pulled in ahead of him. A young Chinese man jumped out. It was not Edgar. Colbert rolled his window down. The man stuck his hand in through the window. Colbert placed the USB drive in his palm. "I want you to tell Edgar," he began, and attempted to enfold the man's hand, as he had Lyons's, but the young guy was too quick. His fingers slithered away like fish. "Thank you," Colbert said, giving up.

"Bie danxin," said the man. He didn't even speak English. He went back to his car and roared away.

Colbert sighed. It was now four in the morning. He drove towards Santa Barbara, filled with a somber and yet exalted sense of accomplishment.

The FBI had misrepresented to Ralf Lyons and his colleagues at JPL that they'd be committing treason if they talked … but in fact, Lyons had not even broken the law when he gave Colbert that USB drive.

It was *Colbert* who'd committed treason. When he passed the USB drive to a Chinese national, he'd rendered himself liable for prosecution under the Espionage Act.

However, he did not consider himself a spy, because the law was insane. It reflected the irrational bigotry of the population, rather than any objective principle. Right-wing demagogues made people act in hateful ways towards foreigners, and China came in for the lion's share of xenophobic hatred, when in reality, the Chinese were just trying to get a fair shake.

As the husband of a Chinese woman, Colbert was very sensitive to the ways colonial oppression had distorted the global order. The *Spirit of Humanity* mission exemplified how the West still conspired to exclude China.

Since his election to the Senate, Colbert had been in a position to make reparations for these historical and ongoing injustices. He'd taken action, to what small extent he could, whenever possible. For instance, the Frostbite thing a few years back.

And tonight, he may have contributed to a truly global response to the alien question.

Fortified by these thoughts, he checked into his hotel in Santa Barbara as the sun rose over the Pacific. A weathered building with dead leaves clogging the pool, it was not exactly a senatorial joint. But the Nuclear Age Peace Foundation couldn't afford to put him up anywhere better, and Edgar Ho, of course, had not paid him anything for his efforts. Even if Edgar had offered, Colbert would have refused.

He settled his head onto the not-very-clean pillow and tried to get comfortable on the lumpy mattress.

He wasn't doing this for money.

He was doing it for humanity.

For Xue Hua.

He slid into unconsciousness. The next thing he knew, a rapping noise forced its way into his sleep. Disoriented, he pushed himself onto his elbow. It felt like he'd slept for no time at all. Glancing at the clock, he saw that it was 7:45. He was tireder than before he'd gone to sleep. Sunlight sliced under the curtains, and someone was knocking on the door of his hotel room.

"Senator," the person outside said, softly. "Senator Colbert. Gonna let me in? Need to talk with you."

Panic electrified Colbert. His mind filled with visions of armed FBI agents breaking down the door and arresting him. He did not pause to consider that it might just be someone from the Nuclear Age Peace Foundation, or the front desk. His guilty conscience drove him to the window. This was a ground-floor room. He was halfway out of the window when the door swung open and a blur of motion crossed the room. Gloved hands hauled him unceremoniously back inside.

"You were gonna run out to the highway, barefoot, in your tighty whities?" Colbert's visitor smiled, showing hillbilly dentistry. "That would have made a nice paparazzi shot."

Not a squad of FBI agents. Just one man, with an Arkansas drawl and eyes so pale they almost matched his blond eyebrows. He wore motorcycle gloves that went halfway up his thick forearms.

"Just kidding," the man went on. "There aren't any paparazzi out there. They've got bigger fish to fry than you."

Colbert glanced at the door. The man sidestepped, blocking his path to freedom.

"You should be more careful about security, Senator."

Colbert found his voice. "What is this about?"

"It's about your meeting with Ralf Lyons last night. Like I said, you should be more careful."

Colbert mentally reeled. In a flash, he saw everything slipping away: his career, Xue Hua …

The man smiled at his horrified expression. "We've got geotraces on the cell phones of everyone at JPL," he explained. "Poor amateur son of a bitch didn't even switch his phone off. Neither did you. And half an hour after that meeting, you telephoned a certain Edgar Ho. He's already been arrested, by the way. We recovered the USB drive."

Colbert kept his mouth shut, reasoning that they couldn't prove anything against him. Oh God. Wait. His fingerprints would be on the USB drive! He should have worn gloves …

But the information was definitely in China by now. That kid last night would have uploaded it within minutes of receiving the USB drive. So whatever happened to Colbert, he'd already succeeded.

He mustered defiance. "I haven't done anything wrong."

"That remains to be seen. What did Ralf Lyons tell you about the *Spirit of Humanity* project?"

If they had the USB drive, they already knew, didn't they? Maybe the man was bluffing. Maybe they *didn't* have it.

The man's pale eyebrows knitted. "I'm not playing games here, Senator. What was the substance of that conversation?"

"My wife!" Colbert blurted. "Is she all right?"

"Why wouldn't she be?"

"You goddamn spooks are capable of anything."

"I'll take that as a compliment," the man said. He made a quick twitching movement, and a gun jumped into his hand like it was spring-loaded. An extension on the barrel had to be a suppressor.

Colbert soiled himself.

The man laughed grimly. "Last chance, Senator. What did Ralf Lyons tell you?"

"The *Spirit of Humanity* is a warship," Colbert said. "We're going out there to blow the aliens away."

"Creeping cheetos," the man swore. "That's what you told Edgar Ho?"

"There were emails on the drive. Sketches, he said. Specifications. I don't know."

The man's pale cheeks reddened. "Congratulations, Senator. You've jeopardized America's national security, *and* the future of humanity. Not bad for a night's work."

"So it's true? The aliens are hostile?"

The man's pale gaze seemed to come back from a very long way away. "There are no aliens," he said. "There's just a busted-up old alien spaceship going round Europa on autopilot."

Colbert's jaw dropped. Profound relief spread through him. The man's words dispelled a fear he had scarcely been aware of harboring … only to replace it with an even more immediate and personal fear of the human being in front of him.

Would they tell him this, and then let him walk away?

"Yep," the man said. "The ship is a hulk. You don't even need a telescope to know that. All you need's a brain. If there were any living aliens on board, they would be emitting radio signals, moving the ship, or engaging in some other sort of activity we could detect. My own agency has been trying to raise 'em for four years. Targeted, tailored messages designed by the top experts in the field. Four goddamn years we've been saying hello, hola, bonjour, konnichiwa … nothing. There are no little green men, but there is a pile of money to be made."

"Oh, so that's your game," Colbert muttered.

"I make thirty-five bucks an hour, Senator. How much did Edgar Ho pay you to betray your country?"

Amidst his humiliation, Colbert straightened his back. "I would never stoop to take money for doing the right thing."

The man's mouth twisted in disgust. "So you're not only a traitor, you're also a sucker."

"Is it true," Colbert asked, "that the *Spirit of Humanity* will carry guns?"

The man crossed the room and peeked out of the curtains. Colbert glimpsed East Cabrillo Boulevard and the beach beyond. More people than usual for eight in the morning were outside, wandering along the beach, or just standing there, looking out to sea. The man let the curtain fall.

"Homicide arrests nationwide are up 300%," he said. "Burglaries, muggings … the police are overwhelmed. Yes, the ship will carry guns."

"Not for the aliens," Colbert realized. "For us." He could smell his own excrement.

"The only thing that will save humanity from tearing itself to pieces over this," the man said, "is retrieving that alien spaceship, so people can see for themselves that it is not a threat. The United States has committed to the *Spirit of Humanity* project. Putin's in for a price. The Europeans will do as they're told. The only power that could prevent a successful launch is China … and you've just given them the wherewithal to stop the project dead in its tracks. Still think you did the right thing?"

He shot Colbert in the neck. The silenced Sig Sauer made

a sound like someone clapping their hands.

In his dying moments, Colbert did not think about justice, humanity, or world peace. He thought of Xue Hua. He regretted nothing he'd done. His only regret was that he'd never get to say goodbye to her.

CHAPTER 19

At JPL in Pasadena, champagne flowed. Hannah smilingly put her hand over her glass when Richard Burke attempted to pour for her. "I have to drive later," she said, ignoring the pang of deprivation she felt.

She hadn't had a drink since the first contact event. Things had been moving so *fast!* First, the Night of the Living Fed—as Hannah had dubbed the surreal hours when the FBI descended on JPL and made everyone sign miles of non-disclosure agreements. That had been crazy, and not *good* crazy. "Martial law is here," Ralf Lyons had said. But then, like a bright dawn following a dark and stormy night, the announcement of the *Spirit of Humanity* project had lifted everyone's mood.

Hannah would have preferred it if RADAR-guided thermonuclear weapons were to be sent to Europa, rather than a manned spacecraft. The good news was that the *Spirit of Humanity* would be a manned spacecraft, *and* a weapon. The rumor was that kinetic bombardment weapons would be mounted on the ship.

Mustn't say a word about that, of course. The NDAs covered *everything*. But the Feds couldn't stop the staff of JPL talking to one another. So Hannah knew about the weapons, and she also knew about the data which suggested that the alien spacecraft was a hulk. Whatever destroyed Juno had most likely been an automated point defence system.

And the good news kept on coming. Today—July 15th, one week after the Juno observations—President Obama had announced that the *Spirit of Humanity* project would be spearheaded right here in the USA, at Johnson Space Center.

The project leader? None other than their own Richard Burke.

Hence the champagne, the silly hats, and the cheesy europop filling the office.

Burke was carrying the magnum of Brut around, filling everyone's glasses, even though the party was in his honor. That was the kind of guy he was.

"Go on, Hannah-banana. You deserve it," he said.

He had absolutely zero idea about her drinking problem. In the last week—the longest dry stretch she'd managed since, oh, college graduation—Hannah had gained enough perspective to accept the three little words she'd been avoiding for years: *high-functioning alcoholic.*

She was a high-functioning alcoholic.

She probably always would be.

But she didn't have to be an alcoholic who drank, and so she shook her head again, privately resolved that Burke would never know about the interior struggle this renunciation cost her. "I'm fine, Rich, seriously." Someone bumped into her from behind. Everyone who'd ever worked with Burke had crowded into their office to say goodbye to him. "Guess you won't miss this luxurious workspace," she quipped, moving the ficus plant that was threatening to topple off Ralf Lyons's desk.

"They've already assigned me a corner office in Building 13 at JSC," Burke said gloomily. "I'll miss you guys."

"We'll miss you, too. But we'll still be here." Hannah assumed the Juno team would be split up and reassigned to tasks related to the Spirit of Humanity project. "I wonder where Ralf is, anyway? I would have expected him to be here today."

Burke hesitated. He moved his head, indicating that she should step closer. "Hannah, Ralf doesn't work here anymore."

"Oh my God."

"He violated the NDA, apparently."

"He was pissed about the rumors about the rail guns," Hannah said in sudden anger. "He thought it would be a provocation. Excuse me, Ralf, the ship's automated defences killed our probe without any provocation whatsoever! And you want to send an *unarmed* ship out there? He would not listen to reason. What did he do, tweet about it?"

"Something like that." The crows-feet at the corners of Burke's eyes deepened. "It's a real loss. He was the best navigation specialist we had."

"Oh well," Hannah said. "I expect we'll get a replacement. A Russian, maybe. Or a European. I hope they speak English."

"We're all going to have to work together," Burke cautioned her.

"I know, I know. I'm excited about the international cooperation aspect, honestly. Who was it that said nothing brings people together like an external threat? So I guess that's the silver lining."

"The reason I'm telling you this, Hannah, is I don't want to lose you, too."

"Don't worry. These lips are sealed," Hannah sighed.

"You're the best propulsion tech in this goddamn outfit," Burke said. His eyes were slightly glazed with the effects of the champagne.

"Why, thank you kindly, sir."

"I'd put you up against anyone ESA or Roscosmos has got. But fortunately I don't have to justify my decisions. To accelerate the ramp-up, they've given me authority to fill certain key positions in-house. So … welcome to the Spirit of Humanity project, Hannah. If you accept, I'd like you to take the lead in propulsion systems development."

Hannah stared at him, thunderstruck. She did not underestimate her own abilities. But she had less experience than many of her counterparts in Russia, not to mention a lack of familiarity with nuclear propulsion systems. "Rich, are you drunk?"

"Is that a refusal?"

"N-n-no, it's a huge honor. I'm just not sure I'm ready."

Burke's focus on her sharpened. "It is not an honor. It is a huge fucking *responsibility.* The estimated budget for this project is $300 billion. The Spirit of Humanity will be massive in every sense of the word. The only vehicles that humanity has constructed on this scale before are ocean-going ships. It's several orders of magnitude bigger than anything we've done in space before, and the only reason it's being done now, instead of the fifty years it should have taken us to reach this stage, is because the whole world is shitting themselves that aliens just turned up on our doorstep. Yes, all the evidence we have suggests the alien ship is a hulk. But we don't know for sure."

Hannah bit her lip. "No, we don't," she agreed. "And *if* there are real, live aliens on board … if they're hostile …"

Burke lowered his voice. "The *Spirit of Humanity* is our only chance to preemptively strike at them. This ship may be all that stands between us and annihilation."

Hannah shivered. "You have a very reassuring way of putting things."

"It's the truth. You know it and I know it. Either we get this right, *first time,* or we may not have a second chance." Burke resumed speaking at a normal pitch. "So do you want the job?"

A huge responsibility. The words resonated in Hannah's mind. Could she handle it?

High-functioning alcoholic Hannah, who spent most of her evenings getting wasted, and her weekends in a stupor, could not handle it. No way.

But maybe high-functioning alcoholic Hannah, who stood here now, in the midst of a drunken celebration, with a glass of sparkling water in her hand, could do what was asked of her.

Either we get this right, FIRST TIME, or we may not have a second chance.

Burke's summation of the Spirit of Humanity project rang true.

But people were not spaceships.

This is *my* second chance, Hannah thought. Right now, right here.

"Yes," she said. "I'll do it."

Without giving her time to reconsider, Burke climbed onto a desk, shouted for quiet, and announced Hannah's appointment as head of propulsion systems.

This was the way they'd be doing things from now on, Hannah realized. Seat of the pants, on the fly, making crucial decisions at office parties, racing to meet deadlines. She wasn't going to have *time* to drink. The thought made her smile.

"Will I get a corner office at JSC, too?" she called up to Burke. "Because I'm going to need peace and quiet to bone up on nuclear electric propulsion technology!"

*

Hannah got her own office at Johnson Space Center. It wasn't a corner, but it was nice and big. Pretty soon it no longer felt big because every surface was hidden by piles of paper, 3D printed models, and coffee mugs.

Her first month on the job got eaten up by hiring decisions.

Other people's decisions, that is.

Burke had rushed through her own appointment, and several others, before organizational structures had time to rigidify. But now they had, hiring was being handled by Human Resources. Even at Hannah's level, she didn't get to decide who would be working with her on the daunting task of building a new spacecraft engine.

She just had to work with whoever they sent her.

On August 15th, they sent her Inga Pitzke.

Skyler Taft shepherded the German woman into Hannah's office. Skyler was one of the vaguely mysterious 'Feds' who hung around JSC nowadays, watching, listening, and occasionally offering a hand with bureaucratic difficulties. If you needed strings pulled, you could butter up one of the Feds. That was how it worked now. Hannah didn't like the open politicization of the *Spirit of Humanity*, but she recognized that it was inevitable with a project this high-profile. Anyway, Skyler was one of the nicer Feds. He wore a peace symbol around his neck and a raggedy friendship bracelet on one ankle. He reminded Hannah of her college boyfriend. He had found her a plasma dynamicist last week.

And now he'd found her a metallurgist.

"Great," Hannah said. "We need someone to work on the composition of the sintering powder to 3D-print the engine components."

"Inga's got a lot of experience in that area," Skyler said. "And I think she might also be able to help clarify the engine selection issue."

Hannah stretched her arms over her head and screamed at the ceiling. No one jumped. Around the clock, seven days a week, people were screaming and shouting and throwing tantrums at Johnson Space Center. It was a combination of stress, and blowing off stress.

"The freaking engine selection issue," Hannah moaned.

"This is a fraught topic," Skyler said to Inga.

Hannah rocked forward in her chair. "Inga, I'm assuming you have project-level clearance?" The German woman nodded. Since Skyler had brought her in, it was a given that she had all the clearances she needed. Hannah just had to ask, because security around the project was tighter than ever. A bunch of technicians and analysts had been let go last week, for no other reason than that they were of Chinese heritage. That was bullshit, in Hannah's opinion. But she had to work within the system.

"Inga spent three years working at the company that developed the water plasma engine," Skyler said.

"Aha," Hannah said. She pointed at the German woman. "You're here to try to convince me that piece of crap will fly."

Inga said, startled, "Why do you say it is a piece of crap?"

Skyler laughed. "We're kind of informal around here,

Inga. Don't take offense."

"None meant," Hannah clarified. "But let me explain where we're at with this. There are three competing engine design proposals. Well, there are actually about twenty. But these are the big three." She ticked them off on her fingers. "TEM. This is the Russians' experimental nuclear drive. It uses a gas-cooled nuclear reactor to produce electricity, which is in turn used to run a xenon-based electrical propulsion system, probably magnetoplasmadynamic. They have a workable reactor design, but haven't yet managed to produce a propulsor unit with sufficient thrust. Then in this corner we've got NASA's preferred propulsion system: chemical rockets. Big, *big* chemical rockets. They're huge, and their fuel is unthinkably heavy, but we already have good, reliable vacuum-rated designs that we can start to scale up. And lastly, the underdog challenger, the magnetoplasmadynamic engine developed by some little startup that folded before they could even build a prototype, right, Skyler?"

Skyler nodded, playing with his peace symbol necklace. He had strong-looking, beautiful hands.

"That's the one the NXC is pushing."

Skyler and his hench-Feds belonged to the National Xenoaffairs Council, a formerly unknown agency that had gotten in on the ground floor of Spirit of Humanity, Inc—the world's fastest-growing boom sector. The NXC had become an indispensable partner to NASA in terms of procuring resources for the project. But they weren't scientists. Skyler was the rare exception. He had a Ph.D in astrophysics. That didn't make him a propulsion expert.

"It's just office politics to you, isn't it, Skyler?" she needled him. "If we go with your system, you get bragging rights and presidential pats on the head."

Skyler bowed his head and twirled one of those beautiful hands in the air. "Pay no attention to me. I'm just here to take the abuse."

"Everyone needs a hobby," Hannah said. "My hobby is tormenting federal agents."

"I was human once, you know."

"So you bring in Ms. Pitzke here to sell me the system, because what, the plural of anecdote is data?"

Inga Pitzke looked from Hannah to Skyler and back again with a horrified expression on her face.

Hannah laughed. She stood up and grabbed her bag. "Let's blow this joint, Fraulein Pitzke. Come for a coffee and convince me that your piece of crap actually works."

CHAPTER 20

They went to Fuddrucker's, on the far side of E. NASA Parkway. It took half an hour just to extricate themselves from JSC. "This is why I sleep under my desk most nights," said Hannah. They had to queue up at a security chicane of concrete crash barriers. Security guards inspected Hannah's car, and both women had to get out and walk through body scanners. That's the way it was now.

National Guardsmen patrolled the six-mile perimeter of JSC, leading muzzled Dobermans that panted in the August heat. Hannah drove cautiously behind a flatbed loaded with enormous pipe segments.

JSC was expanding at breakneck speed. The park south of Space Center Boulevard had transformed into a giant construction zone, tainting the hot, heavy air with dust. Floodlights lit the gantries. The clangor of heavy machinery assaulted Hannah's ears as they crossed the Fuddrucker's parking lot. Work on this new truss assembly building continued around the clock. Some local residents had complained—and had been shamed on social media for it. The entire population of America, give or take a few fussbudgets, had lined up solidly behind the *Spirit of Humanity* project. The knowledge of this broad support invigorated Hannah. What a change from the old days when politicians used to berate NASA for 'wasting' money!

She spun a menu across the table to Inga. "What are you having?"

"I like American food," Inga said. "American beer, no." She ordered a half-pounder hamburger and a premium beer.

Hannah had honestly been planning just to have a coffee.

Too many suppers consisting of snacks from the JSC vending machines had taken their toll on her waistline. But after all, that was a good reason to eat a real meal for a change. She ordered a salad, nachos—and a coffee.

"So," she said. "Why is the water-based magnetoplasmadynamic engine the best choice for the *Spirit of Humanity?*"

Inga nodded. "It is the only concept that will allow the ship to return to Earth."

Hannah sat back and considered the other woman. Inga fulfilled her expectations of German womanhood: tall, blonde, unapproachable. She even wore her hair in two braids pinned up behind her head. Hannah wondered whether she was subconsciously prejudiced against her for being German. Her grandfather had died in the camps. She resolved to be absolutely even-handed in her assessment.

"Where did you hear that the *Spirit of Humanity* is a one-way mission?" she asked.

"I did not hear it from anyone. But it makes sense that it would be considered."

Hannah shook her head. "It's not being considered." She hoped she was right.

"OK," Inga said. "But if we go with the chemical propulsion system, for instance, every gramme of fuel that the ship needs to get back has to be hauled out there. It makes the return journey close to mathematically impossible."

"That's my main objection to that system," Hannah admitted. "Actually, I'm one hundred percent in favor of nuclear propulsion. But you have to understand I'm not the ultimate decision-maker on this. That's the design committee."

"I know, but they will accept your recommendation. Skyler said so."

Hannah suppressed a smile. "Skyler has way too much confidence in my powers."

She stopped talking as the waitress brought their food. Foam dribbled down the side of Inga's beer glass.

Yearning momentarily fogged Hannah's brain. She knew intellectually that she had placed herself in a trigger situation. The cheesy Top 40 music, the buzz of after-work chatter around them, the smell of unhealthy fried food—this was exactly the kind of environment where she used to do her drinking in the days of Hannah's Rules.

The real question was why she'd placed herself in this situation. It had been her choice. She could just as easily have taken Inga to one of the cafes in Starport Building 3.

Come on, Hannah. You don't even *like* beer.

She ate a nacho. "The NXC is a dream factory," she said. "We have to be realists. Nuclear propulsion is the only way to go. I'm not disagreeing with you about that. But the political obstacles to turning engine design over to the Russians ... yikes. That's the only reason I'm listening to you."

Inga was ignoring her meal, scribbling on a napkin. "Is it OK to draw?" she said, glancing up at the ceiling.

Hannah took her meaning. *Security*. "It's OK. This place is practically an extension of JSC." All the booths around them were filled with techs, analysts, and construction workers jabbering about SoHP-related topics. There were more NASA lanyards to be seen than Houston Texans t-shirts. Nevertheless, Hannah glanced up and confirmed that the nearest security camera was too far away to capture a scribble on a napkin.

Inga pushed the napkin across to her. "This is a sketch of the MPD engine."

"What's this?" Hannah said, touching an unlabelled bubble.

"That is the steam generator. The unique feature of this engine is that it uses water as the reaction mass."

"I know. Just like the alien spaceship." By now, everyone had put two and two together. The plume of water plasma observed by the IRTF in 2011 had come from the alien spacecraft's drive as it decelerated into Jupiter orbit. The spaceship had travelled however many light-years—coasting most of the way, for certain—on *water*.

Unexpectedly, Inga flushed pink. "Is that a problem?"

"Not at all. The main problem, honestly, is lofting enough water into orbit to reach Europa. H2O is *heavy.*"

"We will have to loft so much stuff into orbit, anyway ..."

"Yep. It's going to take every launch vehicle on Earth, working flat out for the next two years." Hannah loaded a nacho with guacamole and made it fly on a vertical launch trajectory. It had been a long day. Leaning back, she made the loaded nacho orbit above her face. "Pieces of truss, habitation, avionics. And you want them to lift a few hundred tonnes of water, too?"

"No. Only 70 tonnes. The ship only needs enough reaction mass to travel one way, plus a safety margin."

"Huh? Oh—*oh.*"

Hannah brought the nacho down to land in her mouth. Chewing, in a trance, she ran mental calculations.

"Holy smoke, Batman," she said. "Refuel at Europa. It's

made of freaking water ice!"

Inga grinned. It transformed her face, making her look like a fun, lively person. "You see? Land on Europa—"

"No, *no.* The *Spirit of Humanity* is not going to be launch-capable. Oh sure, it could land—that's easy, just crash. But it couldn't get away again. No, we send an advance lander. Or maybe two of them. Automated electrolysis systems. Send them now. They sit there for the next three years, making reactants and collecting water. By the time the Spirit of Humanity gets there, they've made enough reactants to loft the water for the return trip! They launch the water tanks into orbit, and the SoH picks them up. It could work. It could freaking well work!"

"Assuming the aliens do not interfere," Inga joked.

Hannah picked a celery stick out of her salad and pointed it at Inga like a gun. "That's what the railguns are for."

She had gradually come to discount the possibility—remote, but non-zero—that the alien spacecraft had a living crew. You couldn't calculate for that, anyway. Hannah now spent her days focusing exclusively on the technical challenges of reaching Europa and getting back again. The mission was worth doing for its own sake. Sometimes, lying awake at night, unable to sleep for the heat-rejection calculations running through her head, she rejoiced that this had come about in her lifetime. The alien spacecraft had given humanity a much-needed kick in the pants. It allowed her to consider way-out ideas—like this water engine—that would never have gotten a hearing this time last year.

Yet her innate aversion to risk still governed her instincts. She leaned forward and fixed Inga with a serious gaze. "What about reliability? Eight people's lives will depend on this."

"Eight people?" Inga said.

"Yes. They want an eight-man crew."

"We fit enough engines and turbines that we always make sure we have N+2 redundancy."

Hannah ate the rest of her nachos, thinking about the unforgiving Tsiolkovsky rocket equation. The more mass you carry, the harder you have to push away part of that mass to get the same amount of movement. But if you don't have to take all the mass you need for the return trip out there with you, you can accelerate to a greater velocity with the same engine design, and get there quicker.

The crew would not be eating nachos on board the *Spirit of Humanity,* anyway. They'd be dining on fresh vegetables and legumes, not an unhealthy snack in sight. Hydroponic gardening was the only possible way to keep the crew alive for that long. The life-support department was working on a setup that would deliver an optimal supply of calories and nutrients. They might even include live fish.

"Has the crew been chosen yet?" Inga asked, interrupting her ruminations.

"I think they're being chosen as we speak. Of course, I'm not involved in that at all. It's pure, cut-throat politics." Hannah sighed at the reminder of the looming risk that political considerations might warp the mission at any stage. With the hundreds of other scientists and engineers working on the project worldwide, she was absolutely determined to fight that threat tooth and nail. *Nobody's* pet political agenda should take precedence over getting the *Spirit of Humanity* safely to Europa … and back again.

And yet she had to work within the system.

Game the system, if that was what it took.

Of course the NXC had their own agenda, too. But that didn't mean Skyler and his buddies couldn't hit a home-run from time to time.

An American-sourced propulsion system might make everyone happy … except the Russians. *Wait.* What if the American propulsion system was powered by the Russian gas-cooled reactor? Yes, that would work! It would keep the Russians happy too, and she wouldn't have to worry about the iffy-looking water-cooled reactor used in the original MPD drive proposal. She would need to bring in someone with gas-cooled reactor experience to check the Russians' work, but she could get Skyler to do that for her. Didn't the Brits use gas-cooled reactors for electrical power? It looked like this was really going to fly.

If the mass ratio could be finessed within the crucial parameters.

She pushed aside her empty nachos plate, and her untouched salad. Inga, chewing her burger, raised her eyebrows. Hannah tugged the napkin dispenser closer and borrowed Inga's pencil.

"My freehand drawing skills are craptacular," she muttered, fifteen minutes later, after scrumpling up several failed attempts. (Those napkins went in her bag. She'd shred them back at her office.)

Her sketch showed a truss tower with the MPD engine at one end. The truss narrowed to two-thirds of the way up, supporting radiator vanes, and met a disc labeled *Bioshield.* Above that, several cylindrical modules like a string of beads. One, by far the largest, she'd labeled *Main hab. Spin gravity. 60 m diameter min – Coriolis.*

Inga had watched her sketching in silence. Now she said, *"Schön. Wunderschön!"*

"I actually know what you mean," Hannah murmured. Emotion rose in her chest. The *Spirit of Humanity* had sprung to life in her mind, growing with every stroke of her pencil, each component supporting the others in an exquisite balance. Sure, she was basing this off of ballpark figures. But the ratios worked.

Inga picked up her beer glass and found it empty. "I must have another beer to celebrate. You?"

"No," Hannah started automatically. But the emotion surging through her called for release. A thought flickered momentarily through her mind: *It's OK to have a drink, because Skyler isn't here.* What a strange thing to think! She decided not to examine it. "OK, you win. Just one beer …"

Just one beer.

Lie of the freaking century.

CHAPTER 21

Skyler picked Inga Pitzke up from JSC at 11:30 p.m. and drove her back to the Budgetel Inn near Starpark, where she was staying until NASA found her somewhere to live. She might be here for a while. The *Spirit of Humanity* project had placed a giant thumb on the scales of the Houston real estate market. In the forecourt of the Budgetel Inn, people leaned against the sides of pickup trucks, drinking and talking noisily about construction and launch schedules. Inga shrank from them, not realizing, perhaps, that they were all NASA personnel like herself.

Skyler didn't go into her room with her. She was a shy woman, and might be intimidated, even though she was taller than him. He leaned against the doorjamb. "So you think she'll go for it?"

Inga stood in the dreary little vestibule, clutching her handbag. "I think she is convinced it's the best engine concept. It *is* the best engine concept. Best specific impulse you can achieve." Inga was a ferocious partisan of the water-based magnetoplasmadynamic drive. That's why she had done what she'd done.

Skyler had been trying to come up with a tactful way of asking his next question, but he couldn't. "Did she ask you about Firebird Systems?"

Inga took a step backwards. "No, she did not mention it. We talked only about the drive."

"OK. That's good," Skyler said. "No need to bring it up unless she mentions it."

Inga burst out, "What does Hannah know about Firebird? What is her understanding about ... about where the

IP came from?"

The truth was that the IP had come from Inga herself. Back in March, she'd stolen the entire contents of Firebird's server and quit, planning to take the IP down the road to one of Firebird's competitors. There was more to this earnest, reserved German woman than met the eye. The NXC had swooped in before Inga could make the career-ending mistake of offering the IP to another aerospace company. They'd had their eye on Firebird Systems for a while, and had actually tried to purchase the company, only to be rebuffed by the founder. So Inga and her stolen data had fallen like manna into their laps.

Hannah Ginsburg, of course, knew none of this. "I don't think she's given it a second thought," Skyler answered honestly. "She's a hundred and ten percent focused on the science. Why would she give any thought to stuff that should be handled by the legal department? She assumes we either have a license for the technology, or acquired it outright at some point. We're the *Feds,* after all."

And now they were in a bit of a pickle. Given time, they *would* establish legal right to the Firebird IP. They just hadn't done it yet.

But that wasn't Inga's problem, so Skyler smiled at her. "Don't worry about the legal issues. Just do your job. I think you'll fit right in here."

A chorus of *American Pie* crashed over them from the parking lot. It was first contact syndrome, as Skyler thought of it. Ever since July 8th, it seemed as if no one wanted to go to sleep. People stayed up carousing to put off the moment of facing the darkness alone.

Inga cringed at the noise.

"I know they sound like drunken rednecks," Skyler said, "but they're mostly NASA scientists."

Unexpectedly, Inga grinned. "You know what comes to me, when I'm at JSC? Talking with Hannah, meeting the team—*mein Gott,* they're all so brilliant!—I feel that this must be like the Manhattan Project. The best minds in the world, doing battle with the unknown. This is *our* Manhattan Project. I'm so honored to be here. Thank you, Skyler." Swiftly, she crossed the vestibule and gave him a peck on the cheek.

Skyler stood outside the closed door. The Manhattan Project? Under his breath, he quoted Robert Oppenheimer. "'I am become Death, destroyer of worlds.'" Jesus. I hope not.

He went slowly upstairs to the second floor of the Budgetel Inn.

He and Lance were staying here, too.

Houston real estate: not for guys on federal housing allowances.

He bypassed his own room and knocked on Lance's door. First contact syndrome—he had a touch of it, too. Anyway, he wanted to find out what, if anything, Lance had heard from the design committee.

Lance opened the door with a beer in his hand. "We did it," he said jubilantly.

"Holy crap, that was fast," Skyler said, following him into the room.

"Everything's moving fast. Decisions like this—would've taken years before. Now? One conference call, boom, done. Seems like the launch and construction subgroup really liked the concept."

"I knew they would," Skyler said, playing it cool. "What happens next?"

"The propulsion group builds a unit to run vacuum tests."

"Hmm," Skyler said.

"What? It's great. This *is* the best concept, right?"

"Yes," Skyler said. But he was uneasy. The truth was, he suspected there might be a flaw in the design somewhere. He had looked at the schematics and it seemed to him that the water cooled reactor design didn't add up, and the steam generator didn't seem to have any means of steam separation without gravity. Inga admitted that she didn't know how Firebird Systems had ultimately worked out the freefall fluid dynamics. She had quit while they were still knee deep in it, and that's why the NXC had wanted to obtain Firebird's server. They wanted to know if Oliver Meeks and his team had worked out the answer in the months after Inga left the company.

Well, they hadn't managed to nab the server. But probably it was no big deal. Probably fluid dynamics was *easy.* Inga, after all, was a metallurgist, not a propulsion engineer. And God knows Skyler was not a propulsion specialist, either. But someone like Hannah would probably be able to see the answer in a single glance.

Skyler sighed. He went and looked out the window. In the parking-lot, the tailgate party had moved on to the oeuvre of Tina Turner. Skyler's fingers itched. *Rollin' on the river …* He hadn't picked up his guitar in weeks.

Lance, oblivious, had gone back to his computer. Typing like crazy, he was exchanging messages on SDIMP—Secure Discussion and Instant Messaging Platform—with NXC colleagues in other parts of the country, and overseas. In a month, the agency had grown like a mushroom. They were building new competencies in fields ranging from xenolinguistics to nutrition. Lance, hunched over his computer in his boxer shorts, was actively managing fifty full-time agents and twice as many experts on retainers.

Skyler, to his own bemusement, had also been anointed a manager. Director Flaherty had put him in charge of the deliberately vaguely named Spaceflight Innovation section. In practice this meant everything to do with the water-based magnetoplasmadynamic drive.

He got himself a cold one out of the minifridge and lay on his stomach on Skyler's bed, tapping on his Surface Pro.

First stop: Twitter.

Skyler stalked all the players in the worldwide spacecraft propulsion ecosystem. Most of them practiced extreme circumspection online.

Tonight, Hannah Ginsberg had posted her first tweet since July. It was a photo of her own hand holding a Bacardi Breezer. Caption: "I freaking earned this today!!!"

It had already been retweeted 176 times by followers of the *Spirit of Humanity* project. Well, no harm done.

Skyler gazed at the pixels that formed an image of Hannah's hand. He had a powerful urge to reply to the tweet. "Where's mine?" Something dorky like that.

He didn't do it, of course. It would be counter to NXC protocol. Anyway, she was probably asleep under her desk already. She really did sleep in her office. She'd shown him the sleeping bag, camp mattress, pillow, and eyemask that she kept in the bottom drawer of her filing cabinet. It was like a little spaceship under there.

He'd stop by her office tomorrow. Congratulate her on resolving the engine selection issue. He felt a pleasant tingle of anticipation at the thought—which dissipated like a hit off a cheap joint.

She didn't know he'd stolen the goddamn MPD drive from the guys who invented it. She could never know.

"Hey, Skyler," Lance said without looking around from his computer.

"What?"

"This just in from Sean at the INR."

"Uh oh."

The INR—the Bureau of Intelligence and Research—was the State Department's intelligence wing. Under a new intelligence-sharing agreement, the INR kept the NXC apprised of geopolitical rumblings that might affect the *Spirit of Humanity* project.

"New analysis of all-source intelligence. The CCP is about to fold CNSA into the command structure of the PLA. Expect some kind of announcement within the next few days."

"They're upping the ante, huh?" Skyler sighed.

Minus the acronyms, State had just told them that the Chinese government was about to place the Chinese National Space Agency under military command. Any way you sliced it, that did not amount to the long-awaited Chinese endorsement of the *Spirit of Humanity* project.

"What did I say, you cannot trust them," Lance said, banging his fist on the rickety table where his laptop sat.

The Obama administration had sought to appease China by extending billions of dollars in trade concessions. Clearly it had not produced the desired rapprochement.

"There's always the nuclear option," Skyler said. "Pay off all foreign holders of US treasuries." He was partial to this solution himself. It had an elegance about it. At the click of a mouse, the Fed could tank the Chinese economy. And the Chinese knew that, too. That was why, in Skyler's opinion, Xi Jinping's opposition to the *Spirit of Humanity* project would ultimately turn out to be no more than face-saving bluster.

The news from the INR sounded bad, sure. But it was just a red flag waved at the G8 powers to see if they'd blink. He expounded this perspective to Lance, but got the feeling Lance wasn't really listening.

Lance had been on edge these past few weeks. Either he had a massive dose of first contact syndrome, or something bad had happened to him that Skyler didn't know about. Skyler leaned towards the latter theory. It had started when they failed to prevent that disastrous leak to China. Lance had taken a lot of the blame for that. Shit rolls downhill, and when he came back from California he'd been sour, completely uncommunicative. Skyler had a feeling that Lance might have killed someone. Maybe that senator, or the JPL guy who turned up dead shortly afterwards. Or both of them. He was certainly capable of it.

On top of all his other responsibilities, Skyler felt responsible for pulling Lance back from the brink.

"Anything new related to crew selection?" he said, changing the subject.

"It's proceeding," Lance said, in his normal voice. "The ESA's picked their guy. The Russians have filled one of their slots, and they've provided a shortlist of xenolinguistics mission specialist candidates. Anyway, the crew have to start training by the end of September, at the latest."

At the pace they were moving, it felt like the launch of the *Spirit of Humanity* was scheduled for tomorrow, not 2019. Skyler grinned. "We'd better get on the ball," he said.

When he reached around to put his empty Heineken can on Lance's bedside table, he knocked a copy of *Men's Health* onto the floor. Under it lay Lance's Sig Sauer, suppressor attached.

CHAPTER 22

Hannah did penance for her uncontrolled night of binge drinking by working harder than ever. Yes, that was possible. It was always possible. She now had the green light to build a prototype of the water-based magnetoplasmadynamic drive for vacuum tests. She nagged the propulsion group to bust their asses, and leant on Skyler to work his black magic and get them extra time on the 3D metal printers to build the prototype parts.

They delivered the prototype to Building 32 for vacuum tests on the afternoon of Saturday, August 27th. Hannah sent everyone home to get some rest, made a half-hearted stab at tidying up the lab, and drove home herself, feeling unaccountably blue.

'Home' wasn't really home. It was a furnished condo in League City. She'd 'lived" here for more than a month and still didn't know how to work the washing machine.

Her phone rang while she was stuffing clothes into the accursed maw of the Electrolux. She touched 'accept,' dizzy with tiredness.

"Aunt Hannah? I can only see your ear!"

"Oh. Facetime," Hannah said, smiling. She sat down with her back to the washing-machine and balanced her phone on her knee, so she could enjoy the sight of her niece's bright little face. "I have to get with the program, huh? Are all the cool fourth-graders using Facetime these days?"

"No, only me," Isabel said seriously. "When are you coming to see us? The swimming pool's finished."

Isabel's love of swimming had blossomed into a real aptitude for the sport. Could a ten-year-old have an aptitude for competitive swimming? In Pacific Palisades, she could. Bethany and her husband, David, had recently built a 10-meter pool in the backyard for their budding Olympian.

"Let's have a race," Isabel said. "I bet I would beat you!"

"I bet you would, too, Izzy," Hannah said. She knew this was Isabel's way of trying to entice her out for a visit, and felt bad that she couldn't promise anything at the moment.

Bethany's voice grew louder in the background. "I said don't bother her, Isabel, she's very busy!"

Isabel's face slid out of the screen. Bethany frowned. "Sorry, Hannah. We won't keep you."

"It's OK," Hannah sighed.

"What is that behind you?" Bethany said. "Is it part of the *Spirit of Humanity?* Is it a habitation unit or something?" Even Los Angeles soccer moms now knew the lingo associated with the project.

Hannah laughed. "It's a washing machine." For some reason she couldn't stop laughing. "I am an honest-to-God rocket scientist," she gasped, eyes streaming, "and I can't figure out how this fucking washing machine works!"

"Oh, Hannah," Bethany said. "OK. First of all, you select the cycle ..."

Calmly, Bethany walked her through the process of getting her clothes on the way to clean. She did not reproach Hannah for her many broken promises to visit. She did not pull the guilt-trip shtick she had inherited from their late mother. Towards the end of the call, she said, "So, are you coming out for Izzy's birthday?" When Hannah started her usual stumbling litany of 'maybe' and 'hopefully,' Bethany cut her off with a genuinely warm laugh. "It's OK, Hannah. She would like you to be here, but if it happens, it happens.

If it doesn't, it doesn't."

Hannah hung up the phone feeling like something had changed between them. Her sister accepted her life, at last, for what it was. All it had taken was an alien spaceship.

She crashed on her unmade bed and enjoyed her first full night's sleep in a month.

The next day was Sunday. Hannah did not have much difficulty talking herself into going to work. She had to finalize the staff rota that she'd been putting off for most of last week, the vacuum chamber team was expecting a test suite to run once they'd get her engine installed and ready, and she also had to bring Koichi Masuoka up to speed as soon as possible.

Masuoka was a 32-year-old JAXA astronaut. He would be crewing on the *Spirit of Humanity* as the reactor and propulsion mission specialist. He'd arrived at JSC last week for training. Talk about being thrown in at the deep end. Hannah had to teach him everything she knew, and also the things she *didn't* know yet, such as how to make a steam generator and separator that worked in freefall.

She passed through the JSC security checkpoint, pondering whether to just bombard the liquid with enough microwaves to both flash it to steam and turn it to plasma. She barely noticed the tense and snappish attitude of the security guards.

Getting out of her car, she stopped dead.

Raised her sunglasses.

Lowered them again.

The giant banner that hung across the admin building across her office window should have read *Spirit of Humanity*.

She was absolutely sure that's what it had said yesterday.

Now it read: *Spirit of Destiny.*

"It's too early in the day for hallucinations," Hannah said aloud.

On her way into the building, she noticed a cluster of East Asian people being escorted along the hall by security. More personnel of Chinese descent getting fired? She hadn't thought there were any left. But she shouldn't jump to conclusions. Maybe they were compatriots of Masuoka's, come to join in the insanity.

She entered the propulsion group's office, still marvelling at the mystery of the banner. "Hey, Ross," she called across the office, to the only other person here. "Did you see the banner out front?"

Ross Ferguson, a design engineer, said, "Log onto your computer."

"I'm talking about the banner."

"Just do it."

Hannah went into her own office and booted her desktop. She immediately saw what Ferguson meant. The login screen used to display the *Spirit of Humanity* project's snazzy logo. The logo had changed. It was now a stylized dove, rendered in a deep blue colour that looked familiar, but she couldn't place, flanked by olive branches. And it read, yup, *Spirit of Destiny.*

"What the hell," Hannah said. At least her login still worked. She opened up her email, and found an all-hands announcement extolling the name change in terms of "more clearly reflecting our mission." There was a link to a press release.

Chinese Space Agency CNSA Joins Historic Spirit of Destiny

Project.

Other emails informed her that she was going to get a bunch of new people added to the propulsion group. She also learned that they would now be outsourcing the entire drive subframe assembly to China.

She went back out to the general office space. A couple more people had trickled in. "Don't you guys have lives?" she said, smiling. She was so proud of them. Her blood boiled at the very thought that the politicians might fuck up what they were accomplishing here.

She strode to the bank of elevators, seething while she waited for one to arrive. Impatient, she waited for less than 10 seconds before turning to the stairwell, slamming the door open with a crash that echoed in the stark space. She stomped up the stairs to Richard Burke's office and walked in without knocking.

Burke stood talking to three Chinese (she assumed) men whose formal business suits marked them out as strangers to JSC.

"Hannah, just a moment, if you don't mind!"

Burke's curt tone felt like a slap in the face. Hannah went and got herself a coffee from the vending machine down the hall. Her hand shook with anger, and coffee spilled onto the carpet tiles. A little while later the three Chinese men passed her on their way to the elevator. Their bearing made her think *military*. Their business suits might as well have been uniforms. She went back to Burke's office.

"So," she said. "Without warning, I come into work to find out that the name of the project has changed, and my team's workload is going to double," she took a deep breath before launching into the rest of her tirade in an even harsher tone, "because CNSA is now participating in the project, and this was all announced in a press release back-dated to 11:59 p.m. on Friday. I love that detail. Did they think if they change everything around over the weekend, we won't notice?"

"I didn't get advance warning, either," Burke said. He sat in his desk chair, looking out the window at the construction site where the truss assembly building was going up. He spun his chair around to face her. "You know where I should be right now? At home in Pasadena with my wife and kids. It's goddamn Sunday morning. I shouldn't be here." Burke was a Lutheran, devoted in an understated way to his faith. "Candy says the services have been packed over the last month. Worshippers spilling out of the doors. And here I am in Houston, debating a goddamn logo change."

"It isn't just a logo change. All our workflows will have to change. We'll have to coordinate with Yantai as well as Star City. That adds an extra layer of complexity to a project that is already pushing the envelope of what we can handle."

"It is what it is, Hannah."

"Politics."

"Yes. Look on the bright side. This is now a truly global project. And they've got some top-flight people at CNSA, especially in the realm of remote sensing and optics."

"Those guys you were talking to?"

"'Liaison officers,'" Burke said, making air quotes with his fingers.

Hannah sat down in the low-slung chair at the corner of his desk. She sipped her still-too-hot vending machine coffee. "What changed?"

"Apart from the logo?"

"No, no. Incidentally, that dove? *Barf.* But I mean, what's the political 411? Three years ago we banned Chinese nationals from entering a NASA facility. Last week, we were firing people because they had a Chinese grandmother. Now we're welcoming PLA officers into our maximum-security development facility." That was a shot in the dark. Burke's eyes tightened. He didn't deny it. "There has to be some explanation," she prodded, still angry on behalf of her team, who would be stuck with needless administrative work as a result of the reorg.

Burke stood up. Hannah reacted, scrambling to her feet. She spilled coffee on the decorative rug in front of his desk. She bit back the apology that sprang to her lips.

"They threatened," Burke said, "to shoot down the ship if they could not participate."

Hannah dropped her paper cup of coffee.

"The threat was apparently credible. Remember that weather satellite? The president and the other G8 leaders decided to take it seriously."

"They threatened … to blow up the *Spirit of Humanity?* In orbit?"

"The *Spirit of Destiny,* Hannah. The *Spirit of Destiny.* I gather it sounds good in Chinese."

"I can't freaking believe it."

"The stakes are high. They've never been higher. We've discussed this. It was wrong to leave the Chinese out in the first place, in my opinion. That has now been rectified."

Hannah shook her head, thinking that it was going to be next to impossible to work with the new Chinese colleagues she'd been promised. What a freaking mess.

As if reading her thoughts, Burke said, "It isn't the Chinese people who are the problem. It isn't their scientists. It's their government. We have to keep that distinction in mind."

"What, so those suits *weren't* Chinese army officers?"

"They were. But we have to remember the PLA isn't some kind of monolith. There are guys in there who genuinely favor international cooperation, and others who don't. Remember the Senkaku Islands thing?"

"Oh yeah, when they shot down those Japanese fighters."

"Yup. So that tendency—"

"To shoot things down—"

"—is real. But certain people got very sharply reprimanded over the Senkakus incident. They're licking their wounds at the moment. So we'll just have do our damndest to get this ship built, and fueled, and on its way, before the bad apples regroup and throw a spanner in the gears."

Hannah pointed at him. "Signs that you've become an uber-bureaucrat: when you talk about apples using spanners."

Burke rolled his eyes. "How's the prototype coming?"

Hannah gratefully retreated to safer territory. "We delivered it to Building 32 yesterday. While we wait for the results of the vacuum tests, I'm going to get started on designing Brayton cycle turbines to use with the Russian reactor design. I've already discussed this with Nikolai Petrov, the propulsion reactor design lead at Rosatom. We're looking at helium as the working gas, and discussing what output and return temperatures the reactor needs. It looks promising, although we'll need to bring in a specialist to do the heavy lifting. Actually, I'd like to fly to Star City to take a look at their working prototype."

"Keep me updated on your travel plans. Anything else?"

Hannah hesitated.

While driving to work, she'd reached the conclusion that she needed more detail on the steam generator. She couldn't find the answer in the documentation she'd been given, and Inga was no help on that question. She wasn't hopeful that the results of the vacuum tests would resolve it, but maybe she could get herself a ride on a vomit comet that would. Anyway, she didn't want to bother Burke with technical issues, when he had so much else on his plate.

"No," she said. "That's it right now. Sorry about your carpet."

"It's only a rare Persian antique," Burke said, with a wink, letting her know they were still cool.

"Want me to wash it for you? I just figured out how to use my washing machine."

"Little victories, Hannah-banana. Little victories."

CHAPTER 23

On the morning of Friday, August 2nd, Skyler got a text from Hannah. "Can you come upstairs? Important."

Skyler abandoned the emails he was ploughing through in the NXC office two floors below Hannah's office. He hurried upstairs, telling himself not to be ridiculous. She was ten years older than him. She was most definitely not anyone's idea of a lust object. Didn't matter. Skyler had the curse of being attracted to women for their minds.

As he threaded through the cubicle farm on the fifth floor, he noticed the heavy salting of East Asians among the propulsion specialists. Some of them might be Japanese. The majority were probably Chinese newcomers. More than a hundred CNSA-accredited personnel had descended on JSC this week, charging the rah-rah atmosphere with new tensions.

"Half of them aren't even scientists," Lance had said earlier this morning. "They're spies."

Skyler wryly reflected that the influx of Chinese made the place look more like every astrophysics department he'd ever known. And if some of them were spies, so what? So was he. He knew he wasn't supposed to be thinking like this, but it was true, wasn't it? Different government, same goal: the successful launch of the *Spirit of Humanity.*

Sorry. The *Spirit of Destiny.*

Hannah stood in her office with her arms folded.

"Uh oh," Skyler said.

"We got the results of the vacuum tests back." Hannah indicated a sheaf of printouts on her desk.

"And?"

"The engine works, it works great," Hannah said, flatly.

"But?"

"They say, and I'm quoting from the email they sent me, you're a bunch of idiots if you think this steam generator is going to do anything other than disassemble itself once in freefall. I was worried about it not working, OK? I'm not used to dealing with steam unless it's shooting out the engine bell after I've combined hydrogen with oxygen. But they think it's going to *explode!*"

While Hannah spoke, Skyler's blood turned to ice. He managed, "I thought the steam separation thing was a minor detail."

"It's a minor detail like cracks in the foam insulation on the *Columbia* were a minor detail."

"If you'd been here in those days, those astronauts would still be alive," Skyler said.

She didn't even smile. He should have known by now that flattery didn't move her. He did know it, but he was panicking.

"I've concluded that the specs I was given were not complete," she said. "I asked Inga about the company that came up with this design. Firebird Systems? She says they're not around anymore. But maybe you can track down someone who knows how they resolved the issue, if they did resolve it."

"I can try," Skyler said. He'd had a gas-station burrito for breakfast. It sat in his stomach like a lump of solid grease, making him feel nauseated.

"I just want to emphasize that this is urgent. I have people in Star City waiting on specs which I led them to believe we would have finalized by the end of the week." Hannah's fingers crushed her elbows, white-knuckled. "I'm asking myself if we picked the wrong engine design. I do not want to be asking this question."

"I'm sorry—" Skyler started.

Hannah overrode him. "Just work your magic, OK?" She shooed him out of her office.

Skyler went back downstairs and explained the situation to Lance. He hadn't even finished talking when Lance closed his laptop and stood up. "We're gonna do what we should have done to begin with."

"What are we gonna do?"

"Pay a visit to Oliver Meeks."

Half an hour later, Skyler and Lance were driving north on Route 45.

*

Guns 'N' Roses blared from the stereo. Skyler wasn't a fan. But it was Lance's car. Skyler shouted, "Any reason we shouldn't fly?"

"Don't want this going into the system," Lance shouted back.

Skyler nodded. Made sense. He gazed mindlessly at the billboards and exit signs flying past.

On the outskirts of Fort Worth, they got snarled in a weird parade. People were walking on the interstate—*walking* on the goddamn *interstate*—monopolizing two lanes and sprawling into a third, with bikers guarding them. The bikers did not look like the bearded Harley-riding species native to Texas. They rode Japanese machines and wore ripped denim. So did the walkers—the ones that weren't wearing tutus, or less. A gigantic sculpture of an eight-armed alien bobbed along in the middle of the parade.

Lance guffawed. "That's a new one for the first contact syndrome files."

Skyler rolled down his window. "Are you going to Burning Man?" he shouted.

"Yeah, man! You got a message?"

"For who?" Skyler screamed.

As the car moved on, he barely caught the answer: "For *them!*"

Big rigs zipped by on the other side of the divider, hazing the air with fumes. Skyler rolled the window up. "They're going to a festival in the Nevada desert," he said, "to send messages to the aliens with smoke signals. Or emanations of togetherness. Or something."

"Thank crap there aren't any aliens," Lance said. "I would hate to imagine their reaction." He laughed. "They've got a long way to walk."

"We have a long way to drive."

And Skyler wished it were further. He did not want to pay a visit to Oliver Meeks. Not with Lance's Sig Sauer and his own Glock subcompact lying on the back seat, covered by the ugly old Blue Devils hoodie Lance kept around for when the air-conditioning was turned too low.

"You're one in a million," Lance sang along with Axl, slapping time on the wheel. "Yes that's what you are. You're one in a million, you're a shooting sta-a-ar …"

CHAPTER 24

Jack wedged his left hiking boot into a crevice and pushed off with his right foot. He wrapped his right hand around a protrusion of red ribbed sandstone and hauled himself up. Sweat poured off his body. Little as he liked to admit it, he wasn't twenty anymore. Gone were the days when he could do 100 push-ups without getting out of breath. Which made it all the more important for him to test himself, pushing the limits of his 39-year-old muscles.

Grunting and straining, he heaved himself onto the top of the sandstone formation. He glanced down at the near-vertical rock he'd climbed, and rose to his feet. The wind licked the sweat off his face. Holding his arms out for balance, he walked along a narrow ridge. The rock dropped away steeply for a hundred feet on either side. The ridge dipped down and then rose again into a bridge—a natural arch carved by wind and erosion. On all fours, crawling like a monkey, Jack reached the top of the arch.

He sat down and gave himself a round of applause.

You had to take your victories where you could get them.

There'd been no victories for Firebird Systems lately.

Following the confiscation of their boilerplate unit, the FAA had filed charges against Firebird for violating the Atomic Energy Act. Meeks had filed a motion to have the charges dropped, but their lawyers warned that it could take months—if not years—before they were cleared of wrongdoing. Meanwhile, their test and launch facility remained off-limits as being 'material to an ongoing investigation.'

The engineering and design team had quit. Not all at once,

but in ones and twos. They were understandably terrified lest Firebird's legal troubles should taint their future careers.

Just as well their salaries no longer had to be paid.

Jack had been absolutely gobsmacked to learn how much the lawyers charged.

Firebird's investors had made clear that they would not be funneling any more money into what they now saw as a lost cause.

So there was no money coming in, nor any prospect of it, and at this rate, they'd soon run out of funds to pay the lawyers.

The process was the punishment.

Firebird Systems hadn't done anything wrong. And no doubt they'd be able to prove it eventually. The facts were on their side. But that didn't matter. The government could destroy a company—for whatever opaque reasons of its own—simply by forcing it to defend itself in court.

Meeks refused to give up. He was still working on the water engine, although there was a limit to what he could do without access to their machine shop and CAD workstations.

He'd also taken up shooting. He had gone out one day and bought a 20 gauge Mossberg tactical shotgun and an Arsenal 1911 .45 caliber handgun. He'd been practicing at the Smokin Gun Club in Mesquite.

It was fairly obvious to Jack that this new enthusiasm hadn't come out of nowhere. Meeks had gotten interested in shooting after Jack's close call at the test and launch facility. But Meeks just said he needed something to do, to kill time.

Fair enough.

What else was Jack doing out here, in the Valley of Fire

state park, but killing time, and trying to forget how shit everything was?

Not that it was working. Here he sat on top of a majestic sandstone formation, gazing at one of the most striking views in America, and instead of enjoying the peace, he was thinking dark thoughts about lawyers' hourly rates.

He shook himself out of it. The wind had dried his sweat. He slid his daypack off one shoulder and swigged some Gatorade. Then he took out his camera and framed a shot of the valley.

The setting sun behind Jack threw the shadow of the rock ridge across the valley floor. Dry gullies and patches of blooming poppies lay in twilight. The rock formations on the far side of the valley, still lit by the sun, glowed a stark red against the darkening eastern sky.

Beautiful.

Somewhere in the distance, a coyote yowled.

The lonesome sound amplified the silence of the desert.

Jack spotted his own tiny shadow on the valley floor. He stuck up a victory sign and photographed the shadow. He had to admit that the superzoom of his new Nikon Coolpix lived up to the name.

Couldn't tell if the shadow had his hand facing out or in.

Either way worked.

Jack chuckled to himself and stowed his camera. His fingers brushed cool wooden beads in the bottom of his daypack.

His mother had sent him a rosary.

Since the first contact event, she and his father had rediscovered their Catholic faith. She wrote that his father—a lapsed Catholic in the mould of so many Irish emigrants—had begun going to Mass every morning. *Every* morning.

Jack looked at his watch. As a matter of fact, his father must be kneeling at Our Lady of the Angels right this moment, a continent and an ocean away.

Sentimentally missing his parents, he started to lift the rosary out of his daypack—

—and his phone rang, destroying the silence.

Was there any wilderness spot in America where you couldn't get a signal these days?

Unknown number. Jack picked up, for the hell of it.

"Hey, Jack! *Privjet!*"

Jack nearly fell off the rock in surprise. "Alexei?"

"How are you doing, you lazy bastard?"

"Oh, racing fast cars, dating strippers, the usual," Jack said, grinning. Although he had avoided getting in touch with his old friend Alexei, as he didn't want to be a downer, he was delighted to hear from him now. "What do you think, then? We're living in the world of Star Trek."

"Star Trek is American," Alexei said. "You should watch some Russian sci-fi sometime. Everybody dies. Anyway, where do you think I am now?"

"I have absolutely no idea."

"I am in Star City for training."

"Did you fail your fitness exam? You've got to lay off the vodka, Alexei."

"Yes, giving up vodka will be hard. I'm going on the *Spirit of Humanity!* You are talking to one of the two cosmonauts selected for the mission."

Jack let the phone fall away from his ear. Eyes squeezed shut, he silently shouted: *Fuck! Oh bloody HELL …*

The unfairness of fate took his breath away.

But his natural generosity overcame his piqued reaction. He brought the phone back to his ear. "That's bloody brilliant, Alexei! Congratulations."

"I hope to get on board before they notice their mistake," Alexei cackled. He was plainly thrilled to bits.

"No mistake, mate. You're the best they've got. What role will you be taking?"

"Co-pilot, EVA specialist, and of course my favourite, hydroponics. On the *Spirit of Humanity,* everyone must have two jobs. Or three."

Alexei had mis-named the ship twice now. "Spirit of *Destiny,* mate," Jack said, sniggering. He couldn't say it without cracking up. "Spirit of *Destiny.*"

"Oh, yeah. You know, that sounds very stupid in Russian."

"It sounds worse in English. I should say, British. *SoD.*"

Alexei laughed, although Jack suspected he didn't get it. Alexei only bothered to learn English slang if it was really dirty. *Sod* was an old epithet, born of a homophobic past and not heard so much anymore, though it still sounded vile to Jack. "To be precise, *Spirit of Humanity* sounds stupid in Russian, too," Alexei said. "But the ship itself, Jack, the ship will be a thing of beauty. The first real spaceship we have ever built!"

"They're being very secretive about it, aren't they? Are you allowed to share any of the specs?"

"Of course, it's not classified," Alexei said blithely. "First of all, the propulsion system will use our new reactor design. So you can imagine how happy the *siloviki* are about that. The engine is from NASA. That's also new. It will use water for the reaction mass!"

Jack froze. "Water?"

"Yes, NASA is copying the aliens!"

Oh no, they're not.

Jack's pulse raced.

They're copying *us!*

Concealing his consternation, he asked Alexei for as many details of the new drive as he could reveal. He hung up at last with good wishes for the intensive training Alexei was about to undergo. He immediately dialed Meeks.

"Leave a message."

"Ollie, I've just learned something rather startling. We've got to discuss this ASAP. I'm on my way back now."

Jack shoved his phone into the side pocket of his daypack. He began to climb down.

It was harder on the way down. That's what Inga always used to say, and she was right.

Jack tended to be defensive of his new hobby, because he knew that it looked wet, as if he'd taken up Inga's favorite pastime as a substitute for Inga herself. That really wasn't it at all. He'd started hiking in the desert because he had the 4WD, and time on his hands.

He reached the top of the ridge, dropped to his haunches, and slid his right foot down the near-vertical rock face he had to descend.

He did think about Inga often when he was out here, but he didn't miss her. They had never been perfectly suited—he'd fancied her like mad, of course, but she was too pragmatic and humorless. He could practically hear her saying now, "It is absurd to go climbing alone."

Well, yes, Inga. It is absurd. Perhaps that's why I do it.

"When you attempt a steep face, you should always rope on."

I can't be arsed with ropes, Inga. Takes all the fun out of it. I always wanted to spacewalk without a tether, too. See what it felt like.

"Bouldering is actually more dangerous than climbing. You can get hurt very badly."

Jack glanced down between his feet. The encroaching shadow bled the color from the sandstone. The distance back to the slope didn't look short, and his arms trembled with tiredness. He'd rested too long, talking to Alexei.

He let go with his left hand and reached down with his left foot, probing for that nice deep crevice he'd used on the way up. The dusk hid the horizontal ribs in the sandstone.

"Anyway, it is important to have the right equipment," Inga said smugly, lacing up the La Sportivas she would wear for an afternoon of bouldering with the local club.

Jack found the crevice. He let his weight down onto his left foot.

His chunky hiking boot slipped.

His body scraped down the rock face, driving his breath out in a shout of fear.

His entire bodyweight hung from his right fingertips. He scrabbled with his left hand and both feet, desperately seeking a hold.

Burning, aching, his fingers gave way. He slid down the rock face with a scream.

CHAPTER 25

As they drove the last miles towards Bunkerville, NV, Lance honked and shot the middle finger at any driver unfortunate enough to wind up ahead of him. Skyler thought about pointing out that he was drawing unnecessary attention, but decided against it. Lance was in a foul temper. Understandably so. Their journey had taken a solid 36 hours—twice as long as they had planned on. For miles around Dallas, and then again outside Albuquerque, they'd crawled along in stop-and-go traffic.

Those parades.

Parades was the wrong word, Skyler had decided. *Movements* better described the crowds of people walking along the highways of the Southwest. Skyler had talked to more of the walkers while traffic was stalled—they were friendly. (Or maybe just stoned.) Many were on their way to Burning Man.

Black Rock City was going to be a megalopolis this year.

Others didn't seem to know where they were going. "Out west," or "To the mountains."

Skyler said to Lance, "I believe what we are seeing here is the spontaneous beginning of a Great American Bug-Out."

A movement, or many movements, planned by no one, coordinated via social media, driven by amorphous hopes and fears.

"If they get up in the mountains," Lance said, "they're gonna die."

"It's amazing how peaceful the whole thing is," Skyler pondered.

The police had clearly thrown in the towel, faced with the

impossible task of removing tens of thousands of people from the freeways. A few patrol cars spun their lights, diverting the movement off Route 40 into central Albuquerque. Like that was going to improve the traffic situation. The walkers blew kisses at the cops, tossed paper airplanes.

"They won't be peaceful for long when they run out of weed and Mountain Dew," Lance said.

And a while later: "Don't any of these people have jobs? Homes to go to? Don't answer that."

The masses had come unmoored long before this, Skyler thought. They were ready now to drift up into the sky.

How was this going to end? He shared Lance's fear that it would end badly.

ENTERING BUNKERVILLE.

Lance clicked the car stereo off, jerking Skyler back from his melancholy musings into an even less inspiring present.

"Can you reach in the back seat and get my piece?" Lance said.

Skyler did as he was asked. Lance laid the gun between his thighs. He turned off into a residential neighborhood. The headlights flashed on trees shading empty sidewalks.

"This kind of burg is dead after eight o'clock," Lance said. "Reminds me of my hometown. Except without the clunkers up on blocks."

The houses stood on full acre lots, with green watered lawns signalling affluence.

"How are we gonna play this?" Skyler said. He was so scared his voice came out croaky. He despised himself for it.

"First we case the place." Lance slowed down. He nodded to their left. "That's it. OK, the lights are on, but there's no vehicle in the driveway. Meeks is home alone. Perfect." He drove on, circling the block. "Meeks shares the house with the test pilot who used to work for Firebird."

"Kildare. I met him at Vegas airport," Skyler said. He couldn't forget Kildare's fury when they confiscated the boilerplate unit. It had been a pleasure to humiliate the arrogant Brit. But as night follows day, Skyler's triumph had turned to shame. He did *not* want to confront Kildare again. "So he's not here? How do you figure?"

"He drives a Toyota truck, parks it in the driveway. Meeks parks his car in the garage, but he needs the other garage space free so there's room for him to get out."

"That's right, he's in a wheelchair."

"Yeah."

They came around the block. Lance backed into Meeks's driveway and parked with the nose of his Escalade facing out. Before they started their journey he had changed the license plates for fake ones, of which they had an official NXC-issued stash.

Too late, Skyler said, "Shouldn't we wait until he's asleep?"

"Dude. No. We need to *talk* to him."

Lance slotted his Sig Sauer into his special holster. The suppressor fitted through the hole in the bottom of the holster, poking down alongside his leg. Skyler wedged his Glock into the waistband of his jeans. He pulled his t-shirt over it, as if to hide what he'd become. As if there was any hope of that, when he was with Lance.

Lance rang the front doorbell, bold as brass.

A chain rattled. The door swung back.

A man in a wheelchair wheeled around the door one-handed, holding the door open with his other hand, and stared narrowly up at them. Stubble shadowed his bony jaw. A tartan blanket covered his lap.

"FBI," Lance said, holding up his badge with his thumb over the NXC logo. "We would just like to discuss a couple of things with you, Mr. Meeks. OK if we come in?"

The man stared at Lance's Sig Sauer. He raised his gaze to Lance's face. Then he looked at Skyler. Recognition flashed. "Last time we met, you were pretending to be an FAA agent."

Lance let out an easy laugh, sliding into his good ol' boy persona. "You got a good memory, Mr. Meeks. In fact, that whole sorry mess is what we're here to discuss with you today. So can we come in, or we gotta do this on the doorstep, like Jehovah's Witnesses?"

"I suppose you can come in."

They followed the wheelchair down the broad, ranch-style hall. Lance nudged Skyler in the ribs and grinned.

*

Jack slid down the rock face like a cat that couldn't climb the curtains. He desperately tried to grab any protruding ledge to break his slide, but he was moving too fast.

A gentle, firm push in the small of his back arrested his slide for a microsecond.

His fingers locked on a horizontal rib. He dug in his fingernails. His grip held.

He hung by two fingers of his left hand, scraping his toes over the rock in search of purchase.

His right foot found a ledge. It was barely two inches wide. Just enough for him to put his weight on his toes.

He balanced there, his body flattened against the rock

face, his breath coming in harsh pants.

"OK. Easy now," he muttered. "Easy, easy."

He descended another few meters, testing every handhold and toehold before he moved. Then he jumped the last bit.

He landed on the sandy slope at the bottom of the rock face and rolled. He lay on his back, panting, looking up at the sky. It was nearly dark now. Stars peeked out in the east.

He was lying on his daypack. It dug into the small of his back.

He sat up, only now realizing that his fingers hurt like hell. He couldn't see the damage in the dusk, but he could feel the stickiness of blood. He took off his daypack and reached inside with his right hand—he'd brought a towel to use as a sweat-rag.

His fingers brushed his mother's rosary.

Abruptly, he remembered the push that had seemed to break his fall for a split second.

He froze, scarcely breathing—and then swore impatiently at himself. Don't be absurd, Jack. Your daypack bumped against your back. Or you imagined it. Anyway, what matters is that you didn't fall and break your goddamn idiot neck.

He stood up, shaking with exertion and shock, and stumbled down the slope. He had brought a torch, which was just as well, for it was pitch dark by the time he reached the Toyota. He checked under the car for rattlesnakes. All clear.

He got in and sat without moving for a moment, resting his forehead on the steering wheel. Then he started the engine.

CHAPTER 26

"It's like this," Lance said. They stood in Meeks's kitchen. Meeks sat in his wheelchair with his hands loosely folded on his lap. He struck Skyler as amazingly self-contained. He'd said hardly a word since he let them in. A laptop, a desktop, and piles of printed documents cluttered the kitchen table. Skyler had not managed to get a glimpse of the screens before they went to a screensaver of a green forested valley. "We need your technology, Mr. Meeks." Lance leaned against the kitchen counter and waited.

A smirk flickered across Meeks's lips. "Honestly, you're going to have to do better than that. You can't simply walk in, ask for something, and get it."

"I understand your position," Lance said. "That is why we're prepared to make you an offer. Understand that this is very unusual. It's only possible under these unique circumstances in which we find ourselves."

Lance's words evoked the alien spacecraft silently orbiting Europa. It was 600 million kilometers away and yet Skyler suddenly felt the oppressive sensation, which he'd had before, that the alien craft was close, *close,* right over their heads.

"Go on," Meeks said.

"We will ensure the FAA drops all charges against Firebird Systems. I'm aware your company has suffered as a result of this legal mess …"

"Yes, it has."

"That can all go away. Tomorrow. You can be back in your facility tomorrow. You'll be able to resume doing business."

"And in return?"

"Everything you have on the magnetoplasmadynamic drive," Lance said. "We need it."

They had to ask for everything. They couldn't just ask for more detail on the steam generator, or Meeks would know that the *Spirit of Destiny* project was illegally using his technology already.

Meeks laughed. "I'm sorry. You have to be joking. You want everything I've got, in exchange for fixing a mess that *you* caused in the first place?"

Lance reddened. Skyler knew how difficult this was for him. He hated being in the position of humbly asking for cooperation. "Take it or leave it, sir."

"If that's your final offer, I'm sorry, the answer is no."

Lance shifted his posture, pushing off from the counter. Skyler quickly spoke up. "It's for the *Spirit of Destiny* project, as I'm sure you've guessed, Mr. Meeks. You must be aware of how crucial this is to the future of humankind. Please don't let these petty legal considerations get in the way. Think of it—your technology could help to enable the success of the project …" He was thinking of Hannah, her strained face, her white knuckles. *Work your magic, Skyler.*

He was trying, but it wasn't working. Meeks shook his head, his lips tightening in anger. He took a minute, as if to compose himself, before speaking. "Petty legal considerations? You've maliciously destroyed my company. That's a petty legal consideration?"

Lance said, "I am saying we can fix that! You want money? We'll give you money."

Meeks wheeled across the kitchen and stopped right in front of Lance. He waited until Lance met his gaze. Then he pointed up. “Do you realize they’re watching us?”

Confusion chased across Lance’s face, followed by scorn. “The aliens? There are no aliens. Leastways, not live ones.”

“You have no way of knowing that. No. Shut up. You have no way of knowing that. You’ve promulgated this comforting lie so that people on Earth won’t go off their heads …”

“It isn’t a lie!” Skyler interjected. “It’s based on observations, so I’d advise you not to spread fear.”

“Apparently you believe your own hype. That is a very dangerous condition. If that belief is shared by everyone working on the project, there’s cause for fear indeed. But don’t worry; I’m not going to go on television talking about our visitors. There are enough people wanking on about that without the slightest factual basis, anyway.” Meeks shifted gears. He steepled his fingers and spoke in a measured, emphatic tone. “If they are there, they’re watching our television broadcasts. They’re listening to our radio programs. What sort of an impression do you think they’ve formed of us as a species? Is it any wonder they shot Juno down?”

Lance said. “You’re full of crap.”

Meeks’s eyes danced, mocking his witless response. “I take it you’re not a great believer in the importance of first impressions.”

“If you’re right,” Lance said, “which you’re not, but just for the sake of argument, that’s all the more reason we have to get out there. And so to get back to the point, we need your technology.”

“No, that isn’t actually the point. The point is that Earth is in danger.” Meeks spoke with building intensity. “Why do you think we have never detected any signs of alien life before this?"

"Because space is big," Lance said.

"That's not actually a scientifically sound answer. The likeliest explanation is because broadcasting your cultural vomit into outer space is extremely fucking dangerous."

Skyler's scalp crawled. Again he seemed to sense the alien spacecraft overhead, a dizzying sensation, as if the air pressure were dropping.

"I assume you're aware of the Big Filter," Meeks went on relentlessly. "It's the theory, one of the possible explanations of the Fermi Paradox, that some obstacle prevents sapient species from gaining interstellar status. Some say it's already behind us. The emergence of prokaryotes, for example, is a candidate for the Big Filter. Others say the Big Filter is ahead of us: like all other civilizations, we'll destroy ourselves with apocalyptic weapons before we can reach the stars." Meeks waved a hand as if to deflect such a risible idea. "I think the evidence now argues otherwise. We're heading into the Big Filter *right now.* It is here. Orbiting Europa."

Skyler had heard this theory before, but never put quite so persuasively. He said, "You think the alien spacecraft is here to destroy us."

Meeks nodded. "Mm-hm."

Lance said, "That's fucking stupid. It's a wreck."

"Have you never heard of playing dead?" Meeks sighed loudly. He rolled away to the far side of the table and touched a mouse. The desktop monitor sprang back to life. The screensaver photo must have been taken from a lookout point above all that greenness. A sign said *Rhondda Cynon Taf.* Meeks clicked it away and began to type, pointedly ignoring Lance and Skyler.

"If you think Earth's in danger," Skyler said, "why won't you help?" His voice sounded too loud.

"Oh," Meeks said. "That's actually got nothing to do with the other. I believe in doing business ethically, you see." He looked up. "You lot come barging in here with guns, and expect me to roll over and sign on the dotted line. You're worse than the bloody KGB! Sorry, I'm not surrendering to that."

Skyler spoke before Lance could explode in rage. "We tried to do this your way, Mr. Meeks. We made an extremely good offer for your company, which your investors were happy to accept, but you rejected it."

"Yes, you mentioned that before. Glad I didn't fall for it."

"Two hundred million dollars," Lance gritted.

"That's significantly less than you offered last year."

"Your options have narrowed, if you've noticed," Lance said. Suddenly, he seemed relaxed. Skyler knew why. Lance had had to go through the motions of offering Meeks options, but Meeks's obstinacy had relieved him of the burden of taking that any further. All three of them were now being funneled towards the only option that remained.

Meeks reached down to the side of his wheelchair and released a brake lever. Sitting upright, he said, "If NASA wants to discuss a collaboration, I'd welcome the opportunity to speak with them. That's really all I have to say on the subject. The door's that way."

"Mr. Meeks," Lance said.

Meeks spun his wheelchair and rolled to the far side of the kitchen, where there was a connecting door leading to the garage.

"OK," Lance said. "Guess this discussion is over." He said to Skyler, "Grab the computers. Just unplug everything." He drew his Sig Sauer.

Meeks turned his wheelchair 180° with an economical push on one wheel. The tartan blanket over his knees fluttered to the floor. He aimed a large-caliber pistol at Lance.

Skyler dived sideways.

Meeks fired his gun. Skyler knew it was Meeks because it made a noise fit to wake the dead.

Skyler crawled under the table.

Another gunshot roared out.

A window shattered.

Skyler could hear a thin and tinny keening tone in the distance, but couldn't hear anything else. Maybe he'd gone deaf. He popped his head up to see what the fuck Lance was doing, at the same time as Lance levelled his Sig Sauer. Blood ran down Lance's face, a terrifying shade of red.

Meeks fell backwards. For a second Skyler thought Lance had got him. That wasn't it at all. The damn wheelchair had gone over backwards! Meeks had popped the wheelchair all the way over with a single large shove as he'd leaned backwards, leaving his legs flailing at the ceiling. He rolled off the wheelchair, his legs landing awkwardly on the floor. He dragged himself under the table, the pistol clattering against the marble-look tiles, and shouted at Skyler to run. Save yourself. Run. It was good advice, but Skyler couldn't take it. Fear held him in place, flat on the floor. Meeks supported himself on one elbow and fired at Lance's legs.

"Creeping cheetos," Lance screamed, seemingly far in the distance.

Skyler hurled himself out from under the table. The

computers, he had to save the computers!

Both Meeks and Lance were firing wildly.

A bullet pulverized the green Rhondda valley screensaver on Meeks's desktop, shattering it into a psychedelic pattern of smashed LCD.

Coffee dripped onto the floor from a shattered carafe.

Blood pooled, spreading like water from a faucet that ran red.

*

Skyler drove.

Lance slumped in the passenger seat, holding his wadded-up Blue Devils hoodie to his head.

Meeks's first bullet had scored a crease along the right side of his scalp. It had bled heavily.

Lance had no other injuries.

Meeks wasn't that great of a shooter. An amateur.

A couple of miles out of Bunkerville, several police cars screamed past them, going the other way.

"Points off for poor response time," Lance said. "To be fair, the Mesquite PD probably got there already. These guys would be coming from the tribal police department in Moapa."

Bunkerville itself did not have a police department. They'd known that going in.

Skyler sped up to 90 mph. He wanted to put the whole country between them and Bunkerville. The headlights swept over endless, unchanging desert scrub.

After a little while, Lance started to talk about how it was all Meeks's fault. He said that Meeks was probably working with the Chinese.

Skyler responded with monosyllables. He now realized

that he hated and despised Lance. Maybe even more than he hated and despised himself. It was a toss-up.

When he'd talked his crackpot theory into the ground, Lance called Director Flaherty. They had a 24/7 number for the director of the NXC that was only to be used in emergencies. Lance explained what had happened. He yes-sired and uh-huhed. He was a completely different person on the phone with Flaherty.

"Yes, sir," he said. "Yes, we searched the whole house. We've got everything. Desktop, two laptops, one iPad, and his phone."

It was all in the trunk of the Escalade now, rattling around. The desktop's monitor had been shattered and they'd left it behind, but the hard drive in the main case should be salvageable. Hannah would have the data she needed.

Lance hung up the phone. Wincing, he leaned forward and got a bottle of extra-strength Tylenol out of the glove compartment. He dry-swallowed several capsules.

"Flaherty's got our backs," he said.

"You sure?"

"Yeah. If there's an investigation, he'll make it go away."

"What if they find our fingerprints?"

"You mean what if they find *your* fingerprints?"

"Fuck you," Skyler said. He remembered the last thing that had happened at Meeks's house. He remembered Meeks's face. He wanted to un-remember it, to make it go away.

"You're such a wimp, Sky," Lance said. "Don't *worry.*"

Skyler was silent. He knew he'd be worrying for the rest of his life, or at least as long as Lance remained above ground.

"Shit, I might even get promoted back to Langley for this. I hope not. Having way too much fun right here." Lance laughed, bitterly. "Cheese and rice. That was a fucking *disaster!*"

Having secured Director Flaherty's support, Lance was now free to chew Skyler's ass off for screwing up their play. He called Skyler a fucking retard, a bump on a log, a five-legged dog, and other choice expressions. Eventually—Skyler had known this was coming—he cooled down and apologized.

Skyler apologized, too, for having failed to so much as draw his gun.

"You're not cut out to be a shooter," Lance said, excusing him. Skyler nodded—it was true. After that, there was silence in the car.

They reached the outskirts of Vegas. Neon defiled the night.

"Keep driving," Lance said.

Skyler kept driving. Lance fell asleep. By the time they reached Phoenix, Skyler was smoking cigarettes to stay awake, using an empty Coke can as an ashtray.

He thought about what Meeks had said about the Big Filter.

Maybe Meeks was right. Maybe the aliens had come here to destroy all life on Earth.

If so, that put things into perspective, didn't it? What was one man's death, next to that?

Shame it hadn't been *Lance's* death, that's all.

CHAPTER 27

Jack turned into their street and slowed down sharply.

Blue light splashed across the lawns and sidewalks.

Police cars blocked the driveway of Meeks's house.

More police cars were parked on the lawn.

I just mowed that, Jack thought absurdly, struggling to process the scene.

An ambulance stood at the curb, back doors open. Paramedics loitered on the sidewalk, smoking cigarettes.

A uniformed officer waved at Jack, indicating he should carry on.

Jack stopped the Toyota in the middle of the street and jumped out. "What the hell is going on?"

"There's been an incident, sir. You can't park in the street."

"I live here."

Jack brushed past the officer and ran up the driveway. More officers intercepted him at the front door. "Sir, you cannot enter this residence. There's been an incident."

"Just tell me what's going on!"

They wouldn't tell him anything. He shouldered through them, panic fueling his strength. He lunged down the hall and skidded into the kitchen, where he expected to find Meeks.

Meeks was there, all right.

On the floor.

Supine.

Staring with open eyes at the ceiling.

His 1911 lay beside his outflung right hand.

Jack dropped to his knees. He slapped Meeks's cheek.

A little bit of dark blood trickled out of Meeks's mouth.

Meeks's head rolled sideways, and Jack saw the exit wound gaping behind his right ear.

Hands fastened on Jack's shoulders, hauling him away.

Gravity rolled Meeks's head back to its original position.

Meeks wasn't staring at the ceiling, Jack realized. He was looking far, far, farther away. Those dead eyes stared eternally at the stars. At *Europa.*

Jack distantly took in the other people in the kitchen—crime scene technicians in masks and paper overshoes—and the broken windows, glass on the floor, bullet-holes in the kitchen cupboards, Meeks's wheelchair lying on its back.

He sat on the three-piece living-room suite that they never used. An officer who smelt of perspiration and Listerine took his details. Jack mindlessly gave his name and address. He had to fish out his phone to provide contact information for Meeks's parents in Wales—he'd only met them a few times. Meeks had not been close to them.

"And what is your relationship to the deceased?"

"We were friends," Jack said.

"Were you visiting him from the UK?" the officer said, picking up on Jack's accent.

"No. I live here. I'm an American citizen."

Another policeman came in. He was severely overweight, and wore a suit instead of a uniform. His dress shirt gaped at the collar. He sat down across from Jack. "Did you observe that Mr. Meeks was depressed recently?" he said.

Jack's head jerked up. "You can't be implying he offed himself."

"Please answer the question. Did Mr. Meeks exhibit any

unusual behaviors, or did you have other reasons to be concerned about his state of mind?"

"Ollie did *not* commit suicide."

"A little over a month ago, he purchased two guns. Never owned a gun before."

"Home defense."

"It appears that his company was in trouble. He was on the edge of bankruptcy."

"Where did you hear that?"

"It's unfortunately not uncommon for people to end their lives when they are facing financial ruin."

Jack clenched his fists on his knees. Needles of pain stabbed through the first three fingers on his left hand. He scarcely felt it. "You can't have missed the state of the kitchen! The windows are blown out, there are bullet holes in the walls!" Another detail of the scene etched in his mind sprang out. "The computers are gone! There were two computers on the kitchen table."

The detective's gaze slipped away. He stared at the wall behind Jack. It was a thousand-yard stare, not entirely dissimilar to the look in Meeks's dead eyes. "The diameter of the entry and exit wounds is consistent with a .45 caliber bullet," he said.

"Then someone else shot him with a .45." Saying it out loud, Jack believed it. He remembered another clinching detail. "The exit wound was on the right side of his head. He was right-handed. If he'd shot himself it would have been on the left side."

The detective stood up. He gestured for Jack to stand up, too. "I understand this is very difficult to deal with, Mr. Kildare." The detective sounded like a robot. "It's a shame you had to see him like that."

"I was in Iraq," Jack said.

"Kidding? Me, too." The detective didn't smile. But his mask slipped for a moment. He shook Jack's hand. "I'm sorry." The words seemed to carry a deeper meaning than the obvious one. "I am genuinely goddamn sorry about this."

Jack nodded wordlessly.

The detective looked at Jack's left hand. Dried blood caked his fingertips. "What happened there?"

"Climbing accident. I was stupid." Two fingernails had been torn off halfway down their beds.

"Do you want medical attention?"

"Thanks. I'm fine."

"Probably wise," the detective said. Afterwards, Jack would replay the words, making sure he hadn't misheard them. "We would have to put you in the system, and you do not want that." The detective cleared his throat. "I'm afraid you will not be able to stay here tonight. There's a motel in Mesquite. An officer will escort you if you want to pack up any of your belongings."

Jack drove out on the road to Mesquite, like he had told the police he would. A mile out of town, he U-turned and drove back through Bunkerville. He blasted down the highway towards Las Vegas.

Sleep?

You've got to be fucking joking.

Now that the reality of Meeks's death had sunk in, rage and grief burned through his system like the ephedrine he used to take before missions in Iraq. This required action. *Immediate* action.

Unfortunately, the vast spaces of America intruded onto his reality. After the day he'd had, adrenaline could only carry him so far. He checked into a roadside inn near Flagstaff, Arizona, and slept like the dead. When he awoke, he lay in bed for a moment, staring at the pattern of lucky horseshoes on the curtains, asking himself if he really wanted to do this.

Answer: Yes. He did.

He got up and went downstairs to the breakfast buffet. The room was full of young people in weird costumes, congregating around the grill station like hummingbirds around a feeder. Jack distinctly smelled marijuana. He leerily eyed the off-beat crowd while he ate.

Back on the road, he slid an Eminem CD into the Toyota's stereo and gunned it in the fast lane.

The fast lane didn't stay fast for long. Traffic conditions were horrible. By the time Jack reached Houston, Meeks had been dead for almost two days.

It felt dreamlike to revisit his old stomping grounds around Johnson Space Center under these circumstances. Scratch that. It felt like a nightmare, the kind you can't wake up from even if you fight it.

Cruising past JSC, he saw that every window in Building 13 was lit up. The NASA administrative personnel used to be nine-to-fivers. Clearly those days were past.

Jack knew he ought to wait for tomorrow morning, but the need for *immediate action* returned powerfully. He couldn't face another night of darkness and doubts.

He circled around, passing by a vast building site where construction work continued under floodlights. That used to be the park where Jack and his fellow astronauts would eat lunch on rare days when the Houston weather was neither wet nor sweltering.

It was sweltering now, even hours after sunset. Jack lowered his window as he rolled towards the new, military-style security checkpoint.

"ID, please."

Jack held up an old NASA visitor pass in a plastic cover.

"Thank you very much, sir."

Jack smiled to himself as he got out of the car to walk through the newly installed body scanner. He'd had to turn his old NASA ID in when he was fired four years ago. But he'd happened to have this one—issued on a day when he'd forgotten his own ID. He'd kept it as a souvenir. Evidently it still passed inspection.

Mentally rehearsing his next actions, he drove on towards the parking lot for Building 4 South, where he used to work.

When he realized his mistake, he circled around, parked outside Building 13, and repeated the ID rigmarole at the security desk.

Could feel the energy in the air as soon as he stepped into the building.

A background hum of voices, laughter, *work*.

Longing tugged at his heart.

God, to be back here again—

No.

Fuck NASA.

He pressed the button to call the lift. He didn't know exactly where to go, but the top floor seemed a good bet.

The lift doors opened and out stepped Inga Pitzke.

Jack jumped. Inga went pink. *"Warum?"* she said, reverting to her native German in astonishment.

"Where can I find the director of the *Spirit of Destiny* project?" was what came out of Jack's mouth, while the gears of his brain whirred furiously.

"Seventh floor," Inga said. She was carrying a laptop bag and her handbag, obviously on her way home. Her V-necked t-shirt outlined the undercurves of her breasts. That Valkyrie hair lay over her shoulder in a thick braid that Jack itched to undo.

"Thanks," he said. As the lift doors closed, he added, "We should have a drink sometime, catch up," and was rewarded by a look of horror on her face.

People eddied in the seventh-floor hallway, talking in bright, absorbed tones. The energy in this place was something else. Jack walked through them, past an unoccupied secretary's desk, and into the office of Richard Burke, the leader of the five-country, 2,300-person team designing the *Spirit of Destiny*.

Burke glanced up from his computer. "What is it?" he said, revealing no impatience with an unannounced visitor. He frowned slightly, as if he thought he should recognize Jack but couldn't place him.

Jack sat down in the visitor chair at the side of Burke's desk. He let his legs sprawl across the carpet. He really was exhausted from driving … from everything. "It's regarding a little matter of murder," he said.

Burke spun his chair to face Jack. He crossed his legs and laced his hands on his knee. His face displayed concern. Confusion. "I'm not sure if we've met."

"Yes," Jack said. "Back in 2009. At the Orbiter Processing Facility 2. You were supervising a payload loading. I was about to fly on the last Hubble servicing mission …"

Recognition flooded Burke's eyes. "Jack Kildare! What a surprise!" Under other circumstances Jack would have been hard put not to laugh, seeing Burke remember him—and then remember that Jack had the rare distinction of being an astronaut who'd gotten fired. "I'm sorry," Burke said. "How did you get in here?"

"The security always was quite crap. Evidently it still is," Jack said with a shrug.

"I hate to say this, Jack, but you'll have to leave." Burke sighed. "If you'd like to schedule a meeting—"

"No! I would not like to schedule a fucking meeting! I would like to discuss the murder of Oliver Meeks!"

Burke physically flinched from Jack's shout. Jack knew intuitively in that instant that Burke was innocent. He knew nothing about Meeks's death. He probably didn't even know who Meeks *was*.

The door of the office opened. Jack lurched to his feet, ready to physically resist eviction, no matter how pointless he knew that would be.

Instead of security guards, a skinny young man came in. He wore jeans and a t-shirt. Tevas. Peace symbol on a thong around his neck. He reminded Jack of the weirdos at the breakfast buffet in Flagstaff. Through the red haze of his anger, Jack initially thought he was looking at an IT guy with bad timing.

Then he recognized the bogus FAA official who'd confiscated their boilerplate unit at McCarran Airport.

Every fiber of his body yearned to take a swing at the guy's face.

CHAPTER 28

In a different universe, a better one, Jack pummelled the twerpy little guy into the floor.

In this universe, there were abundant good reasons not to do that. Granted, Jack rarely did anything in his life for what most people considered good reasons. But rather than the fear of consequences, curiosity restrained him.

The guy stared at him.

Jack stared back, pulse thudding.

The guy moved unconsciously into a defensive posture, holding his forearms. Covering the pale pink scars left by Jack's butcher knife.

He doesn't know that was you, Jack reminded himself. Play it cool. Play it *cool,* damn it.

Burke said, "Skyler, this isn't a great time."

Skyler. What had possessed his parents? Jack had to admit the name suited the little twerp.

"It's *important,*" Skyler said to Burke, with a meaningful glance at Jack.

To Jack's surprise, Burke pivoted obediently. "Jack, give us a minute. You can wait in my secretary's office. Don't steal the office supplies."

Manager jokes.

Jack collapsed on a chair against the wall of the secretary's office.

He stared at a *Spirit of Destiny* poster on the opposite wall.

God, that dove logo was epically awful.

As the brain-fuddling buzz of anger faded, he asked himself again what he was doing here. He had driven twelve hundred miles over two days, chasing a vision of justice for

Meeks. But the vision had soured. Turned into a nightmare.

Vividly, his mind coughed up the memory of the wrecked kitchen. Meeks's wheelchair lying on its back.

A fresh wave of loss crashed over him.

The best part of him had died with Meeks, he thought. If he was the kind of man who cried, he'd have wept then. He wasn't, but he mashed his hands against his face. He hadn't just lost a friend, he'd lost a job, a dream, a future. All that remained was this lousy, destructive impulse to lash out at those who'd done it.

He lowered his hands, blinking rapidly, and stared at the dove logo. The closed door muffled Burke and Skyler's voices.

The outer door opened. An angular, middle-aged woman with cropped blonde hair looked in. Her eyes widened. "Kildare!"

It was Katharine Menelaou, who'd been station captain on the ISS when Jack was there. The last time they'd seen each other was in orbit. Unlike Burke, she was clearly one of those who never forgot a face.

Jack leapt to his feet, flustered.

Menelaou came in, smiling. "I think I'd be less surprised to see the Dalai Lama waiting outside Burke's office. How the hell are you, Killer?"

Her nickname for him.

She carried a stack of folders. She shifted them to her left elbow and they shook hands.

Jack had never warmed to Menelaou when they were on the ISS. He'd felt that she was too high-handed, and casually fomented tensions among the crew. But seeing her now took him back to a better time. As when Alexei had rung him, he responded with unfeigned pleasure. "Kate, it's been a while. I hear congratulations are in order?"

Menelaou's appointment as commander of the *Spirit of Destiny* had made the news last week. That one had come as no surprise to Jack, given that it was inevitable the mission should have an American commander. Menelaou was an active astronaut with command experience, past child-bearing, unattached, with no family history of cancer—important, this—going back three generations.

"'A victory for all women,'" Jack mischievously quoted the headline that had been repeated throughout the media, with minor variations. "What does it feel like to be a trail-blazer, Ms. Menelaou?" He held out an imaginary microphone.

"I told them it feels like volunteering to go to jail for five years," she joked. "Except with worse food." She swatted away his invisible microphone. "And let's not discuss the company." She glanced at the closed door of Burke's office. "Actually, that's what … *aha.*" She measured him with a gaze. "At least you've stayed in shape, I see."

"Just ignore the gray hairs," Jack said, wondering what she was on about.

Menelaou tapped her stack of folders straight with the flat of her hand. "Is he in there with someone? I've got an appointment with him at nine."

The top folder was labelled IVANOV.

Those folders represented *Spirit of Destiny* crew members. There were seven of them.

Belatedly, Jack realized she'd asked him a question. "Er, yes, he's in there with a bloke called Skyler."

"Oh God. *Him.*" Menelaou saw Jack's doubtful expression. "You haven't been around here for a while. Skyler Taft is one of our so-called Feds. Basically, they're spooks. They prowl around making sure we're not stealing classified information, not that it would make any difference now that the place is infested with Chinese nationals. I'm going to be saddled with two of them on my crew, as well. Look here. Xiang … Qiu … how do you even pronounce that?" Menelaou sighed and shook her head. "Hell with this. I'm not standing here waiting for him. If they ever get through, tell Burke to call me on my cell. Oh, and good luck!" she added, as she left.

Jack paced between the closed doors. A security camera above the outer door swivelled, as if clumsily tracking him.

Instinct told him to leg it before he got arrested.

But at the thought of jail, he once more remembered the police detective in Bunkerville. That man, an Army veteran, gone to fat, making a good fist of a bad job, had told Jack as clearly as he could, without putting it into words, that the fix was in. Meeks had been murdered. And *someone* wanted it covered up.

Jack gritted his teeth, clenched his good fist. He was working himself up into a right royal rage again when the inner door opened and Burke waved him back into his office.

Burke's mouth smiled. His eyes were worried. "All right, Jack, sorry about that. We've discussed the situation, and …" Abruptly, the experienced manager seemed to run out of words. "I'll let Skyler explain it to you," he said, and left.

So now it was Jack and Skyler alone in the seventh-floor office with a view of the world's biggest construction site.

Skyler appeared to have the situation in hand. Standing,

he faced Jack across the big desk as if *he* were the manager of the *Spirit of Destiny* project. "You've got great timing," he said. "I mean that literally. I've looked into your NASA record. You were the best shuttle pilot of your generation. You're credited with saving the *Atlantis* after that debris strike."

Jack just looked at him, wondering if this was the man who'd killed Meeks. Spook or not, he didn't look capable of murder. Then again, a .45 was a great equalizer.

"So the point being," Skyler went on, "I hear on the grapevine that you're out of a job again. I have to say I'm very sorry about your—your friend. Suicide is a tragedy like no other."

Jack lost control. He lunged around the desk, grabbed Skyler's forearms, and slammed him against the wall. The back of Skyler's head met the window with a sharp crack. Skyler mewled.

Jack stared down at the younger man with loathing. "Suicide. You should be ashamed of yourself. He was murdered. *You* murdered him." He shook Skyler, making his head snap back against the window again.

"I didn't lay a finger on him!"

The denial sounded genuine. But denial was what spooks were best at.

"You murdered him for our technology," Jack spat. "I've reliable information that the *Spirit of Destiny* is using our engine design. Inga Pitzke must have given it to you." Two and two made four. There was no other reason for Inga to be here at JSC. "But she didn't have everything. So you had to come back." Another shake. "Why didn't you just *hire* Ollie, instead of killing him?" Jack asked. He dropped Skyler's shoulders and stepped away.

"It was too late." Skyler felt the back of his head, checked his fingers for blood. There was none. Visibly mustering his courage, he faced Jack. "It's too late to hire Oliver Meeks. But we would like to hire you."

"You're barking. I'm not a bloody scientist. I'm a pilot."

"Exactly," Skyler said, "exactly! You're a superb pilot." His fast-talking East Coast gabble sped up to warp speed. "We're finalizing crew selection right now. Every other agency has already selected its candidates. The Russians had to give up one of their slots to the Chinese. They were not happy about that, to put it mildly. We had to give one up, too. But we've still got one left."

Jack abruptly remembered: *Seven* folders in Katharine Menelaou's stack.

The *Spirit of Destiny* was to have an eight-man crew.

"We've had a hell of a time finding a qualified pilot. Which isn't exactly surprising when you think about the fact that we haven't got a manned spaceflight program. At any rate, it means bringing back someone who flew the space shuttle. And I've just personally recommended to Richard Burke that that should be you."

Amazement warred with outrage. Jack was conscious of a blossoming urge to dance around the office singing hallelujah. That lasted all of a second before he realized what was going on here.

He glanced up at the security camera on the ceiling.

"It's off," Skyler said.

Just how much power did Skyler have?

The question answered itself. *All* of it. This stringy, peace-symbol-wearing guy, and his shadowy confreres, held the reins of power in this country.

Including the power to commit murder and get away with it.

"You're trying to buy me off," Jack said. "This is a bribe to keep me quiet, so you won't get in hot water."

Skyler shook his head. After a moment, he said, "If it mattered that much, you'd be dead." After another moment, he added, "America needs you."

Jack paced in the narrow space available, his thoughts careening between alternatives.

"England needs you," Skyler said, re-tailoring his pitch.

Jack's left hand throbbed. Blood dotted the gauze he'd clumsily wrapped around his fingers in the parking lot of a Flagstaff drugstore. He must have torn the scabs open when he knocked Skyler around, like a low-rent hooligan.

He suddenly felt disgusted with himself, and weary beyond measure. He wanted to leave. Forget everything. Crawl inside a bottle of cheap whiskey and hide, like a wounded animal hiding in its den.

But Jack Kildare had zero tolerance for weakness. More than the thought of failure, he couldn't abide the idea of surrendering to his own petty flaws.

"Please," Skyler said. "Goddamn it, dude! Do you want me to get on my knees here?"

"Don't be ridiculous," Jack said. He ferociously scrubbed any emotion out of his voice. "Of course I'll take the job."

When Burke came back in, Menelaou was with him. Both of them congratulated Jack, seeming pleased (Menelaou) and relieved (Burke) by his decision. "This is one of those days it seems like God is watching over our mission," Burke declared.

When Jack looked around from having his hand shaken and his ears tugged—a Menelaou trick—Skyler was still standing there. "Let's set a time and I'll introduce you to the team leaders here at JSC," he said.

That was when it dawned on Jack.

I'm going to have to work with this guy.

Impossible.

The pendulum of determination swung back the other way. He drew breath to tell them he'd made a mistake, he couldn't take the job.

His eye fell on that dove on the wall. Burke had one of those posters in his office, too.

Meeks, way back in 2012: *This is the biggest test we'll ever face* … The Christmas lights gleaming on his face, red and green. *Have we got what it takes?*

OK, Ollie. OK.

"Looking forward to it," he said.

CHAPTER 29

Hannah came into work to find an email from Skyler.

Hope this is everything you need.

She skimmed the attached documents, then dug into the specifications for a vortex generator to be installed in the steam drum.

When she next looked up, the morning was almost over. Outside the window of her office, the cube farm was hopping.

She walked out and hollered for everyone's attention.

"I think we've solved our problem." She tried not to grin. Nothing was solved until it had been tested. But she felt good about this. "Prototype team, it's time for another go-round!"

Inga was absent.

"Where is she?"

No one knew, and Hannah dismissed it from her mind until she got home that night. She drowsily checked her email on her phone one last time while brushing her teeth.

Dear Hannah, I'm very sorry. I have resigned from the Project. I go back to Germany.

Best regards,

Inga Pitzke

Suddenly wide awake, Hannah spat out a mouthful of toothpaste, rinsed her mouth, and phoned Inga.

"Hallo?"

"Inga, it's me. I just got your email. What's happening? Something wrong?"

"*Ja*. I did a wrong thing." Inga's voice broke. "I'm sorrry, Hannah, I can't say more. Please don't call me again."

"Where are you?" Hannah heard airport noise in the background.

"Chicago. I fly to Frankfurt now." Inga was definitely crying. "Give my good wishes to the team, Hannah, please. Goodbye."

Click.

"So we're going to need a new metallurgist," Hannah told the team next morning, concealing her private concern.

As worried as she was about Inga, she couldn't go sharing details of Inga's personal life in public.

Not that she actually knew any details …

I did a wrong thing.

That phrase troubled Hannah. But Inga's English wasn't perfect. She might just have meant that something had *gone* wrong. What, though? A relationship? She'd never mentioned a boyfriend …

For days, Hannah couldn't get the sound of Inga's long-distance sobs out of her mind. But inevitably, the matter slipped lower down her priority list. They built a new prototype. It passed the vacuum tests without breaking, exploding, or otherwise disassembling itself. Hannah flew to Russia to kick the tyres of Rosatom's gas-cooled reactor prototype. While there, she was wined and dined every night by hard-drinking Russian colleagues, and had an erotic fumble with a dark-eyed atomic physicist.

Couldn't call it a romantic encounter, when she could hardly remember it.

On the plane back, she sat with a fuzzy head and a dry mouth, ordering glass after glass of white wine from the cabin attendant, and wondering why she felt so … good.

She'd broken *all* her rules in one five-day marathon of

brainstorming sessions, brightly lit Moscow restaurants that smelled of onions, and booze-fueled sex.

But the trip had been immensely productive. They'd determined that the reactor could easily power the magnetoplasmadynamic engine and the design baseload of the *SoD,* and still leave enough power for 'reserve functions'—a euphemism for the ship's weaponry. The Russians had even offered a pair of compact electrolysis units, powered by plutonium radioisotope generators, for the advance landers that would land on Europa ahead of the *Spirit of Destiny,* to manufacture reactants for the ship's return journey. The *SoD* was going to fly. So who cared if Hannah Ginsburg had a few drinks along the way?

Not the Russians, anyway. 'High-functioning alcoholic' seemed to be Russian for *normal.* She smiled to herself. Maybe she'd found her spiritual home …

Back at JSC, the next two months passed in a blur of frenetic activity. They specced the hardware, with the contractors feeding them their expertise and the workers standing around with lit welding torches. Then the performance modellers came back with the grim news that given the ship's wet mass, the MPD engine simply did not have the power to cleanly break Earth orbit. The ship would need a liquid-fuelled booster to help it escape Earth's gravity well.

But how were they to get millions of gallons of liquid fuel into orbit, without massively pushing back the *SoD's* launch schedule? The planet's launch-to-orbit capacity was already maxed out. And you couldn't order up more Soyuzes and Falcons like buying new cars. Those things took *years* to build …

It was Koichi Masuoka who solved the problem.

"Maybe there is a workaround," he said in his careful English. "I sometimes wonder why NASA never took the external tank all the way up to orbit before. Now that the shuttle is grounded, we could fly an ET full of liquid oxygen and liquid hydrogen up to orbit instead of the shuttle. But maybe there are not enough SRBs available …"

Hannah's flung her arms around the Japanese astronaut's neck and kissed him. "If there aren't enough SRBs? We have three hundred billion dollars. Oh yeah, baby! This will work!"

Masuoka flushed pink. "Anyway, let's do the calculations. Do we have the performance specs for the tank and SRBs available?"

They did. But a new problem popped its head out of the weeds.

"The plan works great in theory. Unfortunately, we can't do it just with SRBs," Hannah told Burke. "You can't turn them off once they're lit."

Burke's eyes were turned her way, but she knew that he wasn't seeing her. She waited patiently, recognizing a mind hard at work. And it was a brilliant mind. Burke might be an administrator now, but he was also the man who'd sent the Juno probe to Jupiter, solving hellacious engineering problems along the way. She'd brought this problem to him because she was at her wits' end.

"Liquid fuelled, right?" he mumbled. His hands moved aimlessly, touching his lips or tapping on his desk. It was only ninety seconds by the wall clock, but it seemed an eternity to Hannah.

"Heh," Burke said at last, a broad smile suffusing his face. "Use the engines SpaceX developed for the Falcon Heavy.

You'll have to give them a turbopump upgrade to handle LH2. Bolt two of them into a cylindrical housing. SRBs on the east and west of the external tank, Falcon engines north and south. Should get you up, no problem."

"Might work," Hannah said. "That gets the reactants into orbit. What about the booster itself?"

Burke sketched quickly on a pad of paper. He pointed to the cartoon rocket he'd drawn. "Here's the Falcon-SRB-ET combo. We'll call it Shuttle-Lite. Put it close to the construction zone. Then ..." He sketched an arrow from the Shuttle-Lite to the truss representing the engine end of the *Spirit of Destiny*. "Bolt the Shuttle-Lite's engine onto the *SoD's* truss. There's your liquid-fueled booster."

Everyone called the ship the *SoD*—pronounced *sod*—now. The British gas-cooled reactor specialists had objected in the strongest terms, and Hannah gathered there'd even been diplomatic objections lodged, but no one cared what the Brits thought. What mattered was keeping the Chinese happy.

Yet even that wouldn't matter if the ship didn't fly.

Hannah stared at the sketch. "One isn't going to do the job."

"Nope. See what six will do for you." Burke filled the back end of the truss with cartoon rockets. "Then take the ET and snuggle it inside the truss. It will hold six of them, like a sixpack of microbrews. See? Array them in a hexagon around the exit of the MPD engine's exhaust. Keep the foam, for microimpact protection."

Hannah's mind snagged on the word *microbrew*. She reminded herself that she didn't even like beer, and elation swept the craving away. "That's brilliant, Rich! Standard hardware all around. Bet the tooling and jigs are still in place for the engines, at least."

"Call Elon now. We're going to need sixteen upgraded Falcon engines, for eight Shuttle-Lites."

"Why did six just turn into eight?"

Burke's smile, wide before, seemed about to swallow his ears. She remembered how much he used to love this stuff before they turned him into an uber-bureaucrat. It was great to see him having fun again. "The advance lander team's been making a stink recently," he said. "Begging for launch priority, not getting it. This solves their problems, too."

Hannah got it before he could say any more. "Yesss! Bolt their hardware onto the other two external tanks. Fill up the ETs with reactants. Strap on Shuttle-Lite engines, and off they go to Europa. Woo-hoo!" She pumped both fists in the air, exhilarated. "The guys from the advance lander team are *so* going to owe us drinks."

"Eight flights should do it."

"Ten," Hannah said beadily. "Stuff's gonna fail, you know."

"Get moving," said Burke, giving her a light punch on the shoulder. "Hope it all works out."

Meanwhile, NASA sites throughout America were hiring three shifts to keep up with production demands. Stennis scheduled engine test firings so often that smoke plumes over the Mississippi bayou no longer elicited comment. Thiokol was racing to fabricate SRB segments as fast as they could. It got so frantic that even the infamous PEPCON facility was rebuilt to crank out the solid rocket fuel needed.

It wasn't just NASA who was overtaxed. German engineers were speedily, but carefully, crafting the habitation unit for the SoD. Russian titanium mines were hiring anyone who would swing a pickaxe, forcing other industries to raise wages to hang onto their workforce. Even China relented on their self-imposed quotas for foreign purchases of rare earths, so that exotic alloys for the nuclear reactor piping could be fabricated.

Hannah hadn't seen Skyler for ages. He'd vanished from JSC, and so had a couple of the other Feds.

The rumor was they were off in some God-forsaken place, observing tests of the *SoD's* 'reserve functions.'

It had to be railguns. Hannah knew of no other offensive technology that required such huge energy accumulators. Well, maybe lasers, but all high-energy laser systems also required piping for the exotic chemical reactants involved. There was none of that in the *SoD's* design. Just massive power leads and stacked high-farad capacitors.

Hannah shook her head. Railguns. If the *SoD* encountered anything that needed that much stopping, humanity was already screwed. But on the other hand, she fully concurred with the principle of better safe than sorry.

If it was railguns, they'd be made in Sweden, probably by Bofors, or whatever they called themselves now.

Maybe Skyler was in Sweden.

Hiking the fjords, falling for some blonde, beautiful … railgun designer?

Hannah tried her best to put him out of her mind. After all, disappearances were hardly unusual these days. The sheer scale of the *Spirit of Destiny* project, and its ballooning importance in the eyes of the world, had sparked an ongoing bureaucratic fight to the death for control. The top echelons of NASA, ESA, Roscosmos, JAXA, and CNSA (a.k.a. the aerospace division of the People's Liberation Army, as people were always muttering) warred bitterly for increments of decision-making authority. Unpredictable hurricanes of money swept away whole sub-organizations, broke them down to their components, and scattered blinking and stressed individuals around the globe. Hannah counted it a victory that she had managed to remain at JSC this long, and keep her core team together. She owed that largely to her friendship with Richard Burke, who'd developed into a world-class bureaucratic gladiator.

Their greatest victory by far was retaining control of the entire engine development and construction process.

And so, fourteen months later, Hannah stood on the glass-smooth concrete floor of the brand-new Orbital Processing Facility 1, a hangar-like building that stood beside the equally new truss assembly building. She watched technicians carefully slide precision-wound coils onto the main shaft of the ion channel for the *Spirit of Destiny's* magnetoplasmadynamic engine.

Turning to the flat-panel workstation where the designs were displayed, she smiled to herself. Gone were the days of a sheet of plywood on sawhorses, with three-ring binders and rolls of blueprints. This all-electronic construction cleanroom reminded Hannah of the days when she'd worked on Juno's engine at the Lockheed Martin facility—in retrospect, maybe the happiest days of her life.

She adjusted her goggles where they sealed against her crinkly blue microfiber 'bunny suit.' Sure was nice not to have to worry about whether your fashion choices projected sufficient authority. Her nametag did the job by itself: GINSBURG (Propulsion Group Leader). She'd never been prouder of her title than she was at this moment.

"Hannah."

She barely heard Burke's voice over the staticky noise of her hood.

"Hannah? She's been down here since … actually, yesterday. I don't think she sleeps anymore."

"No, I just die at sunrise," Hannah said, turning from the floating images on the screen. "Watch out, Rich, you're looking pretty tasty in that blue onesie."

Oh, hell. Burke had someone with him. The tall, broad-shouldered man extended a gloved hand. "Nice to meet you, Ms. Ginsburg."

Despite his blue bunny suit and enclosing goggles, Hannah recognized Jack Kildare, the mission pilot. She had met all the other crewmembers as they cycled through JSC for training, but this was the first time she'd ever met Kildare in the flesh. He'd been in his own coffin, the flight simulator at the other end of the flight line.

"The man who punched a US senator," she greeted him. "It's an honor."

Kildare looked uncomprehending. "I didn't punch a senator."

"At the *Atlantis* hearing?"

"Oh. No, I'm afraid not. I didn't even spill coffee on a senator. Only on myself."

"Too bad," Hannah said lightly. US senators were slightly less popular at JSC than tarantulas. The kumbaya moment of unity after the first contact event had not lasted long. "Well, nice to meet you, anyway. I guess you've come to see my baby?"

She gave Kildare a quick guided tour. Burke tagged along

with them, interjecting an unneeded comment or quip whenever Hannah paused in her spiel. The result was Jack Kildare couldn't get a word in sideways. Not that he seemed to have anything to say. Hannah took his glaze-eyed expression for the typical non-engineer's reaction.

"It's vital that we keep the reactor running at a low power level throughout the coast phase, to preserve the stock of fissile material and keep out of the xenon pit," she said. "This means we will be generating far more power than we immediately need. We'll be running Sonic here pretty hard, about eighty percent of redline."

"Sonic?" Jack said, looking around cluelessly.

Hannah gestured to the engine, recognizable as such only by its length and slightly flared nozzle. Technicians were carefully aligning the helical coils with laser micrometers and sealing them in place with clear, evil-smelling glue. "Just our nickname for it. 'Magnetoplasmadynamic engine' is a bit of a mouthful."

"Ah," Kildare said.

Hannah wondered again why the powers that be had selected Kildare as the pilot of the *SoD.* Not only had the man got fired from NASA for punching a senator—or whatever it was he had done—there was a big old gap in his resume between then and now. His official bio said he'd spent the missing years in Nevada, rock-climbing. There had to be better qualifications to pilot the first spaceship humanity would ever build. Hannah instinctively mistrusted anyone with such a take-it-or-leave-it approach to authority—regardless of how much she liked the idea of senator-punching.

"Epoxy?" Kildare asked, sniffing the air. "Isn't that rather brittle for this application?"

Hannah smiled. "That's just to hold it in place before we pour in the Glidcop."

"Copper ceramic composite?" Kildare's eyes widened behind the goggles. "For thermal conductivity, of course."

Hannah nodded. She was surprised; Glidcop wasn't well known.

"That's brilliant!" Kildare said.

"Whoa there, curb your enthusiasm," Hannah joked. "It's OK. All you have to do is fly it."

"Koichi will be responsible for the care and feeding of the propulsion system," Burke said. "In fact, there he is!"

Burke waved to Koichi Masuoka, who came over to them with a glue gun in hand. Masuoka had left JSC to observe at the Rosatom fab for a while, then come back to participate in the engine construction process, at his own insistence. Hannah admired his dedication. He said that no one could fully understand a system unless they'd been there on the production line with a wrench—or a glue gun. Hannah fully agreed, and they'd become buddies, searching out Houston's best ramen together on their rare evenings away from the production floor.

"Great to see you, Jack," Masuoka said. "As you can see, we're making gradual progress."

"Koichi, they let you on the floor? Listen to, er, Hannah, here. They're encasing the whole ion channel in Glidcop. I wondered how they would get rid of the induction heating!"

Hannah frowned. Contrary to her previous assumption, Kildare seemed to be clued-up about the engine. *Uncannily* clued-up. "Well, um, Jack," she said, "I guess you didn't waste your time away from NASA."

"Not quite all of it," Kildare said.

"Where did you say you worked in the private sector?"

Burke started to intervene. He actually put a hand on Kildare's arm. Kildare stepped away and said, "A little startup called Firebird Systems."

*

The otherworldly glow of two smartphone screens illuminated the interior of Hannah's beat-up Camry. The air-conditioning blew stale air in Hannah's face as she looked up from Google. She glanced sideways at Koichi Masuoka. "Are you coming up with anything?"

"Give me a minute," Masuoka said, typing with one thumb.

As they were leaving work, she'd asked him if she could borrow his Google-fu. "Any reference to Firebird Systems," she'd said. "Or just Firebird."

For some reason, she didn't feel comfortable Googling it from her work computer.

"OK," Masuoka said after another minute. "I found this."

He showed her a corporate website for Firebird Systems. It featured a lot of snazzy images and zero technical detail, as per usual for aerospace companies. Still, it was more than Hannah had found. "How'd you find this?"

"It's on the Wayback Machine. Not on Google anymore." Masuoka looked as unhappy as Hannah felt.

She clicked on "Company."

Only one individual was listed.

Founder and CEO: Oliver Meeks.

@firebirdmeeks.

It had to be him.

*

"He's dead, isn't he?"

"Yes," Skyler said. "He's dead."

"What happened? Skyler, you have to tell me the truth."

Hannah hunched over her phone. She'd called Skyler from the JSC parking lot, and he'd called back when she was halfway home. She'd pulled off the highway into the parking lot of a strip mall. Silhouetted figures moved around the entrance of the single open store, which seemed to be a vape shop.

"I found this," she said. No need to mention that actually, Koichi Masuoka had found it. A thread on a Japanese space otaku forum discussing the death of Oliver Meeks, allegedly by his own hand, on August 4th.

Half-serious Japanese space otaku consensus: the aliens had done it.

Hannah suspected otherwise.

"Skyler, there is nothing about Firebird, nothing else about Meeks, *nothing* on the internet. It's the dog that didn't bark."

Skyler was outside. City lights blurred behind him as he walked, holding his phone up in front of him.

Facetime. All the cool Feds are doing it.

She knew, though, Skyler's real reason for using Facetime was Apple's NSA-proof end-to-end encryption.

"I'm in San Francisco, Hannah," he said.

She wanted to ask him what he was doing there, but held her tongue. It was probably something to do with weapons guidance systems.

"Things are falling to pieces out here. Google—*Google*—is falling apart. The customer-facing stuff is still running OK. The problems go deeper than that. If you were ever out here before the MOAD …"

"MOAD?"

"Mother Of All Discoveries. That's what they're calling it now. The alien spaceship."

"I see."

"Anyway, there was this optimism—this turbo-charged optimism, on a cultural scale, that things were going to get better. Silicon Valley was in charge of the future and the future was a high-tech John Lennon song. These people believed in *transhumanism,* OK? Even if they didn't drink the singularity koolaid, they believed in their capacity to uplift humanity through technology."

"Then this happens," Hannah said, understanding.

Skyler nodded. The wind in San Francisco blew his hair around. Colorful crowds surged at the perimeter of the screen.

"Then this happens," he said. "And all of a sudden, *they're not in charge anymore.* The power to save humanity has passed to a bunch of uncool engineers in Houston. To the extent that there's overlap, it only makes the humiliation worse. SpaceX is having launch contract terms dictated to them by the *SoD* consortium. And Google is implementing takedown orders from the NXC."

Behind Skyler, something exploded. Skyler flinched, turned. Hot light oranged his face. "Fireworks," he said.

"Where are you exactly?"

"Maiden Lane. I wanted to buy a new guitar."

"Did you kill Oliver Meeks?"

Skyler's face crumpled. The picture jostled up and down. Hannah saw stars bursting over the rooftops.

Skyler's face came back, too close. "I can't say anything

about that."

"Tell me the goddamn truth!"

Now all she could see was his blurry, distorted lips. "I could lose my job—*I* could be murdered, Hannah, for telling you this."

"Tell me!"

"Yes, he was murdered. Please believe me, I've felt completely shitty about it ever since. But I did not kill him."

"No," Hannah said, "you didn't." Tears welled in her eyes. "I did."

"You're crazy."

"If I hadn't asked for more information about the steam generator … That was it, wasn't it? He refused to give up the goods, so you guys killed him and took what I needed." The tears spilled out, warping her voice, so she sounded closer to fourteen than forty. "If I'd had the courage to dig into the problem myself, I could have figured it out."

"That's not what you said."

"It would have taken time. I thought I didn't have time. But basically, I was being goddamn lazy."

She wept into the phone, baring her self-hatred to this kid she hardly knew. Her laziness had murdered Oliver Meeks. No matter what she did to make up for it, that knowledge would blight her life forever. "I can't go on," she sobbed. "I can't go on."

"I'm coming," said Skyler. "Stay there. I'm coming."

That made her laugh bitterly. "You're in goddamn San Francisco."

"I'll get on a plane."

Someone blurred behind Skyler, running. Yodelling cries fuzzed out the mic of Hannah's phone.

"What's going *on* there?" Hannah cried.

"Oh, it's just this Earth Party," Skyler said. "Google's lost half their top people: they're running for the hills. These are the ones who got left behind. They'd rather set fire to a Chinese restaurant than curse the darkness. Same old, freaking same old."

Knuckles rat-tatted on the window of Hannah's car. She looked up to see a bulky silhouette looming outside the car.

"I'll call you back, Skyler," she said, dry-mouthed with fear. She dropped the phone in her lap. Cracked open the window. "What is it?"

The smell of some sweet vape drifted in through the window. "It's not safe here, ma'am. Wouldn't stop here if I was you."

"Why?" Hannah said, on the verge of panic. On her lap, her thumb clicked her iPhone dark. San Francisco and Skyler vanished.

"Some of the boys talking 'bout jacking your car." The large man—who, it appeared, had come to warn her off for her own safety—jerked a thumb at the group in front of the vape shop. "Not the regulars, they cool. It's the git-outta-town gang."

In the darkness, Hannah dimly saw a banner under the eaves of the strip mall where she was parked, stretched across the fronts of two unoccupied stores. It said: EARTH PARTY.

She had literally learned about the Earth Party two minutes ago, from Skyler. She'd been so immersed in her work, she never even glanced at the news. She vaguely speculated that the Earth Party must be something like the Tea Party, with bonus arson and carjackings.

"OK," she said. "Thanks for warning me. I'll—I'll be on my way."

"You do that." The man slapped the roof of her car and stood back.

She drove back to her home that wasn't a home, eyes blurred with tears.

When she got there, she popped open her MacBook, and discovered that her own goddamn Twitter timeline had been messed with.

The night they lost Juno, she'd exchanged tweets with some random guy who used the handle @firebirdmeeks. That must have been Oliver Meeks. If only she'd kept up that connection, Meeks might be alive today. Her immersion in her work had come at a hideous cost. She had completely forgotten about @firebirdmeeks until tonight.

Now, his tweets to her had vanished. But she remembered some of them.

@hannah_a_banana A mai tai sounds good right now!

Yes. Yes, it did.

She stopped at the liquor store on her way home. She never did call Skyler back. He Facetimed her again and again in the following days, but she never picked up. Eventually she blocked his number.

CHAPTER 30

"If you wanted to kill the *Spirit of Destiny,* you'd design something just like the Earth Party."

That was *SoD* commander Katharine Menelaou speaking, in November 2018, 400 vertical kilometers above the United States.

Menelaou's voice crackled into the airlock of the ISS's new Inochi module, where Jack and Alexei were resting and breathing 100% pure oxygen.

"I have no problem with people thinking the MOAD is a hoax, or even saying so. Freedom of speech. But someone should've drawn the line when they began to sabotage the political process. Do we have to wait until they actually bring down the federal government?"

The occasion for Menelaou's tirade was the daily news digest sent up to the ISS. Wikileaks had exposed that a group of hackers affiliated with the Earth Party had monkeyed with electronic voting machines across the US, flinging control of Congress to the Democrats in the recent mid-term elections. The revelations had plunged the machinery of the American government into chaos. No change there, then, thought Jack.

"This needs to be *fixed,"* Menelaou said. "If we don't have a functioning government, we don't have a mechanism to provide funding to NASA and the *SoD* project. Of course, that's a feature not a bug, from the Earth Party's point of view." Menelaou sighed loudly. "Step one: Persuade 90% of Americans that the government made the MOAD up. Step two: Discredit the government. Step three: anarchy, I guess. Who knows what the fuck they want?"

Alexei coughed discreetly. "I was ten when the USSR fell, but I remember it well. Step three is brief, and leads very rapidly to step four: A few people get filthy stinking rich."

Menelaou laughed. "I'll tell you what, Alexei, the Russian system of government is looking better all the time."

Alexei agreed wryly, "This couldn't happen in Russia. No funding mechanism? The president signs a check." A timer beeped. "OK, that's two hours. Let's go, Jack."

Jack pushed off from the wall and flew, legs first, straight into the lower torso assembly of his EVA suit, which was affixed to the opposite wall of the airlock. "Didn't even touch the sides," he whooped. He'd been practising this maneuver. Had plenty of chances to practise.

"Careful out there, guys," Menelaou said, adding sarcastically, "Not that either of you ever takes any risks."

Down on Earth, various parts of the globe might be spiraling into anarchy, but in low earth orbit, a group of twenty-five men and women doggedly continued to assemble the *Spirit of Destiny.*

Jack squirmed into the rigid top half of his EVA suit. He joined the two halves of the suit together, aligning the water and gas connections for the suit ventilation. Then he put on his gloves, his visor and helmet assembly, and lastly his outer gloves. All actions he'd done hundreds of times now. It was starting to become rote, and therein lay the danger. He and Alexei checked each other's seals.

The final item on their checklist was to increase the pressure in their suits, to check for leaks. None detected.

They picked up their tools and drifted out of the airlock, into the shadow of the ISS.

The daylit expanse of Earth, clouds dotting the blue Pacific, stunned Jack with its beauty. He'd once been bored by Earth views, seeing them with a photographer's eye as cliché and old hat, but the MOAD had changed that. Everything became more precious when it was under threat—and Jack continued to believe the MOAD was a threat, even while people on Earth increasingly assumed that just because it hadn't done anything threatening yet, it wasn't going to.

Tethers describing inertial curves behind them, he and Alexei floated along to the 'clothesline' which stretched a hundred horizontal meters from the ISS to the *Spirit of Destiny*.

The spaceship was almost finished. It resembled a tapered 215-meter scaffolding with a humongous thruster array at one end, and a 60-meter-diameter cylinder at the other. This was the main hab module. Smaller modules snuggled inside the truss, between the main hab and the bioshield tank, which was only a little less big.

Most of the scaffolding was temporary, there to assist construction workers with their tasks. Everything took so much more effort in freefall, where turning a screw, for example, made your whole body turn the other direction. But there'd been no other way. A monster like this could never have been lofted into orbit. Trusses, components, and pre-assembled modules had been built on the ground and sent up separately, ready to be plugged into place. Ditto the engines.

What remained to be done was all that plugging-in.

Welding. Wiring. Plumbing.

Jack used to be an astronaut, now he was a plumber. Alexei had morphed into a welder. It was all part of the job.

They clipped onto the clothesline—a zip line like the ones in adventure playgrounds on Earth. Spider wheels, powered by little solar panel arrays, pulled them along in a smooth gliding motion that felt subjectively like falling towards the *Spirit of Destiny.*

Away off on their left and right, horizontally level with the spaceship, giant nets held construction supplies and discarded packing materials. These nets also corralled the tanks of LH2 and LOX that had come up on the first 'Shuttle-Lite' launches. The construction crew pumped the liquefied reactants into fuel cells moored to the ship's truss, and water and electricity came out. They used the electricity for construction. The water was stored in the bioshield, where it would be used as extra rad-shielding until the *SoD's* engine needed it.

The huge cylindrical tanks—ETs, external tanks dating back to the shuttle era—that had brought the reactants up from Earth had also found their way into the *SoD's* hacktastic mission plan. Two of them had set off for Europa last year, powering the advance landers. Six more had stayed to become part of the *SoD.* They garlanded the engine end of the ship like cartridges in the chambers of a massive revolver. When the *SoD* broke Earth orbit, those ETs would be full to the brim with reactants—fuel for the ship's liquid-fueled booster.

Every gramme of this stuff had cost thousands of dollars to bung into orbit. The *SoD* had monopolized Earth's launch capacity for two solid years. Every space agency and private company that could fling a can of bolts out of the atmosphere had been drafted in. The tempo of launches dwarfed anything in the history of spaceflight.

To sustain the pace necessary to meet their launch schedule, everyone on Earth who'd had EVA training and would sign a release form had been roped into the construction force.

Jack could see a dozen hard-hats at work right now, crawling over the scaffolding, or buzzing to and from the storage nets on 'broomsticks.' Most of them wore white NASA spacesuits. Two red suits identified his future crewmates, Qiu Meii and Xiang Peixun.

He reached out and grabbed the scaffolding, simultaneously releasing the carabiner that held him on the clothesline.

He and Alexei exchanged a careful zero-gee high five and separated to begin their shifts.

Plumbing.

Today, Jack was installing some piping for the engine.

"At least I'm picking up useful skills," he quipped.

"Plumbers make much more than astronauts," someone else on the far side of the structure agreed.

"But welders make even more than plumbers," Alexei put in.

"On the other hand," Jack mused, "there's not much call on Earth for lines carrying liquid oxygen …"

Everyone bantered to pass the time. Except the two Chinese. Jack had tried several times to strike up a friendly relationship with them—especially with Qiu, it had to be said. Nothing availed. It wasn't as if they could not speak English. They just preferred to keep themselves to themselves, it seemed.

Both Xiang and Qiu were working at the hab end of the ship today, installing external sensors.

An hour into his shift, Jack rested in the shadow of the mighty engine. A drop of perspiration detached from his head and floated in front of his face. He blew at it, making it adhere to the inside of his visor.

The water-based magnetoplasmadynamic engine, the size of his parents' house, triggered the same complex feelings as when he'd seen it in a half-finished state in the cleanroom at Johnson Space Center.

Pride. Meeks had invented this lovely monster. Jack had helped. They'd put their stamp on history, and what did it really matter who got credit?

Rage. Meeks bloody well deserved credit. He did *not* deserve to be dead.

Jack drank a mouthful of water from the nozzle in his helmet. Forget it, he told himself. You have to let it go and move on. There's no other way.

His intensive work and training schedule over the last 25 months—culminating in this plumbing job at the world's highest construction site—had helped him to avoid dwelling on the whys and what-ifs of Meeks's murder. But he could never shake off the shame of knowing that he'd personally benefited from it. So what if he was the best person for the job? If Meeks hadn't been murdered, the pilot slot would 100% have gone to someone with a better track record of respecting authority.

Out of piping. Need to get more from storage.

He moved forward along the scaffolding until he reached a tethered broomstick. Swinging his leg over, he twisted the throttle and rocketed away from the *SoD*.

The broomstick took the prize for best space hack since the astronauts of Apollo 13 built a CO2 scrubber out of socks and duct tape. It was a small LOX tank with a heater and a nozzle attached. Park and ride. There'd been jokes about quidditch at first. The very name 'broomstick' came from Harry Potter. But by now, everyone took the near-miraculous convenience of the little mobility vehicles for granted.

Buzzing towards the storage net, Jack passed into the shadow of the ISS. For a moment, he was in utter darkness. His helmet lamp beam lost itself in the infinite blackness of space. Reflexively, he twisted his head to look in the direction of Jupiter.

Light splashed over him from behind, casting his shadow over the broomstick's handlebars.

At the same time, the radio erupted with screams and curses.

Disaster scenarios warred for space in Jack's mind. He leaned over, shifting his weight to swing the broomstick around.

Flickering white sheets of exhaust hid the *SoD's* engine.

CHAPTER 31

The *SoD* was on fire. That's what it looked like, as clouds of exhaust hid the MPD engine, lit brilliantly from within.

"The ullage motors are firing!" Alexei's bellow rose above the crosstalk.

Jack seesawed between relief that the whole ship hadn't blown up, and aghast incomprehension. All eight ullage motors—tiny engines that would nudge the *SoD* forward to settle the tanks previous to main engine ignition—had fired at once.

And done their job.

The *SoD* was moving.

The whole mulligatawney of scaffolding surged away from the ISS, leaving behind clouds of exhaust, and the ullage motors themselves, still attached to their endplate—it'd broken off the truss.

People spun out from the *SoD* on their tethers, jolted loose by the sudden movement.

The clothesline strained, with the mass of the *SoD* on one end and the ISS on the other.

Jack experienced a nightmarish sense of déjà vu. He remembered piloting the *Atlantis* through the aftermath of the fatal debris strike, desperately fighting the shuttle's uncontrolled rotation.

The memory told him what to do.

He turned his broomstick and raced to the clothesline. Just before he got there, he whipped around in a 360° flat turn. Earth spun like a saucer beneath him, and the broomstick's hot exhaust burnt through the clothesline.

Jack ducked, the long end sailing over his head as it

snapped back towards the ISS.

"Alexei!" he cried. "Stay with the *SoD!* Keep everyone on the structure!"

An awful scream interrupted him. It was the more awful for being female. Crosstalk erupted again. Everyone was saying Qiu Meili's name.

"I'm coming for you," Jack shouted. He turned his broomstick once more and raced back to the ISS.

Inside, it was chaos. A dozen hands seized Jack as he floated out of the airlock. He shook them off, fought his way through the Inochi module. "We have to go after them!" Through the American module. "It's getting further and further away!" And so to the Russian module, where the current ISS station chief, Grigor Nikolin, had anticipated the necessary maneuver and prepared burn parameters for the Soyuz.

One or more Soyuzes stayed attached to the ISS all the time. They were lifeboats—although, with so many people up here now, any evacuation order would have turned into a grisly lottery. They also served as engines for the ISS itself. When the space station's orbit had to be adjusted, they fired up the Soyuz for a while.

Now, the Soyuz was their only chance of saving the *SoD,* and the people clinging to her.

The *SoD,* half-built, couldn't stop or turn around. It had no working propulsion system. So the ISS would have to chase it.

Nikolin shoved Jack into the capsule by standing on the 'ceiling' and pushing on his shoulders. Twist, wriggle, and squeeze. Boarding a Soyuz was like going back into the womb, if your mother was a robot. Wrong size seat, too. He couldn't have got in at all if he'd not stripped off his spacesuit. Sitting in the Soyuz's right-hand seat in his underwear, he punched in the burn parameters that Nikolin had scrawled in pencil on a page from an assembly manual.

Slowly, slowly, the ISS began to move.

While he was down in the Soyuz, Jack's only means of communication was shouting. Following Nikolin's instructions, he throttled the Soyuz's engine up. In a slow-motion chase through low Earth orbit, the ISS gradually overhauled the runaway *SoD*. Then Jack had to maneuver the space station into sync with the half-built spaceship once more—another hour of fiddly, high-stakes tapping on the console.

The clothesline was restrung.

One by one, the stranded hardhats returned 'home' to the ISS.

Only then did Jack have time to wonder: "What the hell happened?"

*

He got no answers from Nikolin, who was busy talking to Mission Control. He went to meet Alexei at the Inochi airlock. The cosmonaut looked like he'd lost half a stone sweating into his spacesuit. He guzzled water.

"Is Qiu all right?" Jack said.

Alexei nodded. "She's fine. A piece of truss whacked her in the belly. Some bruising, that's all. What the hell happened?"

"That's what I was about to ask you."

"Let's talk to Menelaou."

They found Katharine Menelaou in Center Dock with Nikolin, who'd got off the blower with Mission Control.

They had probably chewed his ear off. The station chief looked to be in a foul mood. "The ullage motors fired. They will have to be replaced. That may mean an extra launch. It'll screw up the schedule."

"But *why* did they fire?" Menelaou demanded. "It shouldn't have happened."

"Why are you asking me? Those motors were made in America."

Qiu Meili floated subjectively below the pair, over the porthole that looked down on Earth. Wearing only shorts and a skimpy tank top, she looked like she was curled on the floor. She was a small, fragile-looking woman with pixie-cut hair, and let's face it, she was cute as hell.

Giddy with exhaustion, Jack shot Alexei a mock-salacious leer. He drifted down to Qiu. "All right?"

"That was frightening," she said in a small, flat voice. "I thought I was going to die."

"All's well that ends well," Jack said, giving her a pat on the shoulder. The touch sent her bobbing against the floor, while Jack rebounded in the other direction.

She uncurled and straightened out in the air. "Yes, we can order new motors and replace the endplate. We can go back for the storage nets. They can be towed with broomsticks."

Xiang Peixun squeezed out of the tunnel leading from the new Chinese module. He was a short, powerfully built man who resembled, in Jack's opinion, a jaundiced toad. He snapped something in Mandarin. Qiu lowered her gaze, said, "Excuse me," and followed Xiang towards the new Chinese module that now opened off the Russian module.

Menelaou gazed after them unhappily.

Jack could guess what was going on in *her* mind. In the

old days, Menelaou had viewed their Russian partners as opponents to be fenced with and watched carefully. But now that the Chinese were in the picture, they'd moved up into the No. 1 enemy slot. Meanwhile, Menelaou was all sweetness and light with the Russians.

She said to Grigor Nikolin, "We'll need to go through the helmet cam footage from everyone who was outside when the ullage motors fired."

Nikolin regarded her steadily. "We already know what happened. The ullage motors malfunctioned. Made In America isn't what it used to be, perhaps."

Evidently Menelaou's new resolve to cozy up to the Russians was not wholly reciprocated.

"They could not possibly have been faulty," Menelaou said, and that told Jack she was rattled. You just couldn't say that. *Anything* might be faulty.

"If the motors were not faulty when they left Earth," Nikolin said, "someone here induced a fault in them." He shrugged.

The station chief's speculation, so calmly uttered, hit Jack like a punch in the gut.

Alexei blurted out what Jack was thinking.

"Sabotazh?"

"Da," Nikolin said. "Sabotage."

*

"But what can be done?" Alexei said. "Nothing. There's no way to prove it."

Koichi Masuoka said, "Why would anyone want to sabotage the *SoD?"*

Jack said dryly, "Stranger things have been heard of."

The sabotage—maybe-sabotage, maybe-not-sabotage—attempt had pushed the three crewmates closer together. Jack felt that he could trust these two men. During the voyage, they'd all be entrusting their lives to one another, anyway. Now, they were united by their skepticism about NASA's supplier network. They came to share a conviction that the ullage motors must have been interfered with before they left Earth.

But their hushed discussions in the cupola of the ISS led to nothing. The powers that be dropped the investigation like a piece of rubbish out of the window of a speeding train.

Faster, faster! Move along, nothing to see here! The *Spirit of Destiny* was scheduled to depart in six months. Every television network in the world had already teased the big event, and ad time had been sold. Construction *had* to be completed on deadline. Overtime, what's that?

So replacement parts were sent up on the next scheduled Falcon 9 launch. Work continued, with only the excitement of dropped tools and botched arc-welds to break up the monotony.

On November 27th, with 150 days to go until launch, Jack flew back to Earth, together with the other Americans on station.

They didn't need to cram into Soyuz capsules anymore. SpaceX had rushed its reusable Dragon 2 crewed spacecraft into service, just in time to provide shuttle services for the *SoD* construction crew. The Dragon 2 capsule held four astronauts. It was slightly less comfortable than the Soyuz, and much noisier—until reentry, when the engines shut off, and the Dragon 2 deployed its parachutes for the last stage of its descent through Earth's life-giving skin of air.

The quiet got to Jack. His months on the ISS had accustomed him to constant noise. Silence had no place in spaceflight. Although he knew the parachutes were functioning as designed, he didn't take a deep breath until the capsule touched down in the Mojave Desert.

Still wobbly from months in freefall, he flew to New York together with Katharine Menelaou and Adam Hardcastle, the third American member of the *SoD* crew, who'd serve as the communications mission specialist and co-pilot.

The three of them went on 'The Early Show,' 'The Tonight Show,' 'The O'Reilly Factor,' and other talk shows Jack had never heard of. This was the opening salvo of the *SoD's* publicity tour, a gimmick dreamt up by the *SoD* consortium to win support from an increasingly skeptical world. Jack told the host of The Tonight Show that he expected the MOAD would turn out to carry a crew of cryogenically frozen leprechauns. The audience laughed.

After that, Menelaou and Hardcastle vanished. Jack only found out where they'd gone by chance, when Richard Burke phoned to reprimand him for the leprechauns remark.

"Jack, we're trying to make the public understand the importance of our mission—"

"Yeah, I'm very sorry about that," Jack said. "I see I'm supposed to be flying to LA tonight. I don't think the glitterati are going to take to me. Or vice versa."

"Katharine and Adam will actually be joining you for the Emmy Awards."

"Where have they gone, anyway?"

Burke went quiet. After a moment, he said, "NXC business, Jack." The veteran administrator sounded very tired.

"Believe me, you'll find out about it soon enough."

Jack hung up and looked down from his hotel room at the crowds in Fifth Avenue. The famed avenue had become a pedestrian mall—a de facto victory for the Earth Party. But the people down there didn't look like they were on a 'walk,' as everyone now called the Earth Party's meandering, carnival-esque migrations from nowhere to nowhere. They looked like shoppers intent on scoring designer trinkets. As if nothing had changed.

Jack made another phone call.

"I'm sorry, His Excellency is not available."

"My name's Jack Kildare. *Spirit of Destiny?"*

"I see. Just a moment, Mr. Kildare."

Jack pictured a Sloane Ranger tapping buttons with French-polished fingernails. He'd visited the British ambassador's residence in D.C. after his selection. It was a haven of subdued elegance in an ugly city.

"Jack, marvellous to hear from you. What can I do for you?"

Jack took a deep breath. "Well, Your Excellency, it's like this …"

Evening found Jack on a Virgin America Airbus, flying west.

But he was not headed for L.A. and a dire round of parties and red-carpet photo ops.

Even in this day and age, Her Majesty's Government still had *some* pull.

Jack changed at LAX for a flight to Honolulu. Arriving bleary-eyed at the end of what had by now been a very long day, he was whisked into a SUV which drove him to the Navy base at Pearl Harbor.

An Osprey awaited. Glum fly-boys spurned Jack's weary attempts at banter.

He slid into sleep, lulled by the noise, and awoke high above Bikini Atoll.

CHAPTER 32

Sunlight blazed down on endless miles of what appeared to be empty ocean. Jack was assured that Bikini Atoll lay approximately 15 kilometers to the west, but he couldn't see it without the binoculars, which Katharine Menelaou was hogging.

The *Zumwalt*-class destroyer *USS Michael Monsoor* sliced through tall waves. The deck rolled underfoot. Adam Hardcastle caught his balance on the railing. His chubby face was pale. "I'm seasick," he said to Jack in tones of indignant disbelief. "Never been spacesick—and I get seasick. What gives?"

Hardcastle was a nice guy. Wife and kids—the only *SoD* crew member to have dependents. Jack sometimes wondered how the conversations between Mr. and Mrs. Hardcastle went. Honey, I'm going to Europa. Don't wait up for me.

Hardcastle and Menelaou had joined the *Michael Monsoor* yesterday, aboard the Sea King helicopter now parked on the flight deck at the back of the ship. It had transported them from the aircraft carrier supporting the *Michael Monsoor*, out of sight in the distance.

Hardcastle had greeted Jack's unscheduled arrival with a grin and a fist-bump. Menelaou, not so much.

Jack kept his thoughts to himself, watching the seamen ready the ship's electromagnetic railgun. Three gunner's mates occupied the barbette, a foot-thick metal shell on the foredeck of the destroyer, which enclosed the breech of the gun. Jack stood just inside the door of the barbette. He didn't want to get in the gunners' way, but he wanted to see this beast fire.

Behind him, the deck baked in the tropical sun. The breeze carried the smell of baking paint, gear grease, and diesel smoke—so much for refreshing sea breezes. Hardcastle clung to the railing. The chemical miasma couldn't be helping his sea-sickness.

The captain of the *Michael Monsoor* strode across the deck. In Jack's very brief acquaintance with the man, he came off as a snarling, obnoxious prick. "Gentlemen, we are about to fire the railgun," he said.

"Excuse me?" Katharine Menelaou said.

"Sorry. Ma'am." The captain smirked, another insult having successfully found its mark. Then he went on, "This is the most advanced projectile weapon in existence today. We will now demonstrate its firepower, targeting Bikini Atoll."

"Why here?" said Hardcastle.

"Because there are miles of empty ocean in every direction in case they miss," Jack murmured.

"Because we don't want the Chinese to see it," Menelaou said.

"Actually, *ma'am,* exactly the opposite. We're showing our Chinese friends what this asset is capable of. There's a PLA Navy cruiser over there, not far away."

Jack glanced in the direction the captain pointed. Smoke stained the northern horizon.

At the captain's command, the sailors swung into action. The senior gunner's mate racked a slide of projectiles under the breech and triggered the load lever. Each member of the gun crew—targeting, electrical, range safety, and telemetry—flashed a thumbs-up. "Safety!" the senior gunner's mate barked. A loud horn sounded and a red strobe started flashing outside the barbette. In combat, of course, there wouldn't have been any klaxon or strobe light.

Jack put on the dark goggles and earplugs he'd been given. So did Menelaou and Hardcastle, now crowding the doorway of the barbette beside him.

The gunner's mate inspected the projectiles resting between the twin rails of the railgun. They were stamped with the name of their maker: BAE Systems. That was where Meeks used to work before he left to start Firebird. Jack felt a tiny pang of sadness as the gunner locked the cover closed

Each of the sailors slapped the next on the shoulder—a final safety poll. A crackling sounded from below their feet, as the capacitors in the underdeck charged. As the *Michael Monsoor* rose from a wave, the gunner's mate toggled the trigger.

Heat and light splashed over them.

Zzzzoik! God it was loud!

And again—*zzzzoik, zzzzoik!* A sound like Jack had never heard before, an eerie sound that came from the future. One projectile followed the next, like bolts of lightning erupting from the railgun. Wind filled the barbette as the air bottle discharged, blasting toxic ozone out to the deck. A stench of acrid smoke rose from the rails. The electrical arcs were actually vaporizing metal off the surface of the rails.

The gunner's mate secured the trigger. The roar of the air bottle ceased. A gray contrail hung over the waves.

A split second later, a thistledown puff of smoke materialized on the horizon.

The sailors exchanged high-fives. Menelaou whooped girlishly. Jack—transported back to his RAF days of dropping things at high speed on other things—crowed, "Mach 5 balls of molten steel, baby!"

"Bull's-eye," said the captain with a satisfied smile.

"Sir!" cackled a sailor sitting at a screen inside the barbette. "Take a look at this feed from the tracking camera on the beach."

As everyone pushed past Jack to see the screen, a mop of dark curly hair appeared through the hatch leading to the weather deck.

Followed by a sharp-featured, intelligent face.

And a peace sign hanging out of the neck of a khaki t-shirt.

Jack already knew that Skyler Taft was on board. Hardcastle had told him. It was an unexpected bonus.

The NXC agent crossed the deck to them. He nodded coolly to Jack, and peered past him, into the barbette.

On the screen showing the feed from the beach tracking camera, a torpedo-shaped projectile—one of those the destroyer had just fired—travelled in slo-mo towards a towering wave. It drilled a hole straight through the wave. A split second later, the top of the wave blew off in a V shape.

"Pretty cool," Jack said.

"How the fuck did you get a ride in an Osprey?" Skyler said.

"Apparently the British ambassador went to school with the Chief of the Defence Staff, who rang someone at the Joint Chiefs of Staff."

Jack enjoyed Skyler's discomfiture. After a moment Skyler said, "This was supposed to be an Americans-only thing."

"Yeah, that's what the captain told me. He'd like to use me for target practice. But I am an American, after all, so he doesn't quite dare."

Skyler nodded. "You just don't sound like it. That's what trips everyone up. And in complete sincerity, *aren't* you reporting back to London?"

Complete sincerity was not an attitude Jack associated with Skyler Taft. As for himself, he still had the completely sincere desire to punch Skyler in the face, even after these two years. Skyler might not have murdered Meeks—he wasn't capable of it, Jack thought—but he almost certainly knew who had, and he wasn't telling.

If that wasn't enough, every time they met, Skyler did or said something new to piss Jack off. Like now.

The devil got into Jack, and he drawled, "Reporting back to London? What would I have to report? Oh, we had a slight problem the other day with the ullage motors. But there's really nothing to see here; move along."

"Yeah, that," Skyler said. He was wearing Navy khakis. He looked gormless in them, but less gormless than usual, as if he might actually have been putting in gym time. "It wasn't looked into as thoroughly as it could have been."

"You're telling me."

Skyler glanced towards the railgun. "Aren't you going to take a turn, since you're here?"

The gunner's mate was showing Katharine Menelaou how to insert a projectile into the cradle breech. She staggered, laughing. Heavy! That's what they were here for. To learn how to shoot the railgun.

Americans only.

"The *SoD's* guns will be smaller than this. The rails will only be a meter and a half, and they'll only need a 750 kiloamp supply, since they don't have to shove a projectile through ten klicks of air," Skyler said. "Obviously, our hope and expectation is that it'll never be needed."

"I hope the *SoD's* gun will be inspected properly before it's sent up," Jack said.

Skyler gave him a displeased look, as if he had hoped this subject had been dropped. "It's actually a very simple design, and yes, of course they'll be inspected. And tested. And tested again."

"But weren't the ullage motors also inspected and tested?"

"There was a cosmic ray burst. It fried the relay chip. When that chip failed, the voltage surged into the detonator, and the ullage motors fired."

Jack didn't believe a word of it. "If these electronics aren't hardened against cosmic rays, that is one hell of an oversight, isn't it?" Of course the electronics were hardened. And if there'd been a cosmic ray burst big enough to overcome them regardless, *everything* would have shorted out, and the construction workers would've been glowing in the dark.

Another storm of lightning bolts and futuristic screeches from the railgun interrupted. Skyler cringed, fumbling his goggles on.

"Dammit," Menelaou joked loudly. "Missed the Chinese warship."

"You know, it actually wasn't a cosmic ray burst," Skyler said. "We've pretty much traced the problem to the supplier of the power distribution units used in the ullage motors."

"And who's that?"

"Dong Yangfun Industries. Headquartered in Shenzhen."

Jack stared incredulously. "Components for those motors came from China? They're only supposed to be supplying the Shenzhou crewed lander."

"Spirit of togetherness," Skyler said, sketching an airquote with one hand.

"You've got to be joking."

"I am. They were the lowest bidder. Three hundred billion dollars isn't actually an infinite amount of money."

"What about the ground inspections? They should have caught the problem."

"Outsourced those, too."

Jack slowly digested the fact that Skyler wasn't joking.

"It can't have been deliberate," he said, knuckling the bridge of his nose. "An astronaut almost died when the motors fired. Qiu Meili. She's Chinese."

"They'd have had no way of knowing she would be outside when it happened," Skyler said. "Anyway, look at it from their point of view. When you've got 1.3 billion people, what's one more or less?"

The captain yelled, "Taft! Come and show the space cadets how it's done." Grinning, he beckoned Skyler.

Jack said. *"You're* approved to fire that thing?"

"One of the many perks of being in the NXC," Skyler said. "We get to play with all the coolest toys."

He winked at Jack and bounded into the barbette. That expression stayed in Jack's mind. Winks suited no one, no matter if they had a somewhat theatrical personality, like Skyler. But in that moment the NXC agent's face had looked tortured.

And no wonder.

Jack had thought all along that the accident that nearly destroyed the *SoD* must have been sabotage. But that was before he knew about components and ground inspections being outsourced to China. That threw it wide open. Sabotage? Or shoddy workmanship? Or underpaid workers cutting corners at the inspections facility? He didn't envy the NXC having to untangle *that* mess.

But then again, they weren't the ones who'd be boarding the *SoD,* with more potentially defective parts still undiscovered.

CHAPTER 33

Skyler poked his head into the cabin alloted to the NXC. "They're leaving," he said.

The cabin held eight berths, and it had occurred to Skyler before that the crew of the *SoD* would have less room to spread out than the sailors of the *USS Michael Mansoor*. He himself had done time in orbit last year, helping with construction. That's how he thought of it—doing time. The ISS was a prison. A smelly prison, where you might end up with turds floating around the living area, courtesy of an under-trained Brazilian astronaut whom Skyler still remembered with strong dislike. The *SoD's* main hab would be bigger, but would offer even less privacy. The *Michael Mansoor* at least had normal toilets.

Lance lay on his bunk, reading a fitness magazine. He looked up. "They gone?"

"No, they're going now," Skyler said patiently.

The other NXC agents left off playing with their various screens and devices, put on their shoes.

Laura: thirty, blonde-ponytailed, an electronic engineer and markswoman who'd nearly made it to the Rio Olympics.

Guillermo: fluent in three languages, a kick-boxer, who'd finished medical school and done a stint in the CIA.

Curtis: a former F-16 pilot who'd joined NASA just before the MOAD hit the fan, and was still pissed that he would never get to go to Mars.

Skyler had recruited them all, and many others, in his latest role as the NXC's human capital advisor. God knows why, Director Flaherty thought he was a good judge of people. Maybe he was. He felt proud of these three, anyway.

They'd all come through their training with flying colors. Any one of them could do the job and do it well.

Lance came out to the flight deck with him to see the astronauts off. The three *SoD* crew members weren't supposed to know anyone else from the NXC was on board, but Lance made his own rules.

The Sea King's rotors spun up. The clattering noise mingled with the wuthering of the wind. Waves crashed on the *Michael Mansoor's* hull, and the destroyer's mighty engines rumbled. Skyler had never suspected before this that seafaring was so damn noisy.

Menelaou came out and walked towards the helicopter. "Safe journey," Skyler called, waving, but she glanced neither left nor right, and never saw him and Lance.

Kildare followed her. *He* saw Skyler and Lance. He checked his stride, as if he were thinking about coming back for a chat. But it was too late—the helicopter's rotors had sped up to a blur in readiness for takeoff. He vaulted in, and disappeared from view.

Lastly, Adam Hardcastle came out of the superstructure. He jogged over to Skyler and Lance. "Guess I'll see you in China," he yelled over the noise. "That's the next stop on the great publicity tour."

"Looking forward to it?" Lance said.

Hardcastle rolled his eyes. "I think I'll survive a few months of the celebrity treatment."

With a flinty look on his face, Lance watched Hardcastle jog across the flight deck and clamber into the Sea King. The helicopter lifted off. The *Michael Mansoor* ploughed on through the waves, steaming back towards its home port of San Diego.

"It might be him," Lance said.

"Hardcastle?"

The Sea King shrank to a dot in the vast blue sky.

"Yeah," Lance said. "He might be trying to make sure his family are provided for."

"Jeez, Lance."

"It's got to be one of them," Lance said, shrugging. He turned to go back in. Skyler followed him, after a last wistful look at the sea.

"Let's not start suspecting the crew," Skyler said, "until we've ruled out sabotage at the factory."

"Or at the ground inspections site …"

"Anyway, if we're looking at the crew, I nominate Kildare as prime suspect."

"Boisselot? He was up there at the time."

"So was Ivanov."

"Let's suspect them *allll,"* Lance said with a grin.

They arrived on the foredeck to find Laura, Guillermo, and Curtis being instructed in the operation of the railgun. It was the same lesson that the astronauts had received yesterday, and the NXC agents were learning how to use the fearsome weapon for the same reason.

They were America's second string.

If one of the American astronauts had to drop out for any reason, the NXC would have a readymade replacement standing in the wings.

For sure, Skyler thought, every country involved in the mission had trained up its own understudies. But none of them could compare to his kids. He was younger than all of them except Laura, yet he thought of them as his kids. He'd handpicked each of them, and felt confident that they were the cream of the crop.

He looked on with pride, seeing how fast they absorbed what the gunnery sergeant had to impart.

But as he recalled his conversation with Lance, his thoughts took a dark turn.

How did it really feel to be Laura, Curtis, or Guillermo? What was it like to train for a mission that you'd never go on … unless someone else got kicked off it?

For example, because they were a Chinese spy?

The incident with the ullage motors had completely blindsided the *SoD* consortium. All their safety inspections had failed to catch the faulty power distribution units. The logical conclusion—Lance's conclusion—was that someone up at the ISS had screwed with the units.

Skyler still held out hope that they'd find the problem lay with Yang Dongfun Industries, which would be bad, but better than if one of the crew turned out to be responsible.

Zzzzzoik!

A wave of heat and light crashed over the deck.

Another projectile, travelling at approximately Mach 5, smashed into poor, abused Bikini Atoll.

The captain, standing just inside the barbette, beckoned to Skyler. "Taft, you shoot better than any of these pussies. Give them a demonstration."

Same thing as yesterday! The captain really was an asshole. He knew how much Skyler *didn't* enjoy shooting the railgun. Liked tormenting him. Ordering the unaccountable, almighty NXC around, now that he had them on board his ship.

Well, not for much longer, thank God.

Skyler racked a new slide of projectiles. The load lever

felt warm under his hands. He knew it was because so many other people had been touching it, but the metal felt like it might be alive, an illusion aided by the slight vibrations coming from the gun.

"I'll do it," Lance said, watching hungrily.

"No, he's better than you are," the captain said.

Both of them gritted their teeth and sucked it up.

"Safety," Skyler yawned, wishing he dared ignore the safety protocol, just to see them jump.

*

Two days later, they arrived in China. Lance had vented his feelings in a flurry of emails and sat-phone calls that rearranged their schedule. The Osprey was there, together with its peeved crew, so why shouldn't they use it? Thus the sickeningly expensive and fancy VTOL aircraft, which had left its home base at the whim of the British ambassador, returned to Pearl Harbor in the role of a taxi for the NXC.

"This is the life," Lance deadpanned.

They left Laura, Curtis, and Guillermo in Hawaii, to run up and down mountains, something they could do just as well there as anywhere. Skyler and Lance flew to Hong Kong amidst hordes of homeward-bound Chinese tourists. Then they took a train to Shenzhen.

Skyler had been to China before. But this was a different China. The level of crowding in Shenzhen's streets was simply unreal. It reminded him of the way the Earth Party's 'walkers' would occupy the hearts of American cities, maybe indulging in some light looting, but mostly just sitting around. However, everyone in Shenzhen seemed to have a destination in mind, and to be intent on getting to it ASAP, even if they had to jaywalk and knock other people out of their way.

"Does China have anything like the Earth Party?" he said, thankful for the taxi that cocooned them from the mob.

"Figure they don't," Lance said. "If they did, they'd crush it Falun Gong style."

A military APV blocked an intersection. It didn't look like there'd been an incident. It was just a show of force. A soldier aimed his rifle at their taxi, eyes dead and cold under his visor. Skyler didn't breathe until they were through the intersection.

"We've been hearing chatter about a split between the PLA and the CCP," he noted.

"There has been a split between the PLA and the CCP," Lance said, "since Mao died. They're not buddies. Their interests just happen to coincide."

"I wonder if they share an interest in stopping the *Spirit of Destiny.*" But it just didn't make sense. The ChiComs had moved heaven and earth to get included in the mission … not to *stop* it.

Lance pointed to the top of a nearby skyscraper. Big screens flashed advertisements, lurid beneath the overcast sky.

One of the screens showed the *SoD* crew. The two Chinese astronauts, Xiang and Qiu, posed in front of the others, as if they were the stars of the show.

Skyler laughed. "They look like Power Rangers."

Now Xiang and Qiu smilingly quaffed energy drinks, accompanied by dynamic text effects.

"Tell you what it is," Lance said. "They want to take over the mission. Look at that ad, they've literally pushed us into the background."

Skyler sighed in frustration. "And therefore they sabotage the ullage motors ...? Maybe it was an accident."

They escaped the city traffic and drove north. Industrial sprawl scabbed the land. The Dong Yangfun Industries Inc. factory loomed over a back road. At the gates, they had to wait for their interpreter to show up before they could be admitted. Lance shook hands with the podgy, cheerful little interpreter without cracking a smile. Skyler knew what he was thinking: This is pointless.

They toured the factory, accompanied by their interpreter and a manager. Skyler was shocked. He'd expected the production floor to look like something out of a brochure from Foxconn, Shenzhen's largest and most famous electronics supplier. It looked more like a sweatshop. Young men and women sat bent-backed at long rows of tables. They weren't even wearing masks, let alone head-to-foot protective gear. They worked with soldering irons, crimps, and tweezers.

"This is where we assemble the power distribution units," said their interpreter.

Skyler moved closer, and almost tripped on the cables trailing over the floor. None of the assembly line workers even looked up. Maybe they'd been told not to talk to the *gweilo* visitors. Or maybe they had quotas to make.

The *Spirit of Destiny*—and ultimately, the outcome of humanity's encounter with the MOAD—depended on the dexterity of overworked twenty-somethings in the armpit of Shenzhen.

Mindboggling.

"Let's see the test area," Lance said.

Another room filled with rows of desks. More young people, system-level-testing the units with tabletop electronic measurement instruments. More bowed heads.

They left the factory the back way, past the ventilation fans of the company cafeteria. The smell of pork soup blew into their faces. Rain began to drizzle down.

"I wouldn't entrust the safety of a goldurned Christmas hog to that assembly and test process," Lance said, watching their interpreter run through the rain to his own car.

Skyler nodded. "Quality assurance ultimately depends on the test equipment. So what are we gonna do, chase down the makers of the measurement instruments?"

"This whole thing is a wild goose chase," Lance said bitterly.

"Flaherty has to cover his ass."

"At least you email him. Tell him we gotta massively tighten up the ground inspections. This shit is frightening."

Skyler, in full agreement, got out his phone and began to type. He had the SDIMP platform installed on the device.

A worker dashed across the yard to them. She looked about seventeen, and carried a plastic bag. When she reached them, she gasped, *"Spirit of Destiny?"*

"Hey honey, what can we do for you?" Lance said.

"Please give." She pushed the bag at Lance. *"Spirit of Destiny* … Qiu Meili. For her!"

The plastic bag turned out to contain a teddy-bear. It held a soft white ball emblazoned with the word *EUROPA* in English.

Once the girl had run back inside, Skyler laughed out loud. "And you thought she might be a whistleblower …? Just a Qiu Meili fan."

"Yup, that's pretty funny," said Lance, and tossed the teddy-bear out the window on the highway.

But they had gained valuable information, Skyler thought. No way on earth would that girl have knowingly sabotaged a component meant for the *Spirit of Destiny*. Nor would any of her coworkers, he guessed. Chinese support for the mission ran broad and deep.

Which meant it was looking more and more like the sabotage must have occurred in orbit.

Shit.

They were stalled in traffic again. “I got better things to do,” Lance fumed, without specifying what those better things were.

Skyler looked at his phone. “The *SoD* crew are landing right about now.”

So they flew to Beijing.

CHAPTER 34

China!

The skyline of Beijing imprinted itself indelibly on Jack's brain. No matter that he'd seen this cityscape many times on TV, the reality came as a shock to the system. He stared out of the high-speed train—a goddamn *maglev!*—like a country bumpkin.

London had *nothing* on this place.

New York? L.A.? Hickvilles.

This was the big city. This was the future, for better or worse. Not just a few, not just a few dozen, but hundreds of skyscrapers stabbed into the low, leaden clouds. The big screens on their summits flashed like technicolor lightning, veiled by the haze and the gathering twilight.

"Pollution," Menelaou said. She handed out surgical masks.

People hurried along with their heads down like New Yorkers used to do in the days before the Earth Party took over. Few of *them* seemed to be wearing surgical masks.

"Oh, Jack!" Qiu giggled, pointing. "There's you!"

He missed it that time, but caught the same advert five minutes later on a different skyscraper. His enormous image grinned whitely, stuck his thumbs up, and climbed into a capsule resembling a Dragon 2 with the serial numbers scraped off. It was the most cringeworthy thing Jack had ever seen. Good thing Alexei wasn't with them—he'd have laughed his arse off. "What was it an advert for?"

"Razors," Qiu said happily. Breathing the particulate-matter-enriched air of her native land seemed to pep her up. "Don't you remember the shoot?"

"No." He vaguely remembered signing something.

"It is probably CG," Xiang Peixuan said. "I am advertising beer."

After that it became a game, spotting their own faces on billboards and screens. Qiu and Xiang won by lengths. Understandably, they were the most popular members of the crew here.

There was a black-tie reception that night, and then on the morrow a tour of the Forbidden City. Jack, hungover, got in trouble for taking pictures in the wrong place, or with the wrong kind of camera, or at the wrong angle, or something—he couldn't understand the soldier who told him off, and the soldier couldn't understand him, and they ended up shouting at each other until someone from the consortium hurried along to smooth things over.

After that, Jack was in no mood for *another* nine-course dinner with *another* bevy of officials and celebrities.

Shark's fins again, I bet.

Birds' nests, too. Or some other bloody endangered thing.

He quietly slipped out of their hotel and sloped off to Sanlitun—a district characterized by Google as an 'upscale expat haunt'—where he had an appointment with Theodore Zhang.

The appointment amounted to a text from Jack this afternoon, after his row with the PLA soldier— "In your neck of the woods. Drinks on me" — and Theo Zhang's reply, which was mostly four-letter words, but expressed warm enthusiasm for the idea of drinks.

Theodore Zhang had been one of the first people to invest in Firebird Systems. Well, his fund had been. But his fund was a one-man band, headquartered in NYC, with a branch in Beijing which was actually Theo's home. He had inherited piles of green, was Jack's impression, and unlike most Chinese princelings, had also inherited a brain to go with it, and a nerd's fascination with aerospace.

"They blackballed me from the *SoD* project," Zhang said. "I have a company specializing in aerospace telemetry and precision guidance systems. We bid on the inertial guidance system contract, but it went to a different company."

"It's a feeding frenzy," Jack said. He was drinking a Tsingtao. He'd had a hell of a time getting here. Took the wrong train, had to backtrack. People staring. They were staring at him here, too. No wonder, as he was the only white person in the bar. He and Zhang sat at a shabby wooden table. Graffiti adorned the bare concrete walls. Loud Chinese pop played. "You know, Theo, this doesn't strike me as an upscale expat haunt."

"Sanlitun? Upscale? Where'd you hear that?"

"Google."

"Oh, Google's wonky. Their search algorithms have been compromised," Zhang said, as if Jack should have known that. "Anyway, Google doesn't have a presence in China. The Party kicked them out. In this country, you have Party connections, or you have nothing. That's why my company didn't get the *SoD* contract."

"No doubt, mate. It's a racket."

Zhang drained his beer and opened his second one by banging it on the edge of the table. He had five bottles lined up in front of him like bowling pins. He wasn't looking very well, Jack realized. A former distance runner in his Harvard days, he used to exude preppy good cheer. Now he seemed sour. His clothes were seedy, too—a baggy black blazer and matching trousers. Flipflops on his feet. "How's Ollie?" he said.

Jack's world turned sideways for a moment. Zhang didn't know Meeks was dead!

Throwing caution to the winds, he related the whole sordid story, including his belief that Meeks had been murdered by the NXC. As he told the tale, anger crowded out sadness. It was a good trade-off for Jack, and one that he made every time he remembered that night.

Zhang's eyes got bigger and bigger. But when Jack finished speaking, he didn't respond immediately. He toyed with the beer caps lying on the table. "That's a shame," he said eventually.

Jack closed his teeth. "Yes, it is a shame," he said.

"Ollie would have been very interested in something I saw recently."

"What's that?"

"When I got your text, I thought, OK, I can tell Jack and he'll tell him."

In a way that would still be true. Meeks was with Jack. He never entirely went away. "Tell me."

"I can't leave the country, did I mention that?"

"No, you didn't. I thought you had an American passport?"

"It's useless when they stop you at the airport. Anyway, this is all because my company bid on the *SoD* contract. We should have got that fucking contract. We were this close! They were considering our bid. That's when I visited Unit 63618."

Jack shook his head. "Am I meant to know what that is?"

"It's in western China. It's a launch facility."

"Oh, part of the Jiuquan Satellite Launch Center?"

The Jiuquan facility was where CNSA launched most of its satellites, and also its payloads destined for the *SoD*.

"Near there," Zhang said. "But not very near. The Gobi desert is pretty big." He took another gulp of beer. "Unit 63618 is a hit-to-kill launch site."

Jack sat back. Suddenly conscious of the people around them, he glanced uneasily at the drinkers. Most of them looked like goths, Beijing version. Two guys in bomber jackers, sitting at the bar, stood out. But they had their backs to Jack and Zhang and they were chatting with the barman.

"It's OK," Zhang said. "You may have noticed that most people in China don't speak English. So anyway. I saw the main base, the launch pad, and the instrumentation sites. That's what they wanted our technology for. Precision guidance for long-range missiles. It wasn't for the *SoD* at all, although the same agency was managing the procurement."

"CNSA?"

Zhang waggled a hand in a very American gesture: kinda sorta.

"Right," Jack said. "CNSA is a wholly-owned subsidiary of the PLA. So they're testing hit-to-kill interceptors?"

"That's been going on for years," Zhang clarified. "This is bigger than the American SLS. With our guidance system it could hit a target as far up as geostationary orbit."

Jack felt a chill. "Maybe it's for destroying space debris? There'll be a lot of crap left behind in orbit when we go."

"Maybe," Zhang said. He opened his fourth beer. His face had flushed red in blotches. "So anyway, let's talk about something different. What's it like to be famous?"

"Oh, the adverts. It's bloody embarrassing."

"Everyone in China knows your face," Zhang laughed. "You're bigger than Tom Cruise."

Christ. It hadn't even dawned on him. *That's* why people had been staring at him all night, of course.

"Theo, is it all right for you to meet with me?"

"Of course it's all right," said Zhang, who was starting to slur his words. "It's a free country. Oh, wait." He theatrically slapped his forehead.

"I wouldn't want you to get into trouble." Jack pushed back his chair and stood up.

"Where are you going? I'm telling you, it's fine. The Party's blacklisted me. I've been un-personned. I no longer exist. At least I still have savings in the US."

"I can't help you get out of the country," Jack said. "But I'm going to get you home."

He heaved Zhang to his feet. They walked out of the bar into raucous noise. Stalls and open-air seating spilled into the right of way. Jack dragged Zhang through a crowd of girls who were defying the November cold in hot pants and microminis. Something odd: they all had patterns of little red dots on their faces, like Hindu bindis, but many more of them, clustered like freckles on their cheeks and foreheads.

"What's up with the little red dots?" he said to Zhang, to distract him from complaining that he wanted to carry on drinking.

"Oh, that. It's a thing. No Earth Party here, but acupuncture isn't illegal yet. I'm not going home. It's not even nine o'clock."

It was ten thirty. "Listen to your Uncle Jack. You've had enough." And if Zhang was telling the truth, it wouldn't be good for him to be seen with Jack. Zhang might not care what happened to him, but Jack did.

He flagged down a taxi on the main drag and climbed in with Zhang, who reluctantly volunteered his address. This turned out to be a ritzy highrise on the Chaoyang Road. Jack said to the taxi driver, "Wait." He watched until Zhang weaved into the foyer.

Uneasily, he settled back against the grubby white seat cover. "Four Seasons Beijing," he said.

"Shen me?"

"Four Seasons Beijing. Hang on." Jack fished out the city map he'd picked up in the hotel's foyer. He pointed to the name of the hotel. "Here."

"Dong le."

The taxi started. Jack folded his arms and watched the city slide past.

Unit *what was it?*

63618.

In the Gobi desert.

A launch facility for hit-to-kill interceptors.

With a jolt, he clocked where the taxi was. Zipping along in a river of traffic. Streetlights illuminated gray Stalinist cubes set well back from a typically broad Beijing street. Trees. This wasn't the way they'd come. "Hey, are you sure this is the right way?"

"Wo ting bu dong."

Jack perched on the edge of the seat, all thoughts of Unit 63618 driven from his mind. The taxi sped on. Now the neon of the city center lay behind them. Ahead was nothing but traffic and darkness.

Hell with this. Jack waved his hand beside the driver's face. "I want to get out."

"Wo ting bu dong." The driver moved his head aside as if Jack's hand was an annoying fly.

Jack remembered things he'd seen on Google when he was researching Sanlitun. Travellers' stories of being taken for a ride, way out into the country, charged the earth. Robbed of all their belongings.

You couldn't trust Google anymore, Zhang had said. It was glitchy.

But Jack trusted the evidence of his eyes, and this was definitely not the way back to the Four Seasons.

"I said stop! I want to get out!"

The driver didn't bother answering him at all this time, but he had to stop at the next red light, because there were dozens of cars ahead of them, and the moment the taxi came to a halt, Jack threw the door open and stepped out. The driver yelled in surprise. Jack slammed the door and ran across four lanes of halted traffic, zigzagging through diesel exhaust fumes. The light changed. A lorry blared its horn. Jack leapt onto the pavement and the lorry accelerated, missing him by a hair.

Panting, he glanced up and down the long, empty sidewalk. Where the hell was he?

What an arsehole that driver was!

Better get off this street before he comes back.

Jack did not know why the driver should come back, instead of cruising for an easier mark elsewhere, but in the back of his mind he heard Alexei relating horror stories about the USSR. How people used to *disappear.*

Alexei was talking out of his arse, of course. He was too young to remember the USSR. And even if that kind of thing used to happen—this wasn't Moscow circa 1990, was it? This was Beijing in 2018.

Jack hastened back the way they'd come. It would be good to get back to the bright lights and the crowds, anyway. Safety in numbers.

He reached a cross street. The city was a grid. He'd parallel on the next street over.

As he turned the corner, he looked back and saw two men walking after him, briskly.

Jack's stomach formed itself into a cold, hard knot.

He walked faster. The traffic noise from the wide street behind him swallowed the sound of his trainer-clad feet. He looked back again.

The two men turned the corner, following him.

Jack fished his phone out of his coat. It was a special NASA phone, which exclusively utilized voice-over-internet protocol. Alexei was in bloody France, so he dialed Koichi, who'd come with them to China.

Ring. Ring.

He crossed a traffic-less street and turned another corner.

"Jack?"

"Yeah, Koichi, it's me. Sorry about this, but can you swing transport? I need a pick-up."

"When?"

"Ideally, now."

"Where are you?"

"Somewhere in Beijing. Use the phone location app …" Jack turned for another look at the two men behind him.

They'd closed the distance to half of what it was.

They were just passing under a streetlight.

Jack recognized the two bomber jackets who'd been drinking at the bar while he and Zhang talked.

As he stared, not quite believing his eyes, trying to convince himself these were two different men, they sped up. One of them called out to him in Chinese. It sounded like a command.

The other one drew his hand out of his jacket pocket, holding a compact gun.

Jack broke into a sprint, not caring where he was going. *Away.*

CHAPTER 35

Skyler was supposed to be at the banquet at the exclusive Diaoyutai State Guesthouse, where the Minister of Science and Technology and a pair of reality television stars would fete the *SoD* astronauts, and the whole thing would be packaged as a special on state television, but fuck that. Lance had told him he wouldn't be attending. And Skyler was supposed to go in his stead? Don his penguin suit and hover around the astronauts, in case Kildare broke out that dry British sense of humor, or Menelaou said something about human rights, or Hardcastle … well, Hardcastle wasn't likely to put a foot wrong. And Giles Boisselot, the ESA astronaut, had his own minder from the DGSE.

Basically, Skyler was sick of doing whatever Lance told him to.

And to be honest, he didn't do great with Chinese food. The very smell of it made him feel queasy at this point.

So he ditched the banquet.

Bad nanny!

Changing into jeans, he reassured himself that Director Flaherty would have his back if anyone (Lance) made a stink about it. The lay of the land had shifted recently at Langley. Lance had formerly been Flaherty's blue-eyed boy, but the director had lately been issuing smoke signals indicating that Skyler was his new favorite. A consequence of Skyler's work with the 'second string,' maybe. Anyway, it was a reversal that had been way too long in coming.

Despite this shift, there also existed the possibiity that Flaherty had *told* Lance to ditch the banquet, as a subtle fuck-you to their hosts. In which case, Skyler wanted to be on the right side of that play.

All of which led to Skyler Taft sitting in solitary splendor in Morton's of Chicago, in the Regent Hotel, enjoying a perfectly seared steak, and feeling a slight sense of melancholy as he employed each of the three forks and three knives correctly, as he'd been taught as a child. He was a *Taft,* after all. His parents might've rejected high WASP culture before he was ever born, but some things remained, passed down like old furniture, because it was too much trouble to get rid of them: for example, table manners.

He kept his phone by his plate as he ate, but it didn't ring or buzz.

A little after ten, he paid the check. He left a solid tip—or rather, Uncle Sam did—and rolled out onto the second floor of the hotel. He descended to the mezzanine level, and trailed his fingers along the balustrade, gazing down into the atrium. People sat taking coffee in the café area below. Skyler was a bit tipsy. Loneliness hung like a thin curtain between him and the rest of the world. He envied the couples billing and cooing over their espressos, and then he saw that one of them was Lance.

To be exact, one half of a couple was Lance.

The other half was a Chinese woman.

Skyler had the peculiar sensation that insects were crawling over his scalp. This was what it meant when people said their hair stood on end.

He leaned on the balustrade, casually observing the pair.

He didn't know the woman. A tailored black dress flattered her bony, thoroughbred physique. Her hair was up in a clasp decorated with pearls. A designer handbag sat on the floor beside her chair. She was maybe forty-five. She looked like the kind of person who frequented the Regent Hotel, Beijing.

Lance leaned across the coffee cups, speaking intensely, his fists clasped between his knees. Skyler had never seen him look so … sincere? *Human?*

Skyler took out his phone and photographed them together. His heart thudded. He moved along the mezzanine and took more photographs until he could be sure he'd got good images of both their faces, or as good as an iPhone camera could manage.

He remembered Lance's conviction that one of the *SoD* crew was a Chinese spy and saboteur.

Lance had suggested it might be Hardcastle.

What if the spy was … Lance?

Skyler could see how he'd have pulled it off. Lance had not been in orbit at the time of the incident, but he'd been up before, as Skyler had. And he had visited the ground inspections facility in Shanxi Province several times over the last year. He had the means and opportunity to have sabotaged the *SoD*.

Motive?

Well, Lance wouldn't be the first man to fall for an older woman.

Skyler could personally understand *that*.

As he stood there, thoughts whirling, Lance and his companion rose to leave. Close together, but not holding hands or touching, they walked under the mezzanine, and out of Skyler's sight.

Skyler hurried down the stairs. He stopped on the landing, where he had a view of the foyer. Lance and his companion stood in front of the bank of elevators leading to the guest rooms. Lance was speaking. Skyler recognized the expression on his face now: *you MUST believe me, you MUST accept MY truth,* was the subtext to whatever he was saying.

An elevator opened. The woman walked in. The doors closed. Lance stood there for a moment, and then turned to leave the hotel, head down.

Skyler descended the last few stairs and followed him. It was easy. Lance wasn't looking around. Outside, a bitter wind sliced through Skyler's coat and scarf. Lance crossed the plaza in front of the hotel, his coat open, seemingly indifferent to the cold. The trees sparkled, clothed in blue and white lights.

Instinct urged Skyler to catch up with Lance and ask him what the fuck was going on.

Wisdom told him not to let Lance see him, at any cost. Send the pictures to Langley. Get the CIA to run a facial recognition analysis on the woman.

His dilemma changed when Lance stopped dead. He pulled his phone out and answered it.

Two seconds later, Skyler's own phone rang.

"Taft," Skyler said, skulking behind a tree, watching Lance.

It was the PR woman from the *SoD* consortium who was managing this leg of the publicity tour. "OK, there you are. Wonderful. I'm assuming you know that Kildare bailed on the event. Is he with you or something?" She did not give Skyler time to respond. "I need to know what's going on. This is getting completely out of hand."

"What's happened, Amber?" said Lance, on the phone.

Christ! Skyler pulled the phone away from his ear, confirmed that he was on a conference call.

Twenty feet away, *and* on the phone, Lance said, "Regarding Kildare, no, I was not aware of that, and he's not with me. Maybe Skyler knows—"

"He's not with me, either," Skyler said, heart sinking. You take *one* night off, your first night off in months, and SHTF. I hate my life.

"Wait up, aren't you at the event, Sky?" Lance said, unaware that Skyler was standing twenty feet from him.

"No," Skyler snapped.

"OK, you guys have got some kind of crossed wires thing going on," Amber the PR woman said. "Just put that on one side for a second. The problem is *not* Kildare. He doesn't show, you know, I kinda fucking expect that from him. The problem is Masuoka."

"Huh? What?" Skyler and Lance said, pretty much at the same time. Koichi Masuoka was the steadiest and most reliable of the entire crew. He would do what was asked of him and then do an extra 20% on top of that, on principle.

"Yep," Amber said. "He just ran out of here like someone lit a fire under his ass. What the fuck is going on? I am here kowtowing to the minister, apologizing like I never apologized in my life. Thank God this broadcast isn't going out live—"

Skyler interrupted. "Did Masuoka say where he was going?"

"If he did, would I be asking you?"

Skyler abandoned his spy-versus-spy game. He walked up to Lance and said, "C'mon, let's get on this."

Lance spun, his right hand dropping to his side. Skyler believed that if Lance had been armed, he might well have shot Skyler there and then.

There was a moment of silence.

Skyler shrugged. "I had dinner at Morton's. Couldn't handle another goddamn Chinese meal."

Lance's face relaxed a fraction. He would now be thinking—or desperately hoping—that Skyler had not seen him meeting his Chinese contact. He held up one finger. To Amber, he said, "Skyler's with me. We'll take care of this. I'll call you back if we need anything." He hung up. "Sorry about that. I practically jumped out of my fucking skin."

"No problem," Skyler said, and because Lance would think it unnatural if he didn't ask, he added, "Don't tell me you went for steak, too?"

"No, man, I had something else to take care of." Lance tapped on his phone. "Kildare *and* Masuoka. They've got to be together. Let's see if we can find them on the locator app."

And Skyler's opportunity to confront Lance passed. He let it pass. This was more important.

Their phones had NSA-developed apps that used cell tower data to locate mobile phones. Here in China, the system only worked for American phones. But that's all they needed, as Kildare and Masuoka both had phones issued by NASA.

Skyler activated his own app. They stood side by side in the cold, heads bent over their phones.

"Got Masuoka," Lance said, and then he exploded: "Oh fucking *shit*."

CHAPTER 36

Jack ran.

He didn't know which way he was going anymore. The concrete monoliths blocked out the neon he'd been heading for. All that mattered was eluding the gunmen behind him.

He turned every corner that offered itself, hoping to cut off their sightlines for long enough to get away. It wasn't any use. Every time he slowed for breath and looked back, he saw one of them behind him, running hard. Fucker was fit. Younger than Jack.

Why didn't he shoot?

Didn't want noise, didn't want trouble.

Or he wanted Jack in one piece. For questioning.

The other guy had vanished. Probably circling around to cut him off.

Their footfalls beat an urgent rhythm on the empty sidewalks. Jack's trainers made soft thuds. The guy behind him sounded like he was wearing shitkicker boots.

Trees lined the broad sidewalks, but were sparse, offering no hiding places.

These damn long blocks.

These damn wide open streets.

The city of the future: nowhere to hide.

Scant traffic zoomed past.

Desperate, his lungs burning, Jack stumbled into the street and waved at an oncoming car. "Please! Stop!"

The car swerved around him with an angry parp. Jack had to nip across the street to avoid a wave of traffic coming the other way, and realized he'd inadvertently put a barrier between himself and his pursuer.

He put on a burst of speed, making for the next corner.

The guy behind him bounded recklessly into the traffic. Horns blared. Someone yelled in Chinese.

Jack didn't stop to see whether his pursuer got through, or got turned into roadkill.

He rounded the corner, arms pumping—

—and skidded to a halt. A black-haired man faced him, arms extended defensively.

It's the other guy. He's cut me off.

Jack's adrenaline peaked, and he was preparing to charge the man, when he recognized Koichi Masuoka.

Momentary shame pulsed through him. He dropped his stance. "Koichi! Fucking hell!"

"Get in the taxi," Masuoka said, pushing him. Only now did Jack notice the vehicle stopped by the curb.

"I had a bad experience with a taxi earlier," he joked uneasily.

Masuoka shoved him in and climbed in after him. "What's going on, Jack?"

"Man with a gun," Jack said. He craned forward, watching the cross street. His pursuer limped up onto the sidewalk. "In fact, that one."

"Honto da," Masuoka said. The man held his gun by his side, in plain view. "What did you do?"

"Fuck all." Jack's nerves were unravelling. He shouted at the driver, "Go! What the hell is the matter with you?"

The man broke into a stream of Chinese, lifting his hands off the wheel as if he thought Jack was threatening him, which actually made sense, given Jack's tone of voice.

"OK, I will call someone," Masuoka said, all humor gone from his voice. He dragged out his phone. After a minute he started talking in Japanese. His tone changed completely, to Jack's bafflement. It sounded like a cordial catch-up call.

Jack braced, holding the door handle.

The gunman lurched alongside the taxi and thumped on the driver's side window.

This finally seemed to convince the driver that it would be smart to get moving. The taxi leapt forward, but had to stop at the corner. The traffic had thickened and there was no stop light. It meant a tricky merge and the poor old driver was trembling in panic.

A bullet hit the taxi's rear window.

Jack and Masuoka instinctively dived into the footwell. When Jack popped his head up, the rear window had turned into a crazy frosted jigsaw, and dimly through it he saw two figures approaching.

Both of them now.

The taxi driver flung the door open and got out. He faced the approaching gunmen, hands in the air.

"Fuck," Jack shouted. Panicking, he forced his six-foot-two frame through the gap between the front seats. He dropped into the driver's seat. As he reached for the door to close it, another gunshot barked. The door jumped out of his hand and safety glass cascaded to the street. He left the door hanging open, stamped on the accelerator.

Brakes squealed. Horns played a discordant fanfare.

The swinging door took someone's wing mirror off.

Jack leaned out and hooked it shut, keeping his other hand on the steering wheel.

Masuoka was yelling into his phone all this time. He thumped Jack's shoulder. "Not this way!"

"Which way?"

"U-turn! *Hayaku!*"

"Oh, Christ."

Jack forced the taxi into the leftmost lane. He spun the wheel, fishtailed the rear wheels around, and accelerated into the traffic going the other way. A flight instructor had once said Jack had the best spatial awareness he'd ever seen. Jack had never expected to use it for aggressive driving in a bullet-riddled Beijing taxi.

"Keep going! Turn right up here!" Masuoka shouted. Minus two windows, the taxi was full of wind and traffic noise.

"How the hell d'you know where we are?"

"I can read the street signs! Same characters. Different language."

Jack swung the taxi into the cross street Masuoka indicated, leaving the heavy traffic behind.

"Other side of this street!"

Street was underselling it. The vast intersection they were now entering reminded Jack of Red Square in Moscow. The concrete monolith on the other side also looked like something out of the USSR. High metal fences blocked the building off from a sweep of pavement. A single stripe of windows glowed, high up. Jack pulled over. "Mate, are you sure—?"

He was talking to the night. Masuoka was out of the taxi and running.

Baffled, but still trusting him, Jack abandoned the taxi at the curb. He sprinted after Masuoka.

Across the empty intersection.

Four men in camouflage stood at parade rest in front of the building's fenced-off gate.

Christ! Those were Chinese paramilitary police!

Jack stopped at the edge of the pavement. At this point he suspected everything and everyone, even Masuoka. The wind ran icy fingers through his hair. His muscles were limp, drained of energy. He watched Masuoka approach the paras, his hands in full view.

The paras moved to repulse him.

Another voice rang out from behind them. A frail man in a business suit hurried out of the gate, waving a handful of documents.

Masuoku greeted the newcomer with a glad shout in Japanese, then turned back— "Jack! Come on, quick! My friend has permissions for us to go in."

That was when Jack spotted the flagpole behind the fences. The Rising Sun fluttered in the cold, dry wind from the Gobi desert.

This forbidding building was the Japanese embassy.

He staggered inside.

From the *Daily Mail*, Tuesday, December 7th, 2018:

TYCOON MURDERED IN UPSCALE BEIJING APARTMENT BUILDING

BEIJING, Dec. 7 (Xinhua) – A leading investor in the global aerospace industry was murdered at his home in an upscale Chaoyang Road apartment building, local authorities said.

Residents are on edge following the discovery of Theodore Zhang's body by his cleaning lady on Monday. According to a police press release, Zhang appears to have been tortured before his death. Sources claim that the body exhibited multiple cuts, consistent with the traditional Chinese technique of *lingchi,* or "the death of a thousand cuts."

The grisly punishment of *lingchi,* which involves slicing off pieces of the body, leading to death, was traditionally reserved for traitors. It was outlawed in 1905, but is rumored to still be practiced by the so-called ultra-militarist faction within the Chinese army.

Zhang, 42, held dual American and Chinese citizenship. While he had formerly been a high-flyer in the aerospace industry, he was rumored to have experienced financial setbacks recently, sources said.

No suspects have been named in the case, but local residents suggested the horrific murder may be linked to the *Spirit of Destiny* project. Whatever the truth, the tragedy is likely to further roil the waters, raising new questions whether the $300 billion spaceship will leave for Europa on schedule next year.

CHAPTER 37

The next thing that happened was Koichi Masuoka got fired.

For Hannah, it was the last straw.

She had liked the Japanese astronaut and had even come to depend emotionally on him. They had shared the troubling story of Firebird Systems. Hannah had trusted him not to breathe a word to another soul.

Was that why he'd been yanked from the mission? Had he spilled the beans to the wrong person?

No, Burke said. Nothing to do with that, Hannah-banana.

Burke also knew about the Firebird Systems thing. He'd admitted it when Hannah pressed him on it. The *Spirit of Destiny* had already started to kill people, and it wasn't even finished yet. That sickening knowledge bonded them. Masuoka had been the third member of their conspiracy of silence.

And now he was gone. Unceremoniously bundled home to Japan, without even returning to JSC to say goodbye.

"What *happened,* Rich?"

"It was political," Burke said. He looked tireder than ever these days. "You know the Chinese can't stand the Japanese, and vice versa, right?"

"Yes, and so?"

"Something had to give."

"Don't you just love international cooperation," Hannah said, scowling at the dove logo on Burke's desk calendar. "Why'd it have to be him?"

"He slipped up. Did something that gave the Chinese an excuse to demand his removal from the mission. I do not know what that was, Hannah."

And then the dreaded, inevitable words:

"Don't ask."

Hannah asked, anyway, because asking was what she *did,* as an engineer. But no one had a satisfactory answer, and so she took the rest of the week off and flew home to California.

She spent Thursday and Friday in a Santa Monica roach motel, getting sloshed.

Walking on the beach, she analyzed her own slipshod approach to human relationships. Alcohol stripped away her illusions about herself. In vino veritas. A clear pattern emerged.

Koichi—

I never got close to him. All those late nights talking shop, and I never asked him anything about himself. He used to look at me with those lovely dark eyes and I—I would just look away. I didn't want to—

—end up sleeping with him—

—ruin it.

Inga—

She was one of my first hires on the project. She was a *friend.* And when she quit—

—when she called me from the airport, in *tears* for fuck's sake—

—I never followed up. Never called her again, because I was too *busy.*

The pattern was letting go. Over and over again, Hannah let go of people, let them slip away without even trying to hold on.

Ralf Lyons! Her closest colleague on the Juno project,

he'd got fired for violating his NDA, and had Hannah phoned him to say hey, sorry you wrecked your career?

Yes, she had. *Eighteen months* later. Which was when she found out he'd died. Gas leak in his apartment. He never knew a thing.

Wine from the carton. Canned cocktails. Punching Mules, her favorite.

She drank them all, and passed out on the beach. She woke up astonished to discover she had not been robbed, raped, or beaten up and left for dead.

A half-circle of miniature teepees sat behind her on the sand—people wrapped in blankets. They were dark shapes in the light from the distant Santa Monica pier. A joint glowed. "Just watching over you, sister."

Hannah struggled to her feet. "Th-thank you," she said.

"Be careful now."

"I will."

"They're coming."

Oh God. Whenever someone said *they* with that meaningful emphasis, it meant the aliens.

"Be ready when that day comes, sister."

"I w-will. Thank you again."

Staggering away, Hannah wondered: was this what her life had come to—protected from muggers by walkers?

While the fallout from the Earth Party's mid-term election antics percolated through the political system, the full-time devotees of the movement seemed to have settled down to wait and see what happened next. Instead of occupying city centers, they were now trickling back to their mountain-top hideouts—or, more appealing in November, California beaches.

Hannah circled around numerous groups of them as she stumbled back to her car.

By the time she got there, a new resolve had taken shape.

She might be guilty of letting people go, over and over, but there was one set of people she could not and would not let go: her sister's family. Since the early death of their parents, Bethany and Hannah had been each other's only family. Hannah loved Bee-Bee and her gang to death—even though Bethany knew just how to push her buttons—and it had been far too long since she visited them.

She put the car in gear, resolving that she would go to Pacific Palisades *today.*

It ended up being tomorrow, because she had to finish off the alcohol in her hotel room first. She was still sweating it out as she crawled in her rental car along the leafy road to her sister's home. She figured it was better to show up early, and a little bit drunk, rather than later, when she might be too drunk to show up at all.

"It's eight in the flipping morning, Hannah!" Bethany cried, when she opened the door.

Jetlag, Hannah said, making much of the two-hour time difference between Texas and California. She'd put Visine in her eyes before getting out of the car, but they still looked red, which would support her story that she'd just got off the plane.

"Izzy isn't up yet," Bethany said. She wrapped Hannah in a hug. "Oh my God, I am so happy to see you! You couldn't call to say you were coming? OK, OK, it's fine. Never mind. You're here."

Hannah relaxed into the hug with a profound sense of homecoming. Both sisters inherited heavy hips and large bosoms—their grandmother had dryly called it 'famine insurance'—but Bethany had really packed on the pounds since having kids. Her hugs felt like being enfolded in the world's coziest quilt, all the more so since she was wearing vast patchwork pyjamas, which she'd probably made herself. Hannah smelled laundry softener and milk, and belatedly held her breath lest Bethany should smell the booze on her, although she'd made sure to shower, brush her teeth, and gargle with Listerine.

"Well, well, a stranger comes to town!" David Marshall, Bethany's husband, ambled out of the archway leading to the open-plan living and kitchen area. On his hip sat a golden-haired cupid, thumb in mouth.

Bethany and David had had a second child, to everyone's surprise, when Isabel was eleven. It stunned Hannah to see how big Nathan had gotten since she last saw him, and furthermore to realize—this was really awful—that this was only the second time she'd seen him, in the flesh, since he was born.

"Aw, bubbeleh," she crooned, breaking away from Bethany. "Do you remember your auntie?"

Nathan hid his face in his dad's shoulder.

"Can I hold him, David? Just for a minute …"

But when they tried to transfer Nathan into Hannah's arms, he started to wail. Hurt, Hannah retreated.

"He just needs to get used to you," Bethany said. "David, is that coffee I can smell? *Perfect.*"

Sitting on the deck out back for a breakfast of freshly perked coffee, rolls, cantaloupe, and kefir, Hannah felt like she'd stepped into a dream world where there was no MOAD orbiting Europa. She played peek-a-boo with Nathan, and won a single heart-melting smile from him. She decided that her goal for the day would be winning her little nephew over.

Isabel, now thirteen going on twenty, stumbled past them clad in a bathing suit, her short hair tousled from sleep. Without a word, she dived into the backyard pool and began to swim lengths.

"An hour every morning," Bethany said proudly, "and on weekdays she trains after school, too." Bethany raised her hands in a gesture of helplessness. "It's self-directed, Hannah. We don't push her. Some things just come from inside."

"And I was worried about drinking and boys," David joked.

The reference to drinking made Hannah twitch, even though she knew that Bethany and David didn't suspect she had a problem. "She's driven," she said, watching Isabel flash through the water. Up and down. Up and down.

Although she didn't say this to her sister and brother-in-law, Isabel's swimming reminded Hannah uneasily of the Earth Partiers' walking. On, on, on, going nowhere. Was Isabel swimming for hours every day—overtaxing her barely-teenage body, if Bethany was telling the truth about her training regimen—because there was an alien ship orbiting Europa? It was a horribly un-mathematical idea, but it wouldn't let go, even after Bethany glowingly showed her Isabel's trophies from junior high swim meets. Isabel was no ordinary swimmer, anyway.

"I'm hyper-competitive," Isabel herself frankly acknowledged, at lunch. "I blame this guy." She tweaked her father's apron strings. He was BBQing, the Marshalls having organized an impromptu cookout in honor of Hannah's visit.

Neighbors and fellow parents of toddlers stood around the pool, chatting. "He made his first million before he was thirty, then started his own law firm. And I'm *not* gonna inherit a competitive streak?"

"You better also inherit my talent with a grill," David growled. He deftly thrust the tongs into his daughter's hand. "Keep an eye on the bloody, dripping lumps of flesh while I get a beer."

Hannah grinned widely. They were such a lovely family. In that moment, she'd have given up everything to trade places with her sister.

She trailed after David to the fridge in the kitchen. Bottles of chichi local microbrews, rosé, and sparkling white wine, most of it brought by friends, crammed the spaces in between Bethany's tupperwares of specially prepared food for Nathan. David grabbed a bottle of something called Dead Ringer. "How 'bout a tall one, Hannah?"

She stood paralyzed, staring into the fridge.

This perfect day *needed* a drink to make it complete.

She could already taste that rosé, cool and sweet. That's what she really wanted. Not a beer. Dared she ask for it?

"Oh, forgot, you're driving later," David said, taking her silence for a no. "Got iced tea, iced coffee, diet cherry coke—that shit is disgusting, but don't tell Bethany I said so!"

Hannah laughed. "No, you're right, it is disgusting. Maybe I'll just have one. Same thing you're having."

She didn't even like beer. So she wouldn't be tempted to have another one. That's what she told herself.

"Good call," David said blithely. He plumped the cold bottle into her hand, and talked at length about the qualities of this beer—its rich caramelly taste, its toasted malt aroma—as they meandered back out to the deck.

Everything he said was true. Halfway down the bottle, Hannah wondered how she could've been so wrong about beer.

The afternoon became kind of a blur after that.

At one point, she found herself trapped by the hedge with a man who used to be a partner in David's law firm. He interrogated her about the *SoD*. Word had got out that she worked on the project, although Bethany and David had been great about not giving out any details, and in fact, not even they knew that she was the worldwide leader of the propulsion group. This guy wasn't interested in the propulsion system, anyway. He wanted to know about the ship's armaments.

Everyone wanted to know about the armaments, despite NASA's never having officially confirmed that the *SoD* would carry any.

"Are they nukes?" he asked. "This thing *does* have a nuke, right? I mean, it *runs* on nuclear power!"

"Yeah," Hannah said. "The reactor puts out 1.1 gigawatts. If the heat rejection systems fail, the ship will be instantaneously reduced to an expanding cloud of atoms." The bottle in her hand was empty. She wanted to get away from this guy and get another one.

"So it's like a self-destruct button?"

"I guess you could put it like that," Hannah said. The angel's trumpets growing by the hedge smelled so intense, the scent was giving her a high. The water in the pool sparkled blindingly.

"That's good," the guy said. "Because I guess you know

the MOAD is a trap." He leaned closer to her. His body odor overpowered the scent of the flowers. "They sent it here so we'd see it. And of course, being stupid fucking monkeys, we're going to poke it …" His eyes were bright, crazy. "I hope at least one of the crew survives long enough to hit the self-destruct button."

Bethany materialized at Hannah's side. She cooed, "I'm gonna steal Hannah, sorry, Craig. I hardly ever get to see her …"

"We're leaving L.A. next month," Craig said. "I've got a place in Montana."

Towing Hannah away, Bethany whispered, "Poor Craig. He'd gone totally off the rails. I wish David wouldn't have invited him. He feels sorry for him, I guess. I mean, he used to be a brilliant lawyer …"

But it was clear to Hannah, as Craig stood alone, staring after the women, that *he* felt sorry for *them.* After all, *they* were going to stay behind and die when the *SoD* returned to Earth with its lethal cargo of—alien bacteria? Nano-goo? What did he imagine could have survived a journey of millennia? She wondered what difference he thought moving to Montana would make.

And yet, if you believed in a looming threat to Earth, what else was there to do? A brilliant lawyer wouldn't be able to settle for just walking.

"Is he right, Hannah?" Bethany said. "Is the MOAD dangerous?"

Looking into her sister's frightened eyes, Hannah understood that the lovely normality of this cookout was a lie. Everyone was scared. Hell, how did Bethany and David rustle up twenty-five friends and neighbors at zero notice, anyway? Pre-MOAD, they would all have been busy on a Saturday, doing important stuff by themselves. Now they jumped at the chance to come together. Because they were scared.

She said, "The whole 'it's a trap' theory is so full of holes, I don't even know where to begin. If the aliens who built the MOAD, *if* they had a specific vendetta against humanity, which is implausible for other reasons, they would've invaded us in the first place. Why over-complicate it by making us go to Europa to get infected with alien cooties, or turned into pod people, or whatever the hell these nutsos think is going to happen? No. The MOAD is a hulk, equipped with limited autonomous defence systems. It wound up here the same way driftwood winds up on a beach."

Bethany looked reassured. "Well, that makes sense when you put it like that," she said. "I'm going to go check on Nathan. He's had a long enough nap."

Hannah headed back to the table on the deck, where the drinks now stood in a cooler full of ice. The rosé had already been opened, so she didn't feel bad about pouring herself a plastic cupful, and swiftly draining it (no one was looking, she was pretty sure) and then refilling the cup.

She wandered over to the pool. Some grade-school-age kids splashed around in swim rings. Isabel was back in her swimsuit, patiently teaching a younger girl how to swim with her face in the water.

It was *unthinkable* that all this should be wiped out.

Alien cooties. Oy vey.

Yet her own voice came back to her down a long tunnel of intoxication: *They just wiped out our most advanced space probe ... This is not going to end well.*

That's what she herself had said, reacting to the death of Juno. She'd changed her mind when she got more information, as you were supposed to. But most people didn't have the training to understand the data which proved the MOAD was a fatally damaged hulk. They just had to believe what the government told them. And with good reason, people had lost the habit of doing that.

Bethany came out of the house, carrying Nathan, who was fretful after his nap. David took over. He swung Nathan up into the air until the toddler laughed. "Here's your auntie, buddy. Want to hang with Aunt Hannah for a while?"

Now cheerful, Nathan smiled and held out his arms to Hannah. Utterly charmed, Hannah set down her drink on the lawn table by the side of the pool and took him.

"Is that wine, Hannah?" Bethany said disapprovingly. "Don't you have to drive?"

Damn. She should have had the sparkling white, then she could have passed it off as Sprite. Hugging Nathan, she said, "I can always stay over, can't I?"

Nathan started to squirm. Oh, no! Hannah held him in front of her face and cooed, "How did you get to be so cute? It should be illegal."

Nathan turned his face aside. Maybe he was smelling her breath. He let out a grumpy cry.

Desperate to make him smile, Hannah resorted to what she'd seen David do. She lifted Nathan over her head and dipped him down again. That did it! "That's fun, huh? Air Nathan, preparing for takeoff! Zzzzzoooom!"

Nathan smiled widely. Carried away, Hannah started to spin in circles while making him fly like an airplane. "We're off, we're off to … where shall we go? *Not* Europa …"

"Not too high," Bethany cautioned.

"We're fine. Aren't we, bubbeleh? Zzzzooomm!"

Nathan laughed out loud, and Hannah slipped.

The tiles around the swimming pool, where the children had been climbing in and out, were wet and slick.

Her feet skidded out from under her.

Nathan!

Instinctively, she clutched him to her chest instead of using her hands to break her fall.

Bethany screamed, far away.

Hannah went down full length, hitting her legs on the lip of the pool. She pitched headfirst into the water, and lost her grip on the child. She sank, her arms empty.

CHAPTER 38

"Hannah! I've been trying to reach you all weekend. Why haven't you been answering your phone?"

Hannah thought about all the ways she could respond to Burke's enquiry.

She sat on top of a cliff at Point Dume, wrapped in a blanket. Far below, surf crashed onto the beach. She'd driven north along the Pacific Coast Highway and stopped when she saw a sizable encampment of walkers. She'd borrowed the blanket from them.

"Just personal stuff," she said eventually.

*

"You were drinking!" Bethany had screamed at her, in front of all their guests.

When Hannah and Nathan fell in the pool, David had dived in after them, followed by several others. Isabel—already in the pool—had rescued her little brother before he had time to swallow much water. Turned out she had a lifeguard certificate, too. Nathan had never been in real danger.

But that, understandably, did not appease Bethany.

"I slipped," Hannah said numbly. "The tiles are wet. You should get terracotta."

Cuddling her squalling, terrified son, Bethany yelled, "You did not fucking slip because we were too cheap to get fucking terracotta! You slipped because you were fucking drunk!"

Complete silence. Hannah's gaze drifted to David. His mouth hung open in unfaked astonishment. He hadn't known.

But Bethany had. All these years Hannah smugly assumed her secret was safe from her sister, turned out Bethany had been noticing things.

"You were drunk at Mom and Dad's funeral. You were drunk at *Granny's* funeral. When we sat shiva for her, you kept sneaking away, and I'm like *no one* has to go to the bathroom that much, so I looked in your toilet bag." Bethany nodded at her stunned audience, not too distressed to milk the moment. "She had airline miniatures in there," she told them all. "Vodka, gin, I don't even know what. And I looked in her suitcase and there was a fifth of whiskey, and I'm like, oh so that explains it—she used to get her coffee and take it upstairs, and I thought that was weird but whatever, but she was spiking the damn coffee. And she thought I didn't guess. Right?" she screamed at Hannah. "You thought I didn't notice anything because I'm too *dumb!* I'm just a stay-at-home mom, so I guess that makes me *stupid* as well as *fat,* right? But at least I'm not a fucking alcoholic!"

Hannah stood there, wet to the skin. No one had given *her* a towel to wrap up in. She opened her mouth to defend herself, despite having no idea what she could say. Every one of Bethany's accusations was true.

David spoke before she could. "Jesus Christ, Bee-Bee, are you out of your mind?"

Huh? Why was he angry with Bethany?

"You knew she was an alcoholic? And you let her come here? You trusted her with our *son?!*"

Oh.

Dripping on the deck, David strode over to Bethany and tried to wrestle Nathan away from her. Bethany, weeping, resisted. "She's my sister! I love her!"

David gave up on trying to pry Nathan away from his wife. He faced Hannah, puce with rage. She understood that he felt guilty because he'd offered her a beer, nay, pushed it on her. "Get off my property."

"Please," Hannah said.

"You almost killed my son. Leave, or I'm calling the cops."

Bethany decided to side with her husband. "You may be a great scientist," she told Hannah, "but you're a shitty human being. I've tried with you, I've tried and tried, God knows, and this is what I get for it? Just go away, Hannah. You need professional help. Get it, please." She started crying again.

Hannah stumbled through the horrified, silent guests, out to her car.

The image that stayed in her mind was Isabel—silent, her lifesaving deed unappreciated—diving back into the pool again.

*

And now here she sat on top of a cliff, looking down at the messy camp on the beach.

"I quit," she told Burke.

Maybe she'd join the walkers. Go wherever they were going.

"Hannah? I'm sorry, I didn't catch that."

"I. Quit."

She fingered the contusion on her right shin. That was where she'd hit the lip of the pool. She had bruises on both legs, and this gash on her right leg which had bled like a faucet. No one at the cookout had said anything about it. Hannah herself hadn't even noticed it until she pulled over to cry, a mile from Bethany and David's place. It had started hurting then, and it still hurt now, one night and a handful of Tylenol later.

At last, Burke said, "You can't quit."

"I knew you'd say that, Rich."

"I don't know what's going on with you, Hannah-banana …"

She'd turned as she fell. Twisted, taking the damage on her own body, to protect the child. So at least she had some good instincts buried deep inside. She clung to that meager shred of self-esteem.

"… but quitting isn't an option."

"Why's that?"

Burke uttered the ghost of a laugh. "It's ironic. I actually called to congratulate you."

"On what?"

"Your new job. Hannah, you're going on the *Spirit of Destiny.*"

*

She stood up, leaving her borrowed blanket in a pile, and kicked her Keds off. Barefoot, she began to pace. "This is insane, Burke. I'm not an astronaut."

"We've got five months until launch. That's long enough for you to go up on a bunch of vomit comet flights, get fitted for a spacesuit. You've already done some of the basic stuff. The flight simulator …"

"Everyone did that."

"*Everyone* isn't a world-class expert on propulsion systems."

It hit her then. "This is because Koichi got kicked off the mission."

"You got it. We're short a reactor and propulsion systems

specialist."

"The Russians have plenty of experts."

"They want to put someone up. Sure they do. But we don't want to give them the slot."

"Oh, I get it. This is another international cooperation moment."

"Yeah." *International cooperation* had become universally understood shorthand for vicious international competition. "It was inevitable, the moment Masuoka got yanked. Everyone's jockeying for the slot. The Chinese want it, too."

"They don't have anyone with the expertise, do they? And they already have two crew slots. Whereas the Russians only have one. And we have *three*. It would be fairer to give it to them."

"Since when," said Burke, "is fairness the guiding principle here?"

"Point," Hannah acknowledged bleakly.

"The guiding principle, *my* guiding principle, is the success of the mission. And this is why I am turning to you, Hannah." He was in the office on a Sunday again. She pictured him leaning on his desk, resting his head on one hand. "Not because you're American. But because you understand the *Spirit of Destiny's* propulsion system better than anyone. You're not just a world-class expert—when it comes to Sonic, you're *the* expert."

She didn't argue with that.

"You built that thing. You practically invented it."

"No," she murmured. "Oliver Meeks did that."

"Yes. You figure he would want to see it put into the care of someone else? I think he would prefer the person who built it, who made his dream a reality."

She thought about Nathan, the way David had yelled at Bethany for putting the child into her care. Sonic was even more finicky and breakable than a child. She shook her head. "No, Burke, I can't do it."

"You're being goddamn selfish!" he yelled down the phone, like he'd never ever yelled at her before.

That shook her. Was it true? Perhaps it was—

—because the first, the very *first* thing that sprang to mind when she thought about the mission was *five years without booze.*

And God knows she couldn't live without booze that long. Because she was a sad sack alcoholic. *Right?*

Burke modulated his tone. "Is there something else I don't know about, Hannah?"

She froze, one foot poised, like a deer. "Such as what?"

"I've looked at your medical records. Everything seems fine. But what about your genetics? I know," he said delicately, "your parents passed away prematurely …"

"Oh, you're thinking about cancer," she realized. "Nope. They died in a traffic accident. And speaking of cancer, I'm Ashkenazi, as you know. So I've actually had those tests—for the BRCA1 and BRCA2 genes. My sister and I both got tested. We're both fine, I'm thankful to say."

"That is wonderful news. So there's no obstacle to you joining the mission. But I'm not going to push you, if your heart's not in it."

"Rich …"

"No, Hannah-banana," he said with a deep sigh. "I understand. It's too much to ask. You'd be going where no human being has ever gone before. Beyond the asteroid belt. Into the Jovian system, which we never got to study up close, after all. You'd be facing trials of will and courage that very few could pass, and those few only because they're driven by an insatiable desire to explore the unknown. And if that's not enough, you'd be investigating an alien artefact, potentially dangerous, which may explode the boundaries of human knowledge … or just explode." Burke sighed again. "No one could take that on who wasn't driven, dedicated, infernally curious, and at the same time, a good team player with a sense of humor. Which doesn't at all describe you, of course."

He'd just described the way she was without the booze. The way she wanted to be. "Go to hell, Rich," she said, laughing. "I'll do it. I was just surprised, that's all"

"No, no. I'll tell them we're OK with Nikolai Petrov taking the slot."

"I'll do it! I want to!"

"Are you sure?"

"Yes!"

"I knew you'd jump on it," Burke said in satisfaction. They both laughed. "You do know about the survivability stats," Burke mentioned.

"Oh, rats, I was forgetting about those," Hannah said in mock horror.

The 'survivability stats' had been a thing in the news recently. Someone on the internet had jumped into a bucket full of poorly understood math and come up with figures for the chances of the crew's survival. The *SoD* consortium had debunked them, pointing out that there were too many unknowns to make any such calculations, but the precision of the figures had helped them catch the public imagination. So, according to the internet, the likelihood that at least *one* crew member of the *SoD* would return to Earth was 55%. The likelihood that they *all* would: 13%.

"Even the internet gives me a better than even chance of coming back," Hannah said. "I'll take that."

She walked to the edge of the cliff. Vertigo gripped her. Digging her bare toes into the sparse grass, she gazed out at the Pacific, and then down again at the chaotic camp on the beach. She had thought about joining the walkers. Leaving her whole life behind.

As it turned out, she didn't even need to quit her job to do that.

CHAPTER 39

Jack walked along Wentworth Drive towards his parents' house. The street ahead of him, lined with neat lawns and neat brick houses, lay empty and gray in the rain.

A boy came around the bend, pedaling a bike. He stopped, put his feet down, and stared. Well might he stare.

Behind Jack, reporters packed the street. Juggling their cameras and microphones, they tripped over each other to keep up with Jack's rapid, pissed-off stride. Satellite vans trundled in the rear of the horde.

Jack outdistanced them, heading into the crescent where his parents lived. The Kildare home stood out from the others on the crescent because of the garden. His mother's riot of plants took the place of a lawn. It was March, so the daffodils were in full flower, their trumpets pearled with droplets by the fine English rain.

Warned to expect this invasion, his parents waited on the doorstep with stiff expressions.

There was a Jaguar parked on the forecourt. Had Dad bought a new motor? It would no longer be beyond their means, since Jack was quite well paid these days, and he sent most of the dough home to them. It would be wildly out of character though.

He hugged them, whispered, "Sorry about this," and then eased them inside and closed the door in the reporters' faces. It took considerable willpower not to slam it, much less flip them off as he would have liked to.

His mother said, "Aren't we supposed to do an interview?"

"We can do it later. Let them hang around and get wet for

a bit."

On cue, Jack's phone started to ring. So did his mother's. So did his father's. So did the landline in the sitting-room.

Jack turned his phone off, advised his parents to do likewise, and went into the sitting-room with the intention of pulling the phone out of the wall. This was his last visit home before the crew started pre-launch procedures. He would not see his parents again for five years … if ever. He was damned if he'd let this gutter-dwelling mob intrude for the sake of clicks and ratings.

In the doorway of the sitting-room, he stopped in surprise.

A couple his parents' age sat on the sectional sofa, teacups in hand. They were both expensively dressed and Jack twigged that he was looking at the owners of the Jaguar. As far as he knew he'd never seen them before.

The man rose, transferred his teacup to his left hand, and shook Jack's hand. "We've been following your career with great interest. It's a pleasure."

Jack's mother rescued him, putting in: "Jack and Oliver were so close, they were like brothers, weren't you, Jack?"

Cripes. These were Meeks's parents!

The doorbell rang, and kept ringing. Jack's father left the room, saying he would disconnect it.

Jack mumbled something polite to Meeks's parents. His mother followed up with a remark about how 'Oliver' must be smiling down on them from heaven now.

Helen Kildare, née Robinson, was American. That was how Jack got his dual citizenship. Born in Charleston, she'd lived in England ever since she met John Kildare on a London bus in 1972, and her Southern accent lingered only faintly, but she could and did say sentimental things no Brit would have dreamt of uttering.

Jack expected that remark about Meeks playing a harp with the angels would bring the conversation, such as it was, to a crashing halt. But Meeks's parents surprised him. They eagerly took up the topic of heaven. Jack's father—the relapsed Catholic—plunged onto the end of the sectional and joined in.

Jack sat on the hassock that hovered apart from the sectional, like a detached booster rocket, and smoothed the rain off his hair. He took off his jacket and dropped it on the floor, as was his habit. The dog—Marvin, a spaniel—promptly lay on it.

"Tea, honey?" his mother said.

"Lovely, Mum."

His father expounded a theory, new to Jack, that the resurrection of the body, as preached by the Church, made perfect sense in view of quantum theory. Retired science teacher or not, it was clear he didn't understand quantum theory (nor did Jack), but he explained to the Meekses that quanta—the fundamental building blocks of matter—were capable of remote and mysterious entanglements. This being the case, why shouldn't God reassemble one's body—the *atoms,* mind you, the *very same atoms* that composed one's body now—on the Day of Judgment, no matter where they may have scattered to in the meantime?

Meeks's mother said, "That's an intriguing idea, but isn't God capable of *anything?* Why would He need to go to the bother—"

"Oh well you see, that's the broader theory," John Kildare said. "Everything we see that isn't currently understood—including miracles, even the miracles of Jesus—is evidence of a higher physics. God so arranged the universe that anything should be possible. It isn't *magic.*"

Meeks's mother was a plump woman with hair dyed a shade of blonde that surely hadn't been her natural color. Despite this, she projected faded elegance. She half-rose, hovering over the coffee table as if looking for somewhere to put down her teacup. The coffee table overflowed, as usual, with the trappings of Jack's father's hobby: weather observations charted on graph paper pads, colored markers and a slide rule, measurement units for a wireless temperature logger, and an anemometer, half-disassembled. John Kildare was an amateur meteorologist. The tea tray balanced precariously on a corner of the table.

Jack's mother sprang up to take the unwanted cup. Mrs. Meeks bent and delved in a large handbag. She removed something from it, and came around the coffee table to Jack. "On that note," she said, "that is, resurrection, and so forth—"

She stood on the dog's paw. Marvin howled. Jack, standing, bent to soothe him.

"I'm so sorry," Mrs. Meeks said. "Please do tell us, straight away, if this is inappropriate. But I believe he would have liked it, and …" Her voice failed. She pushed the object at Jack, who turned it over, nonplussed. It was a brushed aluminum capsule about four inches long.

Mrs. Meeks was crying. It was a terrible sight, this carefully made-up woman in her sixties, with tears tracking her mascara down her cheeks. Her husband put an arm around her and guided her back to the sofa. He said, "What she means to say is that we think Oliver would have liked to have his ashes scattered in space."

Jack jumped. The capsule in his hand suddenly seemed to generate a violent electric charge. It was Meeks! It was his bloody *ashes*. Oh, God.

"If you would be so kind," Mr. Meeks went on. "But perhaps you aren't allowed to take any personal belongings up with you?"

Jack blurted, "Of course I'll do it!" What did one *say?* "It would be an honor. Thank you for thinking of me."

Meeks's mother babbled thanks. Jack's mother sat close beside her with a box of tissues.

Jack sat down again. He suddenly felt sick with sadness, as if Mrs. Meeks's grief were catching. What a nice cheerful visit this was turning out to be.

Throughout these years of training, orbital construction work, and more training, the relentless tempo of deadlines and the ever-approaching date of the launch itself had occupied his mind, almost to the exclusion of all else. Firebird Systems, the outrage of NASA's technology theft, and above all, Meeks's murder, had been relegated to a dark cupboard in the back of his mind.

Now it all came falling out, exactly as if Mrs. Meeks had found the cupboard and opened it.

He'd vowed to identify Meeks's murderer and bring him (or her) to justice, and what had he done about it? Fuck all. And now, with just two weeks left to go until launch, it was too late.

He owed Meeks much more than an empty sentimental gesture. But if it brought Meeks's parents some closure, it was well worth doing. He slid the capsule containing Meeks's remains into the pocket of his jeans. That seemed like a poor way to treat it, but the alternative was asking his mother for a plastic carrier bag, which would, he suspected, be worse.

"It'll be no problem," he said. "We're each allowed to take three kilos of personal belongings."

That prompted his parents to bring out the things they had bought or made for him to take, including a a new rosary to replace the beat-up one which had lived in his back pocket for the last two years. "It's made of tungsten," his father said proudly. "Tough enough to stand up to space! And here." A thumb-sized gadget on a keychain. "I'm sure you know what this is!"

"A *radiation dosimeter?"*

"Yes! Amazing how compact everything is nowadays."

"Dad, we've got those in the ship …"

"A portable one might come in handy," his father said.

His mother added, "We also got this made online."

A lightweight travel mug covered with slogans and jokes, ranging from 'I heart Nuneaton' to a cartoon of the *SoD* with the caption 'I can't believe the government is paying for this.'

Jack grinned. "This is definitely coming with me."

The Meekses tactfully left, to give them some time together. The reporters of course besieged them the moment they appeared on the doorstep. Jack and his parents watched from behind the sitting-room curtains. His father muttered, "I'd like to see him mow some of them down with that Jag."

"Weren't they divorced, Mum?" Jack said.

"Apparently they *were,* but they've got back together. It's funny, isn't it? The death of a child often drives couples apart, but in this case it seems to have brought them back together."

The death of a child. The words hung in the air, reminding Jack that he was his parents' only child. Without having an inflated sense of his own importance, he knew they both lived for him and through him. And now they were seeing him off on a journey more dangerous than any of his deployments in Iraq.

He put a hand on each of their shoulders. "Mum. Dad. You may have heard some statistics floating around. Fifty-five percent … thirteen percent? Those come straight from the Department of Making It Up Wholesale. The truth is that no one has any real grasp of the risks, least of all me."

"That's reassuring," his father said dryly.

"Right? But I promise you one thing. I will come back."

Wheeeeeooooow. Beep, beep, beeeep. EEEEEE!

Those spooky noises he'd heard on the Atlantis suddenly echoed in his mind. He never had told anyone about that. He clenched his jaw in irritation. Why should he remember that now?

"I *will* come back," he repeated, forcefully.

Later, autopiloting through the round of interviews the consortium had promised to the British media, he touched the capsule of ashes in his pocket. It helped to distract him from the wretched business of leaving his parents, possibly for the last time.

He *had* to do something more for Meeks. It was a loose end. Yes, Jack planned to return to Earth, absolutely and without a doubt, but how could he set off for Europa in the first place, knowing that Meeks's murderer was still walking around and thinking they'd got away with it?

Maybe there *was* time. In a week, Jack would enter pre-flight quarantine at Kennedy Space Center. The door would slam on the possibility of further action at that point. So he had a few days. But where to start?

Skyler, obviously. If anyone knew the truth, Skyler Taft did. Jack hadn't seen the little twat since Beijing. Where was he, anyway?

CHAPTER 40

Skyler let himself into the Beacon Hill townhouse where he'd grown up. The frigid March wind swept in after him. "Hello," he shouted.

Standing in the hall, he heard faint explosions from upstairs.

"Trek?"

That had to be his brother Trekker playing a video game, but if Trek wasn't going to come down and say hi, screw him. Skyler was only here on a duty call, and duty had been satisfied by the act of walking through the door. He didn't have to actually see any of his family, much less talk to them.

He wandered through to the kitchen. The kitchen table was covered with drying watercolors—Dad's—and the huge natural-gas stove held a collection of pots which, on inspection, contained sour-smelling dye baths, not anything edible. Skyler opened the refrigerator. It was slim pickings, in the nutritional sense, although high-calorie junk abounded. Skyler had skipped lunch. He selected a packet of Reese's peanut butter cups. The salt shaker stood on the counter. Skyler sprinkled salt on the chocolate.

Munching, he went to look out of the double doors into the backyard. Enclosed by high brick walls, it was a green marble rectangle with a wrought iron table and chairs in the middle. You couldn't tell what season it was out there, except for the bare branches of the trees in neighboring gardens poking over the wall. A hefty bronze nude reclined near the table and chairs. It was an original Rodin, although 'original' kinda lost its meaning when, like old Auguste, you turned out copies of your own stuff by the hundred.

That also went for Dad. Skyler frowned at the watercolors on the table. They depicted happy couples, family groups. The photographs Dad painted from were propped against water jars. Avigdor Taft had real talent, in his elder son's opinion, but for some reason he chose to churn out these commercial 'hand-painted portraits,' as if it gratified him to produce middlebrow hack-work. He had an online store, capitalizing on the Taft name and their Beacon Hill address.

Footsteps sounded in the hall. Trekker came into the kitchen. He was unshaven and wore sweats that clearly hadn't been washed for weeks. "Hey, that's my food," he said, spotting a peanut butter cup vanishing into Skyler's mouth.

"You have a whole candy store in that fridge," Skyler replied. "You won't miss it."

All through their childhood and adolescence it had been a theme: don't take Trek's food. The caution had been well-intentioned. Mom and Dad had believed junk food was the devil, and only allowed it in the house because Trek's needs trumped principle. Trek had severe cystic fibrosis, a genetic disease that carried a sentence of mortality in early adulthood. At twenty-seven, he'd already lived longer than the doctors expected. He coughed terribly, and was so skinny you could practically see through him. Hence the attempts to feed him up with whatever had the most calories per bite.

"Dad's?" Skyler said, nodding at the pans of dye on the stove.

"Piper's." Trek did not explain what Piper was doing with

dye. He probably didn't know, or care.

"Is she walking again?" Skyler said, anticipating Trek's indifferent shrug.

Their sister had dropped out of Rhode Island School of Design, and then dropped out of Massachusetts College of Art and Design, both times because she couldn't get her coke habit under control. Nowadays she went on a lot of Earth Party walks with like-minded druggies and dropouts. It was embarrassing.

Skyler, Piper, and Trekker. Of the three of them, only Skyler had achieved something like success—although you couldn't exactly blame Trek for not being a go-getter, with a death sentence hanging over him.

"What are you doing here, anyway?" Trek said, finally evincing some curiosity.

"I'm wondering that myself. I should be in Russia," Skyler said. "This guy I work with? I'm pretty sure he attempted to sabotage the *Spirit of Destiny*. So I've been watching him."

Skyler had no qualms about letting Trek in on this. Trek wouldn't spread it around. Just in case, Skyler was careful to name no names.

"This guy, he's probably also working with the Chinese. I shouldn't say probably. *Maybe*. He says it's someone else."

"He would say that," Trek commented.

"Exactly." Skyler sighed. "I have some dirt on him, but I need more." He had not shared his photos of Lance and the Chinese woman with Director Flaherty, realizing on reflection how circumstantial it all was. A confrontation would achieve nothing at this point except to alert Lance to be more careful. As it happened, Lance had done nothing suspicious since Beijing. But this trip to Russia might give him the opportunity he'd been waiting for. "I think he might be planning to sabotage the gear the astronauts will be taking with them to the *SoD*. I'm gonna go along to keep an eye on him … but the boss told me to come here first."

"Why?"

Skyler imitated Flaherty's voice, not that Trek would know what the original sounded like. "'When was the last time you been home, Taft? Go say hey to your momma.'"

Trek laughed. "Does he know Mom lives in Bali?"

Given the NXC's close links with the NSA, Flaherty certainly did know it, which made his order even weirder. Before Skyler could say this, Trek's laugh turned into a cough. The horrible whooping noise went on and on. Trek's face purpled. Skyler went over to his brother and pounded on his back with loose fists.

Trek got the cough under control. He went to the fridge and drank some milk straight from the carton. "So this guy. Why would he sabotage the *SoD?* What would be in it for him?"

"Money," Skyler said immediately. This was the easiest part of the whole puzzle. "And sex. Although he probably thinks it's love. But mostly money."

"OK. What's in it for the guys paying him?"

"The Chinese."

"Why would *they* sabotage the *SoD?*"

"That is indeed the question. But here's what I think: they have their own mission to Europa waiting in reserve. Our intel sats have seen a lot of activity around the Korla test launch complex in northwestern China. That facility doesn't have anything to do with *SoD*-related launches. So it's possible that they want to take out the *SoD,* knowing that if this mission fails, we'll have shot our bolt. Then the field will be clear for them. They'll reach Europa before anyone else. The MOAD will be all theirs."

Trek nodded. "This is it for NASA, isn't it?"

"Yup. We've put everything we've got into the *SoD*."

"Chances we could start again from scratch?"

"Zero. We don't even have a functioning government."

"At least we still have a functioning stock market," Trek said—an allusion to the millions of dollars their dad had sitting in stocks and bonds, inherited from *his* father. Dividends paid the family's bills, including Trek's hospital bills. When Skyler thought about that, his pet policy idea of paying off foreign investors in Treasuries, immediately and massively devaluing the dollar, seemed a lot less attractive.

"Well, if you get this guy," Trek said, "give him a kick in the nuts for me." He opened the door, letting cold air into the kitchen. Then he lit a blunt.

"Trek!"

"What?"

Skyler waved away the marijuana smoke clouding from Trek's nostrils. "I don't know what's worse," he said. "You're smoking weed … or you're smoking weed in front of a Fed." He considered how hopeless it was to instruct anyone on how to live their life. "Or, you're smoking weed and you haven't offered me any."

Trek laughed. This time, he didn't start coughing. "This shit is amazing. Quality's gone way up since Massachusetts legalized it. Here, try for yourself."

Skyler took a hit off the blunt. He felt the pleasant swimminess spread through his head, and he felt the harsh smoke hitting his bronchioles. He thought about Trek's lungs, which were full of thick, sticky, bacteria-trapping mucus. Smoke of any kind was the worst possible thing for Trek to be inhaling. But he decided not to say anything more about it. He didn't want to lose Trek's love.

The brothers stood by the open door and blew the smoke outside, watching the March wind toss the bare boughs above the wall.

*

Not to be deflected, Skyler flew straight to Russia from Boston. He arrived in Baikonur on the day of the Intergalactic Tennis Open, an annual tradition that had been moved up this year so that the departing astronauts could take part. From high in the standing-room-only bleachers, he watched Adam Hardcastle destroy Alexei Ivanov, 6-4, 4-6, 6-2. Applause was muted.

Hardcastle would be going up to the *SoD* in a Soyuz. So would Ivanov, Qiu, and Xiang. The other four would be going up by Dragon from Kennedy Space Center, known to insiders as KSC.

Skyler took the inevitable call from Director Flaherty while he was loitering in the outdoor market, an open-air Aladdin's cave of space-themed swag and household staples. "What the fuck are you doing there?"

He was being asked that a lot recently, Skyler reflected.

"You're supposed to be in Florida. I told you to go see your momma. Then you were supposed go to Florida, not fucking Khazakhstan." Flaherty—whom Skyler had first met on a front porch in Arlington, under the name of Travis Moore—started laughing. He had too keen a sense of absurdity to stay angry long. It was the secret to his successful career in the mad, mad world of the American intelligence community. "You're not even on the right fucking continent!"

Skyler said, "Hey, did you know you can get a thing of fresh apricots for five rubles here? Or a mug with Alexei Ivanov's face on it. They're gonna be living off us for years to come."

SoD money had crashed into Baikonur like an earthquake, demolishing rickety Soviet-era buildings, replacing them with modern glass and steel. The ubiquitous space-themed monuments and artworks had survived, but had transmogrified into kitsch in their spanking-new surroundings. From where he stood, Skyler could see the ornate entrance of the market, which looked like a cross between an Orthodox onion dome and something out of *2001: A Space Odyssey.* Smells of turmeric and chili tinged the dry, cold air.

"Get your ass on a plane," Flaherty dictated. "I already said I want you at KSC."

To watch over Menelaou, Boisselot … and Kildare … and Ginsburg.

Do *not* want.

"And I want Lance at Baikonur."

To watch over the other four.

But why, anyway? What did Flaherty imagine was going to happen to the astronauts during their pre-flight quarantine? Did he think someone would slip polonium-210 into their food?

Nonsense. Once the doors of the Cosmonaut Hotel slammed shut behind Hardcastle, Ivanov, Qiu, and Xiang at 10 a.m. tomorrow morning, they'd be safe from any outside interference.

Skyler's worry was what might happen to them—and

their gear—in between now and then.

"Just twenty-four hours, boss," he pleaded, knowing that he was drawing down his amassed brownie points. "One more day. That's all, and I'll only be two days late getting to KSC."

After some more back-and-forth, Flaherty relented. The fact that there were no more flights to Moscow today probably colored his decision. Skyler watched the sun sink towards the steppe from Yuri Gagarin Park. Brown grass poked up through trodden snow. Skyler had no reason for being here, apart from that it was easy for him to blend in among the tourists who'd flocked into town for the historic launch. The same rationale had taken him to the outdoor market earlier. He knew precisely where Lance was all the time, thanks to the locator app. All he wished to do was be where Lance was not, so Lance wouldn't know that Skyler was spying on him.

Wouldn't Lance see Skyler on his own locator app? Not if he didn't turn it on and look for him, and why would he do that? He thought Skyler was in Florida. It was a risk worth taking, Skyler thought, with the security of the *SoD* mission at stake.

He ate borscht, fish, and meat dumplings at the restaurant of the Sputnik Hotel. It was just across the street from the Cosmonaut Hotel where the astronauts were staying. Lance was holed up next door in the much swankier Hotel Cosmodrome. His red dot on the screen of Skyler's phone stayed so still, Skyler wondered if he'd turned in for the night. But he couldn't take anything for granted.

Drinking a second cup of grainy, sweet coffee, he wondered how much of this foul stuff he'd need to stay awake all night.

Then Lance moved.

CHAPTER 41

On the screen of Skyler's phone, a red dot exited the Hotel Cosmodrome and crossed the street.

Lance's phone was moving. So, presumably, was Lance.

He was going to the Cosmonaut Hotel.

Skyler threw rubles on the table and galloped out. He lurked in the gateway of the Sputnik Hotel, watching Lance argue with the guards on the other side of the street. Security was tight, with good reason.

To Skyler's disgust, the guards let Lance in.

Skyler waited as long as he dared, and then crossed the street himself. Lance had unknowingly done the heavy lifting for him. Having allowed one NXC agent in, the guards barely blinked at another one who explained that he was "with that guy."

Skyler walked rapidly across the concrete plaza in front of the hotel. It was full dark now. Floodlights lit the grandiose façade. He'd seen Lance go in the main entrance. He went around the back of the building.

Out of sight of the windows, standing beneath a tree, he questioned what he hoped to accomplish here. Lance could be in there planting bombs in the astronauts' gear. He'd been carrying a rucksack. But whatever mischief he was up to, Skyler couldn't do anything about it. He pictured himself charging in there and demanding that Lance's stuff be scanned, Lance himself subjected to a body-search—bend and grab your ankles, dog!

They'd laugh at him.

They didn't know what Skyler knew, which was the depravity Lance was capable of. A man in a *wheelchair,* for fuck's sake. Computer monitors shattering. Coffee on the floor, mingling with blood. And then the crowning horror ... If Lance could do *that,* he could do anything.

The Cosmonaut Hotel had been renovated, in line with Baikonur's overall facelift. The west wing, to Skyler's right where he stood, was the quarantine area. It had its own doors at ground level. During their pre-flight period of isolation, astronauts and cosmonauts could run, swim and play tennis in the hotel's grounds, and take selfies in the Avenue of the Cosmonauts, where each cosmonaut or astronaut planted a tree before their voyage.

Skyler stood near the entrance to the Avenue of the Cosmonauts now. Yuri Gagarin's tree towered at the head of the long double line of trees. It was almost 60 years old, and pretty big.

A man came out of the west wing, carrying a large rucksack. Skyler stiffened. Lance?

As the man crossed behind the main building, the light from the windows revealed his fleshy profile.

Adam Hardcastle.

Huh?!?

Hardcastle angled towards Skyler, who hastily retreated.

The astronaut walked along the Avenue of the Cosmonauts, away from the hotel.

Fascinated, Skyler kept pace with him, walking on the patches of grass where there was no snow, placing his sneakered feet down as quietly as he could.

At the very end of the Avenue of the Cosmonauts, Hardcastle stopped. He looked around expectantly.

Footsteps rang on the intersecting path that formed a

T-junction with the avenue. "Garner," Hardcastle hailed.

Lance!

Minus his rucksack.

The two men talked quietly. Skyler was on fire. He felt certain that Hardcastle's life was in imminent danger. Lance had said several times that he suspected Hardcastle of being a Chinese spy. It was a great way of deflecting attention from himself. And what better way to 'prove' his suspicions than for Hardcastle to end up dead, no doubt with compromising evidence on his body?

Skyler edged closer.

The men were just dim silhouettes against the vast, cloudy night sky. The wind blowing off the steppe made the trees sough overhead, so Skyler couldn't catch their words.

Near the end of the avenue, four holes had been dug in readiness for Ivanov, Hardcastle, Qiu, and Xiang to plant their saplings. Plaques bearing each name already stood in place. Skyler crouched down there, instinctively making himself small.

Would it be his lot to save a life today? To make up, in some screwy way, for the death of Oliver Meeks? Yeah, and how? he mocked himself. He didn't have his Glock on him. Bringing a gun into what was, after all, a Russian military base would have been a bit too audacious.

Lance and Hardcastle shook hands and parted.

Each man went the way the other one had come. Lance walked back towards the hotel, along the Avenue of the Cosmonauts. Trapped, Skyler hunkered close to the ground.

Lance walked past without seeing him, so close that Skyler could hear the zipper of his coat jingling.

As Skyler crouched there, heart thudding, his gaze fell

on the nearest plaque.

The name of an *SoD* astronaut was written in raised white letters on a dark background.

Cyrillic, sure. Skyler's Russian was pathetic, but to facilitate occasional collaboration with Russian intelligence agencies, he'd learned their alphabet.

Those letters did not say *Alexei Ivanov,* or *Qiu Meili,* or *Xiang Peixun.* Or *Adam Hardcastle.*

They said *Lance Garner.*

*

Skyler ran after Hardcastle, who'd taken the other path. He caught up with him near the front gate. Hardcastle had circled around the hotel, instead of taking a shortcut through the main building. Skyler accosted him by grabbing his elbow.

Hardcastle whirled around, shaking him off. When he recognized Skyler, his stance relaxed, but his expression stayed wary. Skyler could see his pudgy face well in the light from the gates.

"You're overweight," Skyler said. "Did you even pass the medical?"

"Yes, I passed the medical," Hardcastle said. "What's that got to do with anything?"

"You're not going on the *Spirit of Destiny,* are you?"

"Of course I'm not going on that goddamn bottle rocket. I've got kids."

Skyler saw it all now. He didn't want to look stupid, even though he felt like the stupidest dweeb in the northern hemisphere. He said, "I just need to ensure your safety."

"Is there some problem?"

Yes, there was a problem. There was a kiloton-yield

problem which had just gone off in Skyler's face. But all he said was, "Where are you heading to now?" He placed a hand lightly behind Hardcastle's elbow to encourage him to start walking again.

"The Hotel Cosmodrome," Hardcastle said, swinging obediently into motion. "That's right, isn't it? I hole up in Garner's room, watch porn, and order room service for the next two weeks."

It was a good plan, Skyler agreed. He said, "I'll scout ahead. There were a lot of hacks here earlier."

There weren't any now. The media would be back tomorrow morning for the symbolic closing of the gates. This had been the perfect moment to make the switch.

Hardcastle followed him out past the guard kiosk, wearing a baseball cap which partially shadowed his face. Skyler accompanied him across the street and into the Hotel Cosmodrome. The security guard on duty greeted "Mr. Garner" with the faintest suggestion of a wink.

So the hotel staff had been paid off. The important people, the officials and ground techs at the Cosmodrome itself, would have been squared away. All that mattered now was hiding the switcheroo from the US media, who'd be shocked, *shocked* if they discovered that one of America's Heroes™ had changed places with a spook.

Yup, they'd be almost as shocked as Skyler was.

Hiding his dismay, he reconfirmed Hardcastle's plans. These amounted to flying home to the US as soon as the 'bottle rocket' left Earth orbit. "Wait here," Skyler said. He ran next door, took his Glock out of his suitcase, checked that it was fully loaded, and brought it to Hardcastle's room in the Hotel Cosmodrome. "You'd better have this."

"What for?" Hardcastle said. He'd already stripped to his boxers and t-shirt. The fake fire in his room blazed. The television yakked. He was making himself comfortable, but his shoulders slumped. Skyler guessed—*hoped*—the man was ashamed of his part in this deception. He was an astronaut, after all.

"Just in case," Skyler said with his enigmatic NXC smile. He placed the Glock on Hardcastle's dressing table. He didn't feel 100% sure that Hardcastle was scheduled to survive this. There was more than one way to pay off a Russian security guard. At least this way, Hardcastle would have a chance to see his kids again.

Skyler went back next door to his own, much shabbier accommodations. He locked the door, opened the window, and lit one of his rare cigarettes.

He'd been played for a fool.

All this time he thought he was Director Flaherty's favorite, it had been Lance, after all.

How long had they been planning this? Long enough to have a custom Soyuz seat made for Lance, anyway.

Those horrible trips he and Lance had taken into orbit, supposedly because they were needed to help out with the construction of the *SoD?* Training. For Lance.

Lance's suspicions of Hardcastle? Prefabricated as an excuse for booting Hardcastle off the mission, when the US media eventually did find out. *(Poor* Hardcastle.)

And all the work Skyler had done with Laura and Guillermo and Curtis, and the rest of the 'second string,' with Flaherty's encouragement and approval, preparing them to step in at the last moment …

… not to mention the work put in by the *official* reserve

astronauts from each country, who were just there for show, but they'd still had to spend years of their lives in training …

… all of it, *all* a complete fucking waste!

Really angry now, Skyler paused in his pacing to ash his cigarette out the window. He glowered at the Cosmonaut Hotel on the far side of the street. Presumably Lance was now settling in, using his good ol' boy charm on his flummoxed crewmates. *Bastard.* In his head, Skyler used the Russian insult: *dog*.

OK. OK, but wait.

Maybe Hardcastle actually was a Chinese spy. In which case his replacement had been wise and necessary.

No, no. That was bullshit, and it always had been bullshit.

This was an NXC power play, pure and simple.

Flaherty and his allies were on the verge of pulling off a coup. Skyler had been incidental to the plot. He'd just been used.

He lit another cigarette, and his phone rang. Flaherty.

"Taft."

"You catch up with Lance?"

A long moment of silence. "Yes," Skyler said. "I did."

"You just gotta find shit out for yourself, don't you?" Flaherty said. "I was gonna put you into the picture next week. Wouldn't have cost a business-class ticket on Aeroflot, either."

"What can I say, boss? I had a craving for borscht."

Flaherty gave his unamused chuckle. "I'll see you at KSC on Monday."

Stubbing out his last cigarette of the night, Skyler replayed the brief conversation in his head.

You catch up with Lance?

Not yet, boss. But I'm going to.

*

Monday. KSC, Kennedy Space Center, the most valorized facility in the entire US space industry.

Skyler sat in a conference room in the astronaut crew quarters with Director Flaherty, who'd put on weight over the years and now carried a pregnant-looking belly above his belt buckle.

In an ironic contrast to the poetic touches at Baikonur, the Neil Armstrong Operations and Checkout Building was a concrete cuboid that evoked the word 'Stalinist.' Down the hall, the astronauts were settling into their bedrooms. Skyler sat in front of a view of a parking lot. Above half-empty bookcases, a guitar hung on the wall. It made him feel sad.

He laid a sheaf of photos before Flaherty. He'd selected, cropped, and printed them off his iPhone. They showed Lance with his Chinese contact in Beijing.

Flaherty leafed through the stack, expressionless.

"And there's this," Skyler said, producing his trump card. He had printed out an itinerary of Lance's that included a swing through Western China late last year. It cross-referenced perfectly with NRO data on the mysterious activities at the Korla missile complex.

"You're taking the position that Lance is … what, Skyler? Tell me."

"Working for the Chinese," Skyler said. "That's why we never tracked down the cause of the sabotage incident."

"In that case, you're gonna have to answer one question," Flaherty said. "Why the hell would the Chinese take the risk of recruiting an American spy, when they've already got two of their own nationals on board?"

Skyler had thought of that. "We're putting Lance on board to make sure nothing else happens. Right? So if they've got to him, there'll be no one to stop them."

Flaherty shook his head. He pushed Skyler's carefully assembled piles of evidence back at him. "You're forgetting something. Lance is a redblooded, flag-waving patriot." His cool gaze reminded Skyler that he himself never had quite come up to scratch in that regard. The taint of the cosmopolitan intellectual elite still clung about him. Of course, it went without saying that a Ph.D from Beacon Hill could never be as patriotic as a redneck from West Virginia.

"They might have convinced him it would benefit the United States if the mission failed," Skyler said.

"How?" Flaherty said.

And to that Skyler had no answer. He sagged. He never had managed to solve the riddle of Lance's motivation to his own satisfaction.

"The woman?" he said.

"No reason an American patriot can't bang a Chinese chick."

Skyler nodded. In Flaherty's ultimately simplistic worldview—which was also Lance's—relations between men and women always came down to *banging*. Skyler tended to over-complicate things. He had thought of a love affair, which didn't really fit … but *banging* did. And the trip to the environs of Korla? A coincidence.

Skyler's suspicions added up to a pile of nothing. He was wrong. He'd pieced together a case against Lance for the reason that he hated his fucking guts, and no other.

"OK, boss," he said. "I just felt that I should bring this

stuff to your attention."

"And I'm glad you did, because it makes me feel good about *you.*" Flaherty started to laugh—the full-on laugh that meant he'd caught a glimpse of the absurdity underlying the surface of life. "Did you think of this, Skyler? Lance's balls are gonna be *blue.* Five years! Five years with no pussy! Heh, heh, heh. Even I am not *that* much of a patriot."

They parted. Skyler walked down the corridor with his heart full of foul, swirling darkness. He might as well unpack his suitcase, since he'd be staying here with the astronauts for the next two weeks.

CHAPTER 42

Down, up.

Down, up.

Exhale and hold.

Jack's arms started to shake. He thought about Koichi Masuoka. They had lifted together a few times. The Japanese astronaut weighed a stone less than Jack, but he had muscles of steel, and more importantly, he *focused*. Now he was gone, because he'd helped Jack that night in Beijing. Saved his life, maybe. Jack still remembered the office in the Japanese embassy where they'd spent the rest of the night: the safety posters featuring cartoon characters; the bitter green tea served by Masuoka's foreign-service buddy, at two in the morning.

Now back in Japan, Masuoka was preparing to go into space again. He'd be stationed at the ISS after the *SoD* left. Hopefully that would make him feel better about not going on the *SoD,* although it couldn't make *Jack* feel better about it.

Down, up.

Malignant forces swirled around the mission, as anonymous as those two gunmen in Beijing. They'd killed Theodore Zhang. Jack had seen it in the news. He'd rung the Foreign Office, told them that Zhang had probably been killed to stop him from talking about Unit 63618. That's fascinating, they'd said. What is Unit 63618? I don't know, Jack had been forced to say. It's not on Google. Oh, I see. Well, thanks, we'll certainly look into this.

Yeah, right.

How many more people would have their lives overturned like chairs at a bad party? How many more people would *die?*

Mother*fucking* MOAD.

Down, up.

He was benching 140 kilograms. Giles Boisselot stood behind him, spotting.

One more rep.

Up. Exhale—

—oh shit—

A grunt tore out of Jack's lungs. His arms shook uncontrollably.

Boisselot's mind, travelling in some distant galaxy, returned to planet Earth. His fingers closed on the bar just before it would have slipped through them and crashed onto Jack's chest.

"Putain de merde!" Boisselot swore. With considerable difficulty, he replaced the bar on the rack. Jack slid out from underneath. "Sorry, Jack!" It came out as *Jacques.*

"No, I'm sorry," Jack said. He stood, feeling a bit dazed. Bench press fails could be lethal, if your spotter wasn't paying attention. So Jack *was* sorry—sorry he'd asked Boisselot to spot for him. He wouldn't make that mistake again.

"You're OK?"

"Fine, thanks. I ought to've known that was one rep too many." Jack toweled off sweat, drank some Gatorade. He moved over to the leg curl machine and embarked on a set.

He was pushing it in the gym, getting stronger, because he'd spend the next five years getting weaker. They'd have 0.3 gees in the habitation unit of the *SoD.* Exercise machines. But no one knew exactly what years of microgee would do to the human body. Jack was trying to stack the deck in his own favor by bulking up. He'd been working on this project for the last two years, and had stepped it up since they entered quarantine, because frankly there wasn't much else to do.

Boisselot evidently did not share his concerns. The Frenchman exercised for the minimum time required, full stop. Now he was doing bicep curls. Jack craned to see which dumbbells he was using. Cripes. Hannah Ginsburg could have lifted those with less effort.

There were two kinds of astronauts, both in general and on the SoD crew. There were those who came from a military background. Jack, Menelaou, Alexei. Qiu, Xiang, Hardcastle. And then there were those who possessed some unique expertise. Ginsburg fell into that category. So did Giles Boisselot.

That pigeon-chested man over there, struggling to lift 10kg dumbbells, was the best xenolinguist in the world.

That's how the media described him. A more accurate description would have been 'the best xenolinguist in the world, who's under eighty, and isn't married, and doesn't have crap eyesight.' And when you took into account the fact that pre-MOAD, the number of xenolinguists in the world could be counted on two hands …

Well, Jack just hoped Boisselot could pull his weight in the other areas he'd trained for. Hydroponics and advanced life-support, God help us.

At least the Frenchman was willing, Jack reflected, as he went over and offered Boisselot some friendly tips on his form. Boisselot accepted these in the wholly non-smug spirit Jack meant them, nodding with his characteristic enthusiasm. He apologized again about the bench press incident when they left the gym together, towels draped around their necks.

"Sacre bleu, don't worry about it," Jack said, massacring the antiquated French phrase to make Boisselot laugh at him, which he did.

Boisselot went into his bedroom. Jack carried on to his.

The crew quarters at Kennedy Space Center dated back to the Apollo missions, and apparently hadn't been redecorated since then. The NASA-blue carpets and wood-paneled walls made the place feel even more cramped than it actually was. At least they had their own rooms, which wouldn't be the case for the next five years. Jack resolved to enjoy his privacy while he had it. Mentally debating whether to select *Platoon* or *American Sniper* for his evening's entertainment, he opened the door to his room.

On his bed sat Skyler Taft.

The NXC agent got up.

Jack, standing in the doorway, said, "I was trying to choose between a classic depiction of the brutality of war, or a feel-good appreciation of a great soldier. I hadn't considered a well-deserved arse-kicking. But come to think of it, that *would* be entertaining."

Skyler said, "Jeez, do you think I'm coming onto you or something?"

It hadn't occurred to Jack. As soon as Skyler said that, however, Jack added *Probably gay* to his mental dossier on the NXC agent, with the obligatory footnote *Not that there's anything wrong with that.*

"What do you want?" he said roughly, closing the door behind him.

Skyler said, "I just wanted to show you this video." He

messed around with the remote control for the television. Jack had time to wonder if this was actually just some training thing. If so, he should feel ashamed of his brazen aggression. Funnily enough, he didn't. He peeled off his sweat-soaked t-shirt, dropped it on the floor, and dug in the drawer for a clean one.

The TV came on. Skyler turned around. He flinched, a tiny but visible reaction to half-naked Jack. That was primal. It was *Holy shit this guy could break me in half.* Jack was angry enough to enjoy this unseemly little victory. He gestured at the TV screen. "What in the fuck is this shit?"

"2010," Skyler said. "The sequel to *2001."* Lugubrious movie music filled the room, so loud that Skyler had to raise his voice. "It's a better movie, in my opinion. And it's got some parallels with our present situation. You should give it a watch."

He plopped down on the bed and patted the Native American print coverlet next to him.

Jack pulled on a clean t-shirt. He wondered if the NXC agent was completely out of his mind.

Then he got it.

He sat down next to Skyler. "What is it, then?"

"Bugs," Skyler said. "I picked this for the loud music. It is good, though."

"What've you got to say, that you don't want the bugs picking up?" Jack had suspected they were monitored around the clock. The confirmation was unsettling … but not as unsettling as Skyler Taft taking steps to circumvent it.

"It's about Oliver Meeks," Skyler said, staring straight ahead at the TV screen.

Jack growled in his throat. He didn't mean to. It just came

out.

"I know who killed him."

"I *know* you know. That's what sickens me. I've been living with this for three years, knowing that you know."

"I should have told you years ago," Skyler said. And then he spoke the name.

Lance Garner.

Jack instantly berated himself for not guessing before. He hunched over his knees. "Why tell me now? If you're just twisting the knife, you're an even more despicable human being than I thought."

He understood without questioning it—and Skyler apparently did, too—that legal remedies would be no remedies at all. It was the law that *protected* Lance Garner from justice. If anyone was going to avenge Meeks it would have to be Jack himself.

"It's better to know than not to know," he acknowledged, half to himself. "But what can I do about it, stuck in here? Ten days to launch!"

"Aha," Skyler said, unsmiling. "Now for the good news."

CHAPTER 43

As it so happened, Lance Garner was the first human being Jack met when they loaded into the *SoD*.

The Soyuz gang had come up first. They had spacewalked from the ISS to the *SoD,* a simple maneuver that got them and their spacesuits on board. They'd had several hours to make themselves at home before the other half of the crew arrived from Florida.

"Hey!" Lance shouted, clinging to the axis tunnel in the middle of the main hab. He had a good smile. It made him look like Tom Sawyer all grown up. "Sorry, we grabbed all the best bunks."

This was a joke. There were no bunks. There were sleeping spaces built into what would be the floor of the hab, when it was spun up. These were spaced out evenly around the aft wall. During construction, the crew had taken to calling them 'coffins.'

One coffin was much like any other, and Jack stowed his satchel of personal belongings in the nearest unclaimed one. His pulse raced. The blood sang in his ears, and it wasn't a reaction to freefall. It was a reaction to Lance Garner. The intensity of it took him off guard. He wanted to kill the man, bloodily, with his bare hands. He was going to have to get this under control.

The hab echoed. There'd been no time to install frivolous touches such as sound-deadening blankets. Stiff groups of tables and chairs, built into the cylindrical floor and into the 'Potter spaces' under the stairways on the end walls, made the place look like an Ikea showroom. Actually, though, the 'wood' was anodized paint; the furniture was made of ultra-lightweight aluminum. The height of luxury.

Otherwise, the place was tolerable. It would eventually fill up with a locker-room pong, no getting around that. But for now, it had a new-car smell—a hint of machine oil, the odor of plasticizer seeping out of the flooring, muted by the low air pressure and sinus congestion that came with freefall.

"I can see water floating in here," Menelaou called, swarming down from the aft tube that led to the other modules. She moved hand-over-hand down the guardrail of the stairs, legs in the air. No point actually using the stairs, in freefall. "Did one of the fish tanks break?" She cast a glance at the sealed tanks full of tilapia strapped to the floor. Battery-powered pumps burbled, keeping the water fresh for the disoriented fish inside. When the hab was spun up, the tanks would be opened, and they'd stack hydroponic trays on top of them to grow vegetables in the same water. Jack foresaw that *everyone* was going to have to become a hydroponics specialist.

"Only one of the tanks leaked a little," Qiu Meili apologized.

"That's gonna have to stop. No spills. Period." Menelaou gave the Chinese woman a wintry smile.

"Life support system is up and running," said Xiang Peixun, drifting out of the aft tube. He would have come from SLS, the secondary life support module aft of the hab where CO2, oxygen, and sewage were managed.

"Evidently. We are breathing," Menelaou said. "Good job, Pei. I really need to use the toilet."

The toilets were closets in the fore and aft walls, or what would be the walls, after the *SoD* escaped Earth orbit. They'd spin the hab up then. At present, this was just another freefall space, like an ISS module—if much bigger. The hab measured a full 60 meters across.

While Menelaou was baptizing the toilet, Jack floated up to the keel tube which opened in the center of what would be the forward wall. The white-padded, intestinal tube took him to the bridge.

"About fucking time," Alexei greeted him. The cosmonaut floated at the main console, which took up all of one wall. Actually, every wall had consoles on it, including the one which would be the ceiling when they were under thrust. No windshield on the *SoD*. Tiny portholes, set here and there among the dials and levers, were ideas rather than functioning windows. Their view of the outside world came mediated via GPUs from the optic sensor array. Alexei pointed to the fine big screen in front of him, which displayed the ISS with Earth's limb behind it. Construction yard cleanup was underway. Several eviscerated external tanks and Falcon Heavy upper stages floated near the ISS, ready to be loaded with debris for disposal via reentry burnup. Alexei explained that the astronauts who would remain on the ISS were cutting the clothesline now. Jack could see them doing it.

"So," Jack lowered his voice, "Hardcastle's changed a bit, hasn't he? Lost weight, dyed his hair …"

Alexei's elated expression faded to deadpan. "Hardcastle? No, no. That is a very advanced, very futuristic Russian robot. Now you see our fiendish plan to sabotage the mission."

Jack let out a burst of laughter. He was so glad Alexei was on board, he could have hugged him. He cast a glance at the tube to make sure they were still alone. "Kate's making it very clear she won't take any shit from the Chinese. She'd hardly got out of the airlock before she criticized Meili and mocked Peixun. I suppose she's starting as she means to go on."

"Xiang is a pig," Alexei said. "It's because he has a tiny dick."

"Speaking of dickless wonders, Boisselot let go of the clothesline during our tow-over. I had to grab him as I went by, or he'd be on the slow boat to Venus. He's a perfectly nice guy, but I question the sanity of the ESA selection committee."

Before they could slag off any more of their colleagues, Menelaou drifted onto the bridge. Without so much as a 'hi,' she said, "OK, Alexei. Calibrate and zero the inertial nav units, please."

"Done," Alexei said.

"Good. Then call Mission Control and get any final nav tweaks they have for us."

Alexei gave her a raised eyebrow, a tilt of the head.

Menelaou took his meaning. "I know you weren't supposed to be in charge of comms," she said crisply. "That was Hardcastle. The NXC guy? We'll train him up as we go. For now, you do it."

Jack understood her mood. The last-minute roster change had been sprung on her without warning, too. She hadn't even had a Skyler Taft tipping her the wink.

"Jack, it looks like Alexei's already got the nav computers up. Check that everything's zeroed correctly, and load the flight plan. We'll burn when engine status is confirmed and our launch window opens." Menelaou pushed off and flew out of the bridge.

Jack and Alexei exchanged a wry glance. Then Alexei took the radio off the loudspeakers and called CapCom. Jack smiled to himself. 'Capsule Communicator' for a spaceship that was most definitely not a capsule. Traditions died hard.

Alexei spoke grumpily in Russian. Then he punched the keyboard for the nav computer. To Jack, he said, "They want us to verify the hash signature after we decrypt the data. What is the use of 5k encryption if you still don't trust the data?"

"I'd rather know that some Earth Party hacker hasn't spoofed our flight plan. Plenty of people down there would rather see us fly into the sun." Jack strapped himself into the pilot's couch. "Let me know when you've got the official flight plan. I want to see if the boffins at JPL have us whipping around the backside of Mars like I told them to. Shave a few months off the trip out."

*

Hannah had her own private domain within the *SoD*. Well, it didn't have her name on the door, and there wasn't actually a door, but everyone understood—she *hoped*—that Engineering was the territory of Hannah Ginsburg. Private, keep out. Trespassers will be fed to the reactor.

She 'moved in' by taping a picture of Bethany, David, Isabel, and Nathan to the wall, above the all-important 'dollar meter.' She then hung an origami Star of David, made by some schoolchild in Israel, over the hexagonal array or reactor status lights, and that was her little kingdom furnished. She could touch the walls with her fingers and her feet if she floated horizontally to the 'floor.'

One of the curved side walls was taken up with reactor

and turbine controls. Pumps, thermocouples, SCRAM controls, the wall had it all. Any visitor, not that there would be any, could see the status of both critical components at a glance.

The opposite wall was dedicated to the engine controls. Everything from tankage pressures to the width and speed of the plasma exhaust was measured, manipulated, and morphed here.

The other two walls, where they weren't crammed with equipment lockers and racks of electronics, were given over to the mundane housekeeping controls for the rest of the ship.

She still couldn't believe she was really here. Her whole career had been dedicated to space, but she was supposed to be the one who stayed home while others took the risks.

Well, at least she wouldn't have to stare at the others all the time. She'd have her privacy. That could make all the difference between acquiring a spirit of adventure, and going insane.

Moments later, Lance Garner invaded her kingdom.

"Go away," Hannah said. "I'm busy."

"Whatcha doing?"

"Cranking up the reactor."

"Can I watch? I won't get in the way."

Hannah made a tight, irritated feel-free gesture. After all, this was everyone's ship. She just hoped he wasn't going to make a habit of it.

Lance floated in the mouth of the keel tube, which opened in the middle of the circular 'ceiling.' There was a hole in the 'floor,' too, which led to the turbine room.

"Family?" Lance said, indicating the picture.

"Yes," Hannah said.

She had made it up with Bethany. There had been a degree of deception involved. She'd let Bethany think that she was 'getting help'… actually, she'd *told* Bethany in as many words that she was getting help. She'd had to, or Bethany might have taken it into her head to tell Burke, or God knows the media, that her sister was an alcoholic. For her own good.

But of course, Hannah couldn't *actually* get help, or Burke and everyone else would know that she had a problem.

It was OK, though. She'd dried out before, in the white heat of the engine design process. She could do it again. At the moment, she hadn't had a drink for two weeks, and she was doing OK.

She *would* be doing OK, if Lance weren't hanging there watching her. It made her nervous.

She really wished she knew why NASA had foisted a Fed on them at the last minute.

She focused on the dollar meter, which reported the amount of neutrons being created by nuclear reactions in the core.

You can get a reactor to ninety cents fairly quickly. It's that last ten cents that give reactor operators nightmares.

The idea was get as close to 'one dollar,' a.k.a. 'criticality,' as you could, without going over. She programmed the slow withdrawal of the control rods as a wave of reactivity swept through the warming fuel channels.

"So the reactor's all the way at the back of the ship. But you can manage everything from here?" Lance said.

Hannah looked up at him. That was such a stupid question, she wondered if he was making fun of her. "When the reactor's running, it emits gamma rays. Yes, it's shielded, but that shielding is primarily to reduce the space radiation that bombards the reactor, otherwise we'd turn into a bright ball of gas. It's not a safety guarantee for us. So there's a bioshield aft of here." She pointed at the wall behind the reactor controls. "Six feet of water in a tank of steel, polyethylene, and lead. That's what prevents gamma rays from washing over us, and killing us all within minutes. If I went back there while the reactor's running? I'd be so radioactive, you couldn't even risk retrieving my body." She paused to see how he was taking this. Perfect poker face. "So, yeah. I can do everything by computer from here. Did you get *any* training?"

Lance wiggled a hand. "Some. But to be honest, there wasn't time to bone up on a whole lot of specifics. That's why I'm asking, you know?"

"That's fine. There are no stupid questions," Hannah said, although she didn't believe this. *Most* questions were stupid.

She watched the dollar meter as the next fifty centimeters of control rod emerged from the center of the reactor. Suddenly, the dollar meter jumped to ninety-five and the hexagonal array indicators flared yellow, indicating coolant temperatures in the operating range. The coolant pumps kicked on with a tactile hum. The meter in the water/steam separator twitched, and various power relays clicked.

"What did you just do?" Lance said edgily.

Hannah smiled. "I made a dollar today. Sorry if it scared you."

"Shee-it. Skyler told me you were kind of a hard-ass." Lance was grinning. "He said you were always busting his chops …"

It wounded her to know that Skyler had spoken about her in such terms, and to this weirdo, of all people. Although she'd deleted Skyler from her contacts list, she hadn't managed to delete him from her memory.

"Now I'm going to set the reactor on auto-pilot."

"Thanks for the warning," Lance said.

Nothing happened, of course, except that wash of yellow light on the reactor array reached out to the border of the display.

Lance laughed. "You had me going there. Skyler wasn't kidding …"

It was that second reference to Skyler that got her. She wiggled her toes out of the stirrups and floated up to him. "Lance, can I ask you a question? What are you doing here?"

"Are you gonna deck me if I say that's classified?"

"Tricky to deck someone, when a) there isn't a deck, and b) there isn't any gravity," Hannah said dryly. "Well?"

"Like they told you at KSC, Hardcastle backed out at the last minute. I'm his replacement."

"I smell something funny in here. It's kind of familiar … oh yeah. It's the smell of horseshit."

Lance grinned, this time seemingly with admiration. Then his humor faded. "Can I trust you, as a fellow American?" he said quietly.

It seemed a strange way of putting it. "Of course," she said.

Lance leaned in closer. "Someone on this ship doesn't want it to leave orbit. They tried to sabotage it once already. Remember?"

Hannah's mouth opened and closed.

"My job is to suspect everybody."

"So that's why you came to watch me crank the reactor up," she managed.

"Yeah. If you just yanked the rods out, all the folks on Earth would see is a new star in the sky."

"If you know that, you know I couldn't push a button and blow the ship up. There are failsafes, and the failsafes have fallback plans, and the fallback plans have their own Plan Bs."

"Yeah, but you're God back here. You could get around all that. No, I'll tell you how I know you're cool." Lance nodded down at the hexagonal array. "Suicide bombers don't hang up a Star of David."

He floated back up through the keel tube.

Her mind swimming, Hannah pushed off and flew to her intercom. "Engineering."

"Bridge," came Menelaou's voice.

"The reactor has achieved first criticality. I'm now waiting for the delayed neutron production to stabilize. Meanwhile, I'm warming up the secondary heat exchanger and getting the steam generator online. We'll be good to go in about three hours."

Three hours and seven minutes later, the reactor achieved stabilization. The steam turbine generator had taken up the ship's baseload power needs, and the fuel cells were finally shut off. Hannah ramped up the output to three quarters of maximum. Not a hiccup, not a gurgle. She sent a mental thank-you to her dark-eyed Rosatom physicist. The reactor was Russian engineering at its finest: simple, even clunky, and guaranteed to work.

The *SoD's* engine took the water created while the fuel cells were running, and pumped it through a fat electric arc, flashing it to steam. The steam rushed down the central cavity, where tremendous pulses of radio energy shattered the bonds that held the atoms together, ionizing the hydrogen and oxygen into a blue-white plasma. Another series of coils shoved the plasma hard, cramming it out of the exhaust bell at immense velocities.

The upshot of all this violent activity was that the *SoD* started to move away from the ISS at a walking pace. Several spacewalkers floated on tethers outside the ISS, waving goodbye from positions safely out of range of the exhaust.

CHAPTER 44

Star sights: valid.

Gyroscopes: spun and locked.

Latest observations of the MOAD from the spiffy new telescope on the ISS: unchanged.

Surprise, surprise, Jack thought. Observations of the MOAD *never* registered any change, except that the heat source in the alien spacecraft's midsection cooled a few degrees more. Media contrarians, in the last fraught days, had even begun to question why we were going to all this trouble for a piece of space junk.

Suck it up, you tedious little bores.

He reconfirmed the *SoD's* distance from the ISS. 50 kilometers. That was far enough.

Good to go.

Jack said to Menelaou, "Everything looks good," and Menelaou said to Mission Control, "We have achieved minimum separation from the ISS. Power generation is stable. MPD engine is online, and thrust is stable. Request permission to punch it."

"*Spirit of Destiny,* you are approved to execute procedure 42, Trans-Europa burn. Full power to the booster and MPD engine," Mission Control said, in a Russian accent.

The *Spirit of Destiny* had two mission control centers. One in Star City and one in Houston. Star City would be taking point at this historic moment, to make up for the fact that there were three Americans on the bridge.

Jack in the right seat. On his left, Menelaou. On her left, Lance.

After all, Lance *was* the comms officer. Menelaou couldn't

kick him off the bridge. Someone had to ensure they were getting good telemetry, and Menelaou did not have the authority to replace Lance with Alexei, much as she may have wished to.

Jack settled his shoulders against his padded backrest, trying to forget Lance was there. He gut-checked himself. Well-rested. Fully adjusted to zero-gee. He'd eaten a hearty breakfast—with fresh orange juice, the last he'd taste for five years—and then recorded a three-minute webchat with a group of second-graders in Ohio.

Now he was ready to make history.

The bank of instruments in front of him looked nothing like the layout in the cockpit of the space shuttle. For instance, the information on the heads-up display was calibrated in thousands of kilometers, with two detents for hundred-thousands and millions. The chronometer had readouts for weeks and years. Most fundamentally, the coordinate system was based not on Earth-based north and south, but on the poles of the Sun.

As for the rest of the controls, there were no rudder pedals, and there was no flipping *stick*. Could you even call yourself a pilot when your bird had no stick? Well, he'd been a pilot when he was flying a 110-tonne brick, a.k.a. *Atlantis*. He'd claim the term again. No one would mind.

Instead of a pedals and a stick, he had three axis precession controls, which used the ship's reaction wheels to change the orientation of the *SoD*. The throttle was firmly in the hands of the computers.

"Full power to the MPD," Menelaou said.

"Roger." Jack keyed in the throttle command.

"Reactor and turbine steady. Full power to the MPD engine," Hannah said over the intercom. "Fuel tanks are settling and pressurizing."

Menelaou touched the intercom. "All hands, prepare for boost." Back in the storage module, the rest of the crew would be strapped into their acceleration couches, staring at the ceiling.

"Hey Goose, I feel the need ..." Jack said.

"... the need for speed!" Alexei said. Both of them cackled wildly.

"Top Gun," Jack explained to Menelaou.

Menelaou shook her head, smiling. "I will never understand the way men quote movie lines to each other, or why you find it so damn funny."

In clusters of two, separated by intervals of mere seconds, the pumps whined up to fever pitch. A deep subsonic drumming announced the ignition of the booster's engines. Jack grinned, thrilled to the core. He accidentally caught Lance's eye—even the spook felt the excitement. Jesus God, the power of this thing!

He executed a 'barbecue' roll, a minute movement of the gimbaled exhaust bells of the liquid-fuelled engines that rolled the SoD on its axis. For most of their trip out, they'd be soaking up so much heat from the sun that the ship would actually *bend,* expanding on the sunward side and contracting on the shadowed side. So, roll against the contraction. Friction from the counter-rotating hab would cancel out both rolls evenly.

He remembered the last interview he'd done before leaving Earth. A one on one with Buzz Aldrin. A rarity for Jack, he'd been practically speechless in the presence of his hero. And Aldrin, *Buzz freaking Aldrin,* had said to him, "If I was fifty years younger, I'd fight you for that seat."

Jack knew the 89-year-old astronaut would be watching now, along with his surviving handful of Apollo comrades. Those lion-hearted octogenarians, the first and last men to walk on the moon, would be cheering on the *Spirit of Destiny* and its crew.

An overwhelming sense of responsibility braced him, while his hands continued to calmly move between position, rate and fuel indicators on his panel. He'd done this exact same thing 1272 times, precisely, in the flight simulator at JSC.

Pilot joke: The computers fly the plane. You fly the computers.

Jack grinned to himself as he glanced from one screen to the other, checking tank pressures, combustion chamber temperatures and pressures. So this was what making history felt like: pushing buttons …

Mission Control spoke in Jack's helmet. They wore pressure suits as a precaution, in case the hastily-built *SoD* should spring a weld.

Instead of the pro forma status update Jack expected, the voice from Star City said, "*SoD,* this is a heads up from the NRO. Satellites have picked up launch indications from China. Flight parameters—"

They lost the transmission there. It happened. Lance scrambled to restore the signal.

"—your orbital inclination," Mission Control said.

"Say again, Mission Control," Menelaou said tautly. "Didn't copy your last."

"Flight parameters indicate the launched object will collide with you." The Russian voice lost its formality.

"Poslusajte, guys, it's a missile. Early warning systems in Siberia and Alaska just picked it up. Three thousand meters altitude. Four thousand meters. Assuming solid booster and second stage, anticipate ninety seconds until intercept."

The words lodged in Jack's gut like bullets.

"Son of a bitch," Menelaou said flatly.

Lance sat unmoving. Jack wondered at that, and then he realized: Lance had *expected* this …

"What's your current orbital inclination, *SoD?"*.

Menelaou read it out. They were still on the same orbital track as the ISS, spiraling out of Earth's gravity well. Altitude: 537 kilometers. Well within range of a hit-to-kill interceptor.

"Tell us what to do, Star City," Menelaou said. "It would be a damn shame for us to die before we even leave Earth orbit."

CHAPTER 45

Mission Control told them what to do.

"Throttle down the booster to zero."

"Roger," Jack said, but he wasn't really listening. He was remembering the taste of beer in a Beijing bar, and hearing Theodore Zhang say, *No, this is something bigger. It could hit a target as far up as geostationary orbit.*

The subsonic thunder of the booster stopped. The three of them stared at the readouts. Lance said, "There it is."

The *SoD's* radar array had picked up the missile at the 200-klick range circle. At the sight of the fast-moving green wasp on the radar plot, Jack's awareness skipped like a scratched CD. Suddenly, he was no longer a forty-two-year-old astronaut. He was a fighter pilot, on his way to deliver another payload of death to Saddam's forces, watching surface-to-air missiles puff up from the ruined hellscapes of Iraqi towns. Evading them was like avoiding ants on the sidewalk. So easy it didn't even count as a game.

This bird didn't have a stick. Didn't even have wings. But it had an engine that packed almost two gees of thrust.

Mission Control told them what to do next.

Modify the booster's programming.

Dump it.

Fly away.

"Roger," Menelaou snapped. She said to Lance, "It's a heat-seeking missile. It's homing in on the booster. So we dump the booster. Get cracking! Fix the programming!"

The plan made sense to Jack … for about half a second. If they jettisoned the booster early? They wouldn't make it out of Earth's gravity well. They'd be stuck.

Sitting ducks for the *next* missile.

Jack said, "I'm taking defensive action." Mind made up, he snapped the yaw control on the booster motors hard to the right, then back to zero. The *SoD* ponderously slewed to point its tail towards Earth. "Garner, don't touch the booster."

"Do it!" Menelaou said to Lance.

Lance twitched into life, like a battery-powered toy that had been switched on. "Hit it with the railguns!" he said. "Blow that fucker away!"

The railgun controls were on Jack's side of the bridge, which was probably just as well. Jack, concentrating on the yaw control, couldn't be bothered to disabuse Lance of his Star Wars-inspired illusions. Menelaou did it for him. "Moron!" she said to Lance. "The guns aren't even fucking loaded! You can't just put a round on the rails and leave it there! Come back the next day, it'll be vacuum-welded to the rails. That's what nearly killed Galileo. Now dump the booster!"

"Creeping cheetos," Lance yelled, still stuck on the railguns. "This is what they're *for!*"

"You wanna sit here and wait for three minutes while we load rounds, and then another five while we power up the rails?" Menelaou purred. She reached over and shook Lance's shoulder. "Missile's gonna get here before that. Dump the goddamn booster!"

But Lance's futile trigger-happiness had bought Jack time to finish planning his own maneuver.

"Hannah!" he yelled into the intercom. "Can you centralize the mass flow?"

"What?" Hannah said.

"Rig the mass flow to be faster in the center of the tube!"

"What's going on? We're in a hard yaw. What are you doing up there?"

"DO IT!"

"Roger," she said in a tone dripping with skepticism. She had no idea how serious the situation was, and Jack didn't have time to explain.

He returned his attention to the radar plot. The missile was closing in.

"Jettison the fucking booster!" Mission Control said, completely forgetting themselves. *"Ty chto, okhuyel?* What are you waiting for?"

Jack was waiting for the missile to get close enough.

He'd trained for every kind of disaster the boffins could think up.

No one had thought of a heat-seeking missile.

But his training had included reorienting the *SoD*. Jack slapped the yaw controls to stop their rotation. At the same time, he killed all the booster's liquid-fueled engines.

Muted crashes told of loose items hitting forward bulkheads throughout the ship.

Lance sat frozen, staring at the radar plot. Jack knew the signs. That was a man who'd given up any illusion of control over his fate, and was waiting to die.

"Okayyyy," Menelaou said. "I see what you're doing. Mission Control, Kildare is going to attempt to take the missile out. It might work."

The missile screamed higher.

Wait.

Wait for it to lock on.

The missile turned, targeting the *SoD*. In another split

second, its kill booster would fire, and they'd be toast.

Now.

Jack engaged the engine. Maximum thrust.

Ionization coils *off.* Auto-ignition controls *off.* Turbopumps for the booster engines *on.*

Clouds of hydrogen and oxygen gusted out of the back of the booster, obscuring their view of Earth. Jack waited ten agonizing seconds, until the engines started spitting out liquid hydrogen and LOX. Then he turned on the reaction control thrusters, shoving the ship away from the cloud of liquid reactants.

"Now for the fun part," Menelaou purred. Lance continued to sit immobile, watching the green dot close in on them.

Jack snapped on the ionization coils. A loud shock wave thundered through the ship. A torus of live steam boiled aft. Jack engaged the engine at maximum thrust, and a tongue of plasma reached back and touched the edge of the cloud of reactants. A blinding light flared from the aft monitor. The cloud had just exploded in flame.

Jack's lips stretched in an unconscious grin. He throttled the engine down, *way* down. Minimum thrust.

He repeated the max-min thrust maneuver three more times, while the *SoD* tried to shake itself to pieces around them. And the missile—

Well, the missile.

The optical sensor array caught its fate on camera.

When the cloud of fuel and LOX ignited, the missile locked on the flaring reactants, drawing it off a precious few degrees.

That was just the beginning.

Donut-shaped rings of plasma bloomed out of the thrusters. It looked like the SoD was blowing smoke rings, except these were rings of 90,000 degree plasma.

The heat-seeking missile died an ironically apt death, soaked in water plasma hotter than the heart of the sun. The series of blasts fried its electronics, reducing it from a hit-to-kill interceptor to a big dumb lump of metal.

It coasted harmlessly past the *SoD.* Soon it would reach its highest altitude and begin its long fall back towards Earth.

"It worked! It goddamn worked!" Menelaou whooped. She leaned into the intercom. "Mission Control, do you read me? Kildare just executed a series of max thrust / min thrust maneuvers that cooked the missile like a Christmas turkey. We are alive and well."

Unable to relax yet, Jack barked, "Star City, this is Jack. Should we expect any more bogeys?"

There might be another missile. In his experience, there usually was another missile.

"Keyhole satellites aren't picking anything up," Mission Control said. As their survival sank in, Jack reflected that he'd come full circle. In 2011, he'd risked his life to repair a Keyhole satellite—and ended up losing his job over it. Now, those very same satellites had saved their lives. It might even have been *Frostbite,* Keyhole-12a, that saw the missile launch and shrilled its electronic warning. "Our missile defense systems are on high alert, and so are the American systems," Mission Control said, perhaps trying to be reassuring. "If there's another launch, we can test them." A Russian chuckle. "At present we would like you to maintain your orbit and await further instructions."

"Good!" Menelaou said. "We've abused the hell out of our engines. We need to check them over."

Jack craned to the porthole nearest him. Of course, all that could be seen through the thickness of transparent aluminum was black space. "I wonder where it's going to fall," he mumbled.

"What?" Lance said.

"The missile. After all, what goes up must come down."

"Eh, it'll probably fall in the Pacific," Menelaou said lightheartedly. She reached over and tugged Jack's ears. "You did it, Killer. How the hell did you even think of that?"

"Cheating." Jack smiled weakly. "Thought of it ages ago, kicking the MPD concept around with Ollie. He had a devious mind." He chuckled at the memory, but it came out sounding like a bark of sadness. "Any high-powered drive is indistinguishable from a weapon. That was his favorite saying."

"Well, I have no idea who Ollie is," Menelaou said. Of course she didn't. The presiding genius of the *SoD* project didn't even exist on the internet anymore. "Well done, anyway."

Lance said, "There was no Ollie."

Jack sat upright, staring at him. "What did you say?"

"You're lying," Lance said. His blue eyes glistened with the shock of their close call. Jack wondered if he even knew what he was saying. "The engine was developed at NASA. We have the documentation to prove it."

"No one ever suggested otherwise, Lance," Menelaou said lightly, which proved just how completely the NXC had erased Meeks from history. It also cued Lance to shut up, which he did.

Jack clenched his jaw. The adrenaline sloshing around his system urged him to knock Lance's head off. Here and now, in front of the mission commander. There'd never be a better time, right?

Yes. There would be a better time. His chance would come. He just had to be ready for it.

CHAPTER 46

Tumbling through space, the 20,000-kg metal cylinder that had been a hit-to-kill interceptor reentered Earth's atmosphere at high speed. Missile defense installations blasted at it, but its unpredictable flight path defeated their targeting. The missile landed in a small town named Meiwa in Gunma Prefecture, Japan. Sonic booms broke windows as far away as Tokyo. Skyscrapers swayed. Thanks to Japan's long experience with earthquakes, anti-seismic construction was the norm throughout the islands. Nothing much fell down. But that was no consolation to the residents of Meiwa. A crater had appeared in the middle of their town.

Where there used to be an elementary school.

Sod's law.

The crew of the *SoD* watched the news in horror. Unlike on the ISS, they didn't have to rely on prepackaged news digests. Their 'Ka' communications system could receive HD television, as well as provide sideband Internet at up to 8Gb speeds.

They followed along in real time as Japan reacted with fury to the 'Meiwa Massacre.' Doctrinal pacifism went only so far, as it turned out. 43 small children and two teachers had died. Two firefighters and a police officer had died in a secondary collapse of the school building as they searched desperately for survivors. This could not be papered over with diplomatic regrets.

The Japanese prime minister went on television blaming China and threatening retribution. The news channels played the sequence from the *SoD's* aft camera over and over. The markings on the missile were translated into dozens of languages.

By now, the whole world knew that the missile had been launched from a secret test launch facility in the Gobi desert.

Unit 63618.

"I warned them," Jack wretchedly confessed to Alexei. He felt as if he could and should have done more. "When I was at the Japanese embassy, I told them everything Zhang told me. So they knew about the facility. They could have ..." Done what, exactly? "It looks as if they didn't do *anything* with the information."

"And that," Alexei said, "is why they're pissed."

The blame war escalated overnight. Warships faced off in the Sea of Japan. Fighter jets performed fly-bys at distances measured in centimeters.

Behind the scenes, diplomats must have been maneuvering frantically, but the media did not care to know about that. Heavy artillery, tanks, and aircraft carriers filled the communal screen in the *SoD's* kitchen.

"Just out of curiosity," Menelaou said to Mission Control, "will we still get our refueling flight if war breaks out?"

Her question had an acid edge. 27 hours had passed since the thwarted missile attack, and the *SoD* remained parked in an elongated low Earth orbit.

Well. Parked wasn't exactly the word, when you were hurtling around the globe at 24,000 kilometers per hour.

The aborted burn had used up 20% of the booster's liquid fuel, so they couldn't make a second attempt without refueling. And all Misson Control had for them on that front was "Wait."

It was going to be damned tricky to send that refueling

flight, Jack thought. The aborted burn had raised the *SoD's* apogee, without altering its perigee. Now, at apogee—the point at which the *SoD* was furthest from Earth—they were running all the way out to 800 kilometers. The best option he could see was to send a Shuttle-Lite to catch up with the *SoD* at perigee, but at perigee, you were travelling much faster … Tricky as hell.

And it got worse. Jack feared the thwarted missile attack might have damaged the *SoD*. They'd seen liquid hydrazine leaking from the rocket nozzle of the missile's booster …

… and that was *all* they'd seen, before the *SoD's* rear-facing cameras glitched out.

Now they had no 'eyes' behind the bioshield. If the engine or the external tanks had been damaged, they couldn't see it.

"Why are the cameras out?" Giles Boisselot queried, innocently.

"Irregular electrical loads." Menelaou jerked her chin at Jack. "It happened when he was dicking around with the engines."

Menelaou's appreciation for Jack's defensive maneuvers had taken a steep downwards turn.

"Hydrazine," she mused darkly. "That's nasty shit. Extremely corrosive." She ran through a litany of potential problems it could have caused. "Crushed insulation on the external tanks … impacts on the engine bells…"

Not to mention thermal damage from the flaming cloud of propellant I ignited, Jack thought. He decided to mention that at a more opportune time.

"Could've eaten through the insulation on the piping … we might be venting cryogenic fluid from the ETs …"

"I could go out there and kick them," Alexei offered. "It often works. Alternatively: duct tape?"

Everyone laughed at the classic astronaut solution. Even Qiu and Xiang, who'd understandably held somewhat aloof from the rest of the crew over the last hours, smiled hesitantly.

Jack felt glad that the two Chinese astronauts were still part of the team. That could have turned nasty. Although Qiu and Xiang had acted as shocked and outraged as anyone else, it was humanly impossible not to wonder if they had known, or should have known, about the missile attack. CNSA had denied any involvement. Unit 63618 was a separate organization, which had gone rogue without anyone's knowledge—that was China's official line, and knowing what he did about silos in behemoth organizations, Jack believed it. And yet … and yet. The Japanese weren't buying it. Should he?

Of all people, Lance had taken the lead in restoring trust among the crew, going out of his way to express faith in Qiu and Xiang. Given his status as a Fed, that had a dispositive effect.

What sort of game was he playing? Jack wondered, watching him with disgust.

*

"Hannah?"

She looked up, startled. Lance again.

"Mind if I visit with you for a minute?"

She liked it that he asked. She wasn't really doing anything, anyway. She was just watching the hexagonal array, like an anxious mother hovering over a child's cot.

Lance eased himself through the hole in her 'ceiling.' He

floated down to her level, hair standing on end. "About the potential damage to the engine—"

"The risk is significant," Hannah interrupted. "I explained this to Kate. I told her all the different ways both the MPD and the booster engines could be damaged back there. It needs to be checked out."

"Well, that's what I wanted to talk about," Lance said. "I'm going to suggest a spacewalk."

"Oh, no," Hannah said immediately. "I wouldn't recommend that. Not at this stage. The reactor's been throttled down, but it's still hot." She thought about embarking on a detailed explanation of dose rates and relative absorption factors, but decided not to. Lance's absorption factor for lectures about radiation was low. Ha, ha. She settled for saying, "You don't want to go back there now. Wait a few days."

"Do we *have* a few more days? The refueling flight is going to come, and then we'll be on our way."

"I'll believe in that refueling flight when I see it."

"It'll come," Lance said, demonstrating a child-like faith in NASA. "And then what? Are we going to burn out of orbit without even checking for damage?"

"I know, I know! It's a problem." Hannah weighed the risk/reward equation in her mind. "Well, I guess you could peek. But I would object very strongly to anyone going behind the bioshield."

"But it's not gonna kill anyone to just take a look from here?"

"No."

"Gotcha. Appreciate it." Lance pushed off and ascended back to the tube.

"If you can get my cameras fixed, that would be great,"

Hannah called after him. "But be careful."

She settled back to watching the readouts and trying not to think about how much she wanted a drink.

*

Lance floated up to Jack, who was mindlessly watching the news. He'd actually begun to rethink the advantages of the Ka communications system. Yeah, it was great having television on board. The downside was they had television on board.

"Hey, Kildare."

"Yeah?" Jack said, as pleasantly as he could.

"Let's go."

"Huh?"

"Spacewalk," Lance explained. "We need to find out if the ship is damaged. This shit is getting ridiculous."

Jack uncurled in the air. He glanced aft from the kitchen area, across the bare expanse of floor that would eventually be their hydroponic garden. Menelaou, Qiu, Xiang, and Boisselot were sleeping, or at least hanging out in their coffins. The cute little red 'occupied' squares were visible on their coffin lids. Alexei was doing his shift on the bridge. Hannah was in Engineering, as usual.

"Kate wants it done," Lance said. "Hannah said it's fine as long as we're careful."

Jack frowned. Without a word to Lance, he floated up through the tube to the bridge and asked Alexei for a location check.

"That's the Andes down there," Alexei said.

"So we're passing through the South Atlantic Anomaly," Jack said. "Fantastic."

The South Atlantic Anomaly was an area where Earth's

inner Van Allen belt dipped down to within 200 kilometers of the surface. The anomaly was like a witch dancing over the Atlantic, foxing satellites and frying chips on insufficiently hardened spacecraft.

"Yes, I am expecting the computers to crash any minute," Alexei said. "Are you getting shooting stars?"

Jack shook his head. "Lance wants to go out there."

"About fucking time!" Alexei exclaimed, employing one of his favorite English expressions. "I'll go with him."

"No, mate, you're on bridge duty. Just monitor the radio."

Jack went back to the hab and said curtly, "You're on."

They flew down to the storage module, which was between Engineering and Secondary Life Support. Eight spacesuits hung on the wall. Each astronaut had his or her own suit. They made a colorful array: gunmetal gray for the NASA astronauts' suits, blue for Boisselot of ESA, red for the Chinese pair, pale khaki for Alexei's Orlan suit, and white for Lance's old-style NASA suit.

Lance had previously explained at length, as if he were some sort of expert, that the older suit was actually superior to the Z-2. The newer design had been rushed into production for this mission; it wasn't field-tested.

Jack didn't care about that. He liked the Z-2 for its greater flexibility. Also, the integrated life-support pack, rising up in a smooth cowl around the back of the helmet, made you look a bit like the aliens from the *Predator* movies.

He climbed into the plastic-smelling garment, amusedly remembering the minor kerfluffle when there'd been an online petition for him to carry a British flag into space.

As it was, all he'd brought from England was a few small things from his parents … and Meeks's ashes.

He brushed his fingers over the bellows pocket on his suit's thigh where the capsule of ashes resided.

They checked each other's seals, and entered the airlock to pre-breathe oxygen. The whole time they were in there, Lance gassed about the political situation on Earth. It was like he didn't want to think about the task awaiting them.

CHAPTER 47

Earth down there. The total blackness of space out here … except for when streaks of light crossed Jack's vision. These were the 'shooting stars' Alexei had mentioned. What they meant was you were taking rads.

A two-hour pre-breathe had brought them right back into the South Atlantic Anomaly again.

Let's just get this over with.

Tethered, Jack moved hand over hand along the trusses, inspecting the outsides of the hab modules. This was the easy bit, so they were doing it first. Lance went up one side of the truss 'tower,' Jack went up the other.

The tower enclosed the turbine room and the 'bottom' three hab modules like a scaffolding. Clinging to the inside of the titanium/aluminum trusses, Jack shone his helmet lamp on the sides of the modules, checking for dings and dents, or any signs of corrosion.

Two landing craft clung to the outside of the truss tower: a Dragon and a modified Shenzhou. Like baby koalas riding on their mother's back, the Dragon and Shenzhou would accompany the *SoD* all the way to Europa.

If they ever made it out of Earth orbit.

The truss tower terminated in a mighty steel disk, built into the bottom of the main hab, which incorporated all of the bearings and seals. If the hab were rotating at the moment, Jack would've had to turn back here. It wasn't, so he repositioned his tether and floated around the outside of the main hab, between the rim thrusters. That took him to the bridge.

Bolted onto another disk on the 'top' of the hab module,

the bridge was the only non-cylindrical module, sporting a nose cone to deflect microimpacts. The rule still held that all spaceships had to be gray. There was no color on the *SoD* at all. The exception that proved the rule was an engraving of that daft dove logo on the outside of the nose cone, done in hard-wearing pink and green enamel.

Jack maneuvered to one of the bridge portholes. He tapped on the transparent aluminum with his emergency torch.

On the radio, Alexei shouted, *"Blin!!"*

Jack had been intending to pretend he was an alien, but Alexei's mild swear cracked him up. *"Pancake?"*

"It's a well-beloved curse word, asshole," Alexei said over the radio, with dignity.

"So much for your *krutoi* image." Mr. Tough Guy. "Pancake, pancake."

"I have heard you saying 'Sugar' instead of 'Shit' when Meili is listening."

"That's different. It's this thing we have called chivalry, you may have heard of it."

"Don't let Kate catch you talking about chivalry. She'll throw you out without your spacesuit."

Chuckling, Jack suddenly pictured Lance listening to all this, and felt ashamed. "No damage to the modules that I've seen," he said, getting back to business. "Lance?"

"Everything looks fine over here," Lance said. "I'm going back to inspect the engine now."

"Don't be stupid," Alexei said. "It's too hot."

"Hannah said it was OK."

Jack thought: How do I wish to kill thee? Let me count the ways … "I'll sort this, Alexei."

He scrambled back along the truss tower. On the way, he suffered two more shooting stars.

Lance clung to the bioshield, as if standing on a parapet, looking down at the view of Earth. His head and shoulders were above the rim of the massive steel shield / tank. As Jack floated up towards him, Lance floated higher, up through a gap in the truss. His tether belled out behind him in a loop. Jack grabbed it in one hand and yanked him back behind the shield.

"What's the point of being out here if we don't check the engine?" Lance said. He had a point, certainly.

Jack attempted the mental arithmetic. South Atlantic Anomaly + residual reactor radiation. The latter was the biggie. But the other factor in the equation was Jack's life-time dose of radiation. After all the time he'd spent in space, he was already rather warm. And he had five years to go.

"Too much fun stuff coming out of the reactor," he said, trying for a jokey tone. "We'll peek. That's all."

Letting go of Lance's tether, he climbed to the edge of the bioshield, holding onto the trusses above his head. He popped his head up. He was looking down the length of the truss tower, past the radiator fins that stuck out through the trusses, and the convex heat reflector between the fins and the external tanks. Holding still, he strained to see any wisps of vapor. If the hydrazine spill had holed the ETs, or the piping, that would be the giveaway.

Nothing.

"Looks fine," he said.

"Yeah, but we should go down there."

Lance started to climb over the bioshield.

Jack grabbed him by the top of his PLSS, the life-support

backpack attached to his spacesuit. "If you go down there, you won't come back!"

As the words popped out of his mouth, it dawned on him that Lance might have a good reason for going down there.

To screw with the engine.

Going back there would chop Lance's life expectancy down to a few days, but maybe that would be worth it to him. Or his masters.

Jack remembered the panic on the bridge as the missile raced towards them.

Lance freaking out: *Use the railguns, use the railguns.*

Wasting time which they could have used to dump the booster, like Mission Control wanted.

Surely Lance must have known that the railguns weren't even loaded …

His time-wasting failure to obey orders would have killed them all, right there, if not for the 'fiery rings of doom' that Jack and Meeks had dreamed up one rainy day in Wales.

So the missile attack had failed—

—and now Lance was trying another way.

"You go back there, then!" Lance said, as Jack pulled him back down behind the bioshield. "Are you pussy or something?"

Jack blurted, "Did you know about Unit 63618? Did you know they were going to try to blow us out of the sky?"

It seemed unbelievable. But Jack had learnt the hard way that the federal government would go to any lengths, and sink to any depths, to cover up their own guilt.

So—had the NXC plotted with the Chinese to destroy the *SoD,* to cover up the evidence of their original sin of destroying Firebird Systems and murdering Oliver Meeks? Quite conceivably, yes. It was all about institutional longevity for these boys.

Lance twisted around. "Yeah, I knew about Unit 63618," he snapped. "I even snuck up to their perimeter one time. Soldiers chased me away. But no, I did not know they were going to shoot a freaking missile at us. We thought they were building their own spaceship. They take out the *SoD,* launch their own mission—the MOAD's theirs. But for that to work, it has to *not* be obvious to the whole world that they shot down the *SoD*. So yeah, dude. I was surprised."

"Lance—"

"But it still doesn't feel right to me. I still think there's a spy on this tub. A saboteur. It ain't me. Is it you?"

Jack stared at him in horror. His reaction had nothing to do with Lance's tirade. Lance was oblivious to the fact that his sudden twisting motion had had a disastrous effect. The fabric cover of the PLSS had torn loose in Jack's hand. It undulated behind Lance like a superhero's cape.

Now Lance's back bumped against the bioshield, and the hard cover of his PLSS came off and floated away.

Jack instinctively dived past Lance to grab it.

Stupid goddamn noob hadn't even made sure the cover was latched properly!

"Hey! What the fuck?" Lance said.

"You've lost your PLSS cover," Jack gasped. Seizing the wandering plastic rectangle in one glove, he grasped the edge of Lance's PLSS with the other. The interior of the unit was a tangle of pipes and connectors, crammed in around the liquid oxygen tank. To Jack, it was like looking at his mother's garden: everything beautiful, everything in its proper place.

"Lemme go," Lance said.

"Don't move!"

"Are you OK out there, guys?" Alexei said.

"Yes," Jack said. "We're fine."

Liquid oxygen tank.

LOX heater.

A skinny little tube connecting the two.

Jack whispered, so quietly that he could hardly hear it himself, "How does it feel to be helpless, Garner? Does it give you a little more sympathy for others?"

"What? What'd you say?"

"Ollie was helpless. He was in his fucking *wheelchair* when you shot him." Jack's vision tunneled, so that he seemed to be looking through the wrong end of a telescope. Everything was far away but crystal clear. He reached into the PLSS, grasped the tube connecting the LOX tank to the heater, and yanked it loose.

Then he replaced the cover.

"OK. You're good to go," he said, giving Lance a light slap on the shoulder.

"What the hell was that about?" Lance said suspiciously.

Then he spasmed. His arms and legs splayed out rigid to the extent that his spacesuit allowed.

A coughing gurgle splashed onto the radio channel.

Alexei shouted, "What was that?"

Liquid oxygen is stored at very low temperatures. 90 *Kelvin.* That's two hundred degrees below zero.

Heating gasifies it.

But if your heater gets broken, or disconnected, now you've got LOX hitting the regulator, which controls the flow of air to your suit. That'll FUBAR it right quick.

Diaphragm fractures.

Liquid oxygen floods into your helmet.

You die.

Jack knew all of this. He had known it as he yanked out the heater connection, and he rehearsed it once more as he clung to the truss, watching Lance's spacesuit drift higher, tether trailing out behind it.

Way above the bioshield now.

That suit was soaking up whatever funky stuff the reactor was putting out.

Better safe than sorry.

Jack stayed where he was and pulled Lance's spacesuit down, like reeling in a man-shaped kite.

Alexei yelled at him over the radio, begging for a sit-rep.

"We may have a slight problem," Jack told him. "Give Hannah the bridge. Meet me at the airlock."

CHAPTER 48

Jack, Alexei, and Lance floated in the storage module.

Lance was still in his spacesuit.

The LOX that filled the inside of his helmet had gasified, leaving his face clearly visible. His skin was pink. He did not look frozen.

But his eyes had burst into mounds of ice crystals.

A horizontal icicle—frozen spittle—protruded from his lips like a mutated, spear-like tongue.

"He's dead," Jack said.

"He might be only mostly dead," Alexei said. "But I think you're right. He's all dead. In that case there's only one thing to do."

Jack dredged the next line up from his memory. He said in unison with Alexei: "Go through his clothes and look for loose change."

Alexei laughed. He flipped the spacesuit over, hiding that terrible sight. The cover of the PLSS flapped open again. Alexei clicked his tongue against his teeth. "The heater connection," he said, almost under his breath. He looked up and met Jack's eyes.

Knackered from his spacewalk, stripped to his underwear, soaked in sweat, Jack nodded.

"OK," Alexei said. "Give me the 13 millimeter flare nut wrench. Over there in the locker."

He reconnected the tube Jack had yanked out. Then, using the titanium nut wrench, he worked away at it.

"What are you doing?" Jack said.

Alexei just shook his head. When he was finished, he beckoned Jack over.

The connection now appeared to have frayed loose. It could have got that way over time, if a tyro astronaut didn't bother to check his equipment properly.

"Work of art, mate," Jack managed. He felt nauseated.

Alexei snapped the PLSS cover closed. He reattached the fabric cover. "Now we wake Kate. You'll have to tell her what … *happened.*"

Jack scrambled for the medical supplies locker. He found a barf bag and pressed its seal to his face, just in time.

Alexei floated in the air, watching him vomit. After a couple of minutes he drifted closer and steadied Jack with an arm around his shoulders.

Jack lowered the barf bag and sealed it. He felt really ropey, unlike himself. Everything had a dreamlike quality. He tried to joke, "Must be the rads."

"I'll let you know if you start glowing."

"He wanted me to go behind the shield. Actually, if you were listening, he tried to taunt me into proving my masculinity, or some fucking thing—are you chicken, are you pussy? Maybe that works on the sort of guys he normally hangs around with." Jack caught himself referring to Lance in the present tense. He shuddered.

"But you didn't go back there," Alexei said.

"Of course not."

"Then you should be OK."

"Christ, yeah. I'm fine," Jack said. On the other side of the storage module, Lance's spacesuit moved, as if waving weakly at them. Jack clamped his lips shut.

Alexei sighed. "It's OK," he said, patting Jack on the back. "It's your first time, right? It's natural to puke. I puked my first time, too. Although, maybe that was the vodka."

Jack stared at his friend. "Hang on, you've …?"

"Oh, sure."

"In Chechnya?"

Alexei had flown an Su-25 during the second Chechen war. It was something they both had in common. They'd fought in ugly, asymmetrical wars, and lost comrades to ugly, asymmetrical tactics.

"Sure, I dropped plenty of bombs in Chechnya. But that's different."

Jack nodded. He, too, had killed people with bombs dropped from on high. It *was* different. The reaction he was having now had nothing to do with deservingness; it was down to the visceral, overwhelming horror of having slain another human being with his own hands.

"It was during the war," Alexei said. "We were headquartered in Dagestan. Of course they hate us down there. I got into a bar fight, I don't even know who started it. Some shithead Dagestani pulls a knife. Ha! I smash the vodka bottle, stab him in the fucking face." Alexei related the story as calmly as if it had been a shopping trip.

Jack shook his head in amazement. You never really knew someone, did you? "Right, I'll think twice before I pull a knife on *you.*"

"If I'm not drunk, probably it's OK." Alexei smiled briefly, before pushing off. He floated towards the keel tube. "We raise the alarm now. It looks bad if we wait too long."

Jack caught up with him. "Did you hear what he said about Unit 63618, the Chinese government—a spy on board? What did you make of that?"

"Ha! *Everyone* on board is a spy. Aren't you?"

Jack shook his head. The British government had wished

him well and put his likeness on a commemorative pound coin. That was the full extent of his relationship with Whitehall.

"I'm supposed to plant a Russian flag on the MOAD when we get there," Alexei said, cackling. "Now I will only have to push two Americans out of the way."

Jack noted that Alexei did not count him in the tally of Americans. "One down, two to go," he quipped.

Pull yourself together, Kildare.

He had to take a cue from Alexei. Be tough. *Krutoi.* There was no exact equivalent in English. To *krutit* was to walk a steep and winding road with aplomb, carrying a broken vodka bottle.

Gripping the rim of the keel tube, Alexei paused. "One thing I must ask. Who's Ollie?"

"Friend of mine."

"So I have one more question. What took you so long?"

Alexei pushed off and flew up the central tube, shouting in feigned panic.

CHAPTER 49

"Hannah come home," Skyler sang. "There's a hole in the bed where you slept, and it's growing cold …"

C, Em7, B, he put the guitar that hung in the KSC crew quarters through its paces. When he took it down, it'd been so dusty it looked like he'd emptied a vacuum cleaner bag in the air.

"And I'm leaving the light on the stairs—no I'm not scared; I'll wait for you. Hey Hannah, it's lonely. Come home."

The quarantine floor of KSC was quiet now. When the astronauts moved out, the reserves had moved in—the actual, official reserves, and the NXC's second string. They would not be stood down until the *SoD* left orbit. Skyler had been instructed to stay here and keep an eye on them. However, since no one expected the reserves would actually have to step up at this point, they spent most of their time watching TV and surfing the internet. Understandable. The ongoing dramas on Earth and in orbit were hypnotic stuff. But Skyler did not care to be hypnotized by the 24/7 news coverage. In his position, he was all too aware that the news only told a fraction of the story.

He sat crosslegged on the large conference table, guitar in his lap. "Hannah, the spread on the bed, it's like when you left, I kept it for you ..."

He couldn't imagine actually sharing a bed with Hannah. Well, he could *imagine* it. Her typical uniform of jeans and a t-shirt melted away in his mind, revealing the luscious curves that her frumpy outfits never hid as well as she thought they did. But the fantasies carried a searing charge of regret. She was on her way to Europa.

The intercom squealed. Director Flaherty boomed, "Holy hell, Taft."

"Did it sound that bad?" Skyler parried, aiming an embarrassed grin at the security camera on the ceiling. He hoped Flaherty hadn't caught him changing the lyrics.

"Let's just say Jimi Hendrix you ain't."

"Damn, and I already sent my resume to the Walkers," Skyler said, referring to the Grateful Dead-like megaband that had grown out of the Earth Party movement. "What's up, boss?"

"Come down to the interview room."

Skyler hopped off the conference table, replaced the guitar on the wall, and lolloped down the hallway. The interview room was where astronauts historically did their pre-launch press conferences. One wall was a plate glass window. Flaherty stood outside it, wearing a headset.

Ignoring the chairs, Skyler put on one of the headsets on his side of the window. Now they could talk in privacy

"News," Flaherty said, and paused, as if wondering how to break it.

"China's declared war on Japan?" For the first time since the Meiwa Massacre, Skyler felt a twinge of alarm. He, and the whole of the NXC, figured that the face-off in the Sea of Japan would sputter out. It would suck to be wrong about something that big. "Japan's declared war on China? Jesus, *we* haven't declared war, have we?"

Flaherty shook his head. "No one's declaring war, unless it's the PLA declaring war on the CCP. Tanks in the streets of Beijing, 'keeping the peace' ... all it takes is for them to turn around and point their guns the other way. We would tentatively welcome that development if it happens."

Skyler uh-huhed. Overseas military coups, in general, were good for US interests.

"But so far, it hasn't happened," Flaherty said. "No, what I got to tell you is something completely different." He met Skyler's alarmed gaze through the glass. "Lance is dead."

One of the most useful things Skyler had learned in the NXC was how to control his body language. On hearing Flaherty's words, he did not blush, exaggerate his shock with an open mouth, or hold Flaherty's gaze with a fake stare of disbelief, like an amateur would. He most certainly did not pump his fists and shout "Yessss!" which was what he would have done if alone. He blinked, letting his gaze dart away, and raised one hand to rub under his eye—a gesture which reliably indicated astonishment when a person had heard something too shocking to take in. "Say again, boss? *Lance?*"

"He insisted on that old suit. He should've taken one of the new ones. Piece of shit malfunctioned while he was spacewalking."

And I'm the Wizard of Oz, Skyler thought.

Who needs a guided missile when you've got Jack Kildare?

Arm, trigger, and walk away.

He fought back his grin of triumph. Guilt supervened when he saw the glitter in Flaherty's eyes. For the director, this must feel like losing a son. "This is a complete fucking disaster," he said, aiming to take Flaherty's mind off his personal loss by referencing the NXC's mission.

"You're telling me." Flaherty accepted the emotional lifeline. He stood up straighter. "We *have* to have someone on that ship."

"Yup." Skyler's mind flew to his 'kids.' "Assume there's a realistic possibility of sending up a replacement …"

"There is, thank the Lord. That refueling flight. It's gonna be touch and go, but they're saying they can pull it off. Rendezvous at the *SoD's* apogee."

"Thought that was gonna be an unmanned flight?"

"It is. But there's room for one person in the trunk, provided they're on the scrawny side."

Skyler grimaced. That let out Curtis, whom he'd otherwise have favored. It would have to be Guillermo or Laura. Another problem intruded. "Hang on, are we using the Dragon 2? Can the Falcon 9 booster make it up that high?"

"Aha," Flaherty said. "With a second stage, yes it can."

Skyler blinked. Two extra stages turned SpaceX's Falcon 9 booster rocket into a Falcon Heavy. Certified in time to participate in the last few months of the *SoD* construction process, the Falcon Heavy had only ever done unmanned launches. This would be its maiden flight as a manned spacecraft. "Hang on. *Two* stages? The Heavy has three."

"They're going to switch out the third stage for a LOX tank for the *SoD.* Astronaut sits in the Dragon 2 capsule up top."

Skyler weighed his choices. It felt heady, spiritually perilous, to wield such power. He had only to speak a name to send that person into space for the next five years of their life, maybe never to return.

He realized, however, that it was pretty dumb to feel this way when he'd just murdered someone by proxy. *That* was power. *This* was an administrative decision.

"Laura," he said.

But Flaherty was already shaking his gray-frosted head.

Smiling.

"My bad, Skyler. I shouldn't be teasing you. I know how you felt, stuck here on the ground, left behind while Lance joined the mission. Going into space—that was *your* dream, and he was the one who got to go? Not fair. I shoulda picked you in the first place."

Flaherty drew himself up and rendered a snappy salute. Skyler thought he saw regret lurking in the director's sad smile—if he'd picked Skyler in the first place, Lance wouldn't be dead.

"Congratulations, Taft. You're going to Europa."

Skyler's return salute had all the snap of wet spaghetti.

*

It wasn't that he didn't love space. Ever since he first got his hands on a telescope in grade school, he'd been addicted to the stars. Watching them, learning about them, dreaming about them.

That's why he had become an astrophysicist.

Not an astronaut.

These two things are not the same, sir.

If I wanted to be an astronaut, I'd have got a degree in turd-dodging and mindless macho posturing.

How could Flaherty have got him so colossally wrong?

He'd pictured himself watching the skies for the *SoD's* return, playing melancholy songs on a new and better guitar. Coordinating observations from the new telescope on the ISS, maybe even heading up the worldwide MOAD-watching team. That job would have suited Skyler Taft down to the ground.

But obviously, Flaherty had seen things differently all

along.

Skyler had never even fucking noticed that all the time he was training his 'kids,' he'd been training alongside them.

Training to be Lance's replacement.

And now, well, it was over, that's all. Years as a federal agent had conditioned him thoroughly. When Flaherty said jump, Skyler said "How high?" even if the answer was 400 million miles.

They'd got a spacesuit all ready for him. One of the new Z2s, of course. It was the one that had been made for Laura. Skyler had never noticed, or never cared to notice (because frankly it was a bit embarrassing), that he was the same size as Laura: 5'8", 140 pounds.

On the scrawny side.

*

His last glimpse of Earth: the drive along NASA Parkway East to Cape Canaveral. The water of the Banana River sparkled in the spring sunlight.

Boats.

Seagulls.

He couldn't even smell the sea air, or hear the birds crying, stuck inside a van sealed up like a biohazard unit.

He recalled his last phone call home. Dad had seemed distracted, as usual, barely taking in the news. Piper hadn't been there. Trek had screamed down the phone: "You lucky bastard I am so fucking JEALOUS of you right now," and then started coughing.

Skyler smiled at the memory of his younger brother … and wondered if he'd ever see Trek again.

If Trek would live until he got back.

If Skyler ever would get back.

Let's not kid ourselves, Taft. What's going on here? It is *fear.* Correction: it's *just* fear. Fear is an emotion, that's all it is. (He'd been into Zen meditation for a while when he lived in California.) Experience it, and let it go. It has nothing to do with reality.

OH YES IT FUCKING DOES, his mind screamed when he saw the Falcon Heavy standing on the launch pad, obnoxiously phallic, poised to punch a hole in the cloudless sky.

*

"We have a five-minute launch window," the ground techs told him. They were snarling, yelling, rushing around like mad dogs, and if there was a method to their madness Skyler Taft did not perceive it as he was lifted 230 feet above the launch pad and thrown into the Dragon capsule like a side of beef.

Five. Four. Three. Two. One.

Fear is just an emotion just an emotion—

Fuck Zen meditation, Skyler decided as he hurtled out of Earth's gravity well with three gees pinning him into his seat.

CHAPTER 50

Jack and Xiang Peixun floated outside the *SoD's* airlock. Lance was with them.

They'd powered Lance's spacesuit down and stuck him outside to freeze. Sure, his head had been frozen already. But the rest of him was still warm when he died. This way, he didn't rot in his suit. Less horror for whoever unpacked him on the ground.

He'd be going home in the Falcon Heavy, when it got here.

"There it is!" Xiang said.

A spark glowed against Earth's nightside. The Falcon Heavy had launched from Cape Canaveral in broad day, but had had to circle halfway around the globe before catching up with the *SoD*.

It grew brighter and closer.

"This is going to be like hitting a topspinner," Jack muttered. "And we're the wicket."

"No speakee cricket," Menelaou said amiably from the bridge. "Peixun, the fuel tank is programmed to release at the Falcon Heavy's point of closest approach. I want you to secure that tank. Jack, your job is to talk the replacement in by radio. I don't know who they ended up sending us, but chances are he or she is not a proficient broomstick rider. Make sure they get in OK."

"Roger," Jack said.

Whoever NASA had sent up, they would have to be an improvement over Lance Garner, at any rate.

*

Skyler's fear had gone away.

It was pretty hard to be scared when you were concentrating every fiber of your being on not vomiting.

He'd puked on his first trip to orbit. That had been bad enough. If he puked now, it would be a disaster. He was wearing his spacesuit. A glass bubble enclosed the front of his head, seamlessly joined to the rigid cowl of his Z-2. The puke would have nowhere to go.

Weightless, he bobbled in his harness, staring at the tiny screen ahead of him in the capsule's cockpit.

The *SoD* grew from a pixel to a blot to the familiar shape of a child's stacking toy stacked out of order, with the largest piece near the 'top.' And then it started to shrink again.

"It's pulling away!" Skyler shrieked.

"Sit tight," CapCom said.

CapCom had a warm voice. Skyler trusted her. He sat tight, mouth-breathing. Do not puke. Do *not* puke.

"The *SoD* is now approaching its apogee," CapCom said. "It will slow down significantly. Watch."

No lie. The *SoD* grew again, and grew. The Falcon Heavy was gradually overhauling it.

"On my word," Capcom said.

"Ready." Skyler opened his lips as little as possible, lest the saliva collecting in his mouth escape.

"Release your harness."

"Roger."

He floated into the middle of the cockpit.

"Grab your broomstick."

It was riding next to him in one of the unoccupied couches. "Got it."

"Go up to the hatch."

He towed the broomstick up to the hatch overhead.

"Roger."

"You remember how to get out, right? Knock on the hatch three times and say 'Open sesame.'"

Intent on following orders, Skyler had raised his gloved fist to knock before he got the joke. Quit trying to put me at my ease! he thought. Just get me safely to the *SoD*. "What next?"

"Vent the cockpit to space and undog the hatch," CapCom said. *Dumbass,* she didn't say.

The cockpit vented its air. The hatch swung open. Skyler fell 'up' into the vacuum. The broomstick, tethered to his wrist, followed him.

Feeling tiny in the void, clumsy in his spacesuit, Skyler swung his leg over the broomstick's cylindrical body. Like all the best inventions, the broomstick was absurdly simple: a LOX tube with a heater, a nozzle, and handlebars. A motorbike, basically, without wheels. Skyler had never ridden one of these babies when he was at the ISS. But how hard could it be?

"I'm handing you over to the *SoD* now," CapCom said. "Godspeed."

The *Spirit of Destiny* floated subjectively overhead. It was over 200 meters long, three times the length of the Falcon Heavy, but it looked about the size of a semi-trailer. That's how Skyler knew it was some distance away.

Two tiny figures floated outside the string of modules between the main hab and the bioshield.

Skyler had to reach them. Straddling the broomstick, he twisted the throttle control in his right handlebar.

The broomstick rocketed away from the Falcon Heavy at a shocking speed, and Skyler puked.

Retching, eyes watering, he struggled to turn the broomstick towards the *SoD*. He was veering all over the place. "Help," he yelled, and then realized he'd forgotten to chin-press the toggle to switch his comms to the *SoD's* channel. He pressed it, as puke drooled out of his mouth.

"—out! *Straighten out!*"

The British voice yelling into his helmet could only be Jack Kildare. Skyler was in so much distress, he didn't care. "I'm trying!"

"You're veering away from us! Turn to your right!"

"I'm TRYING," Skyler screamed, and retched again. His vomit splashed against his faceplate. A film of puke covered the glass. He couldn't see.

"Have you engaged the gyroscopes?" Kildare yelled.

Oh God! He hadn't! He felt for the control on the left handlebar. It was like trying to type in mittens—

The gyroscopes locked. The broomstick stopped massively overreacting to every twitch.

"That's better," Kildare said. "*Now* turn to your right. I'll talk you in ..."

*

Whoever was on the broomstick, Jack knew he'd puked in his helmet, because his voice sounded underwatery—vomit clogging the mic. Another tyro, Jack thought bleakly. The FNG was, at least, good at following orders. Obeying Jack's careful instructions, he chugged towards the *SoD*.

The two spacecraft had achieved a stable separation distance. But this couldn't last long. Soon, the Falcon Heavy would fall behind again, as the *SoD* plunged back towards Earth.

No time to spare.

As soon as the replacement got within reach, Jack unceremoniously yanked him off the broomstick. Vomit covered the inside of his faceplate, hiding his face. "Go in and get cleaned up," Jack said, stuffing him into the airlock.

He released his tether, flung his leg over the broomstick, and wrangled Lance's frozen corpse in front of him.

Hold on tight, buddy.

That ride across the void to the Falcon Heavy taxed Jack's mental resilience. Face-down across the cylinder, Lance rocked back and forth, his stiff legs bumping against Jack's arms. The dead man wore his satchel, duct-taped to the back of his spacesuit. They'd cleared out Lance's coffin, packed up his belongings.

They'd found no evidence that he was a spy and saboteur.

But then, there wouldn't be, would there?

A smart Fed doesn't leave his secret diary lying around.

Jack clung to the belief that he'd done the right thing. There had been no more missiles, no more insider sabotage attempts. What more proof did he need? No more bad guy, no more problems. It was going to be smooth sailing from here on out.

He turned the broomstick, nosed it alongside the Dragon 2 capsule, and killed the thrust. The hatch hung open. Cramming Lance and his pathetic belongings inside, Jack thought of Hansel and Gretel cramming the wicked witch into her own oven. But he felt more like the witch.

The oven comparison wasn't inapt. After separating from the *SoD,* the Falcon Heavy would fire its second stage once more. It would curve back towards Earth, dumping the second stage along the way, and fire its retros at perigee for a hot landing. Lance was going to get a bit singed.

Jack slammed the hatch shut. There was an emergency access port on the outside of the capsule. Juggling the broomstick, he redogged the hatch and felt it latch securrly.

As he straddled the broomstick once more, a slow-moving torpedo glided over his head. The Falcon Heavy had released the fuel tank it carried instead of a third stage. The computer-controlled release looked to be well-timed, but just in case, Jack rode the broomstick up to the tank and nudged it with his knee, guiding it towards the waiting Xiang.

This maneuver hadn't been in the original mission plan, but the whole idea was that they'd come prepared for anything. Xiang carried the *SoD's* magnetic harpoon gun. He fired it, and the grapple locked onto the tank. Easy as falling off a log.

"Well done," Menelaou said over the radio. "Now we need to transfer the fuel into our booster."

"Someone else can do that," Jack said, before she could order him to do it. Not only was he tired, he wanted to be on the bridge during the fuel transfer maneuver. It could result in a loss of trim, and as confident as Menelaou might be in her own piloting skills, Jack didn't quite share her confidence.

Besides, he had one more thing he wanted to do before he went inside.

He pushed the broomstick into the airlock.

His tether trailed from the fitting on the hull adjacent to the airlock, ready to be clipped onto his belt.

About to grab it, he paused.

Then he let his hand fall.

Always wanted to spacewalk without a tether.

With the tiniest fingertip push against the hull, he turned his back on the *SoD*. Although he floated within arm's reach of the airlock, the sensation of peril thrilled through his brain like a siren. He was deliberately ignoring the single most important rule of spacewalking, the one drilled into him over years of training and experience … and it felt like a cocaine high.

Earth turned below him.

Sunrise painted a silver arc over the Pacific.

Tears pricked the corners of Jack's eyes.

"You should've been here, Ollie," he whispered under his breath. "Goddammit."

He could imagine it so clearly, it felt almost like Meeks *was* with him. Spacesuited, helmeted, chattering zealously about the adventure ahead of them.

The imaginary vision, like a mirror, reflected Jack's loneliness.

He clumsily extracted the aluminum capsule from his thigh pocket. A twist opened it. He shook it. The contents misted out. A fine grey haze, and then nothing.

Jack bit his lip, refusing to say goodbye.

"What the hell are you doing out there, Kildare?" Menelaou said. "You're tying up the airlock. Need you to get in here and look after the new guy." She added in a lower voice, "Wait till you see what they've landed us with this time. *Total* mess, and I mean that literally."

CHAPTER 51

Menelaou wasn't kidding.

Crawling out of the airlock, the first thing Jack saw was the skinny figure of the replacement. Half in and half out of his spacesuit. Puke in his hair. Face in a barf bag.

Globules of vomit, large and small, floated around the storage module.

Boisselot was chasing the mess with the handheld vacuum cleaner, whose roaring redoubled the usual noise of fans. He shot Jack a Gallic eye-roll—conveniently forgetting that he'd had more than one puking episode himself.

Jack stripped off his spacesuit and the sweat-saturated liner he wore under it. He wanted to towel down, but the replacement obviously had the greater need. He grabbed a towel and floated over to the guy. "I know how much it sucks right now, but I promise …"

I promise it'll wear off.

That's what he had been going to say, before he saw the peace sign floating on a cord around the replacement's neck.

Oh, no.

No goddamn way.

They did *not* send us …

"Skyler Taft?"

Skyler lowered the barf bag. He blinked bloodshot eyes. His hair was so sticky with sweat and puke that it lay flat to his head, instead of rising into a zero-gee halo. "One of my ancestors was a president," he croaked. "We've got senators, generals, ambassadors in there too. I had to find some way to rise higher than them all."

*

Alexei Ivanov flew into the storage module. He tossed a neutrally pitched greeting to Skyler, and began to suit up for a spacewalk. Kildare said something about the fuel transfer maneuver. Ivanov replied. Boisselot threw in a comment. They were speaking English but it might as well have been Chinese.

Skyler methodically scrubbed his face with a towel. Why had he let himself be shanghaied into this?

Director Flaherty's last words to him echoed in his mind.

"The mission of the SoD is to investigate the MOAD and determine whether it is, or is not, a threat to humanity.

"Your mission is to secure as much alien shit as you can get your hands on, and return it to the United States."

Yeah.

That's why.

He guessed Flaherty would never know that the first guy he charged with this mission had been a Chinese spy. The NXC had dodged a bullet there.

And Skyler felt like he'd taken that bullet, right in the gut.

But the nausea would fade. Whether the amazing impression of competence he'd made here would fade … that seemed questionable.

Real impressive, wobbling all over the sky with a helmet full of vomit.

He hung up his spacesuit, and detached his satchel of personal belongings from the limp garment. It was a little bit bulkier than anyone else had been allowed to bring. That's because it held a Glock subcompact with a modified trigger grip, to permit a gloved finger to fit in.

Suddenly, Hannah flew into the module. Skyler barely had time to grip one of the grab handles on the wall before she cannoned into him, hugging him. "Skyler! This is so freaking awesome! They didn't tell us who was coming."

Her enthusiastic embrace astonished him—especially given the state he was in. "Watch out, I stink," he said weakly.

"My nose is so stuffed up, I can't smell it anyway." She squeezed him once more, to prove it. It was a hell of a wasted opportunity. Her breasts pressed against his chest. In freefall, she was seriously pneumatic. And he didn't even dare give her an innocent, brotherly kiss on the cheek, with Kildare and Boisselot and Ivanov looking on, no doubt wondering why this nice woman was letting Skyler get his noob cooties all over her.

She pushed off, drifting away from him. Her smile didn't reach her eyes. That tipped him off that this was a performance.

"Come down and see me in Engineering when you get cleaned up," she said.

*

It had taken Hannah ten minutes to work herself up to that. In an ideal world, she'd have helped Skyler out of his suit and held his hair while he puked. But her spontaneity seemed to have vanished along with her access to alcohol. Instead, she'd lurked in her lair, listening to the men's voices 'above,' gradually psyching herself up to go and hug him.

He hadn't bought it. She knew that the instant he appeared in the keel tube entrance to her kingdom. His eyes were wary.

"So this is where the magic happens?" he said.

The tragic thing was, she had meant that hug. As much as she didn't know about Skyler's involvement with the Firebird Systems mess, he had still been one of her best friends at JSC. They'd had a real connection, charged with potential. She had often regretted pushing him away. This was a heaven-sent second chance.

But they could never mend their relationship if she wasn't up-front with him right now.

"Come on in," she said.

The hexagonal array pulsed. Skyler glanced uneasily at it.

"We're cranking the output up again," Hannah explained. "Commander Menelaou wants to be ready to boost when we get the green light from Mission Control."

"Yeah, she said in about two hours." Skyler looked a bit stunned, as if everything was happening too fast for him. Hannah sympathized. She'd felt that way ever since that day on a California clifftop when she took the job.

Skyler had cleaned himself up as well as you could with wet wipes and dry shampoo. His hair had recovered its natural exuberance.

Hannah pushed her own hair back self-consciously. In zero-gee, it had an infuriating tendency to escape a scrunchie. "I have something to show you."

She dived aft, through the short section of keel tube that led to the turbine room. Skyler followed. "Wow. What are those?" He stared at the massive machine housings riveted to opposing walls of the rectangular room. One was the size of a jet engine, the other was much larger.

"They're the most important things on board, short of the reactor," Hannah said, over the roar. "That's the housekeeping turbine, and that's the one that generates power for the MPD engine. That stuff back there is the generator. We use that when we're running the ship's systems off the reactor, although right now, because all the reactor power is going to the engine, we're running on the fuel cells."

She dived down to the housekeeping turbine cabinet and opened it up. She reached under the turbine itself, into the warm dark space between the turbine and the wall, where she had stashed some personal stuff. She took out a single sheet of airmail paper.

"I helped clean out Lance's coffin," she said. "I found this in his stuff. No one else has seen it. I thought … I don't know. I don't know what it is. Maybe you do."

Skyler snatched the sheet of paper. Elegant handwriting covered the fine blue sheet on both sides.

He read out: "'Please believe that I forgive you. When we met in Beijing, I saw how this has tortured you. I'm a Christian, Lance! I believe in the possibility of repentance. And although you kept saying you could not understand how I could forgive you, I do. Our Lord taught us to forgive seven and seven times seven times, no matter how serious the sin—'"

Skyler stopped reading. Hannah knew why. She had read the letter herself, and knew what came next.

…*Even if it's murder.*

Skyler flipped the sheet over and kept reading. When he got to the end, he read out: "'Sincerely yours in Christ, Xue Hua Colbert."

"Do you know who she is, Skyler? Do you know why he kept it?"

Skyler looked up. "She forgave him for murdering her husband. How is that even possible?"

"Don't ask me. I'm Jewish," Hannah said. "We believe in an eye for an eye."

She regretted her flippancy a moment later. Skyler knuckled his eyes. His cheeks flushed. "I was wrong." His voice was a subterranean croak. *"I was wrong."*

"Huh? I don't get it."

"The woman he met in Beijing. It was her. The widow of Senator Colbert."

Now the name rang a bell. "Oh my God! I remember that! He was murdered right around the time we discovered the MOAD. You mean *Lance* … killed him?"

"Yup," Skyler said. "I always suspected it. Now we have proof. Lance did that … but he didn't do anything else." He shook his head wildly. "Take that away, and everything else can be explained. It all falls to pieces." He dropped the letter. Hannah caught it. "Oh God. Oh God. Oh God."

"Skyler," Hannah said cautiously. Fearfully. "Have *you* done something?"

She braced for his confession. But then a shutter came down. The man was gone. The Fed was back. "Can I have that?" he said, reaching for the letter.

Hannah pushed off with one toe and floated out of range. "Nope," she said. "No one's getting it."

She tore the letter across. Then she tore it into smaller pieces. Then stuffed the pieces into her pocket, to be flushed down the crapper later. She looked him in the eye. "It's gone."

EPILOGUE

"Mission Control, this is the *SoD,"* Katharine Menelaou said. Her singsong intonation emphasized that this was their *second* try at making history.

"Reading you loud and clear, *SoD."*

"Power generation is stable. MPD engine is online, and thrust is stable." Abruptly, Menelaou veered off script. "So do we have permission to haul ass before sod's law strikes again?"

She'd got that from Jack—sod's law. She winked at him.

"Spirit of Destiny, you are approved to haul ass," Mission Control sent back.

"Hey Goose, I feel the need … " Jack called out.

"… the need for speed!" Alexei called back.

Jack laughed out loud, and keyed in the throttle command to send full power to the booster engines.

Spewing superheated plasma, the *Spirit of Destiny* bulled out of Earth orbit.

Next stop: Europa.

*

Down in the storage module, Skyler observed the other crew members. They were all strapped into their acceleration couches, lined up across the floor of the module.

Which of you is it?

Boisselot.

Xiang.

Qiu.

Hannah was down in Engineering. He knew it wasn't *her.*

Ivanov had taken the co-pilot's seat on the bridge for the burn. It might be him.

Also on the bridge: Menelaou. (Please let it not be her.)

And Kildare.

What if it was *him?*

What if Lance had been murdered by *the very saboteur he was seeking to expose?*

Lance had been no spy. Skyler knew that now. A red-blooded, flag-waving American patriot, that's all he had ever been, and his trigger-happy methods just demonstrated his high-proof Americanness. Flaherty had been right, Skyler had been wrong.

Skyler might as well've murdered Lance with his own hands.

He'd made a colossal, life-changing mistake. But it was too late to fix that now.

The boosters roared. Gravity pressed down on Skyler's body, a full two Gs. He struggled to breathe. It was a terrifying, exhilarating sensation, but one thought filled his mind.

If Lance had not been the saboteur, then *the saboteur was still on board.*

THE STORY CONTINUES IN
SHIPLORD
EARTH'S LAST GAMBIT, VOLUME 2

THE CREW OF THE *SPIRIT OF DESTINY*

Commander Katharine Menelaou (US)

Pilot Jack Kildare (UK / US): EVA specialist, advanced medical support

Mission Specialist ~~Koichi Masuoka (JP)~~ Hannah Ginsberg (US): reactor and propulsion

Mission Specialist Alexei Ivanov (RU): co-pilot, EVA specialist, and hydroponics

Mission Specialist Giles Boisselot (FR): xenolinguistics, advanced life-support

Mission Specialist ~~Adam Hardcastle (US) Lance Garner (US)~~ Skyler Taft (US): communications, hydroponics

Mission Specialist Qiu Meili (CH): optics and sensors and electronics, hydroponics

Mission Specialist Xiang Peixun (CH): EVA specialist, advanced life-support

59386769R00228

Made in the USA
Lexington, KY
03 January 2017